Vendetta

Book Nine in Detectives Daniels and Remalla
J. T. Bishop

Eudoran Press LLC

Eudoran Press LLC.
6009 W. Parker Rd. #149-913
Plano, TX 75093

The story, all names, characters, and incidents portrayed in this production are fictitious. No identification with actual persons (living or deceased), places, buildings, and products is intended or should be inferred.

Book Cover by J. T. Bishop
Vendetta/First Edition 2025

eBook ISBN 978-1-955370-59-2
Paperback ISBN 978-1-955370-70-7
Hardback ISBN 978-1-955370-71-4

To my family.

Writing makes me happy, but you make me whole.

I love you with all my heart.

Other Books by J. T. Bishop

Previously...

Two men have been murdered and branded with a star, and Daniels and Remalla are asked to investigate. They travel to Los Angeles to meet with another detective on the case and to escort Rhonda, a supposed witness, back to San Diego. But nothing is ever simple for Rem and Daniels, and as they are preparing to leave, they spot Daniels' father, Raymond, speaking to a young woman he refuses to identify. And once on their way, Rem and Daniels encounter Lexie Logan, a reporter who is convinced Rhonda is a killer instead of a witness.

The team stay overnight in Elmwood, where Rem and Daniels realize there is a lot more at stake than escort duty, or even the two murders—they survive an assassination attempt by two men they nickname Tex and Tommy, and notice that both killers bear the tattoo of a black bird on their wrist. The truth about Rhonda - Lexie was right all along - emerges once they return to San Diego, where Rhonda disappears.

When Rem notices his cousin Cain bears the same tattoo sported by Tex and Tommy, he and Daniels begin to suspect that the black bird tattoo is a clue to what's behind the murders and possibly something even more complex. Through Cain, Rem and Daniels meet Erin, the same mystery woman who Rem and Daniels spotted talking to his father. Keeping her relationship to Raymond Daniels secret, she still offers to use her relationship with Cain to go undercover and feed Daniels intel on the black bird society and Cain's involvement.

But Cain and Rhonda are not the only problems. A seemingly fresh case emerges when several protestors against a real-estate development, headed by Pinnacle Properties, go missing. As they dig deeper, Daniels and Rem learn that one of the missing men, Nathan Briars, is an old friend of Rem's girlfriend, Mikey, from her days in Victor D'Mato's cult. Nathan visits Mikey and stirs up flashbacks of a terrible night - one where she witnessed her friend Vera being shot by a masked man smoking a cigarette. The man is friendly with her sister Margaret and Victor, and Daniels and Rem believe this man is Margaret's accomplice, nicknamed Winnie, who they know is responsible for several murders and assaults - including those against the kidnapped protestors, and Rem and Daniels.

Daniels, Rem, and reporter Lexie Logan now realize there is a larger conspiracy at play, likely connected to the shadowy "black bird society." When Ackerman, a former Pinnacle employee who also bears the tattoo of a black bird, gives Daniels and Remalla a box of secret information connected to the society before blowing himself up, the trio realizes the organization is real, and deadly.

And in the background, a new, insidious connection is revealed. Detective Manetti's partner, Monk, is undercover in the worse possible way - deeply connected to Rhonda, the murders, and whatever plot is behind it all.

Find out what happens next, in *Vendetta*...

Cast of Characters

Detective Aaron Remalla - a detective based in San Diego

Detective Gordon Daniels - Remalla's long-term partner and friend

Marjorie Daniels - Daniels' wife

Captain Frank Lozano - the head of the squad

Mikey Redstone - works at SCOPE with her brother Mason, is Rem's girlfriend

Margaret Redstone - Mikey's psychopathic sister and a former high-ranking member of Victor's cult

Mason Redstone - medium, paranormal PI, and former Texas Ranger. Brother to Margaret and Mikey

Victor D'Mato - cult leader

Detective Luca Manetti - A detective in the same precinct as Remalla and Daniels

Detective Frank Monk - Manetti's partner

Lexie Logan - investigative journalist

'Rhonda Champlin' - an assassin

Marvin Ackerman - former Pinnacle Properties accountant

Cain Carson - Remalla's cousin

Erin Gerard - a woman associated with Raymond Daniels and Cain Carson

Reginald Durning - defense attorney for Crenshaw, Ingram and Willoughby

Josh Durning - Reginald's son and a state prosecutor.

Jerry Lee Caruso - son to Patricia Caruso and grandson to Sammy Caruso

Sammy Caruso - a powerful politician from Chicago with mob connections

Vera Canmore - A former cult member and close friend of Mikey

Ben Crenshaw, Barbara Ingram, and Charles Willoughby - partners in the law firm of Crenshaw, Ingram, and Willoughby (CIW)

Delaina Desmond - Ben Crenshaw's personal assistant

Martha Cravitz - Reginald Durning's personal assistant

Miguel - front receptionist at CIW

Lena - shaman and grandmother to Kyle, Mikey's co-worker

Elsa Crow - police captain promoted from the Special Crimes unit and daughter of Chogan Crow

Chogan Crow - city council president and Elsa Crow's father

Phoebe Reinart - former detective and now FBI agent

Damien Rook - founder of Rook Enterprises, which owns Pinnacle Properties

Agents Alicia Brady and Vern Lattimore - FBI agents investigating Reginald Durning

Tex and Tommy - nicknames given to two men who tried to kill Rem and Daniels in the town of Elmwood

Chief Ronald Patterson - Chief of Police and Captain Lozano's superior

Jennifer Chambers - Aaron Remalla's deceased girlfriend

Raymond Daniels - Detective Gordon Daniels' father.

Melinda Daniels - Gordon Daniels' deceased sister

Chapter One

JERRY LEE TRIED NOT to stare. The pretty redhead standing beside the older gentleman who was checking in to the hotel ran her hand down the man's chest to his abdomen and lower, but the high counter prevented Jerry from seeing how much lower. The man sucked in a breath, though, and the pen in his hand jerked as he signed the paper Donald, Jerry's boss at the front desk, had given him. The woman grinned, chewed some gum, made eye contact with Jerry Lee, and winked at him.

Jerry Lee blushed and looked away. He'd just returned to reception after delivering a guest's bags to a room and hoped the man checking in with the sexy redhead also had bags for Jerry to deliver. The redhead was the best-looking woman to enter the lobby all day, and probably all week.

Curious, Jerry glanced over Donald's shoulder and saw the man's name was Reginald Durning. He didn't recognize him, but it looked like Reginald was only staying the night, and glancing at the redhead again, Jerry Lee could assume why. He spied a wedding ring on Reginald's finger but not one on the redhead's. Jerry Lee had worked at the hotel long enough not to be surprised. It happened frequently.

Donald took the signed form. "Thank you, Mr. Durning. Do you have bags with you?" He gestured toward Jerry Lee. "Jerry here can help you with them."

Hopeful, Jerry Lee waited. He guessed Mr. Durning might be a good tipper, and ogling the redhead a bit more would be an added bonus.

Reginald smiled at the redhead. "No bags, Donald. Thank you."

Jerry Lee deflated.

Reginald put his arm around the redhead. "C'mon, beautiful."

The redhead giggled and put her arm around his waist. "I can't wait to get you into bed."

Jerry Lee widened his eyes, and Donald glared at him. "Why don't you go to the kitchen, Jerry Lee?" asked Donald. "See if room service needs any help."

Jerry Lee sighed. It was definitely one of those nights. Check-ins had been light, and Jerry had struggled to stay busy. He still preferred working at the front desk, although room service wasn't bad. He just didn't like Marty, the man who ran the kitchen. He was short-tempered, stressed, and hard to please. Once he'd found out who Jerry Lee was related to, Marty had called him "Little Mobster" ever since. Jerry Lee hated the name, but didn't dare tell Marty. "Sure thing, Donald."

Reginald stopped on his way to the elevator and looked over his shoulder while the redhead clung to him. "Room service," he said. "That's a great idea." He smiled at Jerry. "How about you bring some champagne to our room, kid?"

Jerry eyed the redhead, who still clung to Reginald. "That's a great idea, baby." She spoke to Jerry Lee, and her eyes glimmered. "Something expensive."

"The nicest bottle you got," said Reginald. "Room 302. Charge the card on file."

"Of course, Mr. Durning," said Donald. "Jerry Lee will bring it up right away, sir."

Reginald pulled the redhead closer, and she giggled again and glanced back at Jerry. "Thank you, Jerry Lee." She narrowed her eyes and almost cooed. "See you soon." They headed to the elevators and Reginald hit the *Up* button.

Donald smacked Jerry Lee's shoulder and whispered. "Would you stop drooling? You're embarrassing yourself."

The elevator dinged and opened. Reginald and the redhead stepped on and disappeared when the doors closed.

Jerry Lee closed his mouth, which had been hanging open. "Man, she's pretty. Did you see that outfit she was wearing?" He couldn't stop thinking about the woman's short skirt, which had revealed her long shapely legs, and her snug short top, which had exposed plenty of cleavage and her toned midriff. He didn't care much for all the heavy makeup she wore and the ostentatious jewelry. He guessed she'd be much prettier without it.

"What our guests wear is none of your business." Donald went back to the computer. "But yes. I saw. It was hard to miss." He typed something. "I've requested the order. Now go get the champagne. And don't act stupid when you deliver it." He rolled his eyes. "Marty won't be happy if you look foolish."

"How's Marty going to know?" asked Jerry. "He doesn't have eyes and ears everywhere."

Donald arched an eyebrow at him. "How do you think Courtney got fired?"

Jerry Lee recalled Courtney Givens getting the boot after flirting with a celebrity from a reality show when she delivered a steak dinner to his room the previous week. "Seriously?" asked Jerry. "That was Marty?"

"That was Marty, so behave yourself. Now go."

Jerry nodded, turned and headed toward the kitchen, wondering how Marty could have known about Courtney. Jerry could only guess that the celebrity had complained. Courtney had been forward with the staff and apparently the guests, too.

Walking down the hall, Jerry Lee thought of the redhead and wondered if he'd ever check in to a nice hotel with a sexy woman on his arm. At the rate he was going, it wouldn't be soon. Although if his grandfather had any say in it, Jerry would have gorgeous women on his arm day and night. But his mother had insisted that Jerry limit his time with his grandfather and with good reason. His grandfather was Sammy Caruso, the well-known senator from Illinois, whose powerful connections had almost gotten him into the White House. When one of those connections turned out to be the mob, and one of Sam Caruso's opponents had been shot and almost killed, the presidency had slipped away. But it didn't make Sam Caruso any less powerful.

Jerry Lee barely knew his dad, but he knew he'd been a big Jerry Lee Lewis fan. After his mom had given birth, his dad hadn't stayed long, and his mom had moved back to Chicago. Jerry Lee had been raised among the influential men who'd sworn loyalty to his grandfather, and the women who'd raised the children and kept the homes of those men. His mother, who'd never wanted Jerry Lee to join the ranks of their political family, had done her best to shield Jerry Lee from the activities surrounding his grandfather, but Jerry Lee had seen some things, and grown up fast. No matter how much his mother had tried to protect him, his grandfather wanted the opposite, until his grandfather had been indicted for racketeering and tax evasion two years earlier. By then, Jerry Lee was graduating from high school, and his mother had endured enough. She packed her and Jerry Lee's bags, and they'd moved to San Diego.

The transition had been difficult at first, but Jerry had enrolled at a community college and his mother had found a good job that paid the bills and a decent boyfriend that treated Jerry well. Jerry made friends and had come to love the California lifestyle. His mother liked the change, too, and they'd settled into their new life. Although his grandfather frequently requested they come home, with the trial looming, the unrelenting press coverage, and her father's political future in limbo, his mom refused. She would not reconsider until her father's issues were settled.

Jerry Lee entered the hotel kitchen and saw a nice champagne bottle in a bucket of ice with two champagne flutes beside it sitting on the counter. Jerry moved them to a tablecloth-covered cart and pushed them toward the door.

"Watch yourself, Little Mobster."

Jerry startled and turned to see Marty staring at him from the other side of the kitchen. His dark curly hair, angular cheekbones and jaw, and beady brown eyes reminded Jerry of some of the men who worked for his grandfather. "Remember what happened to Courtney." He sneered at Jerry and walked away.

Wondering if Marty had ESP or maybe secret spies in the lobby, Jerry pushed the cart through a set of double doors and headed toward the service elevator. Once on it, he hit the button for the third floor and the elevator ascended. After reaching the floor, he pushed the cart to door 302 and knocked. "Room service," he said.

The door swung open, and Jerry Lee saw Reginald. His tie was undone and his shirt unbuttoned. "Bring it on in." He opened the door wider. Jerry pushed the cart into the room and set the champagne and glasses on the table beside the bed and tried to hide his disappointment when he didn't see the redhead.

He heard a high-pitched voice from the bathroom. "Is that the champagne, baby?"

"It is," said Reginald. "Better get out here and drink some with me."

"On my way," she said with a giggle.

"Thanks, Jerry." Reginald pulled some cash from his wallet, paused, eyed the tray, and glanced at the bathroom door. "You know what? Let's surprise her." He grabbed some more cash. "Go get some strawberries and whipped cream, too." He handed Jerry Lee the money with a grin. "And make it fast."

Jerry took the cash. "Yes, sir." He put the money in his pocket and pushed the empty cart toward the door.

Reginald walked with him. "And if you knock and we don't answer," he raised the side of his lip, "just leave it outside."

Jerry nodded. "Yes, sir."

"See you, kid." He closed the door.

Pulling out the money, Jerry headed toward the elevator with the cart. The elevator was still on the floor, and after entering it, he counted the money and whistled when he realized it was a hundred bucks. Not believing his luck, he returned to the kitchen, told the staff what he needed, what room it was for, and to hurry. The strawberries didn't take long to prepare, but apparently, the whipped cream was missing. No one could find it until Marty appeared, yelled at the staff, told them they were idiots, and found the whipped cream himself. He spooned some out in a bowl, and without calling Jerry any names, stormed away, still yelling. Glad not to be the object of his hostility, Jerry pushed the cart with the strawberries and cream back to the elevator and rode it up to the third floor. Hoping he might get another hefty tip, he pushed it to the door of 302 and knocked again. "Room service, Mr. Durning."

There was no answer. Guessing Reginald was getting lucky, he pushed the cart against the wall and knocked softly again. "Strawberries and cream are outside, sir, when you're ready."

He started to walk away when a distinct odor made him stop. It smelled like something was burning. He returned to the door and sniffed. The smell was definitely stronger near the door. Uncertain of what to do, he recalled his training. Fire was a major concern at a hotel. Was something on fire inside Reginald's room?

Jerry Lee recalled entering the room earlier with the champagne. A candle had been lit beside the bed. The hotel didn't provide candles, so it must have belonged to Reginald or the redhead. Had the candle caught the bed sheets on fire? The odor grew stronger, and it had an unpleasant tinge to it—something Jerry had not smelled before, but it made him wince. The acrid smell worried him, and he knocked again softly. "Mr. Durning? Is everything okay?"

There was no answer.

His worry grew, and he imagined unpleasant scenarios. What if the room was aflame and Reginald and the redhead had succumbed to the smoke?

Or had Reginald and the redhead accidentally set the fire and now they were trying to put it out without getting into trouble? Jerry eyed the fire alarm on the wall across from him. Should he pull it?

About to knock again, Jerry heard a thump in the room, and knew someone was inside, but no one had answered. Thinking he had better check, he pulled out his key card, which gave him access to the rooms. He suspected Donald would disapprove, but he'd rather be yelled at than have a guest injured or risk a fire. He spoke as he waved the card in front of the reader. "Mr. Durning? I can smell something burning. I'm coming in to be sure you're okay."

The light flicked to green on the reader, and he pushed on the handle. The door opened, and he spoke before looking. "Mr. Durning? Ma'am? It's Jerry." The smell was much stronger, and he almost gagged. Something was definitely wrong. "Sir?" He poked his head inside and dropped his jaw when he saw Reginald, partially clothed, lying on the floor beside the bed. His eyes were partially open and there was a wound in his chest. Blood ran from the wound to the carpet. Looking closer, Jerry saw what looked like a star burned into Reginald's thigh. Shocked into silence, he started to enter when the redhead stepped out of the shadows. She held a weapon in her hand, and she pointed it at Jerry.

"Hi, handsome," she said. Her top was open, and Jerry caught sight of her lacy black bra. Her short skirt was pulled slightly down, exposing a black tattoo on her hip. "You really should have left the strawberries outside."

Jerry froze, but the gun in her hand told him she meant to kill him, and thinking of his grandfather, who'd been the target of more than a few enemies, he darted backwards and raced through the door just as he heard a thunk and a piece of the wall near his ear exploded into shards. Shrieking, he raced out of the room, pulled the fire alarm, and as the sirens wailed, he made it to the stairwell and sprinted down the stairs to the garage. Terrified, he passed the parked cars, ran out into the street and sprinted away from the hotel.

Chapter Two

DETECTIVE AARON REMALLA WALKED past a parked police car with swirling lights. Hotel guests wandered around the parking lot, many of them in robes and sweatpants. A fire truck was in the front driveway and its flashing lights brightened the entrance to the hotel. Seeing his partner, Gordon Daniels, waiting for him outside, he stepped up onto the sidewalk and approached the sliding glass doors that led to the lobby. "Long time, no see."

Daniels pushed off the brick wall he'd been leaning on. "No kidding."

"You been here long?"

"Couple of minutes."

They headed into the lobby, where more guests wandered, and an officer was speaking to a man behind the reception counter. On their way to the elevator, Rem and Daniels flashed their badges at an officer standing guard, and he told them to go to the third floor.

Tired, Rem swiped back a strand of his long dark hair and tucked it behind his ear. He'd been ready to hit the hay when he'd received the call from Captain Lozano about the body found in the hotel. Another murder in the city was part of the job, and Rem hadn't thought much of it, until Lozano had informed him that a star had been burned into the victim's thigh. That had changed everything. Rem had quickly dressed, kissed Mikey and told her not to wait up, and headed out to meet Daniels, who Lozano had already called.

"You thinking what I'm thinking?" asked Rem, as he hit the button for the elevator.

Daniels smoothed back his gelled blond hair. "Another vic with a star branded into them means our Star Killer is back, and I'm wondering why."

The elevator arrived and opened. "It could be a copycat."

They stepped on to the elevator and the doors closed. "You believe that?" asked Daniels.

"The other two murders were in seedy hotels. This one's way nicer."

"So our vic prefers the swankier places. That doesn't mean much."

"I guess we won't know for sure until get up there." Rem eyed the illuminated buttons as they ascended.

"That's the reason I partnered with you." Daniels tapped his fingertip on his temple. "All those brains of yours."

Rem smirked at his partner. "Anybody ever tell you you're weird when you're tired?"

The elevator stopped. "At least I can use fatigue as an excuse," said Daniels. "What's yours?"

Rem smirked again as the doors opened, and they stepped out into a lobby buzzing with activity. Officers stood in the hall leading to a room with an open door. Rem and Daniels flashed their badges again and approached the room, where a member of the forensic unit handed them gloves and shoe coverings. After putting them on, they stepped into the hotel room, where one forensic tech was dusting for prints, and a third took photos. A woman wearing a jacket with *Coroner Unit* etched into the fabric of a pocket stood beside a covered body lying near the bed. She typed notes into a tablet.

Rem could see the blood seeping into the carpet beyond the covering. "Hey, Gillespie." He stepped closer. "Ibrahim getting his beauty sleep tonight?"

Sharon Gillespie looked over at Rem. She wore dark-rimmed glasses and had her dark hair pulled back into a ponytail. "He's out of town at his son's college graduation, so I pulled the short straw."

"Lucky you," said Daniels. He sniffed and winced. "It stinks in here."

Sharon nodded. "That's burned skin." She slid her tablet into a wide pocket in her jacket, squatted, and lifted the covering from the victim. "He's been branded with a star."

Rem grimaced. The victim was a white male around sixty years of age. Partially dressed, he had what looked like a bullet wound in his chest. Blood had spilled down his sides and soaked the carpet beneath him. Rem squatted next to Gillespie and studied the black star burned into the victim's skin. "Looks like our guy." He glanced up at Daniels, who was also studying the victim.

"Sure does," said Daniels. "You got a time of death, Sharon?"

Sharon straightened. "I'd say around two hours ago. The fire department found him after someone pulled the alarm."

Rem stood. "Someone pulled the alarm? Do they know who?"

Sharon shrugged. "You'll have to talk to Brann about that. He's got all those juicy details."

Daniels scratched his jaw. "What else can you tell us?"

Sharon pulled out her tablet again. "He's got a close-range gunshot wound to the chest, which is likely your cause of death. I'll know more when we get him on the table."

"Any ID?" asked Rem.

"There is, but Brann's got it. I'm just here for the body."

"Thanks, Sharon," said Daniels, as she pulled out her phone and walked away. He looked around the room. "No signs of a struggle."

Rem pointed. "There's a candle by the bed." He gestured at the vic. "And he's half naked. Plus, there's champagne and two glasses. That suggests a romantic interlude."

Daniels shot a thumb back toward the door. "Did you notice the cart in the hall? I saw strawberries and whipped cream."

"Yup. He was definitely gonna get lucky until his luck changed."

"It all follows the same pattern as the other two vics. A lovely lady lures her target into a hotel room with the promise of sex, but she kills and brands him instead."

Rem recalled the two previous victims who'd been murdered and branded—Rex Beelson, who'd been killed three years earlier in LA, and Donald Morgans, who'd been murdered in San Diego four months ago. "Seems like she's escalating."

"We need to find out about the vic, and who pulled the fire alarm."

Rem turned toward the door and, stepping away from the body, noticed the damage to the wall near the doorframe. "Check that out."

Daniels turned and frowned. "Looks like one shot missed." He moved to the door frame and studied the damage. "That's not part of the pattern." He glanced back into the room toward the bed. "How could she miss when he's that close?"

"Maybe he pushed the gun away?"

Daniels knitted his brows. "And what? He gave her more time to fire a second round? If he shoved the gun away, he would have either run and been hit in the back, or he would have tackled her and tried to take the weapon. There would have been a struggle, but there's no indication of that."

Rem looked around the room. "Doesn't add up. Nor does the fire alarm. She didn't pull it."

"Someone else did," added Daniels.

Rem raised his brow. "What are we saying here? That someone walked in on the murder, got shot at, pulled the alarm and ran?"

Daniels pulled on his glove. "If that's true, then we've got a witness."

Rem's heart thumped. "That changes everything."

"There's something else to consider," said Daniels. "You remember Lexie's theory about who our hit woman is?"

Rem thought of Lexie Logan, the investigative reporter they'd been working with recently. "I didn't forget. If Lexie's right, that means Rhonda did this."

"And if there's a witness who saw her...," said Daniels, his face tightening, "we may have a way to catch her."

"Assuming the witness lives long enough. If Rhonda's working with this secret black bird organization, they aren't going to allow loose ends." Rem flashed back on their history with Rhonda and a covert organization whose members sported black bird tattoos. All they knew about it was that it was led by someone who extorted people in powerful and influential positions and killed those who didn't pay up.

Daniels eyed the damaged wall and shook his head. "If there is a witness, he'll have a target on his back as big as ours."

Rem grunted and poked his head outside the door and saw two officers at the end of the hall talking to Brann, the officer in charge of the scene. "Let's talk to Brann."

He and Daniels stepped out, and Brann headed in their direction. "Sorry, guys," said Brann. "I needed to talk to Everman. He got a statement from the man at the front desk who checked in our vic." He raised an open notepad. "Names Donald Winters."

"Our vic?" asked Rem.

"No," said Brann. "The guy at reception." He glanced at his notes. "Our vic checked in a little after eight o'clock with a woman. Winters didn't get a name for the woman, but she was around thirty, five foot six, with jaw-length layered red hair and long bangs. She wore lots of makeup and jewelry, and, in his words, the two were affectionate." He used his fingers as quote marks.

"We get the picture," said Daniels.

Brann read his notes. "Vic wore a wedding ring. She didn't. On the way to the elevator, the vic ordered the hotel's nicest bottle of champagne, and the two went upstairs. About twenty, maybe thirty minutes later, the fire alarm went off. Everyone evacuated and the fire department came. They didn't find a fire, but they found our dead guy."

"Who is he?" asked Rem.

Brann flipped back a page in his notebook. "We found his wallet on the floor. Had two hundred in cash, and his cards and license were still there. His name is Reginald Durning."

Daniels' eyes widened, and Rem knitted his brow. "Reginald Durning?" asked Rem "You're sure?"

"I'm sure," said Brann. He looked between Daniels and Rem. "You two know him?"

"No," said Daniels. "But we know Josh Durning. A prosecutor for the state. We've worked a few cases with him." He spoke to Rem. "Isn't Reginald his dad's name?"

"I think so," said Rem. "Lozano is friends with him. He'll know."

Daniels pulled off his gloves and grabbed his phone. "I'll call Lozano." He stepped away.

Hoping they were wrong and weren't about to tell a friend his father had been murdered, Rem faced Brann. "Anything else? Any sign of the woman?"

Brann shook his head. "Nope. But the good news is we have video from the hotel lobby and the elevator. Everton's going to talk to security and get copies sent to us."

"That's something at least." Rem tipped his head. "Did you notice the damage to the wall near the door in the room?"

"We did. Forensics will retrieve the bullet. We're working on talking to the guests, but with most of them wandering around downstairs, it's been tough."

"I bet," said Rem, "but keep working on it. We need to know if anyone saw anything."

"We will." Brann lowered his notebook. "Donald Winters told Everton that a staff member by the name of," he glanced at his notes, "Jerry Lee Caruso delivered the champagne. He's twenty years old and has worked for the hotel for six months."

Rem perked up. "Where is he?"

Brann lowered his notes again. "Nobody knows. Everton talked to the kitchen too. Apparently, the vic ordered strawberries and cream after the champagne. Caruso took it up, and then all hell broke loose."

Rem looked down the hall. Had Caruso delivered the strawberries and walked in on the murder? "We need to find this Jerry Lee Caruso. Pronto."

"Everton got his name, address and phone number, but Caruso's not answering his cell."

"Send all that info to me and Daniels. We'll start looking."

"I got his mother's number, too. She's his emergency contact."

"Send it."

Brann nodded as Daniels walked up, his face somber. "Lozano says Durning's dad is Reggie Durning. He's a defense attorney for a large private firm. He and Lozano used to work together when Lozano was a detective and Reggie was a prosecutor. They still played golf now and then, but Lozano says he hasn't seen Reggie in almost a year."

"Hell," said Rem.

Daniels sighed. "Lozano's on his way. He wants to ID the body, so Josh doesn't have to. Then we'll notify the family." He rubbed his neck. "Damn. This sucks."

Rem dreaded this part of the job, and knowing a member of the victim's family made it worse. "Yeah, well. Better we tell Josh than some stranger."

"I guess," said Daniels. "But now we have to figure out why Josh Durning's father was murdered in a hotel room and branded by a killer."

"There's one bit of good news," added Rem. "We may have our witness. A Jerry Lee Caruso. He delivered the strawberries and hasn't been seen since."

"Does that mean he's dead or alive?"

"One way to find out." Rem's phone dinged with a notification.

"I sent you the info on Caruso," Brann said to Rem.

"Thanks," said Rem, pulling off his gloves and shoe coverings. He eyed Daniels. "While we wait for Lozano, we need to make some phone calls. The sooner we locate Caruso, the better."

Daniels squinted at Rem. "Strangely, you're way more positive when you're tired."

"Enjoy it while it lasts." Rem headed down the hall.

Chapter Three

EXHAUSTED, DANIELS PUSHED THE doors open to the squad room, walked to his desk and fell into his chair with a groan. Rem followed, but headed straight to the coffee machine, where he poured himself a cup after grabbing a mug from his desk. "I don't know about you, but I'm running on empty."

Daniels pushed up in his seat. "After that large soda, mile-high cheeseburger, and chili-covered fries you ate in the car, I'm surprised you aren't doing high kicks."

"If I'd gotten more than two hours of sleep last night, the food would have helped." Rem added sugar and cream to his coffee.

Daniels rested his chin in his palm. "I guess that's what happens when you get older."

Rem turned with a smirk. "I don't see you doing any jumping jacks after eating that salad with raw tuna." He made a face of disgust.

"Yeah, but I look good. You, on the other hand..."

Rem eyed the chili stain on his shirt. "Mikey looks past my stains, and she likes what she sees just fine."

"For now..."

Rem tossed his stir stick into the trash. "If Marjorie can put up with you for as long as she has, then Mikey's got it made."

Daniels rubbed his face. "Mikey does have stamina. I'll give her that." He moved a loose folder to a stack of them on his desk. "Any luck with her trying to find that lost dog?"

Rem sat at his desk. "Not so far."

"Sorry to hear it."

After the overzealous Detective Monk had almost arrested Mikey for murder, Mikey had been working on retrieving her lost memories of D'Mato's cult with Lena, a shaman and grandmother to her coworker, Kyle. Determined to find Vera's killer, who Mikey saw but couldn't identify, she and Lena had been meeting twice a week.

Rem sipped some coffee. "She and the neighbor have tried a few tactics to find the dog with no luck so far, but the neighbor's hopeful."

"Good." Daniels eyed the quiet squad room. Monk and Manetti weren't there, and none of the detectives sitting at the other desks seemed interested in Daniels' and Rem's conversation. Despite that, he and Rem continued to use the "finding a lost dog" story as a metaphor for Mikey attempting to retrieve her memories. If anyone was listening, it wouldn't make them suspicious.

"You have any time this past weekend to look at potential vacation sites?" asked Rem.

Daniels recognized the other metaphor they were using to describe their review of the contents of Ackerman's box, which Lexie had copied to three USB drives. "I did, but I didn't see anything I liked."

"Me, either." Rem sipped his coffee. "Frustrating. I know there's a decent place to visit out there, but none of it fits the requirements."

"There are an awful lot of vacation spots to check out, though."

Rem dropped his head and gripped his temples. "Tell me about it." He sighed, lifted his head, and set his coffee down. "Okay. Let's get back to what we can deal with. Jerry Lee Caruso."

"Get back to what? The kid has vanished. We've spent all night looking for him. All the places his mother suggested were a bust, and she's panicked. His friends and coworkers don't know anything, and his phone was found in a trash can near the hotel." He leaned back in his chair. "I hate to say it, but it's looking like our hit woman got to him."

"Don't you mean Rhonda?"

"We can't be a hundred percent positive it's her. You saw the video."

"I saw a woman who's likely wearing a wig and put on enough makeup and jewelry to easily disguise herself."

"Well, if it is Rhonda, then that doesn't bode well for Jerry Lee."

"Until we find his body, we have to keep looking."

"Any idea where?"

Rem rested his head back against his chair. "Let me think. I think that chilidog and cheesy fries are kicking in."

Daniels snorted. "I'm not encouraged. You can't even remember what you ate."

"Tomato. Tomahto. Same difference." Rem closed his eyes.

"If you say so." Daniels eyed Lozano's empty office. "I guess Lozano is still with Mandy Durning."

Rem opened his eyes and raised his head. "I guess. She was devastated about her husband. I'm sure Lozano wants to help however he can."

"And try to get information about why Reggie checked into a hotel with a woman who was not Mandy."

Rem eyed his watch. "I suspect we'll know soon enough. When Lozano gets back, we'll get the scoop."

"Yeah." Daniels sighed. "Josh handled it pretty well last night." He recalled meeting with Josh and his mother to tell them about Reginald. While Lozano had stayed with the family, Daniels and Rem had gone through Reginald's home office. They'd found little of interest but had brought his personal laptop back to the station for the tech guys to review.

"That was brutal." Rem sat up. "But I'm familiar with hiding your grief until you're alone. Something tells me he fell apart after we left."

"I'm going to assume that the Williamson trial will be postponed, which means so will my testimony."

"Judge Voorhees may give Josh a few days, but that's it. That trial's been put off long enough as it is."

"Yeah. Maybe." Daniels poked at the edge of a folder. He lowered his voice. "You think we should tell Josh about the whole black bird thing?"

Rem paused and picked up his mug. "Not yet. We need more information."

"His father was branded with a star. Which means he owed someone and didn't pay up. He was a high-profile defense attorney. God knows what kind of trouble he'd gotten himself into."

"Yeah," said Rem. "And if we find something bad, we'll have to tell Josh and his family."

"You heard Josh last night. He wants the killer behind bars, and if we tell him about the black bird group, he's going to want to go after them too."

Rem looked around the room and kept his voice down. "We're not investigating the black birds, remember?"

Daniels kept his voice low. "Since the last three months have been quiet, that's easy to say, but now we have another murder on our hands. What are we supposed to do? Not investigate the elephant in the room?"

"That's the thing about elephants, Daniels. They can smush you without a second thought."

"They're also big and lumbering, and they leave a giant trail behind them."

Rem blew out a heavy breath. "I'm not saying we don't follow that trail. We just have to be careful how we do it, which means we leave Josh out of it." He leaned over his desk. "Any word from your friend?"

Rem meant Erin Gerard—another mystery player in a giant game of riddles. Erin's connection to Daniels' father had yet to be revealed, but she continued to date Rem's cousin, Cain, who sported a black bird tattoo on his wrist and had his own elusive connection to the society. Daniels eyed the squad room and rolled his chair closer to Rem's so he could speak quietly. "Nothing recent. I guess Cain's been out of town a lot." Daniels groaned. "I hope he's not onto her. If something happens…"

"Don't worry about it. She did this on her own. You told her the risks. And don't worry about Cain. He's not smart enough to realize that a woman could dupe him." He paused. "She just needs to push a little harder."

Daniels sat up. "What are you saying? You want her to get killed?"

"Of course not. But she's there, and she offered to help. Why not use her? She's the only asset we have right now."

"She's not an asset. She's flesh and blood, and if Cain catches on, I don't want Erin to wind up dead with a star branded into her skin."

Rem studied Daniels. "You're getting attached to her, aren't you?"

"I'm as attached as I would be to any informant. I worry about her safety. Don't you?"

Rem paused. "Just be careful, partner. We still can't be sure who she is or whose side she's on."

Daniels hesitated. "You think she's lying to me?"

"I didn't say that."

"But you didn't not say it."

Rem set his coffee mug on his desk. "How do I not say something?"

"You do it all the time."

"Really? I had no idea."

Thinking about Erin, Daniels massaged his tight neck.

"Listen," said Rem, keeping his voice quiet. "All I'm saying is to be wary. And since she claims to be helping, we need to use that. It's been three months. That's more than enough time to get on Cain's good side. At some point, though, she either needs to get the goods or get the hell out of there."

"You try telling her that."

"I would if I could ever meet her." He reached for his mug, but his eyes widened, and he pointed. "That's what we should do."

Daniels smirked. "I'm afraid to ask, but I have no choice because I know you'll tell me, anyway. What should we do?"

"Invite her to dinner."

Daniels recalled the last time he did that. "I tried. She ran off like a frightened deer."

"I know, but that was a while ago. Let's try again." He rocked back in his seat. "Only this time, try a different tactic."

"Like what?"

Rem sat up with more energy than he'd shown all day. "Have Marjorie invite her."

Daniels wasn't sure he heard right. "Are you out of your freaking mind? There's no way I'm getting Marjorie involved in this. Did you forget that she's barely three months pregnant?"

"Of course not. But does that mean she can't invite Erin to dinner?"

"I don't want her involved."

"She's already involved. Erin followed her, remember? To supposedly find out more about her? Erin's obviously curious about you and your family. Let's use that."

"What exactly are you proposing? That Marjorie and Erin go to dinner? There's no way they're meeting without me."

"No. Not just them. But if you're so sure Erin is telling the truth, then what are you worried about?"

"That's not fair. We're talking about my wife. And you know she's had a rough first trimester. The doctor told her to take it easy."

Rem raised his brow. "Is it anything serious?"

"No. But the morning sickness has been a lot tougher than J.P. And she's exhausted."

"Then you cook." Rem leaned his elbows on his desk. "And we'll make it the whole group. Ask Marjorie to invite Erin over. I'll come and bring Mikey. Keep it casual. We can chip in and help, and Marj can take it easy."

Daniels paused. "I don't want to put Erin at risk, either."

"What risk? If Cain's using her to get to you, then wouldn't he and this organization want her to get closer? Let them think that she's on their side.

That may spur Cain to start talking to her more about his little secret group of brothers."

Daniels wanted to object but could see Rem's point. If the black bird group thought Erin could help them, the more likely they'd bring her into the fold, and she might get information. "I really hate this double-agent crap."

Rem softened his gaze. "This double-agent crap will work just fine, as long as we can trust her. If you don't, then leave it alone. It's your call."

Daniels set his jaw but nodded. "I hear you." He sighed. "I'll talk to Marjorie about it."

"Good." Rem picked up his mug and sat back.

"It's still a long shot. I think Erin's terrified to meet my family. Especially you."

Rem's brow furrowed. "Me? Why me? I'm the fun one of this duo." He smiled and drank his coffee.

"Which makes me the brains."

"You wish."

"But you're also the intense one. And I think she senses your doubt."

Rem held his coffee. "If she's on the up and up, then she's got nothing to worry about, but if she's lying to you..." His face fell and he turned serious. "I'll bury her ass."

Daniels noted Rem's tone and understood it. Over the last three months, he'd grown closer to Erin even though they'd spoken little. It surprised him that he'd come to care for her. But if she gave him reason to doubt her allegiance, he knew what he'd do. He eyed Rem with a similar intensity. "You and me both."

Chapter Four

JERRY LEE TRIED TO relax on the small cot in the dark and dank basement. One measly light bulb hanging from the ceiling provided the only light, but it cast eerie shadows in the room, giving Jerry the sense that he was not alone.

He'd tried to sleep, but every time he closed his eyes, he could see the redhead with the gun pointed at him, standing over Reginald Durning's dead body, and he'd smell that awful odor. Jerry chastised himself for the millionth time. Why the hell had he opened that door? He should have called security or just pulled the alarm. Then he wouldn't be in this mess.

He thought of his mom and his chest tightened and tears sprang to his eyes. He imagined how worried she must be, but Jerry couldn't go home, and he couldn't call her. He'd spent enough time with his grandfather to know that the woman who'd killed Mr. Durning wouldn't abide a witness. Jerry could see it in her eyes, and the whiz of the bullet past his ear was all he needed to know. If he talked to his mother, he would put her safety at risk, and he couldn't do that.

After racing out of the hotel, Jerry had dumped his phone into a trashcan on the street because it was traceable, and walked the streets, trying to figure out where to go. Friends weren't an option because it would risk them too. After an hour of wandering, he saw the street he was on and realized he was close to Arnold Bertrand's pawn shop, where Jerry Lee had taken his first job after arriving in the city. His mother had never been a fan of Arnie's, but he'd paid Jerry well and had been a decent boss. He also knew things about the city and the people in it and was street smart, like Jerry's granddad. He also kept a very large gun behind the counter.

Jerry walked to the darkened shop with the iron rods over the windows and rang the bell outside the door. Although the shop was closed, Jerry Lee remembered that Arnie frequently slept in the basement and occasionally assisted late-night customers who needed cash fast.

He waited and when no one answered, he rang the bell again and was rewarded when the light inside the shop brightened. Tucking his hands into his pockets and keeping his hood up, Jerry waited until the curtain on the other side of the door shifted and Arnie peeked around it with a dubious look. Jerry waved, and Arnie's eyes widened. The locks disengaged, and Arnie pushed the door open. "Jerry? What the hell are you doing here?"

"Can I come in?"

Arnie pushed the door open. "Get your ass inside."

Jerry slipped into the shop, and Arnie closed the doors and relocked them. Jerry didn't miss the large gun in his hand. "I'm sorry, Mr. Bertrand, but I need your help."

Arnie looked him over and raised an eyebrow. "Is it drugs, kid? I told you to leave that shit alone. If you're dealing—"

"No, no, no. It's not drugs. I...I saw something."

"Saw something? Like what? Is your mom okay?"

Jerry bobbed his head up and down. "She's fine. It's not about her. I was at the hotel."

Arnie scoffed. "I bet you've seen things. Places like that are a haven for pedophiles and traffickers." Arnie had always been a bit of a conspiracy theorist, and he trusted few people, and the government, banks and the police even less. "Did somebody proposition you?"

"I...I saw a murder." His turmoil and emotions stirred, all the tension and fear caught up to him, and it was hard to speak. "And I don't know what to do." Tears sprung into his eyes and all he wanted to do was go home. His throat tightened, and he tried not to cry.

Arnie took his arm. "Come with me." He guided Jerry to a back door, which led to the basement. Arnie flipped off the lights to the pawn shop and guided Jerry down the stairs. Trying to hold it together, Jerry entered the sparse, cold room with a cement floor and brick walls. A cot with rumpled sheets was pushed against the far wall, and there was a small table and two chairs beside it. Arnie had a small fridge and TV, plus a cabinet with shelves, and there was a small window in the upper corner.

Arnie pulled out one of the chairs. "Take a seat. I'll get you something to drink."

Jerry sat in the chair, sniffed, and swiped his eyes.

Arnie opened the cabinet, pulled out two glasses and a bottle. He set his gun down on the table along with the two glasses. He opened the bottle and poured some dark liquid into each glass.

Jerry saw it was bourbon. "I don't drink bourbon."

"You do tonight, kid." Arnie set the bottle down and sat beside Jerry. He picked up a glass, handed it to Jerry, and took one for himself. He clinked it against Jerry's. "Bottoms up." He knocked the glass back and swallowed its contents.

Jerry hesitated, but then did the same. The liquid burned and Jerry almost coughed it up. His eyes watered again.

Arnie leaned his elbows on the table. "Now, tell me what happened."

Jerry told him everything, and when he finished, Arnie poured him another dose of bourbon, which Jerry drank with less difficulty than the first glass. "What should I do?" asked Jerry. "Go to the cops?"

Arnie put the cap back on the bourbon. "You're going to stay here while I go out."

"Go out? Where are you going?"

Arnie stood and pushed his chair in. "To find out what the hell is going on." He gestured toward the cot. "Try to get some rest. I'll be back by morning."

"But what about my mom? I have to let her know I'm okay."

Arnie paused. "I'll get word to her. Just stay put. Don't call anyone, especially the cops."

"I don't have my phone."

"Even better." He headed to the stairs and turned back. "You eat?"

"I'm not hungry."

"I'll bring us some chow for breakfast." He headed up the stairs.

"Mr. Bertrand?"

He looked back.

"Thank you." His throat tightened again.

"Don't thank me yet, kid. Let's find out what we're dealing with first." He resumed his walk up the stairs. "Get some sleep."

· · · • • • • • · ·

Detective Luca Manetti entered the squad room, holding his apple and bag of seaweed crisps. He saw Daniels and Remalla murmuring to each other; Daniels had slid his chair close to Rem's and their heads were together. Seeing Manetti, Daniels straightened and wheeled himself back to his desk. "Hey, Manetti," said Daniels.

"Rem. Daniels. You two planning something secret?" asked Manetti on the way to his desk.

Rem swiveled in his seat. "Daniels' birthday is coming up. I'm planning a surprise party."

Manetti set his apple and seaweed down. "It's not much of a surprise, is it? If you're talking to him about it."

"I guess that's true." Rem eyed Daniels. "Sorry, partner."

"It's okay," said Daniels. "Just the fact that you remembered my birthday is three months away is all the surprise I need."

Rem's eyes widened. "Three months? I thought it was two."

Daniels rolled his eyes. "Just don't buy me another double fudge chocolate cake from that bakery."

"What? You like chocolate."

"It's not about the flavor, although I could do without the double fudge. It was in a shape not appropriate for most birthday parties. Marjorie couldn't take any pictures with the cake in it, and especially none of J.P. digging into it with his little hands."

Rem shrugged. "I didn't know it was that kind of bakery, which is probably why I got it at a discount when the lady at the register told me it was meant for a bachelorette party that got canceled."

Daniels shot out his hand. "Would it kill you to pay full price for something?"

"Do you know how much a large double-fudge chocolate cake is? Besides, it was a good cake, despite the shape it was in."

Daniels aimed his finger at Rem. "Next time, no cake without Marjorie's approval."

"Fine, but don't blame me if you get a one-layered plain vanilla with buttercream icing."

Daniels spoke with exasperation. "That's exactly what I want."

Rem moved a folder to a pile on his desk. "Details."

Daniels grumbled.

Manetti chuckled at the pair's banter. "You two have any progress with your latest case?" Manetti sat at his desk. "I heard your victim got branded."

"He did," said Daniels. "And what's worse is the victim is Josh Durnings' father."

Manetti sucked in a breath when he recognized the name. "You're kidding."

"I wish we were." Rem drank some coffee. "We had to break the news to Josh earlier. It was awful."

His hunger waning, Manetti set his seaweed chips to the side. "Isn't his dad some bigwig attorney?"

"He is," said Daniels. "How'd you know?"

Still surprised, Manetti shook his head. "Monk and I worked with Durning on the Speedman case. Josh and I got to know each other, and he mentioned his dad. They were close."

Rem sat his coffee cup on his desk. "Yeah. It's a tough one."

"Any leads?" asked Manetti.

"We may have a witness," said Daniels. "But we can't find him."

"Spent all night looking with no luck," added Rem. "We're hoping he's still alive."

"Damn," said Manetti. "You think he can ID the brander?"

"We're hoping," said Rem. "So say some prayers he's still breathing."

"I will." Manetti sat back, still absorbing the news, when the squad doors opened and his partner, Frank Monk, walked in.

He wore his usual dark slacks and button-down shirt with a loosened tie around his neck. His wire-rim glasses were perched on the end of his nose, and he slipped off his jacket as he approached his desk. "Morning, Manetti."

"Morning, Monk." Manetti didn't miss how Daniels and Remalla went back to work without acknowledging Monk, and Monk ignored them, too. The relationship between the three had been frosty ever since Monk had gone after Rem's girlfriend, Mikey, for a murder she hadn't committed.

Following Mikey's exoneration, Monk had given a half-hearted, but necessary, apology, yet Rem and Daniels' view of Monk remained unchanged, despite Manetti's attempts at reconciliation. "Did you hear about Josh Durning's dad?" asked Manetti.

Monk pulled out his chair and sat. "No. Why would I hear about Josh Durning's dad?" He pushed his glasses up his nose.

"Because he's dead. He was murdered and branded with a star last night. Just like the other two cases." Manetti nodded at Rem and Daniels. "They're on it."

"Really?" Monk looked over at Rem and Daniels. "Durning's dad?" He whistled. "I wonder what he was into?"

"Why do you say that?" asked Manetti.

Monk smirked. "The other two vics who got branded weren't random. I'm guessing they were targeted and this one's no different."

Manetti glanced at Rem and Daniels. "Is that true?" asked Manetti.

Rem looked up. "Durning was found in a hotel room."

"After checking in with a woman who wasn't his wife," added Daniels.

Manetti deflated. "Poor Josh."

Monk scooted his chair closer to his desk. "Let's hope he's not involved."

Rem and Daniels perked up.

"Why would you say that?" asked Manetti.

"The sins of the father frequently become the sins of the son." Monk shrugged. "Something to consider."

Rem closed the folder he'd been studying. "What are you saying, Monk? That Josh Durning is involved in whatever got his father killed?"

Monk jiggled his mouse, and his computer monitor brightened. "I'm not saying anything, Remalla. Whatever happened to Durning's dad is for you two to figure out. Just don't let friendship taint your judgement. Josh is just as capable of poor decisions and may have been aware of whatever his father was involved in."

Daniels narrowed his eyes. "Do you know something, Monk?"

"Don't know a thing," said Monk. "Just making some basic deductions."

Rem swiveled his chair toward Monk. "Reginald Durning was friends with Lozano. Based on your brilliant theory, are you suggesting Lozano may have known what Durning was involved in too?"

Monk knitted his brow. "Lozano knew the vic? That's even more interesting."

Rem stood with a huff and filled his cup with coffee. "I forgot that's how you work, Monk. Blame first. Get evidence later."

Monk straightened. "I just don't have a bleeding heart, Remalla, unlike you and Daniels. You two would protect Charles Manson if he were your buddy."

Daniels scoffed. "And you'd arrest your mother if her neighbor was murdered after bringing her cookies."

Manetti leaned forward. "C'mon, guys."

Rem set the coffeepot back on the burner and stared at Monk with a look that Manetti wouldn't want directed at him.

Monk eyed the duo and chuckled. "Knowing my mother, I probably would." He lifted and splayed out his hands. "Just giving my two cents, fellas."

"You can keep it," said Rem, with that same intense gaze.

Eyeing Rem, Monk rocked in his seat.

Manetti was about to step in again when the squad doors opened, and Captain Lozano entered. He wore his normal pressed suit with a colorful tie that suited his brown skin. His round belly tested the lower buttons of his wrinkled shirt, and his loose tie, red eyes, and haggard face told Manetti he'd been up a while and was tired.

"Morning, Captain," said Manetti. "I heard about Reginald Durning. I'm sorry for your loss."

Lozano walked through the squad room. "Thank you, Manetti. Daniels. Remalla. Let's talk." He strode past them and went into his office.

Daniels stood. Rem quickly doctored his coffee, followed Daniels into the office, and shut the door behind him.

Manetti sat back in his chair and eyed Monk, who was typing on his keyboard. "Why do you do that?"

"Do what?"

"Antagonize them? You're only making it worse."

"Just saying what I think, Manetti. That's how I roll."

Manetti sighed. "You think you could slow your roll a little then? You don't have to say anything at all."

Monk picked up a pencil and twirled it between his fingers. "Am I wrong? You and I both know Josh Durning will have to be questioned about what he knows about his dad's activities. His mother, too."

"You didn't have to make it sound like he was up to something. He's our friend."

Monk snorted. "You, Rem, and Daniels should get together and sing camp songs around a roaring fire. Make s'mores and shit. Then braid each other's hair."

"C'mon, Monk. You know what I mean."

"All I know is there's a killer running around branding her vics with a star. She lures them to a hotel room because they want to get laid, and she takes her revenge because they've somehow pissed her off, or at least someone off. This is vic number three that we know of, and the way it's going, there will probably be more. At this point, I'd be investigating the victim's dog." He pointed toward Lozano's office. "And I sure as hell wouldn't have those two on this case."

"You're just mad because they proved Mikey Redstone innocent when you were certain she was guilty."

"I was doing my job, Manetti, and if I had that case again, I wouldn't change a thing."

"They know what they're doing."

"Well, if Josh ends up protecting his dad, he's got the right detectives on the case. Those two will waste loads of time and tax dollars before they dare upset Josh. And they sure as hell won't get in Lozano's face either." He went back to his typing.

Manetti rested his elbows on his desk. "They may not have to. Apparently, there's a witness."

Monk's fingers stilled, and he glanced at Manetti. "What?"

Manetti nodded. "Someone saw the crime and took off. Rem and Daniels have been looking for him."

Monk leaned forward. "Someone caught the killer in the act? How much did they see?"

Manetti shrugged. "I don't know." He looked over at Lozano's office, where he could see Rem and Daniels talking to their captain through the glass. "I suppose that's what they're talking about right now."

Monk glanced toward the office, too.

Manetti grabbed his bag of seaweed crisps. "They find that witness, and bring him in, they may have their killer behind bars before dinner, and poor Josh will be off the hook." He pulled out a crisp. "Wouldn't that be nice?" He popped the crisp in his mouth.

Monk, his face a little paler, didn't answer.

"Monk?" asked Manetti.

Monk glanced at his watch. "Hell."

"Something wrong?" Manetti dug through his files. "We need to prep for the Desmond deposition today. You ready?"

"Sure," said Monk, standing. "I forgot, though. I got to make a phone call. Give me a sec."

Surprised by his partner's abrupt shift in subject, Manetti watched Monk pull out his cell and hurry out of the squad room.

Chapter Five

REM DRANK HIS COFFEE while Daniels updated Lozano on their unsuccessful hunt for Jerry Lee Caruso.

"His mother hasn't heard from him?" asked Lozano. "You think she'd tell you if she had?"

"She was pretty distraught, Cap," said Rem. "If she's lying, she's good at it."

"We told her to get in touch if Jerry Lee contacts her," said Daniels.

Lozano sat back in his chair. "Let's hope she does." He blew out a long breath. "You two think this could be Rhonda's dirty work?"

"Seems likely," said Rem, "although there's no way to be sure. It's just a theory now."

"If that theory proves true," said Lozano, "it could mean Reggie somehow pissed off this black bird group."

"It could," said Rem. He could see the concern in his captain's eyes. "But that's not certain. We don't know enough yet." While Lozano didn't know about Ackerman's box, he knew about Rhonda's potential connection to the black bird group, and Lexie's theory that Rhonda could be the hit woman who was branding men as some sort of retribution.

"Yeah," said Lozano with a sigh. "I know."

"How'd it go with Durning's wife?" asked Daniels. "Did you tell her where her husband was found?"

"I did." Lozano grunted. "It didn't go well."

"Sorry, Cap." Rem sat his coffee cup on the edge of Lozano's desk. "This whole situation sucks."

Daniels scratched his knee. "She had no idea?"

Lozano shook his head. "Not about the affair, but after she calmed down, she told me he hadn't been himself recently."

"How recently?" asked Rem.

Lozano rubbed his eyes. "The last six to eight months. Said he'd been drinking more, working longer hours, and not sleeping well. She told me he'd blamed it on work. Said he was vying for a partnership at the firm, but she thought there was more to it than that."

"She didn't suspect another woman?" asked Daniels.

"No," said Lozano. "Said that was out of character for Reggie, and I agree."

Rem sighed. "You hadn't seen him in a year. It's possible things changed."

"I know that, Remalla." Lozano leaned back in his chair. "I want you two to interview his friends and family and visit Reggie's firm." He picked up a piece of paper and read from it. "Crenshaw, Ingram, and Willoughby."

Daniels grabbed a piece of paper from Lozano's desk and a pencil. "That's a mouthful." He wrote on the paper.

"Get Reggie's list of clients and talk to them, too. Find out why the hell my friend ended up in that room with a bullet in his chest and a star branded into his thigh." Lozano set the paper down.

"What about our witness?" asked Rem.

"You've done all you can for now," said Lozano. "There's an APB out on him, and an officer is with the mother. The kid's friends and the hotel staff know to get in touch if Jerry Lee shows. All we can do now is wait."

Daniels glanced at the piece of paper. "Crenshaw, Ingram, and Willoughby might not be too forthcoming about that list of clients."

Lozano's tone hardened. "Get a warrant if you have to, but we need those names. Something tells me this has something to do with his work.

I'll be curious to learn how helpful Reggie's fellow associates are when it comes to finding his killer."

Rem stifled a yawn. "Lawyers aren't known to be generous with that type of information."

"And detectives, especially you two," Lozano pointed, "aren't known to care."

Daniels sat back. "Translation...figure it out."

Rem glanced at his partner. "Maybe you should take Spanish classes."

Daniels stood. "What for? I already speak Rem."

"That won't get you far on a resumé," said Lozano.

"But it will get me plenty far on this case." Daniels spoke to Rem. "You ready, partner?"

Shaking off his fatigue, Rem groaned and stood. "Any chance we can take a nap first, Cap?"

Lozano pulled off his tie. "You can nap when you're dead, Remalla." He turned on his monitor. "Keep me posted."

Rem pushed his chair toward the desk. "It was worth a shot."

Daniels headed toward the door but turned back. "You okay, Cap? We'd understand if you need to take the day."

Lozano snorted. "Taking the day won't get us closer to finding a killer. Go find this guy." He ran his hand over his head. "I'll be fine."

Rem nodded. "You need anything, let us know."

"What I need is answers." He swiveled in his chair and stared out the window. "Now get going."

"Will do, Cap," said Rem, after a pause. Opening the door and following Daniels, he left the office.

•••••••••

The wood popped, and the fire crackled as the flames brightened the circle within the grove of trees. Victor stood beside the fire, his eyes reflecting the light. Margaret stood beside him, holding a gun, and beside her stood a man. Tall and broad shouldered, he wore a mask that covered the top half of his face, and a lit cigarette hung from his lips. Smoke from the cigarette trailed into the air and the breeze caught it like the smoke from the fire, blowing it toward the two others at the fire's edge. A man and a woman, both on their knees, waited silently as Victor spoke to Margaret and the man wearing the mask.

Mikey knew the kneeling man and woman. They were fellow cult members and her friends, Nathan and Vera. From her perch behind the trees and just below the grove, Mikey watched the activity around the fire, wondering why Nathan and Vera had been summoned to the grove.

Seeing her sister Margaret sneer and speak to the masked man, Mikey's fear ramped up. Her stomach twisted, her heart raced, and her breathing quickened. Nathan and Vera's faces tensed when Margaret held the gun out to Nathan and said something Mikey couldn't hear. Nathan shook his head and Vera leaned back from the fire, her face etched in terror. She looked around as if considering ways to escape.

As if sensing her plans, Victor stepped closer to Vera as the argument between Margaret and Nathan intensified. Nathan raised his voice, and Mikey clearly heard him say "no" just as the man in the mask stepped forward, took the gun from Margaret, and aimed it at Vera. He smiled, pulled the cigarette from his mouth with one hand, and raised the weapon with the other.

Mikey heard him speak. "It's nothing personal," he said.

Vera barely had a second to scream before the boom of the gun made Mikey scream too, and she opened her eyes.

Clutching her chest, Mikey blinked several times, trying to come back from the grip of the memory.

"Mikey. Do you hear me?"

A woman's voice penetrated her fog, and Mikey felt a hand on her knee. She blinked again and focused on Lena sitting in front of her.

Lena spoke soothingly. "You're back. There is nothing to fear." Her long black and gray hair ran down her back in a braid, and the wrinkles around her eyes deepened. She took Mikey's hands and squeezed her fingers. "Feel my touch and ground yourself. You are safe."

Mikey's heart rate slowed, and she took a deep breath. The memory of what had happened in the grove lingered, though, and the knot in her stomach remained. She nodded. "I'm okay."

"Deep breaths, Michaela." Lena rubbed her palm over the back of Mikey's hand.

Mikey felt the flow of Lena's energy run up her arms and into her torso. The warmth helped ease her fear along with the knot in her stomach. "I'm better now."

Lena studied her for a moment before sitting back. "How was it this time? What did you see?"

Mikey rubbed her arms. "Pretty much what I see every time. The fire. The people." She bit her lip. "The gunshot." She closed her eyes. "It's awful every single time."

"Think about each detail. Is there anything new? It could be a small thing. The hoot of an owl, the whisper of a word, the movement of anyone at the scene."

Mikey sighed. "No. I didn't—" An image flashed in her mind. "Wait."

"What did you see?"

Mikey opened her eyes. "It's not what I saw. It's what I heard. He spoke. The smoking man said something."

"What did he say?"

Mikey swallowed. Just the memory made her queasy. "He told Vera it wasn't personal. He said it before he shot her." Her stomach rolled, and she clutched it.

Lena put her hand on Mikey's arm. "Breathe through it. Relax. Move the dark energy down into the earth. Release it. Don't hold on to it."

Mikey took several long and slow breaths. The first few times after working with Lena, she'd had to run to the bathroom when her stomach rebelled, but her control was better now, and she allowed the horror of the moment to move from her stomach down an invisible cord that led into the earth. Her midsection settled, and she relaxed. "It's okay. I'm okay."

"Good." Lena sat back. "You've done well today."

Mikey relaxed and sat back against Lena's couch. She was sitting in the middle of Lena's living room floor where Lena had created a sacred circle. Mikey could practice her meditations safely here, without fear of succumbing to the darkness of her recall. At first, Lena had been the one to guide Mikey in and out of the meditations, but now Mikey could do it on her own. "I've done well? He said three words. That's the most I've remembered in weeks. I feel like I'm getting nowhere."

"You must let go of your expectations and surrender the outcome. You will remember when the time is right. Rushing will only delay your progress."

Mikey held her head. "It's hard not to rush. This man killed Vera and almost killed Nathan. He's out there somewhere and he's dangerous."

Sitting on the floor, Lena crossed her legs and rested her hands on her knees. "How is Nathan? Is he safe? Has there been another threat against him?"

"He's safe. There hasn't been another threat." Mikey thought back on her meeting with Nathan not long after he'd left the hospital. He'd been relieved to know that what had happened to Vera was out in the open and seemed eager to get back to his life and not dwell on the past. "He's recovered from his attack and has returned to his routine. He doesn't think his kidnapping and assault had anything to do with Vera." She groaned in frustration. "Even though someone called him and offered him money to dig up Vera's grave and call the cops, which means whoever contacted him was at the grove when Vera died. Since Victor's dead and Margaret's institutionalized, that leaves our masked man." She tossed out her hand. "How can Nathan not be bothered by that?"

Lena tipped her head. "Maybe you should take a hint from Nathan."

"You mean bury my head in the sand as if nothing happened?" She rubbed her face. "I can't do that. The man who murdered Vera needs to be caught."

"I'm not saying he doesn't. I'm saying if you push too hard, you'll only push your memories further away." She stood and walked over to Mikey. "Your anger and guilt create a wall, and the higher you build it, the harder it becomes to breach." She sat on the couch.

Frustrated, Mikey got up and sat beside Lena. "I don't know how to do that. Every time I relive this memory, it stirs up all the emotion inside me. I should have helped Vera, and my fear stopped me." She hung her head. "I'm ashamed of myself."

"Vera doesn't blame you."

"Which makes it even worse."

"Then maybe we're going about this the wrong way."

Mikey raised her head. "What do you mean?"

"Maybe we should try to reach Vera, instead of trying to unmask the mystery man."

Mikey recalled the initial ceremony she'd done with Lena to help her deal with her traumatic memory of the grove. During the meditation, Vera had spoken to Mikey and told her she didn't blame her. "We did reach Vera."

"Just the one time. Perhaps you should speak to her again to help resolve your guilt."

Mikey ran her hands through her hair. "Oh, Lena. That just takes more time."

"Your impatience only adds to that time. And your impatience is tied to your shame. It's all connected, Michaela."

Mikey sighed. "Why do you have to be so reasonable? Can't you be angry and frustrated, too?"

"You asked for my help. Help means I tell you the truth. There is no other way."

Mikey leaned back on the sofa with a groan.

Lena smiled softly. "How's that handsome detective of yours? I'm sure he can be frustrated and angry along with you."

Mikey eyed the ceiling and thought of Rem. "He can be, but he's acting cool as a cucumber. He tells me to take my time and not rush it."

"Hmm," said Lena. "He's a smart one." She poked Mikey's knee. "That's good advice."

"His motives aren't so pure. I think he's scared. He knows if I remember, it puts me at risk."

"That's understandable."

Mikey looked over at Lena. "So it's fine if he's upset and scared?"

"He's not the one trying to retrieve lost memories. Nor is he ashamed."

Mikey resumed her stare at the ceiling. "Maybe not, but he's got his own issues to resolve."

Lena's brow furrowed. "What does that mean?"

Mikey regretted her words. "Nothing."

Lena shifted to face Mikey. "Your difficulty in remembering isn't solely tied to your anger and shame. Troubles in other areas also affect your connection." She paused. "Are you and Remalla having problems?"

Mikey grabbed a pillow from the couch and set it in her lap. "No. We're fine. We're good." She poked at the edge of the pillow.

Lena's face softened. "It's okay to say if there's a problem. Healthy relationships have them, too." She leaned closer. "What troubles you?"

Mikey let go of a long breath. "It's stupid."

"If you've hesitated to speak with him about it, then you don't think it's stupid." She paused. "Whatever it is scares you. Why?"

Mikey bit back another groan. She hadn't prepared herself for working with Lena, who, as a Native American shaman and a spiritual guru, was highly intuitive. Finding Vera's killer meant digging deep, and Mikey had to push through some hard layers to get to the heart of her issues. "I...I don't know."

"Yes. You do."

Mikey gripped the pillow. "You know I moved in with him when I started with you."

"I know. How is that going?"

"Great. Fine. We live well together."

"But...?"

Mikey shrugged. "The closet space isn't great in his house, and I...I want to use the closet upstairs, but..." she picked at the hem of the pillow, "...Jennie's things are in there. I mentioned it once, and he agreed to clean it out, but that was months ago, and I'm...I'm..." She sighed. "I don't know. I feel like I'm competing with a ghost."

"And you're reluctant to talk with him about it?"

"Of course I am. Jennie...she was the love of his life, and it almost killed him when she died."

"And you think you're competing?"

"It feels like I am."

"Why does it feel that way?"

"Because he retreats from that closet and doesn't want to deal with it, which tells me he...he..."

"He what?"

"That he's still in love with her."

"And if he is?"

Mikey looked away, her heart hammering. She'd voiced what had been sitting in the back of her mind since she'd first opened that upstairs closet. "If he is, then maybe he doesn't love me, or at least doesn't love me as much as he loves her." She dropped her head. "Maybe I don't measure up." Unexpected tears welled in her eyes. "See? It's stupid." She sniffed and swiped her eye.

"I see." Lena paused. "So you doubt his love for you?"

Mikey eyed Lena. "No. That's not..." She shook her head. "I mean, I know he loves me."

"But?"

Mikey held her head. "Why are you making this so hard?"

"This isn't hard at all. Do you love him?"

"Yes. I do."

"And he loves you?"

"Yes. He does."

"Then what is the issue, because it can't be a closet of another woman's things if you love each other."

Mikey bit her bottom lip. "How come when you say it, I feel silly?"

Lena put her hand on Mikey's knee. "Love isn't constricted or uncertain, and it isn't competitive or lacking. Love is big and bold. It's abundant and soothing and calm and knowing. It makes you feel better, not worse."

Mikey sniffed again and wiped away a tear that spilled down her cheek.

"If Remalla loves this woman, then that is a good thing. It doesn't mean he loves you any less. There is plenty of love to go around for all of us." She paused. "Are you okay with that? Or would you rather he only love you and no other?"

Mikey swallowed. "Well, when you put it that way, no. I don't want him to feel as if I'm trying to push Jennie away. I understand why he loves her."

"Then also understand his hesitation. Like you said, revisiting memories stirs emotion. The same is true for him. Going through her things is difficult, and it's natural to avoid it. And if you don't talk to him, he'll continue to ignore it. Communication is key, Michaela. Don't create problems that don't exist because you're afraid to ask the questions you've assumed the answers to."

More tears welled up, and Mikey cleared her throat. "Are you telling me I'm overreacting?"

"I'm telling you to talk to him. Something tells me the moment you do, he'll clean that closet and you can be there to help him through it."

Mikey wiped her eyes with her shirtsleeve. "Okay," she whispered. "I'll talk to him."

"And after you do, I think your sessions here might show some progress."

Mikey cleared her throat. "You still think we should try to contact Vera?"

"Yes. I do. She came through once, which shows she's willing."

"And once she does, I talk to her about my guilt?"

"Talk to her about whatever comes up. And be prepared. Opening the door to this means she could visit at any time. Not necessarily in one of our sessions."

Mikey moaned. "Wonderful."

"There's another thing we should consider."

"I'm afraid to ask."

"Your memories. They might not be enough to reveal this man's identity."

Mikey dropped her jaw. "Could that be a reason I'm struggling?"

"Perhaps. We'll continue to work on it and see what is revealed. But it's possible Vera knows him."

Mikey straightened. "Are you saying...?"

Lena nodded. "You get in touch with Vera, and if she's willing, she may tell you exactly who this man is."

Chapter Six

DANIELS STEPPED OFF THE elevator onto the top floor of a downtown skyscraper occupied by Crenshaw, Ingram, and Willoughby, along with the floor below.

Rem followed and, pulling his badge from his pocket, Daniels approached the receptionist sitting behind a counter at a wide desk at the front. On either side of him were two double glass doors that led to the main offices.

The man sitting at the desk wore a crisp brown suit and yellow tie, and he looked up from his computer. "May I help you?"

"Yes," said Daniels. He eyed the nameplate on the desk. "Miguel?"

Miguel smiled. "That's me."

"Miguel, I'm Detective Gordon Daniels and this is my partner. Detective Aaron Remalla." They held out their badges. "We'd like to see..." He thought about it and glanced at Rem. "Which one?"

Rem leaned against the desk and spoke to Miguel. "Either Crenshaw, Ingram or Willoughby."

Miguel frowned. "Um...Do you have an appointment?"

"No," said Daniels. "We're investigating the death of Reginald Durning."

Miguel's face fell. "I heard. It's just horrible. Mr. Durning was a nice man." He lowered his voice. "Is it true he was murdered?"

Daniels nodded. "Yes. Which is why we need to speak with Mr. Durning's superior."

Miguel gasped. "Do you think someone here did it?"

"We don't know," said Rem. "That's why we're investigating. How well did you know Mr. Durning?"

Miguel widened his eyes. "Me? Not very well. I only saw him coming and going."

"No office gossip?" asked Daniels. "No problems with the staff, or anyone else?"

Miguel shut his mouth and shook his head. "I can't tell you."

"Why not?" asked Rem.

"I was told the police might stop by and I was not to speak of Mr. Durning unless you had a warrant and I had an attorney present."

"Really? You have something to hide?" asked Daniels.

Miguel's eyes widened. "No. I mean, all I could tell you is who I've seen Mr. Durning speaking to as he came and went."

Daniels suspected he knew more, but wasn't going to say a word.

"Okay, then." Rem rested his elbows on the counter. "So, which one of the bosses can we talk to?"

"Let me check." Miguel typed on his keyboard. "Barbara Ingram is out of town, and Charles Willoughby, he's meeting with a client and is out of the office."

"What about Crenshaw?" asked Daniels.

"He's here." Miguel eyed the doors and tightened his jaw. "But he's not good with last-minute appointments."

"How is he with dead attorneys? Especially murdered ones that worked for him?" asked Rem.

Miguel paused. "Let me make a phone call." He picked up the phone.

"You do that," said Daniels.

Miguel dialed and spoke into the phone. "Delaina?" He lowered his voice and turned away from his desk.

Daniels straightened and looked around the small lobby with a leather sofa and two leather chairs surrounding a glass coffee table. The dark brown walls and the gold tile floors with no rug gave the space a drab feel. "Quite the place." There were no plants or paintings; the only items on the wall were the large gold initials of C, I, and W, which hung above the couch. In the upper corner, behind Miguel, a muted TV played a news channel, and captions scrolled at the bottom of the screen.

Rem looked around too. "It's got all the warmth of a parking lot."

Daniels glanced at Miguel, who was still talking on the phone. "You think Crenshaw will talk to us?"

"You kidding? Two detectives show up to discuss the murder of one of his high-powered attorneys should be important enough. And avoiding us only makes the firm look more suspicious."

Daniels glanced at the TV. "Look at that." He pointed. A news reporter was interviewing a man Daniels recognized.

Rem looked up and squinted. "Is that...?"

"...Damien Rook. Remember talking to him?" Damien Rook was the founder of Rook Enterprises, which owned Pinnacle Properties.

"Hard to forget." Rem studied the screen. "He still looks like the most interesting man in the world."

Daniels recalled Rem comparing Rook's appearance to a man from a beer commercial. The broadcast cut to a shot of protestors marching in front of Pinnacle. "They're not giving up, are they?" said Daniels.

"Nope. They're not, even though it's a lost cause. That development's going in come hell or high water."

"Especially if Rook has anything to say about it."

Waiting for Miguel, Rem tapped on the counter and watched the footage of the protesters. "Just so long as none of them goes missing."

The footage of the protests ended, and the broadcast cut back to the interview with Rook. "No kidding."

Miguel swiveled back. "Thank you, Delaina." He hung up. "Mr. Crenshaw's assistant is on her way. She'll take you back."

"Thanks, Miguel." Daniels glanced at both sets of double doors. "Which side?"

Miguel pointed to his left. "That one."

"Great," said Rem, facing the doors.

"Just one note of advice," said Miguel in a low voice.

Daniels leaned closer. "What's that?"

Miguel whispered. "Ben Crenshaw is a sneaky bastard."

Rem turned back and Daniels raised his brow. "Is that so?" asked Daniels.

Miguel nodded. "The last time we had cops here was when Janice Desmond, one of our interns, threatened an attorney and assaulted her in the conference room with a bronze statue of Mr. Crenshaw."

"Why'd she do that?" asked Rem.

"The attorney slept with the intern's husband, but that's not the point," whispered Miguel, looking around.

"What's the point?" whispered Daniels, wondering why they were whispering since no one was in the lobby.

"The cops left in a snit. They told me my boss was an ass, and afterword, Crenshaw threatened to sue the SDPD unless the officers were reprimanded." He shook his head. "It was bad."

Rem leaned closer. "We'll be careful, Miguel, but we have some experience with this."

"Thanks for the heads up, though," said Daniels.

Miguel sat back. "Just so you know, I'm a sucker for true crime. I love all the serial killer documentaries, and I listen to all the murder podcasts."

"Then this is right up your alley," said Rem.

Miguel spoke low again. "I'm pretty sure I know what happened to Jonbenét Ramsey."

Daniels almost choked. "Really?"

"You should call the Boulder PD," said Rem. "They could use the help."

Miguel gasped again. "Maybe I should do my own podcast about Mr. Durning's murder. I've always wanted to do something like that." He narrowed his eyes. "Maybe you two can slip me some inside info?"

Rem pursed his lips. "That's not the way it works, Miguel. If anyone's giving any tips, it should travel from you to us."

"Speaking of which," Daniels pulled out his card, "if anything comes up you'd like to share..." he lowered his voice, "...away from the office, feel free to reach out." He held out his card.

Miguel hesitated and took the card. "I'll keep that in mind."

"Good," said Daniels.

Miguel tucked the card into his suit pocket. "There's Delaina."

Daniels turned to see a tall brunette in a navy-blue business suit, wearing bright red lipstick and a string of pearls, approach and open the glass door. "You're the detectives?" she asked.

"We're not the window washers," said Rem, heading toward the door.

Daniels followed Rem into the main office.

"Right this way," said Delaina.

She walked down a carpeted hall, past an open room where several men and women, also in suits, sat at various desks with monitors. Some glanced up as Rem and Daniels walked by, but most ignored them. Daniels noticed several large offices lined the hall and the perimeter of the floor. They walked past them and went through another set of double doors and into a second reception area, this one much different from the outer one. Pictures of various colorful landscapes hung on the paneled wood walls. Potted plants sat beside another leather sofa and on either side of Delaina's desk, where she sat in her leather chair. Two high-backed upholstered chairs were against the opposite wall, with a potted plant between them. A closed door was behind Delaina. "Have a seat." Delaina waved toward the couch. "Mr. Crenshaw will see you soon."

Daniels eyed the couch. "Do you have an estimate of when?"

"Just a few minutes." Delaina smiled. "He has a busy schedule today, but he'll fit you in as best he can." She began typing on her keyboard.

Rem raised a brow at Daniels and sat on the couch. Daniels joined him. Twenty minutes later, Delaina was still typing, and they were still sitting.

"Excuse me, Delaina," said Daniels. "But it's been a few minutes."

She stopped typing. "It shouldn't be much longer." She went back to typing.

Rem glanced at his watch. He whispered to Daniels. "You get the feeling Crenshaw is playing games with us?"

Daniels whispered back. "You mean making us wait to show us who's boss?"

"Yup."

"I'm not good at playing games."

Rem huffed. "No. You're not. I thought you were going to punch me the last time we played Uno."

"That's because you cheated."

"Nobody said J.P. couldn't play with me."

"Playing cards is one thing, but he was hiding your cards in his pants."

Rem frowned. "Was that wrong?"

Daniels rolled his eyes. "C'mon. Let's hope Crenshaw doesn't cheat like you do." He stood.

Rem stood too. "Something tells me he's a lot better at it."

Daniels approached Delaina's desk. "Sorry Delaina, but my partner and I are busy, too. We can't wait any longer."

"Oh." Delaina flipped a page in a binder. "Would you like to reschedule?"

Rem chuckled. "No. We would not." He walked around her desk. "We'll see ourselves in."

"Wait a minute." Delaina stood as Daniels followed Rem, who opened the door behind Delaina's desk. She tried to stop them. "You can't go in there."

"Oh, but we can," said Daniels.

They walked into an opulent office with an impressive view of the city, a large oak desk, an oval conference table, and an ornate oriental rug that covered almost the entire polished wood floor. A sitting area was arranged across the room from the desk.

Seated in the tall leather chair behind the desk was a small older man with dark-rimmed glasses and thinning hair, wearing what certainly was a custom-made suit. He looked up when they entered, closed a file on his pristine desk, and stood.

"I'm sorry, sir," said Delaina. "These are the detectives."

"It's okay, Delaina. I was just about done." He gestured toward the sitting area. "Why don't you two have a seat? Did Delaina offer you any beverages? Would you like some water or coffee?"

"We're fine. Thanks," said Daniels.

"Thank you, Delaina," said Crenshaw. "You can go."

Delaina turned, scowling at Rem and Daniels, and closed the doors behind her.

"Sorry to barge in," said Rem. "But we need to ask about Reginald Durning. I assume you're Ben Crenshaw?"

"I am." Crenshaw walked around his desk. "I apologize for keeping you waiting. An appointment would have been better."

"And if Reginald Durning wasn't dead, we'd agree," said Daniels.

"We assumed you'd like to find his killer as soon as possible," added Rem.

Crenshaw offered a flat stare. "Of course." He held out his hand. "Have a seat."

Daniels sat next to Rem on the sofa, and Crenshaw sat in a chair across from them.

Crenshaw smoothed his jacket. "How can I help?"

"What can you tell us about Reginald Durning?" asked Rem.

"He was a fine attorney and represented the firm well. Was in line for a partnership." He sat back and crossed one leg over the other.

When Crenshaw didn't offer more, Daniels guessed they'd have to get specific. "How was he for the last six to eight months? Any issues with staff or superiors?"

Crenshaw appeared to think about it. "Other than the usual conflicts, no."

"What are the usual conflicts?" asked Rem.

"Oh, work that should get done but doesn't. An intern drops the ball. A deadline gets missed. A case goes south when it shouldn't. All part of the job."

"Are there any cases in particular Durning was working on that went south?" asked Daniels.

Crenshaw rested his elbow on the armrest. "Nothing that couldn't be handled."

Rem shot a steely look at Daniels and sat forward. "Um, Mr. Crenshaw, we would appreciate it if you could offer more detail."

"What sort of detail?" asked Crenshaw.

Rem sighed with impatience. "Reginald Durning was murdered in a hotel room last night after checking in with a woman who was not his wife. He had a star branded into his thigh. We need to know if he had any issues here at work that may have some connection to his death. Now, according to his wife, Durning was working longer hours, was overly stressed and wasn't sleeping well. He told her it was because of work. Can you verify that?"

Crenshaw waved his hand. "As I told you, he was in line for a partnership. That requires hard work and dedication, and personal life and family often take a back seat. Now, if the man was having an affair, I can't help you with that. I suspect he wasn't the only attorney at this firm who cheated on a spouse. But I have no reason to believe his death had anything to do with a case he'd been working on."

"There was nothing else that you're aware of that was causing him stress?" asked Rem. "Doesn't have to be work related. It could be anything."

"None," said Crenshaw. He shrugged. "Sorry. I wish I could be of more help."

Rem's phone rang. He pulled it from his pocket, eyed the display, and silenced it.

"Did you ever spend time with him outside of work?" asked Daniels. "Did you go to dinners? Happy hours? Company parties?"

Crenshaw's expression maintained that irritating calm. "We didn't socialize."

Returning his phone to his pocket, Rem narrowed his eyes. "Do you even know his wife's name?"

Crenshaw made a soft grunt in the back of his throat. "I don't see how that's relevant, Detective."

Irritated by Crenshaw's cavalier attitude and seeing they wouldn't get much out of him, Daniels took another route. "We're going to need a list of his clients. We need to talk to them, too."

"Plus, we'd like to search his office and get his work laptop," added Rem.

Daniels waited for the expected outburst and demand for a warrant.

Crenshaw brushed something off his knee. "Of course. You're welcome to look through his office. You can have his work laptop, too, but be aware we've had to remove sensitive files. It's company property and we don't want to break attorney-client privilege. And I've already requested Delaina put a list of clients together for you. She'll have it when you leave."

Rem furrowed his brow. "No objections?"

"We've notified Reginald's clients of what's happened to him," said Crenshaw. "They are as shocked as we are and want to cooperate. They're as eager to find the killer as we are." He smiled, but it didn't reach his eyes.

"We'd also like to interview any staff who worked with Durning," said Daniels. "Especially his assistant."

"Martha Cravitz," said Crenshaw. "She didn't come in today, for obvious reasons. I've asked Delaina to add her name plus other relevant staff names and numbers to the client list. I'll let them know to expect your call and to answer any questions you may have, within reason, of course."

Although Crenshaw was cooperating, something about him was triggering Daniels' radar. "We appreciate that."

Crenshaw eyed his watch. "Is there anything else? I have a busy schedule today."

"We'll leave our card with Delaina," said Rem, "in case you remember anything you think might be important."

"Please do." Crenshaw stood. "And again, I'm sorry I'm not more help."

Rem and Daniels stood, too. "What about Ingram and Willoughby?" asked Daniels. "Can we talk to them?"

Crenshaw nodded. "Certainly, but Barbara won't be back for a couple of days. Doug is out of the office today, but I'll let him know you'd like to speak with him."

"We'd appreciate that," said Rem.

Crenshaw gestured toward the exit. "Delaina will get you that list and escort you to Reginald's office."

Daniels headed to the door. Rem followed and stopped before leaving. "Just one more thing, Mr. Crenshaw."

Crenshaw paused on his way back to his desk. "What's that?"

Rem tipped his head. "If Reginald Durning was involved in something at this firm that caused him undue stress and led to his murder, would you tell us?"

Daniels caught the brief tightening of Crenshaw's face before he relaxed. "What are you implying, Detective?"

Rem held Crenshaw's gaze. "Only that if you're lying to us, we'll be back, and it will be with a lot more officers, and we won't be waiting for you, or anyone else, to speak with us, because we'll be escorting you back to the station."

"And if that happens," added Daniels. "I don't think anybody's going to want any more of your pretty bronze Crenshaw statues."

Rem zipped up his jacket. "Something tells me nobody wanted them in the first place."

His face flattened. Crenshaw adjusted his tie and returned to his desk. "Good luck in your search, Detectives." He leaned over and pressed a button on his phone. "Delaina, please provide the list I mentioned to the detectives and show them to Reginald's office. Then escort them out when they're finished."

Rem and Daniels left and stopped at Delaina's desk. Delaina picked up several pieces of paper and held them out. "A list of staff and Durning's clients."

Rem took the papers and glanced at the first page. "This is all of his current clients?"

"Current and former."

Daniels eyed the list. "Any way to distinguish who's current and who's former?"

Delaina closed her binder. "That's the information I was told to give you."

Rem raised a brow. "That's an interesting way to put it." He swiped through the remaining papers.

Daniels snorted. "Did Crenshaw tell you to give us the entire staff list?"

"Take it or leave it." She stood.

"Is Martha Cravitz on here?" asked Rem.

"She's under the C names." She moved around the desk. "I'll show you to Mr. Durning's office."

Taking the list from Rem and flipping through it, Daniels followed Delaina and Rem to Durning's office. She stopped at a door with Reginald's name on a nameplate and opened it. "This is it."

They stepped into a clean office a quarter of the size of Crenshaw's. While Delaina waited, Rem and Daniels went through the drawers and cabinets and found next to nothing inside them other than unused calendars, takeout menus, empty folders, and blank looseleaf paper and notebooks.

"This was Durning's office?" asked Rem to Delaina. "Where's all his stuff?"

Delaina shrugged.

"I'll tell you where it is," said Daniels. "Safe from prying eyes. That's where."

"I don't even see any dust bunnies," said Rem with annoyance.

Holding the papers with the list of names, Daniels closed a drawer. "Let's get out of here."

"I'll escort you to the front," said Delaina, standing outside the door.

Daniels and Rem walked past her. "Save your shoes," said Rem. "We know the way."

"But—"

Daniels ignored her, and he and Rem left Durning's office and headed down the hall toward the main entrance. More staff watched them leave.

"That was a waste of time." Rem waved at the papers in Daniels' hand. "And I think he gave us the name of everyone who's ever worked here."

"Should we guess how many on this staff list have never met Durning?"

"I'd say ninety-five percent."

"And that client list? How much you want to bet some of them haven't seen Durning in years?" asked Daniels.

"I'd bet a lot. It's probably more doctored than my Aunt Beverly."

Daniels frowned. "Is Aunt Beverly sick?"

"No. Plastic surgeries. Says she can't get her nose right."

Daniels smirked. "Why do I ask?" He waved his fingers at a worker at a nearby desk who watched them walk by. "It's a classic stall tactic. We spin our wheels while CIW makes sure nothing about Durning blows back on them. They sure cleaned out that office in a hurry." Daniels aimed his thumb behind him. "You buy what Crenshaw told us?"

"I get the feeling Crenshaw lies with ease. And rarely gets called on it."

"He's used to winning and certainly has a healthy self-image." Daniels reached the door to the lobby. "It's smart though. Giving us a lengthy list. We have to sort through the whole thing, and it stops us from getting a warrant." He pulled open the door to the lobby, and he and Rem walked out of the main office.

Miguel poked his head up. "How'd it go, Detectives?"

Rem strode toward the elevators. "You're right, Miguel. Crenshaw is delightful." He punched the *Down* button.

A thought occurred to Daniels, and he eyed Miguel. "You really want to get your own murder podcast, Miguel?"

Miguel sat up. "What do you mean?"

The elevator arrived, and the doors opened. Rem stepped on and Daniels spoke to Miguel. "Just curious." He joined Rem in the elevator and hit the button for the lobby.

Chapter Seven

MANETTI RETURNED TO HIS desk in the squad room. After he and Monk had provided their deposition, they'd headed back to the station. Monk had stopped in the cafeteria on the way up to grab a sandwich and make another phone call; apparently whoever he was trying to reach wasn't answering, and Manetti returned upstairs to eat his leftover keto mushroom pasta Annabelle had made the previous evening.

He flipped on his monitor to review their latest cases—a string of convenience store burglaries, and an auto theft ring that had escalated to murder after someone shot the latest victim who was trying to prevent his car from being stolen.

He ran through his notes, but distracted, gave up and sat back with a sigh. He eyed a folder on his desk and pulled it out. He opened it and read the name at the top. Vera Canmore. Someone murdered Vera after she went undercover to expose the illegal activities of Victor D'Mato's cult. Monk had almost gotten himself fired after pursuing Mikey Redstone for the crime, but after she'd been exonerated, the case had gone cold.

Manetti remembered talking to Vera's mother and her distress. He'd told her they would do everything they could to find Vera's killer, but so far, it had not been enough.

"Manetti? You in there?"

Manetti jumped. Seeing Lozano standing by his desk, he lowered the folder. "Sorry, Cap." He put the folder down. "What do you need?"

"How'd the deposition go?"

Manetti gave Lozano a quick rundown of his and Monk's morning activities.

"You track down any witnesses to the car theft murder?"

"Not so far, but Monk and I are going to talk to the businesses around the street where it happened again. Maybe we'll get lucky."

"And the robberies?"

"We got a lead on an owner's son, who supposedly has a drug problem. An employee said he'd been getting his money from somewhere. It's thin, but we'll follow up."

"You do that." Lozano looked around the quiet squad room. Working detectives sat at some desks, but most, including Rem's and Daniels', were unoccupied. "Where's your partner?"

"Getting some food."

Lozano nodded. "Keep me posted."

"We will. Hey, Cap?"

Lozano turned back. "What is it?"

Manetti paused and picked up the Canmore file. "How come you don't ask about this one?"

Lozano eyed the name on the file. "Do you have any updates?"

"No."

"I suspect you'll let me know if you do?"

"Yes."

"Good."

Manetti set the file down.

"Something on your mind?"

Manetti leaned back in his chair. "We've been spending less and less time on the Canmore case."

"You've got other cases to deal with."

"I know. But I don't like putting it off."

"You're not putting it off. You've done all you can with it. Until there's a new lead, focus on what you can solve."

"She was murdered, Cap."

"I'm aware, Manetti, and I know it eats at you. But not every case is resolved. Some take years. We do what we can with what we have, but you can't ignore other crimes."

"I won't, but I don't want to give up on her."

"I never said you should. Work on it when you're able, but be prepared. You may never find her killer."

"You mean she's a cold case?"

"Pretty much, but you can keep it warm. Do your due diligence. And keep that file clean and up to date. Mention every detail from the moment you discovered her body and the last person you spoke to. There may come a time when another detective picks it up to review it, and you want to make it as easy on them as possible."

"That makes sense. I'll do that."

"And try not to let it get to you. There's always one case that eats at a detective, and if you're not careful, all those kale chips and seaweed won't be enough to keep you from an early grave. And since you're about to become a father, you have other priorities."

"I hear you, Cap." He blew out a long breath. "That's just it, though. I'm about to be a dad, and if someone ever hurt my child, I'd move heaven and earth to find and stop that person, and I can imagine if someone else was expected to do that for me, and they didn't, I'd just go crazy." He thought again of Vera's mother.

Lozano put his hand on Manetti's shoulder. "That's what makes you a good cop, Manetti, but it also makes you a prime candidate for an early retirement, if not worse. You do what you can and that has to be enough. It's the job, Manetti, but we're not superheroes. We have lives of our own. Don't forget that."

"Yeah, I know. Annie tells me the same thing."

"She's a smart lady."

"I know it, Cap. I'm a lucky guy."

"She's due soon, isn't she?"

"Two and a half months, Cap."

"Well, then, I'll give you those months to fret over the Canmore case, but afterward, you move on. I can reassign it if needed."

"That's unnecessary, Cap."

"We'll revisit it in two and a half months, unless something changes. Okay?"

"Okay."

The squad doors opened, and a man and woman walked in. Both dressed in dark suits, they stopped and looked around. "We're looking for Captain Frank Lozano," said the woman.

Lozano faced them. "Well, you found him."

The two approached and took out their badges. "We're with the FBI. I'm Agent Alicia Brady, and this is my partner, Agent Vern Lattimore."

Manetti sat up and eyed their official badges.

Lozano did too. "What's this about?"

Lattimore glanced at Manetti. "Is there somewhere we can talk? In private?"

"How about my office?" Lozano headed to his office door.

"Thank you," said Agent Brady. She followed Lozano and Lattimore into Lozano's office and shut the door behind them.

Manetti watched through the glass as they sat and talked and then he looked back at the Canmore folder. He pulled it back and opened it. After a second, he jiggled his mouse and pulled up the file on his computer. Monk had written most of it and it was fairly complete, but thinking of what Lozano had told him, Manetti could see holes in the information, starting with how they'd identified Vera at the beginning. That minor detail wouldn't matter to most but imagining a future detective reading about this case for the first time, Manetti started typing, adding in how he and Monk had pulled a file from Research with all the names of missing females for a five-year time span in the state that matched what they knew about the bones in the grave. They'd expected a long slog of going through the names, but Monk had gotten lucky and identified a match to Vera quickly.

Thinking about that file from Research, Manetti searched for it in his email. After finding it, he saved and attached it to Vera's file. Every detail mattered, and he wanted it included. He paused after attaching it and recalled pulling up Vera's information and reading about her. Wanting to jog his memory, he opened the research file, typed Vera's name into the search bar and hit enter.

He frowned when the screen went blank, and the search bar displayed *No results found*. Confused, he tried again with the same result. Rubbing his jaw, he wondered if he had the correct research file. He double checked, and verified he had the correct one. He tried multiple spellings of Vera's name, assuming that was the problem. But it didn't help. Her name did not appear.

Wondering what was wrong, he sat back and stared at the screen. If Vera's name was not in the file, then how had Monk discovered her? Had her name been deleted? He sat up and dug a little deeper. He looked into the file's history, but found no sign it had been edited.

Confused because he knew Vera fit the criteria used to generate the list of names, he picked up the phone and called Records.

"This is Jarvis," said the man who answered.

"Hi, Jarvis. This is Detective Manetti from Homicide. I need to ask a question." He explained to Jarvis the situation regarding Vera Canmore's missing name. "Can you explain that?" he asked.

"What's the name again?" asked Jarvis.

Manetti gave him Vera's name and waited. After a minute or two, Jarvis came back on the line. "I found her. She was reported missing, but the original detectives on the case pulled her name."

Manetti recalled flipping through the original case notes but didn't recall reading that. "Why?"

Jarvis paused. "Notes say the vic got in touch with family, so they no longer considered her missing."

Surprised, Manetti thought back to his interview with Vera's mother. She'd been upset that the original detectives on the case had not taken her seriously, and they'd been convinced Vera had run off with Victor's cult after receiving a text from Vera saying she was fine and would be traveling. "Wouldn't that information be noted in the case file?" he asked Jarvis.

"Not if it wasn't added," said Jarvis. "Anything else?"

Manetti's brain was spinning. "No. That's it. Thanks." He hung up with Jarvis and fell back in his seat. He tried to think of an explanation, but returned to the same question repeatedly. If Vera's name had been removed from the Missing Persons list, how had Monk found her?

·•·•·••·•••·

Rem walked out of the building where CIW was located and into the sunshine. He squinted in the sun. "You going to tell me what that was about with Miguel?"

Daniels pulled out his sunglasses and slid them on. "We may need him."

"You mean use him to get information?"

"If we have to." Daniels headed toward the parking lot.

Rem followed. "We do that, and any good prosecutor would eat us alive, and Lozano would be furious if we didn't get a warrant."

He looked back. "Who said *we* would do anything?"

Getting the gist, Rem stopped. "Are you serious?"

"Nope. Name's Daniels."

Rem rolled his eyes. "Why don't we talk to Martha Cravitz before we take that route?"

"You really think she'll tell us anything?"

"One way to find out."

They headed toward their car.

"Besides," said Rem, "we're supposed to be keeping our distance from Lexie, remember?" He unlocked their doors.

"We have been, but like you said at the station, it's been three months, and now there's been another murder. Why not use her?"

Rem got behind the wheel, and Daniels slid into the passenger seat. Rem shut the door. "About that. Guess who called me when we were in Crenshaw's office?"

"See?" Daniels smiled. "What did I tell you?"

"We use her, then we risk her at the same time."

"I think she's made it very clear that she's part of this, whether we like it or not. And it's not like we can ignore her."

Rem put his hand on the wheel. "We call her, and it could stir up this whole black bird situation."

"Maybe it's time we did." He rested his elbow on the window ledge. "We're detectives, Rem, and we've been assigned to find Reginald Durning's killer, and if that's Rhonda, then that means digging into the black bird group. Now, if CIW is going to give us the runaround and play games with us, I say we do the same. If it turns out this is some sort of weird copycat killing and Durning just picked up the wrong prostitute, then what does it matter?"

Rem eyed his partner. "You and I both know that's not what happened to Durning." He pointed at the building. "Based on my gut instinct, Durning got mixed up with a black bird member. Someone who was likely a CIW client. And when Durning either dropped the ball or didn't follow through, he got iced by Rhonda, who apparently takes her orders from someone on the black bird squad." He shifted to face Daniels. "Which means, if we keep digging, we might find someone whose name is on that secret USB file Ackerman hid, which we're all currently searching for." He gripped the wheel. "Cain and Erin could also be on that list, not to mention the man Mikey's trying to recall who killed Vera Canmore."

"Don't forget Frank Monk," said Daniels. "Based on his obsession to pin a murder on Mikey, it makes him a possible victim, or member of the black birds."

"He's settled down the last few months, although his asshole standing is still intact. Plus, he doesn't have a tattoo."

"Not a visible one, at least."

Rem grunted. "Let's not talk about Monk. He's the least of our problems."

"Don't assume anything."

"That seems to be all we're doing."

"Exactly. Which is why you need to call Lexie back."

Rem scrunched his face. "Tell me why again?"

"Rem, we have gone in circles these last three months. We backed off, but we're getting nowhere. Now we have a case we're required to investigate. So let's investigate. There's no rule that says we can't get help. We're not investigating Ackerman's box. We're trying to solve a crime. Let's see where it leads and go from there. And if something should happen and we ruffle some feathers, then we'll reevaluate."

"Ruffle some feathers? That's what you want to call it?"

"What do you want to do, Rem? Shove it all under the rug and pretend these black birds don't exist? You know they'll be back, regardless of what we do or don't do. So, let's be proactive. You're the one who wants me to invite Erin to the house to move things along between her and Cain. You can't have it both ways. Either we're all in, or all out."

Rem hardened his gaze. "What did you put in your Wheaties this morning?"

"Crenshaw pissed me off. He's playing with us. I say we show him we can be sneaky too."

Rem pulled out his phone. "Okay. Just remember. You asked for this." He hit the call back button.

The phone rang on the other end and was immediately picked up. "What took you so long?"

Rem bit back an unproductive response. "Hello, Lex. Long time, no talk. What's up?"

"What's up? What kind of question is that? Is Daniels there?"

"He is."

"Of course he is. You two are surgically attached. Tell him he's just as annoying as you are."

Rem did his best to remain patient. "What do you want, Lexie?"

"Did you forget I am a part of this case? And when Reginald Durning turned up murdered with a star branded into his skin, you should have called me?"

"We've been busy."

"You always say that."

"Because it's true."

"Save it for the people who care, which isn't me."

"We would have called."

"When?"

Rem paused. "I don't know."

She scoffed. "How'd I end up working with Laurel and Hardy?"

"Daniels and I prefer Holmes and Watson."

"Don't flatter yourselves."

Rem flashed a frustrated look at Daniels. "Listen. We'll fill you in on Durning. Plus, Daniels may need your help."

"Daniels? Not you?"

"Okay. Me too."

"I'll think about it."

"You don't even know what it is yet."

"Then you can tell me at my place."

"You want to meet?"

Lexie huffed. "I didn't just call about Durning. I may have something."

"Have what?"

"Get over here and I'll tell you. If you can fit me into your busy schedule."

"Lexie—"

"I'll see you in thirty minutes. And if you take any longer, you better bring me a coffee." The line went dead.

Rem grunted and hung up. "She wants to meet. Says she has something."

"Did she say what?" asked Daniels.

Rem slid his phone into his pocket. "Yes. She told me everything, including what earrings she was wearing and what she had for breakfast." He started the car.

"Sorry I asked. Where and when?"

"Now and at her place." He pulled out of the parking space.

Daniels nodded. "Good. Let's go talk to Lexie Logan."

"First, we're stopping for coffee. And you're buying."

Chapter Eight

LEXIE SAT IN FRONT of her laptop at her small dining table in her apartment. She flipped through the files she'd copied from Ackerman's box and organized into various folders. The last three months she'd done her best to focus on other articles and stories while spending her free time going through Ackerman's information, looking for clues about where he'd hidden his secret file containing the names of black bird members. She'd had various ideas, but each one had been a bust.

It had been tricky flying under the radar. After being attacked in her mother's home by two masked men who'd taken the box and warned her to stay away from investigating anything connected to Ackerman, she'd had her share of nightmares. Not wanting to go through that again, she'd been very careful to look busy with other projects. All of that had gone well, and she'd begun to feel safe again, until she'd heard the news that morning that another victim of the Star Killer had been found in a swanky downtown hotel.

Old fears resurfaced, and she'd taken the morning to consider her options. Investigating this killing meant opening herself up to the dangers of digging deeper into a group that would kill to protect themselves. Was the case worth it? Since she'd been researching the contents of Ackerman's box, she obviously thought it was. But her lack of progress had provided a sense of security. If they couldn't find the names, and without another lead, they'd have to move on, no matter how much Lexie wanted to catch Rhonda and expose the society she worked for.

A case like this, though, was what all investigative journalists dreamed of, and breaking it wide open would change Lexie's career overnight. But what was rarely revealed in cases like these were the risks involved, and now she had to face them head on.

It hadn't taken her long to decide that she was willing to face those risks, even if it meant another possible visit from the two masked men. She'd just have to be careful and take her safety seriously. But there was no point worrying about it until she knew more about the man who'd been murdered—Reginald Durning—and the circumstances of his death. For that, she'd have to talk to Daniels and Remalla, and when they hadn't called her that morning, her annoyance grew until she'd picked up the phone and called them. If they thought they were going to keep her at a distance out of some sense of duty to protect her, she'd have to inform them otherwise. They'd come this far together, and she wasn't going to stop now.

Plus, she'd discovered something in Ackerman's files that showed promise, and it had given her an idea. She needed to tell Daniels and Rem her plans in case they blew up in her face. Considering the danger, she appreciated knowing she wasn't doing this by herself. No matter how much she badgered the detectives, she was glad they were there and considered her safety a priority. There was no way any of them could do this alone.

A knock on the door made her jump, and she checked her watch and stood.

"Coffee delivery," said a male voice she recognized as Remalla's.

She walked to the door and opened it. "It's about time."

Daniels walked in. "You said thirty minutes."

Holding two coffee cups, Remalla entered behind Daniels and handed her a cup. "Your coffee."

"Thank you." She closed the door. "Did you add strychnine?"

"Daniels suggested it, but I fought for you," said Rem.

Daniels shook his head.

Rem walked into the room. "Figured we should at least find out what you got before we off you."

"I appreciate that." Lexie took a sip of her drink. "And what do you mean, find out what I know? How about you tell me about Reginald Durning?"

Daniels eyed her laptop. "We don't know that much. Just that he was shot in the chest, and a star was branded into his thigh."

Rem drank some of his coffee. "After checking into a hotel with a woman who was not his wife."

"That definitely fits the profile of the other two victims," said Lexie. "What do you know about Durning?"

"He's a defense attorney for CIW," said Daniels. "Crenshaw, Ingram and Willoughby."

Lexie had heard of them. "They're a big firm. They've handled some high-profile cases."

"Durning is also the father of one of our prosecutors," said Rem. "Josh Durning."

Lexie dropped her jaw. "Seriously? Does the son know anything about the black birds?"

"Not yet, he doesn't," said Daniels. "We're debating how much to say to him, since we don't want him to get involved if he doesn't have to."

"What about CIW?" asked Lexie. "Did you talk to them?"

"Just left there, and they were as cooperative as you'd expect." Rem pulled out a chair and sat at her dining table.

"I can imagine." Lexie returned to the table and sat in front of her laptop. "I bet they told you everything you wanted to hear, but offered nothing of value. Am I close?"

"Pretty damn," said Daniels. "Ben Crenshaw is as transparent as an oak door."

"And about as nice as one," added Rem.

"Good luck with those guys," said Lexie. "They'll do everything they can to deny and deflect."

"They gave us a staff list a mile long, and a supposed list of Durning's clients," replied Rem. "We're going to talk to Durning's assistant and then make some phone calls."

Lexie set her coffee cup on the dining table. "Where do I fit into all of this?"

"Before we go any further," said Daniels. "Are you sure you want to help? You know what digging into this case might mean."

"It's been quiet the last few months, and this might change that," added Rem. "No hard feelings if you want out."

Lexie had a split second where she considered it but pushed past her fears. "I'm well aware of what it means. I admit I hesitated. But I had my come-to-Jesus earlier and I'm still on board. What about you two?"

"We don't have a choice," said Rem. "We're assigned to the case."

"There's always a choice," said Lexie. "You two both have copies of Ackerman's files, and I may have a lead. But if you'd rather I keep it to myself, I understand."

"If I thought that would matter, I'd consider it," said Daniels. "But I don't think it does. Rem and I were targets from the beginning, and I doubt that's changed just because the black birds have temporarily gone quiet. So the more we know, the better."

Rem glanced at her laptop. "What's your lead?"

Another knock made Lexie jump again, and she glanced back at her door.

"You expecting someone?" asked Daniels.

Lexie shook her head, her mind racing. "No."

Rem, clearly on alert, stood. "Ask who it is."

Seeing him slide his hand under his jacket, her heart thudded. Was she prepared for this? Jumping at any unexpected knock? She got up and walked up to the door. "Who is it?"

Daniels came up on one side of the door and Rem the other.

She looked out the peephole just as a man answered. "Lexie? It's me. Lonny."

Lexie let go of a held breath. "It's okay. It's my neighbor."

Daniels and Rem relaxed, and Lexie opened the door. "Hey, Lon."

Around her age, Lonny was a ghostwriter who worked from his apartment. She'd met him not long after he'd moved in and stopped by to introduce himself. Learning she was a journalist, he'd asked her lots of questions about her work and writing, and it hadn't been long afterward that he'd asked her out for drinks.

Although he was a nice man, and good-looking in an average way, she had no interest in pursuing anything romantic with him, or anybody else. Not one to beat around the bush, she'd told him as much, and he'd understood, but it didn't stop him from coming around. He remained friendly though, and not pushy, so she didn't mind him occasionally stopping by. She wasn't home a lot anyway, and he'd offered to water her plants and get her mail if she wanted him to. Not that she had any plants or had much mail, but she appreciated the offer.

Lonny eyed Daniels, who was near the door. "Oh, I'm sorry. I didn't know you had company."

"It's okay," said Lexie. "You need something?" She pulled the door open wider, and Lonny glanced at Remalla, who came into view.

"I, uh…," His gaze bounced between the two detectives. "…um…yeah. Do you have any ground coffee?" He looked at Lexie.

"Ground coffee?"

"Sorry. Yes. I realized I'm out and I'm on a deadline." Lonny shot another look at Rem.

Lexie half smiled, knowing Lonny ordered his groceries through a delivery service and could get his coffee with a quick online order. Had he seen Rem and Daniels arrive and found an excuse to figure out who they were?

"Sure. One sec." She left the door but didn't bother to introduce Rem or Daniels. She opened a cabinet and pulled out a bag of coffee. "Here you go." She returned to the door and handed him the bag.

"Thanks. I owe you one." He raised the bag.

"Good luck with your deadline." She started to close the door.

"You, uh, okay, Lex?" he asked.

She glanced behind her to see Rem and Daniels staring back at Lonny. They didn't say a word.

Rolling her eyes, she looked back at Lonny. "I'm great. See you."

"You need anything, let me know. Just bang on the wall."

"Thanks, but I'm fine. Bye, Lon."

"See you, Lex." Lon's gaze held on Rem and Daniels as she closed the door.

"Who is that guy?" asked Rem.

She turned toward them. "What was that staring contest all about?"

"Just trying to size him up," said Daniels. "I think he likes you."

"He definitely likes you," replied Rem. "That coffee thing is a total lie."

"How do you know?" asked Lexie.

"Because it's what I would have done," said Rem.

Daniels chuckled. "Probably would have winked and asked her to share a cup with you the next morning."

Rem made a face. "I wasn't that bad." He paused. "Well, maybe in my twenties. But those days are long gone." He shot his thumb toward the door. "Just be careful with him, Lex."

"You want us to check him out?" asked Daniels.

"What are you two?" asked Lexie. "My big brothers? Lonny is harmless. He moved in long before Ackerman's box and any of this black bird stuff. He's just smitten."

"Smitten, huh?" asked Rem. "Does he have any idea who he's dealing with?"

"If he did, he'd think twice." Daniels chuckled.

"Very funny." Lexie crossed her arms. "But you're probably right."

"You change your mind about Lonny, let us know," said Rem.

"Lon is the least of our worries. We have bigger chickens to chase." She returned to the dining table and sat at her laptop.

"Like what?" asked Daniels.

Lexie pulled up her lengthy list of notes. "Well, after running down a few dead ends, I stepped back and looked from a different perspective."

Rem stepped behind her and looked at her screen. "What perspective is that?"

"Ackerman's perspective. Any good profiler will tell you to dig into the mind of a suspect first. Figure out who he is."

"I figured we knew Ackerman pretty well," said Daniels.

"To a degree," added Lexie, "but after observing with a wider lens, what does Ackerman value above all else?"

Rem pursed his lips. "Information?"

"Sticking it to the black birds?" added Daniels.

"Even more than that." Lexie looked up at them. "His family."

Rem knitted his brow. "He was estranged from his family."

"He was from his daughter, but still wanted to protect her. His wife died, but he talks about how much he loved her, and his regrets with each of them. It comes up a lot in his writings."

"How does this help find the lost file?" asked Daniels.

Lexie turned back to the screen. "I did a little digging. Ackerman's wife was Marion Ackerman." She pulled up another file. "I discovered she's still got a storage unit under her name at a local facility."

Rem lowered his coffee. "You're kidding."

"Nope. I'm not."

"Did you go to this facility?" asked Daniels.

Lexie smiled. "Sure did. And it's a good thing. Since he died, Ackerman hasn't paid the bill. The contents were scheduled to go up for auction at the end of the month."

Rem narrowed his eyes. "What did you do?"

"I talked to the owner, told him about Ackerman, and paid the bill." She picked up her coffee cup and sipped it. "The owner gave me access to the unit."

"You did what?" asked Daniels. "Shouldn't it go to his daughter?"

"And it will," said Lexie, "but not until I go through it first. Care to join me?"

"You think that's where Ackerman left his file of names?" asked Rem. "Why there?"

Lexie picked up her coffee cup. "Because he talked a lot about regrets, and even mentioned that what you leave behind after you're gone can tell you a lot about a person, and while he didn't do a good job while alive, he planned to do a better job after he was dead. Other than his daughter, his wife was the one good thing in his life, and she knew him best. He could trust her with anything."

"That's your lead?" asked Rem.

"It's not much, but it's got potential," said Daniels. He eyed Rem. "It can't hurt to look."

Rem shrugged. "I suppose with all our free time, we can schedule a visit to the storage unit and check it out."

"We'll have to fit it in somewhere between talking to Martha Cravitz and all of CIW's staff, plus Durning's clients." Daniels pointed at Lexie. "Which is where you come in."

Lexie closed her laptop. "What do you need?"

Daniels and Rem told her about their visit to CIW and meeting Miguel.

Lexie thought about it. "So you think if I talk to Miguel, he might give me a little inside info?" she asked. She grabbed a notebook from a bag of them on the floor, put it on the table, and opened it. "I'll need details." She wrote Miguel's name and noted his interest in murder and podcasts. "I can use that, assuming I can get close to him."

"Something tells me you can," said Daniels. His phone rang, and he pulled it out. He read the display and answered. "This is Daniels. What's up Burrows?" His face furrowed. "When?"

"Who's Burrows?" asked Lexie.

Rem held up his hand.

"You trace it?" asked Daniels. He sighed. "Yeah. Okay. How's the mom?" He listened. "You stick there in case he calls again, and make sure Lozano knows." He nodded. "Thanks, Burrows." He lowered the phone and hung up.

"What's up?" asked Rem.

Daniels put his phone away. "Someone called Jerry Lee's mother. Said Jerry Lee was fine and not to worry."

"Someone? Who's someone?" asked Rem.

"A man. Didn't give his name. Said he'd keep an eye on Jerry Lee until it was safe for him to come home. Burrows traced the number to a burner cell."

"Who's Jerry Lee?" asked Lexie.

"Jerry Lee Caruso," replied Daniels. "He witnessed Reginald Durning's murder. He works for the hotel and took off after the assassin tried to kill him too, and we haven't been able to locate him."

Lexie dropped her jaw. "And you didn't think to mention that?"

"Lon interrupted," said Rem.

She stood. "Don't blame this on Lonny."

"Don't get mad," said Rem. "We're telling you now. And it would have come up, eventually."

Frustrated, Lexie put her hands on her hips. "Eventually?" She paused. "Listen, you two—"

"Hold up," said Daniels. "Before you berate us, we spent our entire morning looking for Jerry Lee. His mother's a wreck. His dad is not in the picture, and if Rhonda, if that's who our killer is, gets to him first, Jerry Lee is a dead man. Now you know what we know. We're not holding anything back."

She glowered at them.

"He was delivering strawberries and cream when he interrupted the crime," said Rem. "He barely avoided a shot to the head and pulled the fire alarm when he raced out of the hotel." Rem spoke to Daniels. "Looks like he found a place to hole up."

"But with who?" asked Daniels. "Who's the mystery man who's using a burner and is willing to protect Jerry Lee?"

Something about the name picked at Lexie. "What did you say the witness' full name is?" She sat again and opened her laptop.

"Jerry Lee Caruso," said Rem. "He's twenty, and lives with his mother."

Lexie pulled up a file and read it. "Holy—" After a pause, she leaned over and dug through her bag of binders.

"What's the matter?" asked Daniels.

She found the binder she wanted and put it on the table. "About eight months ago, I did a story about political corruption." She flipped through her notes. "You two heard of Sammy Caruso?" She stopped on a page and read through it.

Daniels walked closer. "The senator from Illinois with ties to the mob? Who almost ran for president, but had to drop out?"

"That's him." Lexie sucked in a breath when she read her notes. "I tried to get an interview with him, but he said no. But in case he said yes, I did my research." She turned the page to show them her notes. "I checked out his family. He's got a daughter named Patricia, and a grandson named Jerry Lee. They'd both left Illinois and moved to California."

Daniels and Rem leaned over and looked at her notes. "You mean Jerry Lee is Sammy Caruso's grandson?" asked Rem. He straightened, stared at Daniels, and put his hand on his head. "Son-of-a-bitch."

Chapter Nine

MONK CURSED AND HUNG up the phone. After a third call with no answer, he was angry. Sitting at a table in the cafeteria, he set his phone down and stared at it, debating his next move. If there was a witness to Durning's murder, then it had to be handled. But in order to know what to do next, he needed more information. How much had the witness seen? Could he identify Rhonda? Was Rhonda already on his trail? How much did she know? And more importantly, how had she let a witness escape?

His cell buzzed and hopeful, he eyed the display, but it was not the number he wanted to see. It was the number he'd been expecting, but one he had no desire to answer. At least not until he learned more. Until he could speak to Rhonda, there was no point talking to anyone else, so he let the phone ring until the voicemail picked up. The caller didn't leave a message.

Guessing Rhonda had dumped her phone, and that's why he couldn't reach her, Monk told himself to relax. If anyone could handle themselves in a crisis, it was Rhonda. But it was the not knowing that bothered him. His mind whirled with potential scenarios. Rhonda was either on the hunt, had gone to ground, or had skipped town. He doubted the last two; they weren't Rhonda's style. But if she'd gone with option one, Monk would be her obvious point of contact.

Looking around the cafeteria, he debated getting a sandwich since Manetti would expect him to have one, but he had no appetite. He was a man who appreciated information, and with information came control. Right now, he had neither, and it didn't sit well with him.

Frustrated, he ran his hand over his face and was about to try Rhonda again when his phone rang. This time, it was from a number he didn't recognize. He picked it up and answered. "This is Monk."

"Hey, handsome."

Rhonda's voice immediately settled him down. He kept his voice even. "Where the hell have you been? I've been trying to reach you."

"You heard about last night?"

"I heard there's a witness."

"Stupid kid walked in out of nowhere."

"He saw you?"

"Sure did. But I was in disguise."

Monk cursed. "Could he pick you out in a lineup?"

She paused. "If they put me in a wig and makeup, he sure as shit can."

Monk dropped his head into his palm. "Okay. What do you want to do next?"

"I need his name and whatever you can tell me about him. Has he been to the cops?"

"No. He's hiding. At least that's the last I heard."

"Good. Let's hope he's smart enough to stay hidden. At least until I can locate him."

"I'll find out more and send it to you." He looked around to be sure no one was listening. "You can handle this?"

He heard her scoff. "Honey, when have you ever known me not to? He gets to the cops, though, and it gets trickier."

"Then let's make sure that doesn't happen."

"I want everything. Name, current and old addresses, family, friends, where he hangs out, employers. His favorite foods. Everything."

"I'll get it to you. Use this number?"

"Yes. I got rid of the other phone."

Monk nodded. "When I know something, you'll know something."

"The sooner I can resolve this problem, the better." She paused. "Has *he* contacted you?"

Monk thought of his previous caller. "He tried. I didn't answer."

"Tell him I'll handle it. He's got nothing to worry about."

"Don't worry about him. I'll take care of it."

"I know you will, baby. And when I ice this kid, you and I will celebrate."

Monk smiled. "I'm looking forward to it." He considered his next question. "Will this affect your next job?"

He heard her laugh. "Not if I can help it."

"The timing's critical. This sets off an important chain of events. If you can't—"

Her tone hardened. "I said I'll deal with it."

"No. You said, 'Not if I can help it.' There's a difference."

She went quiet. "You doubt me?"

He heard the challenge in her voice and admired it. "Never."

"Then don't start now. I'll handle both. The timing won't be an issue."

He gripped the phone. "I trust you."

"Just make sure he does, too."

He said nothing about what would happen if that trust was lost. "I'll make sure of it. I'll be in touch."

"Today?"

"Today." He hung up and slid the phone into his jacket pocket. Feeling better, he stood. His stomach rumbled and, eyeing the menu on the wall, he approached the counter and ordered a sandwich.

•••••••••

Jerry Lee sat on the cot and stared up the staircase at the door to the pawn shop. Arnie had been gone for hours. Reruns of an old comedy series played on TV, but Jerry Lee had turned the volume down and wasn't watching it. The only thing he'd paid attention to had been the morning news when they'd covered the murder of Mr. Durning, but they hadn't mentioned Jerry or the woman who'd killed Durning.

Worried about his mom, Jerry had considered many times whether to go upstairs and call her, or the cops. But each time he did, he remembered the look in the killer's eyes when she'd aimed her weapon at Jerry. She meant to kill Jerry, and if he showed himself, she'd succeed.

Emotional, he sat back on the cot, pulled his knees up and wrapped his arms around them. He tried to think positive thoughts. Maybe the police would capture or kill the woman, and Jerry Lee would be safe. If she was captured, though, Jerry would have to testify. Would he survive long enough to do it? Could the police protect him?

He thought of his grandfather. If anyone could protect Jerry, it would be him. But involving Sammy Caruso opened doors that Jerry might never close, and Jerry wasn't sure if that was the right move either.

Jerry startled when he heard the door open, and looked up to see Arnie return, carrying a paper bag. He closed the door behind him and came down the stairs. "How you doin', kid?"

Jerry got off the bed. "Did you talk to my mom?"

Arnie stepped off the stairs and put the bag on the table. "Sure did. Told her you were okay."

"What did she say?"

"She started cryin'."

Jerry set his jaw. "What did you tell her?"

"I told her you'd be staying away until it was safe. Then I hung up."

"You hung up on her?"

"Have a seat, kid. We need to talk." He took off his jacket and put it on the back of a chair at the table. He pulled out the chair and sat.

Perplexed and worried about his mother, Jerry did his best not to cry and sat across from Arnie.

Arnie interlaced his fingers. "You've got yourself in a hell of a mess, kid."

Jerry couldn't prevent his eyes from welling with tears.

"That guy who bought it?" said Arnie. "He's an attorney. A big wig."

Jerry sniffed and swiped his eyes.

"Whoever offed him used an assassin to do it. She's the chick you saw kill Durning, and she's good." He reached inside the bag and pulled out a bag of potato chips. "This isn't her first go round. She's done this before."

Jerry did his best to pull himself together. "How do you know?"

Arnie opened the bag of chips. "She branded Durning with a star, which is what you smelled. Durning's her third victim, at least that the cops know of. Something tells me there are more." He swiveled the open chip bag toward Jerry. "Have a chip."

Not hungry, Jerry grabbed a chip but didn't eat it. "She's going to kill me, isn't she?"

Arnie grabbed a chip. "If she finds you, hell yeah." He ate the chip. "But she won't find you. Not if I can help it."

Jerry's reserves started to crumble again. "What about my mom? Is she safe?"

"She is for now. There are too many cops around her. They know you saw what happened and they're looking for you."

"Shouldn't I go to them, then?"

"You do, and you'll be as dead as Durning. They can't protect you. Too many are on the take."

"Then what do I do?" A tear escaped and trickled down his cheek.

"We wait and see how this all plays out." He ate another chip. "At some point, this chick, or whoever she works for, is going to connect me to you, and they're going to come calling. I'll know more then."

"How long will that take?"

"Not long, kid. Not long." He stood and pulled more food out of the bag. "I got lunch meat and bread. Plus some donuts. You hungry?"

Jerry still hadn't eaten his chip. "There's another option."

Arnie dropped a loaf of bread on the table. "What's that?"

Jerry swallowed. "My grandfather."

Arnie stilled, and holding the lunch meat, he sat again. "Think long and hard about that option, kid."

Jerry straightened. "You know who he is?"

"Course I know who he is. I do my due diligence when I hire someone. I've always known."

Jerry sat back. "You didn't care?"

"Why would I? As long as he's not botherin' me, I ain't botherin' him. But if you call him, I'm out."

Wiping his cheeks, Jerry blew out a breath. "Why?"

"Why?" Arnie snorted. "I don't know how well you know your grandfather, but he's a powerful man, and he works with other powerful men. The kind that don't play around." He set the lunch meat on the table.

"Isn't that what I need right now?"

Arnie studied the table and pursed his lips. "I understand how you'd see it that way, but if Sammy Caruso gets involved, that changes things. And he will get involved if you contact him. Would your mom call him?"

"I'm not sure. She's always told me he's dangerous and to keep my distance from him."

"It's good advice. Probably doesn't matter, anyway. Guy like Caruso will have eyes on you and your mom."

Jerry frowned. "What do you mean?"

"Powerful men have powerful enemies. Enemies that sometimes target another man's loved ones, although that's typically taboo with the crowd Caruso runs with. You don't touch family. That doesn't mean your granddad won't take precautions, though." He opened the bag of lunch meat. "I'm making you a sandwich. You need to eat. Hope you like turkey."

"If my grandfather can protect me, then why not call him?"

Arnie paused, set the turkey aside, and rested his elbows on the table. "I'll tell it to you straight. You call him, and he'll send his goons. They'll pick you and your mom up and they'll bring you back to Illinois, no matter what you and your mom say."

Jerry deflated. He knew Arnie was right.

"And your granddad will take it upon himself to find this assassin and kill her himself." He shrugged. "Which isn't necessarily a bad thing. The problem is that it could take a while, and you'll likely never return to California again. Your whole life here? Your friends? Your job? Your mom's job? Her boyfriend? That all disappears. You prepared for that?"

Jerry hadn't thought that far ahead. "I don't know."

"Not to mention the other problem. Assassins tend to work for powerful people, too. And powerful people run in similar circles. Your assassin's employer, if he's as big as I think he might be, could put a big target on your grandfather's back if he's harboring you or kills the assassin. That whole 'Don't touch family' taboo will go right out the window. You, your mom, and your granddad will never be safe. I couldn't give a shit about your granddad. He's used to being a target. But you're not. Neither is your mom." He sat back. "So think before opening that can of worms. Because once they spill out, there's no putting 'em back."

Jerry tried to think, but nothing made sense. "I'm already a target, though."

"You are, but the goal is to get you back to your mom and your life with as little disruption as possible."

"How do we do that?"

Arnie resumed making the sandwich. "As long as no one knows where you are, that gives us the advantage." He opened the loaf of bread. "Right now, your assassin's got a problem. She screwed up. You can identify her, and she has to find you before the cops do. And that gives her boss a problem. If she's caught, that could lead to him and others in the organization."

"There are others?" asked Jerry.

Arnie stood. "I can guaran-damn-tee it." He went to the sink and flipped on the faucet. "Which is why we need to keep your granddad out of this as much as possible. These two bump heads and you could start a damn war." He washed his hands and dried them on a towel. "So, we wait and see who comes sniffing around, looking for you." He opened a cabinet beneath the sink, pulled out two paper plates, returned to the table, and took out two pieces of bread. "If this assassin can be caught or killed without involving your granddad, then you're good." He dug into the bag. "You like cheddar cheese?" He pulled out a package of cheese and opened it.

"If she's caught, I'll have to testify."

"Maybe. Maybe not. If they can tie her to other crimes, they may not need you. Doesn't mean they won't want you, though." Arnie slapped some turkey and a slice of cheese on the bread and put the bread on one of the paper plates. "But I doubt it will get that far." He handed the plate to Jerry, who took it. "That assassin won't live to see the trial. She'll be dead before she can plead not guilty."

"How do you know that?"

Arnie slapped some turkey and cheese on two more slices of bread. "Because that's the way it works, kid. You f-up, you're a liability. And liabilities don't last. Not with people like this." He smiled and bit into his sandwich.

Jerry Lee stared at his food but had no appetite. "I'm sorry I got you into this, Mr. Bertrand." His stomach rolled. "Are you sure you even want me to stay? If what you say is true, I'm putting you in danger, too."

Arnie chewed and swallowed. "Don't worry about me. I've been in bigger scrapes. Besides," he took another bite of his sandwich and spoke through a mouthful, "this is the most fun I've had in years." He winked. "And I think it's time you call me Arnie."

Jerry couldn't believe what he was hearing.

Arnie pushed Jerry's sandwich closer. "Eat up, kid. You're gonna need it."

Chapter Ten

REM SAT AT HIS desk, set his large thermos of coffee down, and opened the donut bag. Tired, he stifled a yawn and smiled when he pulled out a large chocolate donut with sprinkles from the bag. "Hello, beautiful." He grabbed a napkin from a side drawer, set it on his desk, and placed the donut on it.

The squad door opened. Manetti walked in and spotted Rem. "You're here early." He headed toward his desk.

"I was up, so I came in."

"Any luck finding your witness?" Manetti sat at his desk.

"None." Rem bit into his donut and moaned as he chewed.

Manetti chuckled. "I've got some vegan blueberry bran muffins if you're hungry."

Rem smirked and swallowed. "Yesterday was torture enough, Manetti."

Manetti opened a drawer and set his lunch bag inside. "Suit yourself."

The doors opened again, and Daniels entered.

"Daniels might be up for it, though," said Rem.

Daniels raised a brow at Rem. "I assumed I wouldn't see you for at least half an hour, and what am I up for?"

Rem tipped his head at Manetti. "Manetti's got a gluten-free, vegan, non-fat, organic, keto, decaf, sugar free and definitely taste free bran muffin with blueberries."

Manetti chuckled.

"Sounds delicious, but I've had breakfast." Daniels slid off his jacket and tossed it over the back of his chair. He eyed Rem's donut and rolled his eyes.

"They're all yours, Manetti, unless you can pawn one off on Monk." Rem sipped some coffee from his thermos.

"He's had them before," replied Manetti. "And didn't complain."

"That confirms my suspicions," said Rem. "He's a sociopath."

Daniels sat at his desk. "If that's your barometer for psychopathy, it's going to be a lot easier to catch the bad guys."

"You can stake out all the healthy bakeries," said Manetti with a smile.

"And your house," said Rem. "Which makes you and Annabelle prime suspects."

Manetti raised his hands. "Guilty as charged. Take it easy on Annabelle, though. She won't go quietly. Pregnancy has made her lots more vocal."

"That's just the beginning, Manetti," said Daniels. "That new baby is going to be way more vocal than you or Annabelle combined."

"Can't wait. I'm trying to sleep as much as I can now." Manetti rolled his chair closer to his desk.

"Enjoy it while it lasts," added Daniels.

The doors opened again, and Monk entered the squad room.

The banter between Daniels, Rem, and Manetti ended.

Monk eyed the three men and headed toward his desk. "Morning."

"Morning," said Manetti, flipping on his monitor.

While Manetti and Monk talked, Rem spoke to Daniels. "You get some sleep?"

"A decent amount." Daniels studied Rem. "You didn't? I figured you'd collapse after getting home. Yesterday was rough."

Rem recalled leaving Lexie's and heading over to Patricia Caruso's to talk to her about the man who'd called to tell her Jerry Lee was safe, and ask her about her father, Sammy Caruso. She'd said little about her father other than to insist she'd had no contact with him and preferred he stay out of it. When they'd reviewed Jerry's other male friends and acquaintances in Jerry's life, she'd reluctantly added Jerry's former boss, an Arnold Bertrand, who owned a pawn shop. She didn't particularly like him though and doubted Jerry Lee would rely on him for help.

After leaving Patricia's, they'd contacted Martha Cravitz and arranged for her to come in that morning to talk about Reginald Durning, and then stopped by Bertrand's pawn shop, but it had been closed, and no one had picked up the phone when they'd called. Deciding to check on Bertrand later, they'd returned to the station, gone through the CIW staff and client list and divvied up who would contact whom. Lozano had been out of the office and after making several calls, their exhaustion caught up to them and they'd left for the day.

Rem sighed, thinking about his evening. "It didn't get better after I got home. Mikey and I had a talk." Pensive, he pulled off another bite of his donut and ate it.

Daniels paused. "Now I understand the chocolate donut."

"What do you mean?"

"When something's on your mind, you gravitate toward chocolate."

Rem considered that. "I do?"

"You do."

Rem shrugged. "Hmm. Maybe, but doesn't everybody?"

"Not me. And probably not Manetti."

"I meant normal people."

Daniels smiled. "What's up with Mikey?"

Rem set his donut down. "I could tell something was up." He lowered his voice. "She had a session with Lena yesterday." He looked around to see if anyone was listening. "I guess it stirred a few things up."

"Like what?"

"Things have stalled, and Mikey's frustrated. I guess Lena told her that if she's impatient or pushes too hard, it can slow things down."

Daniels nodded. "Makes sense."

Rem shifted in his seat. "But so can other things, outside of her sessions."

Daniels leaned in and rested his elbows on his desk. "Would that be a reference to you?"

Rem sighed. "Yeah."

Daniels waited. "Don't keep me in suspense."

Rem gripped his thermos. "It's Jennie's closet. When Mikey moved in, I told her I'd clean it out so she'd have more room."

"And you didn't, and now Mikey's upset?"

Rem shrugged. "Not upset. More like uncertain. She doesn't want to bring up a tough subject, but at the same time, she thinks she's playing second fiddle to a ghost."

Daniels paused. "What do you think?"

"She's not second fiddle, but I understand why she thinks that."

"What's holding you back from cleaning the closet?"

His donut forgotten, he made a ragged groan. "Mikey asked the same question. I realize it needs to be done, but I dread it. I know it will stir things up, and I don't want Mikey thinking I'm still stuck on my deceased girlfriend."

"I hate to tell you this, but your plan has backfired."

Rem snorted. "Apparently."

Daniels interlaced his fingers and took a deep breath. "Now tell me the real reason you don't want to deal with the closet."

Rem looked up. "What?"

"I understand it will stir things up. Mikey knows that too. But you two can handle that. You've both dealt with way worse. So what's really bothering you?"

Impressed, but not surprised by Daniels' perceptions, Rem recalled waking early that morning, thinking about the closet. He blew out a deep breath and voiced his fears. "All I could think about was what if she's right? Am I still stuck on Jennie? What if I get in there and it's too much? What if... what if..." He stared at his thermos. "...I can't let go?"

Daniels paused. "That's understandable, but I think you're over-thinking it. These last three months have only added to the pressure of cleaning the closet, and now you've got these huge fears of what *may* happen, when the truth is that it will be hard, but you'll be okay. You and Mikey should do it together, and I think you'll quickly see that Jennie's ghost is no competition to a flesh and blood woman who loves you and is standing beside you."

Hearing Daniels' advice helped, and Rem straightened. "Which is why, after a restless night, I got out of bed while Mikey slept and went upstairs to face the closet alone."

"And how did that go?"

"Better than I expected. I stood outside the door and spoke to Jennie. Told her it was time, but that cleaning out her things didn't mean I loved her any less."

"What did she say?"

"I didn't get a response, but that was okay, because I was saying it more for me than for her." He picked at his donut. "Then I opened the door. I told myself to do one box. That would tell the tale."

"Did you do it?"

"I did." He picked up his thermos and held it. "I had a few touch and go moments, but I needed that to process it. I want to be able to go through her things with my shit together, because I think it would be good for Mikey to do it with me."

"Good for you. You took a big step."

"Maybe." Rem recalled going through the box. Most of it had been cosmetics and toiletries that he'd thrown away, but he'd found it hard to get rid of Jennie's hairbrush. "It still wasn't easy, though."

"I'm sure it wasn't. But are you sitting there thinking about Mikey? Or Jennie?"

Rem understood and half-smiled. "Do you mean am I pining away for my late girlfriend?" He shook his head. "I miss her, but no. I'm thinking about Mikey."

"Then I think you have your answer, partner." He sat back. "You worry too much."

"I suppose so." He sipped some coffee. "That's why I'm here early. That box was all I could handle, and I needed to distract myself."

"Well, you're in the right place for that." He waved. "Eat your donut."

His appetite returning, Rem reached for it. "By the time I get through this closet, I'm going to need to buy stock in chocolate."

"As long as it's chocolate, and not something stronger."

"I'll save that for when the closet's done. I'm going to need it."

"When it's done, we'll celebrate. Have a little get together in Jennie's memory."

"I'd like that." Rem set his thermos down. Seeing Monk and Manetti talking, he kept his voice low. "Any updates on the Erin front? What did Marjorie think?"

Daniels' face fell. "She was as bad as you are. Thinks it's a great idea."

"Course she did."

"She's going to call Erin this morning." He sat back. "Don't get your hopes up, though. I'd be surprised if Erin accepted. Getting her phone number was harder than getting you to give up those ragged jeans with the hole in them."

Rem deflated. "I liked those jeans."

"They were so worn, we could see what color underwear you were wearing."

"That's why I wore blue ones, so you couldn't tell."

Daniels smirked. "I think you're missing the point."

Rem ate another bite of donut.

"Hey, guys," said Manetti.

Rem and Daniels looked over.

"I meant to tell you I talked to Josh Durning. I offered condolences about his dad."

Rem chewed and swallowed. "That was nice of you, Manetti. How was he?"

"About as good as you'd expect. He and his mom are planning a memorial service for his dad at the end of the month. Thankfully, Judge Voorhees gave him a three-day delay."

Daniels rocked back in his chair. "Yeah. Josh called me on the way in and gave me a heads up. Looks like the trial and my testimony could conflict with Marjorie's doctor appointment."

Rem knew Daniels liked to join Marjorie on her appointments, especially now, since she wasn't feeling well. "Can you reschedule?"

"I don't think we should." He pointed at Rem. "I may call on you to help her out. I don't like her going by herself."

"Happy to help," said Rem. "Just let me know."

Monk, who'd been studying his computer, glanced over. "Manetti told me about your witness in the Durning case. You think you'll find him before the killer does?"

Rem prickled at Monk's interruption but stayed civil. He wondered how much they should say in front of Monk. If he actually had a connection to the black bird group, it was better to keep him out of it. But as a detective, it wouldn't be hard for Monk to access the information. "That's the plan, Monk." A thought occurred to him and with a glance at Daniels, he said more. "But I think our assassin may think twice when he or she realizes our witness is the grandson of Sammy Caruso."

Daniels knitted his brow.

Monk straightened. "He's what?"

Manetti sucked in a breath. "You mean *the* Sammy Caruso? From Chicago?"

After a pause, Daniels offered Rem an expression that said he wasn't sure he agreed with Rem. He answered Manetti. "The one and the same."

"Holy shit," said Manetti.

Rem sipped his coffee. "Holy shit is right." He watched Monk, who'd gone quiet. "So far, Caruso's behaving himself, but who knows how long that will last?"

Manetti whistled. "That assassin kills the grandson, then all hell's gonna break loose."

"Which is what we're trying to avoid." Daniels opened his side drawer and pulled out a bottle of water. "If we can catch the assassin first, maybe we can avoid Caruso's involvement."

"Good luck with that," said Manetti.

Rem glanced at Lozano's office. "Anyone see the captain? I figured he'd be here before all of us."

Daniels cracked open his water bottle. "Maybe he stopped to see Josh's mom again, or maybe Josh."

"Maybe." Rem looked a little closer. "His desk is cleaner than usual. I can actually see his desktop."

Daniels sat up and looked toward Lozano's office. "Maybe he got tired of the mess."

"Now?" asked Rem. "That seems unlikely."

"Even you clean your desk once every ten years. So it's possible." Daniels drank some water.

Rem shoved back a pile of folders and added some loose papers to the top of the pile. He swiped some donut crumbs into the trashcan. "I'm due in about another three years."

Daniels moved a jar of pens on his desk into their proper place. "I think it's closer to two."

Rem wiped a drip of coffee off his desk with his napkin. "Don't rush me."

Daniels flipped on his monitor and mumbled. "And I'm the one who's not normal."

Rem started to offer a colorful retort when the squad doors opened again. Expecting Lozano, Rem was surprised to see the chief of police enter along with two people, a man and a woman, both dressed in dark suits.

Rem stood, along with Daniels, Monk and Manetti, and the other few detectives who were at their desks.

"Chief Patterson," said Daniels, smoothing his shirt. "We didn't know you were coming."

The chief spoke gruffly. "That's because I didn't tell anyone, Detective Daniels."

Chief Ronald Patterson, a tall, bald, black man with a barrel chest, narrow eyes, and bushy eyebrows and mustache, eyed the squad room. Rising fast in the ranks, he'd become the youngest person to reach the rank of chief. With his body type, brusque manner and razor-sharp wit, there had been rumors he'd once wrestled. During a poker match at Rem's, the detectives in attendance, after several rounds of beer, came up with wrestler names for the chief. Rem's had been the Brainy Bruiser. Daniels had preferred Cranium Crusher.

"Are you looking for Captain Lozano, Chief?" asked Rem.

"No. I am not, Detective Remalla." The chief prided himself on knowing every detective's name on his force, and as far as Rem knew, he'd never forgotten one. The chief eyed the room. "I'm here to talk to all of you."

Rem looked around, along with the rest of the detectives. The chief was not known to come to squad rooms to talk to his men. An uneasy feeling rippled through Rem.

The chief gestured at the two people with him. "These two are federal agents Alicia Brady, and Vern Lattimore, with the FBI."

The agents raised their badges but didn't say anything.

Patterson continued. "They spoke to Captain Lozano yesterday."

Daniels glanced at Rem and his expression told Rem he felt uneasy, too.

The chief regarded Daniels and Rem. "I know you two are investigating the death of Reginald Durning."

"We are, Chief," said Daniels.

The chief nodded. "I'll get to the point and tell you what I know. Durning was under federal investigation for acts committed during his time as a prosecutor. His death has complicated the investigation but not stopped it. Agents Brady and Lattimore have reason to suspect that Captain Lozano, during his time as a detective, may have some involvement in Durning's acts. As such, I had no choice but to suspend Captain Lozano until Agents Brady and Lattimore finish the investigation and clear his name." He aimed a steely gaze at the agents. "Which, I have no doubt, will be the result."

Neither agent responded.

Rem stood in mute shock, and Daniels dropped his jaw.

"You all will receive emails about the situation," said the chief, "but I wanted you to hear it from me first."

Manetti spoke first. "That can't be true, Chief Patterson."

"What's true is to be determined, Detective Manetti." Patterson looked back at the detectives in the squad. "I spoke to Captain Lozano last night, and he is aware of the decision. I asked him not to contact you. I expect him, and all of you, to not discuss this situation with him until it's resolved."

Lozano's clean desk now made sense. "Chief," said Rem, trying to assimilate the news, "why is the FBI investigating Durning?"

Agent Brady spoke. "That's need to know."

"My partner and I are investigating his murder," said Daniels. "I'd say we need to know."

Agent Lattimore narrowed his eyes. "We'll keep that in mind."

"Keep it in mind?" asked Rem in disbelief. "How nice of you." He tapped his temple. "Anything else in there of any use?"

"I hope so, for Lozano's sake," added Daniels.

Lattimore's expression darkened.

"That's enough, Detectives," said Patterson. "I expect full cooperation from everyone in this squad. If Agents Brady and Lattimore need to speak with you, they'll let you know. In the meantime, do your jobs. It's what Lozano expects, and so do I."

"Who is going to replace Lozano, Chief?" asked Monk.

"I've made arrangements," said Patterson. "Lozano's replacement is on her way."

Just then, the squad doors opened behind the chief and a woman with stick straight black hair, high cheekbones and arched dark brows, wearing a crisp blue suit with a high-necked white blouse, entered. Carrying a briefcase, she walked up to the chief.

"Sorry I'm late, Chief."

Patterson grunted. "Detectives," he studied the group. "This is Elsa Crow. She's from the Special Crimes unit and is now your temporary captain. I expect you to afford her the same respect and assistance you'd give Lozano."

Elsa Crow regarded the detectives in the room. Her gaze stopped on Rem and Daniels. "I look forward to working with all of you."

That icy feeling intensified, and Rem met Daniels' worried look again.

Chapter Eleven

DANIELS SETTLED MARTHA CRAVITZ in the interview room and brought her a cup of coffee. Seeing she was emotional, he patted her shoulder. "Give us about ten minutes."

She pulled a tissue from her purse. "That's fine."

He left the interview room and shut the door behind him. Instead of going to the squad room, though, he headed to the men's restroom.

After the chief departed, along with the FBI agents, Elsa Crow had told them she would take time to familiarize herself with the squad's cases and would be talking to each of the detectives soon. Then she'd entered Lozano's office and shut the door.

Daniels and Rem, along with everyone else in the room, had stood in silence, unsure of what to do. Eventually, they'd all done their best to resume their work without looking like they were talking about the shocking turn of events. Thankfully, it hadn't been long afterward that Shorty had called from the main desk and told Daniels that Martha Cravitz had arrived. Rem and Daniels couldn't get out of the squad room fast enough.

Daniels pushed the bathroom door open and saw Rem leaning against the back wall with his arms crossed. "Martha situated?" he asked.

"She is. Told her to give us a few minutes." Daniels leaned against the wall next to Rem. "So, what do you think?"

Rem sighed and stared at the ceiling. "Durning was being investigated by the FBI and suddenly Lozano is implicated? Right after Durning's murder?"

Daniels shook his head. "It doesn't make sense."

"It does if you look at the bigger picture."

Daniels glanced at Rem. "You think Lozano's being framed? By the black birds?"

"Maybe Durning too." Rem pushed off the wall. "Think about it. Durning's murdered and branded, likely by Rhonda, which suggests Durning got caught up with the black birds and couldn't get out. You and I are investigating his murder and told Lozano about Rhonda and this society. Plus, Lozano and Durning were friends and used to work together."

"Which makes it easy to link Lozano and Durning and make Lozano look culpable in whatever Durning may or may not have been doing."

"It distracts us too, from pursuing the black birds and Rhonda, because now we have to deal with a new captain and clear Lozano's name."

"You heard the chief. We're supposed to stay out of it."

Rem tipped his head.

Daniels narrowed his eyes. "We're going to have to be careful. We get caught interfering, and it could mean our jobs."

"If we don't interfere, it could mean Lozano's career, and possibly our lives. These people aren't going to stop with the captain. This could be the first link in the next chain of events."

Daniels slid his hands into his pockets. "You really know how to cheer a guy up."

"If you have another suggestion, I'm all ears."

"This could be a misunderstanding. Brady and Lattimore could complete their investigation and clear Lozano's name. Maybe Durning's too."

"You willing to bet money on that?"

Daniels stepped away from the wall. "We could wait and see what Elsa Crow says."

Rem pursed his lips. "You think we should trust her?"

Daniels recalled seeing Crow sit at Lozano's desk. It had made his stomach flip. "She's our new captain, Rem."

"Whose last name is Crow, which just happens to be a black bird."

That took Daniels by surprise. "C'mon. You think she's the mastermind of the black bird society? That's a bit of a stretch."

"I didn't say mastermind, but it's a hell of a coincidence, don't you think? And other than she comes from Special Crimes, we know nothing about her."

"So now we're supposed to investigate her, too?" He waved his hand. "You seem to think we have an awful lot of time on our hands."

"No. I mean, we need to be cautious. She may have nothing to do with the black birds, but what about her family? Maybe she's connected like Jerry Lee, and because of her name, someone pulled some strings and put her in charge as a big joke to us."

"That's a big assumption, Rem, and some seriously big strings."

"You heard what Lexie said, and you've seen the stuff from Ackerman's box. This society has put some big money behind some powerful people, including politicians and higher ups in law enforcement. There's no telling how deep this goes."

Daniels set his jaw. Thinking about it, he couldn't deny Rem was right. They had to assume the worst. "If that's true, we're in some deep shit."

"We're gonna have to buy knee-high boots."

"More like thigh-high."

"As long as our heads are uncovered."

"The rate we're going, that may not last long."

Rem rested against the bathroom counter. "Well, there's always Bolivia. I hear it's nice this time of year."

"I'm partial to colder weather."

Rem half-smiled. "Marj already told me she prefers a warmer climate, so you're screwed, unless you're prepared to be all alone."

"Basically, I'm screwed whether I stay or go."

"Seems so."

Daniels recalled Rem's comment to Monk. "And what's up with you mentioning Sammy Caruso to Monk? Don't you think we should have kept that to ourselves?"

Rem ran his thumb over his jaw. "If Monk has any affiliation with the black birds—"

"Which is looking less and less likely. It appears he's just an asshole."

"Maybe so, but if he has some connection, he'll let them know their assassin is going after the grandson of a powerful mobster. That may make this assassin think twice and buy Jerry Lee some time."

Daniels considered that. "If our assassin is Rhonda, you think she'd care? She may see it as a challenge."

"If Rhonda values her life, challenge or not, she may have to back off. I doubt these black birds want to take on Sammy Caruso."

"If they're big enough, they may not care either."

"I guess we're about to find out, because the Carusos and black birds are going to bump heads if we don't find Rhonda first, and Jerry Lee is going to be caught right in the middle."

"Great," said Daniels. "One more thing to look forward to." He groaned and rubbed his neck. "So what do we do now, Einstein?"

"Let's see what Martha has to say about Durning. Maybe she can illuminate us on the lengthy client and staff list. And maybe she knows something about this FBI investigation or Durning's connection to the black birds."

"And if she doesn't?"

Rem froze, stared off, and snapped his fingers. "Phoebe Reinart."

Recalling the detective who'd helped him and Rem investigate the murder of the prominent art dealer, Rowan Laroche, after he'd acquired a famous but cursed painting, Daniels frowned. "Reinart works in the art crime division."

"It's still the FBI. I bet she could do some digging for us."

Daniels had to admit it wasn't a bad idea. "It's worth a shot."

"I'll bribe her with some Taco del Fuegos."

"We want her to help us, not hurt us."

"Hey," Rem pushed off the counter, "Reinart loves those tacos."

"She was just being nice."

Rem smirked. "You're just mad she didn't like your green juice."

"Let's just hope her information is more beneficial than her food choices." Daniels headed toward the door. "What do you want to do about Lozano?"

Rem paused. "Well, if we're meeting Lexie tomorrow at the storage unit, maybe afterward, we stop by and let Lozano know we're thinking of him."

Daniels reached for the handle. "And maybe, while we're there, we can update him on what we know."

"And he can update us." He smacked Daniels' shoulder. "Sounds like we have a plan."

"Should we take bets on how long it takes to fall apart?"

"I give it a solid twenty minutes."

Daniels swung the door open. "Looks like you get the crown for Mr. Positivity."

"Don't worry. I won't get used to it." Rem headed out the door.

· · · ● · ● · · · ·

While Daniels joined Martha, Rem returned to the squad room to grab his coffee and Daniels' water. Seeing the staff and client list provided by Ben Crenshaw on his desk, he grabbed it. Spying Monk and Manetti sitting in Lozano's office with Elsa Crow, he made brief eye contact with Crow through the glass before grabbing the drinks and leaving the squad room. Trying not to think about Lozano losing his job, he entered the interview room where Daniels sat with Martha. Daniels' notebook was open, and Martha was dabbing her nose with a tissue.

"This is my partner, Detective Aaron Remalla," said Daniels.

Rem set the drinks and papers down and sat. "Thanks for coming, Mrs. Cravitz." Thinking of the nosy neighbor from the TV show *Bewitched*, he almost chuckled. "I'm sorry about your loss. Can I get you something to drink?"

"Thank you and no. I'm good," she said with a sniff. "It's been hard. Reggie was a good boss and friend." She held her head. "I just can't believe this happened to him."

"That's why we wanted to speak with you," said Daniels. "You were his assistant, so you probably knew him best. Can you tell us anything about his last few months? Was there anyone or anything strange you noticed? Any arguments with staff? Any odd correspondence or occurrences that stood out?"

Martha rubbed her head. "Let me think. My head's in a fog. I haven't slept well."

Rem understood. "Take your time, Mrs. Cravitz."

"Please, call me Martha."

"Martha," said Rem. He tried to help jog her memory. "We know Reggie was working to become partner and that meant long hours at the office."

"It sure did," she said. "But Reggie was always a hard worker."

"Were there any clients in particular that stood out?" asked Daniels. "That maybe Reggie was having difficulty with or didn't like?"

"Reggie was always good with the clients, but he disliked several of them. He defended some lousy people. But that was his job."

"Anyone he complained about?" asked Rem.

"No. Reggie was too professional for that." She bit her lip. "I'm sorry. I'm not much help, am I?"

"You're doing fine, Martha," said Daniels. "How was Reggie's relationship with the other staff at CIW? Did he get along well with his superiors?"

"He didn't like Ben Crenshaw much. He wasn't too fond of Barbara or Charles either, but Ben seemed to get under his skin." She pointed with the hand holding her tissue. "They had an argument maybe a month before...before..." Her eyes watered. "...before Reggie died."

"Do you know about what?" asked Rem, hopeful they were getting somewhere.

She shook her head. "All I know is that Mr. Crenshaw went into Reggie's office, which was unusual. Usually it was the other way around. Reggie closed the blinds so I couldn't see anything, but I did hear raised voices. After about fifteen minutes, Crenshaw left. Reggie stayed in his office, blinds closed, for an hour, before he abruptly left for the rest of the day."

"Did Reggie say anything to you about that meeting?" asked Rem.

"No, he didn't," she said with a sniff. "He came in the next day acting like nothing happened. And I didn't ask."

Daniels wrote in his notebook. "We've heard that Reggie was stressed the last several months, and that it was about more than just becoming a partner. What were your observations of Reggie this past year?"

She held her tissue to her lips. "That's hard for me to say. I've never been one to believe office gossip or contribute to it. I stay away from all of that."

Rem perked up. "What did you hear?"

She hesitated.

"It's important, Martha," said Daniels.

"Well," she drank some of her coffee. "I heard he was drinking a lot and that he'd go to the bars after work, but I never saw him drunk. He always did his job." She studied her hands.

"I sense a 'but' coming," added Rem.

She looked up. "There were times he was short-tempered, which was unlike him. He'd get impatient or angry at the drop of a hat, especially after..." She sucked in a breath. "I remember now. Two FBI agents came to talk to him."

Daniels glanced at Rem. "When was this?" asked Daniels.

"Oh, I think..." She rubbed her temple. "...maybe three, four months ago. It's in my appointment book."

"Any idea what they talked to Reggie about?" asked Rem.

"No. He never said, but his agitation flared up after that, and he was overly stressed. More so than usual. I was worried about him and told him, but he told me not to be concerned. It was nothing and he would handle it."

Daniels scribbled in his notebook. "Did the agents come back?"

She paused. "Yes, as a matter of fact, but not to see Reggie. I saw them walk through the hall and they went into Crenshaw's office. I think the other two partners were there too. Ingram and Willoughby."

"When was this?" asked Rem.

Martha stared off. "Two months ago, I think? I told Reggie, and he didn't look happy about it. He told me to cancel his appointments for the rest of the day, but he didn't go anywhere. He just stayed in his office."

Rem sat back in his seat. "And he never told you why they were there?"

"Never," she said. "I'm sorry. In hindsight, I wished I'd pressed harder. Maybe...maybe if I had..." More tears welled up, and she pressed the tissue to the corner of her eye.

"It's okay, Martha," said Rem, recalling his own experiences. "Hindsight always sucks."

She swallowed. "Yes. It does." Taking a deep breath, she settled herself.

Daniels tapped his pen against his notepad. "I hate to ask a delicate question, but were you aware if Reggie ever had sexual relationships with women outside of his marriage?"

Her jaw dropped. "No. Never."

"So you never saw him with anyone?" asked Rem.

"I didn't." She paused. "If I'm honest, though, I heard things, and I didn't believe them."

"Like what?" asked Daniels.

She picked at her tissue. "I don't like to spread lies..., but," she rubbed her temple. "...there was some suggestion that Reggie may have had affairs with women in the office."

Eager to hear more, Rem asked the delicate question. "Can you tell us with who?"

She dropped her head into her hands. "I didn't ask. And didn't want to know. It's none of my business, and Reggie never acted like a cheating spouse. He loved his wife."

"When was this? Recently or in the past?" asked Daniels.

She looked up. "More recent."

"What about on the day of his death? How was he acting?" asked Rem.

She tugged on the edge of her shirtsleeve. "He left early that day. Said he didn't feel well."

"Was there anything unusual about that day?" asked Daniels. "Did he speak to any clients?"

She dabbed her nose with her tissue. "He did his normal routine. He spoke on the phone and had a couple of meetings. Nothing strange."

"So he didn't act sick?" asked Rem.

"No. Not that I saw. We got to three o'clock, and he suddenly left the office. Told me he was leaving early because he thought he was coming down with something, and he'd see me the next day." She spoke softly. "Those were our last words."

After speaking with Reggie's wife, Rem knew Reggie had not gone home. "Did he talk to anyone else in the office? Anyone else he was close to he might have confided in?"

She made a snort. "You don't confide in anyone at CIW, not unless you want to get stabbed in the back. Too many money-hungry and ambitious attorneys who want Reggie's job." She paused. "Now I suppose one of them will step into Reggie's shoes." She closed her eyes. "I hope they're prepared."

"What does that mean?" asked Daniels. He put his pen down and sipped some of his water.

Martha crossed her arms. "CIW is not known for its work-life balance. There are high expectations, and Crenshaw is the taskmaster. What he says, goes."

"What about Ingram and Willoughby?" asked Rem. "They the same?"

"They're not as bad. I think they just put up with Crenshaw because they have to, but what do I know?" She shrugged.

Daniels set his water bottle down. "You mentioned an appointment book? Any chance we could see it?"

She looked between them. "The appointments are all on the computer. I tried to access them to cancel any upcoming client meetings, but when I tried to go in, it was all locked down."

"Locked down?" asked Rem.

She nodded. "Yes. It's a calendar software created specifically for CIW." Martha rolled her eyes. "So CIW can see everyone's schedule, I suppose. It's accessed with a password, but mine no longer works." She reached for her coffee. "I guess Crenshaw and company are circling the wagons."

Daniels sighed. "That's unfortunate."

Rem set his thermos down. "CIW works fast."

Martha nibbled her lip again. "But..."

Rem lifted his brow. "But what?"

Martha fiddled with her tissue. "Last year, we had a power outage. The entire system went down, and when it came back, we'd lost everything in the schedule. Some sort of bug, I was told. It was a mess trying to figure out who was doing what and when. So, after that, I kept a backup."

Daniels clutched his pen. "Does CIW know about this backup?"

"Certainly not, but it made me feel better." Martha reached for her large purse, which hung from her chair.

Rem watched as she opened her purse and pulled out a small notebook. "I wrote everything down in here, so I'd always know, computer or not."

Rem wanted to kiss her. "You're a smart lady, Martha."

"Of course, this is between you and me," she said. "CIW wouldn't be pleased."

"Our lips are sealed." Daniels reached for the book. "You mind if we take a look?"

"Please do." Martha set her purse aside. "Although I don't know if it will be of much help."

Rem leaned over to see the book when Daniels opened it. "In our line of work, we assume nothing." Rem eyed the pages, seeing the various appointments. "How far back does this go?"

"A year plus anything in the future," she said.

"That's great, Martha." Daniels flipped through the pages starting from the beginning. He asked about various appointments, which Martha easily explained. He stopped on one dated eleven months back. "What's this?"

Rem read the name Dirk written in bold letters. There was no time noted.

She leaned to look. "Oh, yes. I recall that. Reggie would add that on the calendar and whenever they met, he took the whole day. He'd be gone in the morning and would come back sometime in the afternoon."

"You don't know who Dirk is?" asked Daniels.

"No idea." She sat back and brushed a tendril of hair behind her ear. "I never met the mysterious Dirk and when I asked about his full name, Reggie told me to leave it as Dirk in the calendar, so I did."

Daniels flipped forward and found Dirk in three more places. One ten months, five months, and the latest one was one month prior to Reggie's death. "If you had to guess, was this a client?"

She nodded. "I would say yes. Reggie was a little more on edge the days he met with Dirk, and I noticed Crenshaw was out of the office on those days as well. I don't know if it matters, though."

"Something tells me it does," said Rem. He picked up the papers. "Martha, this is a list of staff at CIW and Durning's clients, both former and current. Would you be able to look through this and mark any current clients? And note if there are any staff you think we should talk to." He took Daniels' pen and handed it to her.

Martha took the papers and pen. "I suppose so."

Daniels flipped to the end of Martha's appointment book. "Do you mind if we make a copy of this?"

"Keep it," said Martha, looking up from the papers. Her voice softened. "I don't need it anymore."

"Thank you," said Rem. "This is a big help."

They waited as she went through the names on the list and made marks next to several of them. "I put a 'C' next to current clients and a 'F' next to former," she said. "If I'm unsure, I put a question mark." She circled a name. "I'll circle the staff that have worked with Reggie. Although I can't be sure it's accurate. I'm sure he's worked with people I'm not aware of."

"We'll take whatever you've got, Martha," said Rem, eyeing her marks. While it helped streamline the list, there were still several names they would have to check.

After she finished, she slid the list back to Rem. "I hope that helps."

"I'm sure it will," replied Daniels.

"Is there anything else?" she asked, her eyes weary.

"Not at the moment," said Rem. "We appreciate you coming in. We may be in touch if we have more questions."

She reached for her purse. "That's fine. I'm happy to help."

Daniels' phone rang, and he reached into his pocket and took it out. "I have to take this." Daniels stood. "Thank you again, Martha."

"I'll see you out, Mrs. Cravitz," said Rem.

Daniels left and Rem walked Martha downstairs. After she exited the building and headed into the parking lot, he returned up the stairs and turned toward the squad room when Daniels called his name. He stopped and saw Daniels approaching, tucking his phone into his pocket.

"That was Marjorie," said Daniels. "Guess what?"

Noting Daniels' concerned expression, Rem hoped the news wasn't bad. "What?"

"Erin accepted a dinner invitation to our house the day after tomorrow."

Rem dropped his jaw.

"You and Mikey better be available, and you're bringing the wine and beer, too." He raised a finger. "And if this backfires, I'm not buying you one more Taco Del Fuego." Before Rem could say a word, Daniels strode past him and headed into the squad room.

Chapter Twelve

RHONDA PULLED HER RENTAL car up to the curb in the small residential neighborhood and parked. Taking a second to study her surroundings, she was glad it was quiet. No one was walking their dog and there wasn't a jogger or bratty child in sight. In her line of work, the fewer people who saw you, the better.

She grabbed her large purse and pulled out the piece of paper. After her conversation with Monk the previous day, he'd contacted her that night and had sent her the information he had on Jerry Lee Caruso, the idiot bellboy who'd caught her murdering the other idiot, Reginald Durning.

Flipping through the information again, she tested herself, memorizing everything on the paper, which included Jerry Lee's address, his mother's name, names of his friends, and his current and former workplaces, of which there were only two–his current hotel employer and his past job at a pawn shop. It's what Monk could get on short notice, but he told her he should have more soon.

Not one to wait, Rhonda made a plan. And once she had it, the unsettled feeling in her stomach relaxed. If there was one thing she understood best, it was people. She assumed Monk's partner, or boss, depending on who she spoke to, would not be happy about the witness, and she suspected that Jerry Lee, who was only twenty, would rely on the people he knew best to get him out of a tight spot. Studying the paper, she didn't doubt that the person Jerry had gone to would be on the list. She just had to figure out who, and the best way to do that, would be to speak to his mother.

Prepared, Rhonda tucked the paper back into her purse and stud-ied her reflection in the rear-view mirror. She adjusted her long, wavy brown-haired wig, pulled a tube of lipstick from her purse and applied the bland color to her lips, and returned it to her purse. She smoothed her long-sleeved sweater, scratched at a stain on her jeans, and pulled off her high heels and put on a pair of ugly flat sneakers that were a current popular brand.

Pleased with her look, she pulled out a pair of sunglasses and slid them on and smiled into the mirror.

Despite her tenuous situation, she took perverse pleasure in it. It afford-ed her a challenge, and she was rarely able to enjoy that nowadays. Most of her work, while dangerous, wasn't particularly hard. But with Jerry Lee's interference, Rhonda had suddenly found herself on shaky ground, and to her surprise, she liked it. It gave her an unexpected opportunity to prove herself. Not only could she take care of other people's problems, but she could take care of hers, too. If she could successfully handle Jerry Lee, that would do wonders for her reputation, and that made her pulse pound. One day, she'd move on from Monk and his boss, and she needed to take advantage of every opportunity to be ready.

Sighing with satisfaction, she started up the car and pulled away from the curb. She drove slowly down the street, checking addresses. She already knew where the house was, but she wanted to look slightly lost, so she took her time. Seeing the patrol car parked in front of Patricia Caruso's house, Rhonda pulled up to the curb and parked. Not paying attention to the patrol, she got out, slung her purse over her shoulder, and shut the car door. She pulled out her phone and, keeping her head down, she strode up the walkway to the front door, where she rang the bell and put her phone away. The patrol car remained where it was, and no one emerged from it. She half-wondered whether the officer behind the wheel was even awake.

After a few seconds, the door opened, and a woman stood at the entry. Around her mid-forties, she wore little makeup, and her hair was pulled back into an unkempt ponytail. Her eyes were puffy and red. She frowned at Rhonda.

Rhonda stepped forward and put on her most somber expression. "Mrs. Caruso?"

"Yes?"

Rhonda held her purse against her body. "I'm so sorry to bother you during a difficult time, but I'm hoping I could speak with you."

Patricia eyed the police cruiser and then Rhonda. "About what?"

Rhonda held her hand against her chest. "I know about Jerry Lee."

Patricia's eyes widened. "Who are you?" She eyed the cruiser again.

Rhonda held up her hand. "I'm sorry. I don't mean to scare you. I'm an investigative reporter." She reached into her bag. "My name's Lexie Logan." She pulled out the fake ID she'd picked up that afternoon. The ID had a picture of Rhonda in her full Lexie makeover. "Detectives Daniels and Remalla sent me."

Patricia narrowed her eyes. "They did? Why didn't they tell me? And why would they send a reporter? They told me they were keeping Jerry Lee's name out of the press."

Rhonda put the ID away. "And they are. Don't worry. I'm independent. I only work for myself. And nothing will be printed until Jerry Lee is safe and sound."

Patricia's eyes widened again. "You're going to write a story about Jerry Lee?"

Rhonda quickly backtracked. "No. No. No." She shook her head. "I'm sorry. I'm writing about the victim. Reginald Durning. And I'll be keeping Jerry Lee's name out of it."

Patricia's leery expression remained. "I don't understand."

Rhonda softened her voice. "I'm sorry. I'm not explaining myself well. And I'm sorry to surprise you like this. I suspect Detectives Daniels and Remalla didn't tell you because they don't want anyone to know that we sometimes work together."

"Work together? They're cops. Why do they need a reporter?"

"Because sometimes reporters can get information they can't. And in a situation like this, that can come in handy. That's why when they told me about Jerry Lee, I offered to help."

She set her jaw. "To get your story?"

"I won't deny this story is big, but we, the detectives and I, have an agreement. I don't print anything without their approval, and that's usually only when it's safe to print. Believe me, I don't want to put Jerry Lee in any more danger."

"What can you possibly do that they can't?"

"Nothing, but what I have, and they don't, is time, Mrs. Caruso. Right now, they've got to hunt down Durning's killer, and since Jerry Lee is good at hiding, they have to rely on an APB and other officers to look for him. And I'm good at finding people. It's a strength of mine, and I'm certain if you and I talk, and you tell me about his friends, and other people Jerry knows, that I can find him. And when I do, I can direct Daniels and Remalla to his whereabouts, so they can bring him home."

Patricia's chin quivered. "That's all I want. I'm so worried about him."

Rhonda took a step closer. "That's all I want too, Mrs. Caruso." She put on her most somber expression and lowered her tone. "I promise."

Patricia hesitated, eyed the patrol car, and then Rhonda.

Rhonda sighed. "But if you'd rather I leave, I completely understand. No hard feelings. I'll wish you well in your search for Jerry Lee and pray he's found in time."

A tear welled up in Patricia's eye and she wiped it away.

Rhonda gripped her purse handle. "I'm upsetting you." She waved a hand. "I'll go." She turned to leave.

"No. Wait."

Rhonda smiled to herself and turned, looking somber again.

Patricia pulled her front door open wider. "Please," she said. "Come in."

. . . ● . ● . ● . .

Holding Martha's appointment book, Daniels returned to the squad room and dropped the book into his desk drawer. Through the glass, he saw Monk and Manetti sitting in Lozano's office with Elsa Crow. Rem went to the coffeemaker. "Looks like the conversations have begun."

"Seems so." Daniels put his bottle of water on his desk and sat.

Rem added coffee to his thermos. "And don't worry about dinner with Erin. It will be fine."

"I hope you're right."

Rem returned the pot to the burner. "I've been thinking."

"Don't hurt yourself."

Rem smirked. "Since we're going to talk to Erin, maybe it's time I reengage with Cain." He added cream and sugar to his thermos.

Daniels rested his elbows on his desk. "You sure about that?"

"I've been giving him his space while things quieted down, but with Durning's murder, Lozano's suspension, and Erin coming over, maybe it's time to put a little pressure on Cain."

Daniels considered whether that was a good idea. "Maybe we should talk to Erin first and see how that goes?" He sat back. "We don't even know if she'll stay. She may get one look at you and bolt."

Rem sat at his desk. "I'll be on my best behavior. I don't want her to bolt any more than you do. And why are you worried about me talking to Cain?" He sipped his coffee.

Daniels shrugged. "If we push him, it could put Erin at risk."

Rem's face fell. "Erin knows the deal. That's the whole point of meeting with her. To find out what she knows about Cain's involvement with the black birds. If I rile things up, it might get him talking, and she might learn more."

Daniels adjusted a folder on his desk. "Maybe."

Rem sighed. "Buddy, if you don't want Erin involved in this, then tell her."

"I didn't say that."

"You didn't have to. It's written all over your face."

Daniels had to admit his strange attachment to Erin made him worry about her. "It's out of my hands, anyway. I told her it was dangerous, but she was determined to do it."

"Which is exactly why this is a good thing. If Cain opens up to her, this could be exactly what we need."

Daniels nodded. "Yeah. I know. It's still nagging at me, though. It's like I know she's doing this for all the wrong reasons."

"Why don't we let her be the judge of that? Maybe this dinner will help with alleviating your fears."

"I guess we're about to find out."

The door to Lozano's office opened, and Monk and Manetti stepped out and closed the door behind them.

Rem glanced over. "How'd it go?"

"You two are up next," said Monk. "She said to give her a couple of minutes and then head in."

Daniels could see Elsa Crow typing on her keyboard. "Any words of wisdom?"

Manetti sat at his desk. "She's definitely not Lozano."

"Be prepared to answer a lot of questions and don't expect logical answers." Monk grabbed a mug from his desk. "Lozano gave us lots of leeway. She likes to know what's going on." He went to the coffee machine and added coffee to his mug.

"It's not unexpected," said Manetti. "She's new at this. I suspect she'll ease up with time."

"Let's hope she doesn't get that time," said Rem, "and Lozano is back soon."

Monk sipped his coffee. "Let's hope."

Daniels saw Crow look up and wave him and Rem in. "That's our cue, partner." He stood and grabbed his water.

Rem stood too, with his thermos. "Here goes nothing."

Manetti swiveled toward them in his chair. "Keep in mind the level of detail you give her. Something tells me she's got one of those photographic memories and what you say could come back to haunt you."

Monk returned to his desk. "Good observation, Manetti. I was thinking the same."

"Good to know." Daniels went to the office door and opened it.

Crow looked up from her monitor. "Come in, gentlemen."

Rem followed Daniels inside. He sat in one chair across from Crow, and Daniels sat in the other.

"Captain," said Daniels.

"Captain," said Rem.

She pushed her keyboard back. "I know you two are busy, so I'll try not to take much of your time." She interlaced her fingers. "What I'd like to say first is that I understand that this change is a shock to you and the squad. I know how much Captain Lozano was respected—"

"—is respected," said Rem.

Crow eyed Rem. "Yes. Of course. I know how long you two have worked with him and I do not intend to take his place. If he's cleared…"

"…when he's cleared," added Daniels.

Crow paused. "My hope is just that." She pursed her lips. "But his situation is in the hands of the FBI and whatever internal investigation Chief Patterson pursues. And that means that I am now your captain. I realize that this change is difficult. It's not easy for me either. I'm aware of how loyal detectives are to the people on their squad and their captains, but I am not the bad guy."

Rem sipped his coffee. "Nobody said you were."

"But you're right," said Daniels. "This isn't easy."

Crow looked between them. "Then I guess we agree on that much." She sat back. "Now that we've gotten that cleared up, let's talk about what you're working on. I've gone through a lot of the current case files, read the reports and Lozano's notes." She pulled a folder over and opened it. "You two are working on the murder of Reginald Durning?"

"We are," said Rem.

"Where are you on it?" asked Crow.

Daniels gave her a brief update on their visit to CIW, the client and staff lists, the visit with Patricia Caruso to discuss the call regarding Jerry Lee, how Tech had found little on Durning's personal and business laptops, and their talk with Martha Cravitz.

Crow took notes while he talked. "Any thoughts about who killed Durning?"

"We suspect it's an assassin named Rhonda," said Rem.

Crow paused her writing. "Is this the woman you escorted from LA to San Diego because you believed she was a witness in a murder trial?"

Surprised Crow knew that much, Daniels sat up. "Yes. That's her."

"And now you believe she's an assassin? Why?"

Rem shifted in his seat. "We learned once we got back that Rhonda had actually framed the person she was going to testify against and killed the husband."

"How do you know that?" asked Crow.

"Because she told us," said Daniels.

Crow nodded. "I see. And you believed her?"

Daniels' tension rose. "We did and still do."

Crow tapped her pen against the notepad on her desk. "The woman is a pathological liar. What makes you think she wasn't lying to you?"

Daniels caught Rem narrowing his eyes. "Because she wasn't," said Rem. "We spent two days with her while she led us all over the town of Elmwood to get us into a position to be killed. She was working for someone, along with the two men who tried to kill us. And when we figured out who she really was, she called and told us the whole story. The entire thing was planned."

Crow glanced at the open folder and read something inside it. "Is this where the alleged back bird society comes in?" She picked up a piece of paper. "Because one of the men who came after you had a tattoo of one on his wrist?" She read more from the paper. "And there was a reporter involved? Who apparently knew from the start that this Rhonda wasn't who she said she was? And you didn't believe her?"

Daniels bit back a groan because he knew how it sounded. "Lexie Logan is the reporter. She was investigating Rhonda, and based on that research, believed Rhonda was a killer."

"And she was right," said Rem. "And the only reason we didn't believe her was because we didn't know her, plus, we were running for our lives."

"And that tattoo keeps showing up," said Daniels. "It wasn't just on one guy."

Crow lowered the paper. "I read about that too." She eyed Rem. "Lozano's notes say your cousin has one of these tattoos?" She glanced at the paper. "And a man named Ackerman, who blew himself up, and almost blew you two up, as well?"

"That's true," said Daniels. "Ackerman admitted to us he was part of the secret organization."

"My cousin, too," said Rem.

"We believe Rhonda has ties to this organization as well," replied Daniels.

Crow nodded. "Have you found any proof of that?"

Rem straightened. "Not directly. But Lexie Logan..."

"The reporter?" asked Crow.

"Yes," said Daniels. "She believes Rhonda is the Star Killer."

"That's right," said Crow, studying her paper. "Because of a conversation she had with Rhonda's ex, who's currently in jail?"

"Her ex said Rhonda threatened to brand him on his ass with a star," said Rem. "That's pretty telling."

"She also could have threatened to slash his throat and put makeup on him. Would that make her the Makeup Artist?" asked Crow, tipping her head.

Not liking where this was going, Daniels set his jaw. "We caught the Makeup Artist, so no. That theory doesn't work."

"Was the Star Killer in the news at that point?" asked Crow.

Rem mumbled something under his breath and sighed. "I believe so. At least the first victim was."

Crow lowered the paper. "You see my point, then. This Rhonda could be taking credit for all sorts of murders and may have nothing at all to do with Durning's death."

Daniels leaned up. "We're not rookies, Crow."

"That's Captain Crow." She held Daniels' gaze.

Frustrated, Daniels sat back. "Sorry. Captain Crow."

Rem spoke up. "Rhonda and this society—"

Crow cut in. "—is some figment of your imagination."

"Excuse me?" asked Rem, his face taut.

She leaned back and crossed her arms. "I realize the thought of chasing down some elusive society is very Dan Brown and exciting for two detectives who're used to big cases and accolades."

Daniels couldn't believe what he was hearing. "We're what?"

"You think we're making this up because we're bored and like attention?" asked Rem. "How the hell did you get picked to take Lozano's place?"

Her face clenched. "Watch it, Detective."

Rem set his coffee on the edge of her desk. "No. You watch it. You've been in this office for all of thirty minutes and you think you understand this case and the mechanics of it by reading a report and some notes?"

"As I was saying," said Daniels. "We're not rookies. Rem and I know a conspiracy when we see one. The black birds are real and so is Rhonda, whether you want to believe it or not." He pointed at himself. "We're the ones who were shot at and almost blown up, and we could still be targets, so we have some skin in this game. So does Jerry Lee Caruso. And Rhonda or not, there's an assassin out there who wants him dead, plus three murdered men who've been branded."

"All I'm asking for is proof," added Crow. "And other than a few tattoos, two of which are on dead men, one on a missing one, and one on your uncooperative cousin, Remalla, you don't have it. And until you do, I have to go with what we know, which isn't much."

Daniels thought of Ackerman's box, which they'd never told Lozano about, and which would offer all the proof needed. "I guess then you're going to have to trust us."

"And maybe our time would be better spent investigating than sitting in a meeting discussing what you think we've done wrong," added Rem.

Crow rocked back in her seat. "I'm all for you investigating, Detective. Just make sure you're on the right path and not on some wild goose chase." She paused. "And what about this Lexie Logan? You still working with her?"

Daniels recalled Manetti's advice to be careful with detail. "We're still in touch."

"She's researching," said Rem.

"Researching what?" asked Crow. "Or should I ask?"

"The black birds," said Daniels.

"I see." Crow sat up again. "I suggest you let her do her thing and you do yours. Keep her out of this investigation. She's not a detective, and it's not her job to do the work you don't have time for. Plus, if she divulges important information..."

"She's not a rookie either, Captain Crow," said Rem. "And we trust her."

"Good for you, but I don't." Crow eyed Daniels. "So, for now, focus on that client and staff list, and on finding Jerry Lee Caruso."

Daniels debated mentioning Jerry Lee's connection to Sammy Caruso but was too annoyed. Rem didn't mention it either. "Reginald Durning was not killed by some random pissed off person," said Daniels. "He was branded and murdered, like two other victims before him." Daniels did his best to keep his temper under control but wasn't sure he was succeeding.

Crow shut her folder. "They were all killed by someone who was likely hired to kill them. Possibly by someone they knew, which is why those lists are important, especially if you can link anyone on those lists to your first two victims." She pushed the folder aside.

Daniels made a half snort. "We know the lists are important, but we also know that Ben Crenshaw has names on there that have no relevance whatsoever to Reginald Durning, and that Durning, and the other two vics, were likely targeted by someone high-powered and influential enough to hire an assassin to get rid of them. From what we've learned, the victims owed a debt to someone and didn't honor it. Going through every name on that list is going to take a lot of time that could be better used in pursuing the most likely suspects."

"And we know it's also critical to find and protect Jerry Lee," said Rem. "He can identify our killer."

"Have you considered using the media?" she asked. "That might help."

"It could also get Jerry Lee killed," said Daniels.

She made a note in her notebook. "You want to find this killer? You need to find Caruso. I'll give you a couple of days, but after that, use the media."

Remaining silent, Daniels bit back the urge to offer his opinion.

"I suggest you two get busy," said Crow, putting her pen down. "You've got a lot to do."

Daniels cleared his throat. "We could move faster if we get help to go through those lists. Rem and I can focus on Jerry Lee and on investigating the most likely suspects."

Crow flipped open a second folder. "For now, you're on your own."

Rem leaned in. "There's no one else who can help make some phone calls and do background checks? What about Silvers? He's great at research."

"Silvers is busy breaking in a new partner," she said. "The other detectives have their own cases, which are no less important than yours. If that changes, I'll let you know."

Irritated, Daniels shook his head.

"You have a problem with that, Detective?" asked Crow.

Daniels tapped his finger on his armrest. "Certainly not, Captain."

"Are we allowed to call people in any order we want?" asked Rem. "Or would you like to organize who gets contacted first?"

Crow glared. "Don't get cocky with me, Detective Remalla. I'm your superior, whether or not you and your partner like it, and since you want to be a smart ass about it, I expect a brief report of tasks you've completed emailed to me at the end of each day."

Rem's eyes widened. "You're serious?"

Daniels stiffened. "So we're being punished?"

She stood and put her palms on her desk. "I don't know you two any better than you know me. Lozano may have put up with your attitudes and BS because he was used to it, and you solved big cases, but you're dealing with me now, and until I'm certain I can trust you, and you're not working with reporters, and chasing secret societies and their mystery assassins, I want to know what you're up to."

Daniels sat in disbelief. Rem gripped his armrest, and the muscle in his jaw flexed. "You want it single or double spaced, Captain?" asked Rem.

"I'll leave that up to you." Crow stared at them, took a breath, and sat again. "That's all I have. You two can go."

A second of silence passed before they both stood. Rem grabbed his coffee and Daniels picked up his bottle of water. His heart pounding in frustration, Daniels kept his mouth shut and went to the door.

Rem did not remain as calm. "Permission to use the john, Captain?"

Crow's glare returned. "You're lucky I respect Lozano and his opinion, but that will only last so long." She went back to studying her monitor. "Now get the hell out of my office."

Rem glared back. "Whatever you say, *Captain*."

Daniels opened the door and Rem stomped out. Daniels started to follow, but his mind raced with all the implications this first interaction with Crow had spawned. Had the black birds arranged for her to take Lozano's place? Did she have something to do with Lozano's suspension? Could she be deliberately impeding the investigation of the black bird group? He glanced back at her. "What exactly do you expect from us?"

Her back straight, she met his gaze. "What every other captain expects, Detective. For you to do your best."

He softened his glare. "That's all we've ever done...Captain." He walked out and closed the door behind him.

Chapter Thirteen

Rhonda parked down the street from the pawn shop owned by Arnold Bertrand. Close enough to watch the front entrance but not close enough to be noticed from inside the shop, she sat and thought.

After her meeting with Patricia Caruso, she felt certain that Arnold Bertrand was the man Jerry had gone to for help. He made the most sense. No one else could provide that kind of protection. Jerry's friends certainly couldn't, and it was unlikely any of the staff at the hotel could or would. Bertrand made the most sense, especially after Patricia had told Rhonda that a man had called to inform her that Jerry Lee was safe and would come home when the killer was caught.

As a pawn shop owner, Bertrand would understand safety. His clientele would expect it. Plus, eyeing the area and seeing the bars over Bertrand's windows, he had to be careful of break-ins. And Patricia had told her that although she never cared for Bertrand, Jerry Lee had liked him and learned a lot from him as a teenager who'd recently moved to California.

Confident she had her man, and would soon have Jerry, she'd made a new plan. She assumed the pawn shop had a back room or basement where Jerry would likely be hiding. Men like Bertrand typically stayed close to their place of business in case of a late-night client. It was possible Bertrand even lived there. She'd ask Monk to do a deep dive on Bertrand. The more Rhonda knew, the better.

She considered going into the shop now, as Lexie Logan, to do surveillance. If she spoke to Bertrand and saw the shop, it would bolster her conviction that Jerry was nearby. And if by some lucky stroke she got access to the back, she might be able to end this problem now. That would mean taking care of Bertrand too, but sometimes collateral damage was unavoidable.

Her heart racing at the possibilities, she started to get out of the car when her phone rang. Annoyed by the distraction, she pulled it from her purse and recognized the number Monk used to reach her. Hoping he had new information for her, she sat back, closed her door, and answered. "It's me."

"Where are you?" he asked.

She eyed the front of the pawn shop. "Outside Arnold Bertrand's shop. I think he's harboring Jerry Lee." She smiled. "This problem might be over sooner than I thought."

"You need to back down."

She didn't expect that. "Why the hell would I back down?"

"The kid," said Monk. "He's Sammy Caruso's grandson."

"Who the hell is Sammy Caruso?"

"You need to pay more attention to national affairs. He's a powerful senator and mobster from Illinois."

"Who the hell cares where he's from?"

Monk sighed. "You're missing the point. You kill Jerry Lee, and you're signing your death warrant."

Rhonda paused. "I'm a serial killer. Haven't I already done that?"

"Only if you get caught."

"Which I'm trying to avoid. This kid can't stay alive."

"Killing him brings down a hammer I can't protect you from."

"Who says I need your protection?" She thought about it. "I can kill him and disappear for a while. The heat will die down."

"We're not talking about the cops, babe. This is a mobster with dangerous connections. They won't stop until they get an eye-for-an-eye. And if they can't find you, they'll take their revenge elsewhere."

Rhonda hesitated. "This is about him, isn't it? Your superior. He's protecting his own ass."

"He's not my superior and of course he is. It's about protecting my ass and yours, too."

"The hell it is. If Jerry lives, and the cops get to him, I'm screwed."

"They've got to find you first."

She gripped the steering wheel. "Is that the plan? I go into hiding, and never come back? Do I have some unfortunate accident instead of Jerry?"

His tone deepened. "No. That's not the plan. We just need time to determine the best way to handle this."

"Bullshit. Your friend wants to figure out the best way to handle *me*." She stared at the shop's entry. "I'm going in."

"Damn it. For once in your crazy life, I need you to stand down. Let me talk to my partner. You know I can handle him. And what's the rush? It's not like the kid's going anywhere."

"If he's this mobster's grandkid, the mobster could swoop in and grab him. And then I've got no shot at all. And this mobster could still target me to keep Jerry safe."

"He does that, and he risks a war. Neither side wants that." Monk paused. "And I've talked to some of my connections. Caruso's still in Chicago."

"If he is who you say he is, that won't last long."

"Which is why I need to work fast. So hang back. For now. Give me time to put a plan together." He made a grunt. "Maybe there's a way to get rid of the kid while keeping you out of it."

Rhonda straightened. "You mean hire someone else? The hell you will. This one is mine."

"That's not what I mean. Maybe you can kill him, but point the evidence elsewhere." He chuckled. "That could be fun, don't you think? I know how you like a challenge."

Rhonda's heart raced. Could they pull something like that off? "I'll admit. It intrigues me."

"I thought so, but it's going to take some planning. We need the proper scapegoat."

Watching the shop, she straightened when another car she recognized pulled up near the entrance and parked. Two men got out, and recognizing Detectives Daniels and Remalla, she smiled. "Can I offer a suggestion?"

He chuckled again. "I figured you might have one. We'll meet tonight. At our usual place. And talk more."

Daniels and Remalla approached and walked into the pawn shop. "I hope we do more than talk."

He moaned softly into the phone. "With you, honey? You better believe it."

"Okay, baby. I'll wait...for now. See you tonight." Her mind whirling, Rhonda hung up. She continued to watch the store front, wondering what she would do if Daniels and Remalla walked out with Jerry Lee. Would it be worth taking a shot from here, or while driving by? Thinking about taking all three of them out, she sighed with satisfaction but realized it would be a death sentence for her. Both the mobster and the entire police force would be after her. Still enjoying the thought, she settled back in her seat and waited. If Jerry Lee was in that building and the detectives found him, she needed to know.

· · • • • • • • · ·

Rem rang the bell at the counter. "Hello? Anybody here?" He rang the bell again. Looking around, he saw the typical items found in a pawn shop. The counter in front of him contained several pieces of jewelry and numerous watches for sale. Various musical instruments, mostly guitars, took up one corner and one entire wall and a second counter contained all types of electronics. Another corner displayed bicycles and skateboards and along the back was a locked-up case of firearms.

Daniels walked through the shop. "Quite the collection."

Rem noted the bars on the windows and a door behind the counter marked *Office*. Another door, marked *Private*, was beside the firearm case in the back. He wondered what was behind that door. Glancing upward, he saw a video camera in the upper corner of the shop. "Daniels." He pointed at the camera. "Think we're being watched?"

Daniels turned and eyed the camera. "Maybe."

Rem waved at the camera. "Hello? Anybody there?" He pulled out his badge and held it up. "Police. We'd like to talk to Arnold Bertrand."

"He's got to be here," said Daniels.

The door marked *Private* opened and a short but stocky, balding man in his fifties emerged from behind it. He wore baggy jeans and an oversized sweatshirt. "Can I help you?" He shut the door and walked behind the counter.

"Arnold Bertrand?" asked Rem, approaching the counter.

"That's me," said the man. He eyed Rem's badge. "You cops?"

Daniels held out his badge as well. "We are," he said. "Detectives Daniels and Remalla."

"What's this about?" asked Bertrand.

"We'd like to ask you about Jerry Lee Caruso," said Rem. "He used to work here."

Bertrand nodded. "He did. But not for a while. He in trouble?" He shook his head. "I told him to stay away from drugs. Said they'd wreck his brain."

"It's not about drugs," said Daniels. "Jerry is missing."

"Missing?" asked Bertrand. "Since when?"

"Since two days ago," said Rem. "He was working and witnessed something he shouldn't have and took off. We suspect he's hiding somewhere. Probably with someone he knows."

Bertrand acted unfazed by two detectives questioning him. "What did the kid witness?"

"A murder," said Daniels.

Bertrand's eyes widened. "You're kidding. Jerry saw a murder?"

"Which is why it's important that we find him," added Rem. "And fast."

"How come none of this is in the news?" asked Bertrand. "Wouldn't that be the fastest way to find him?"

"We're trying to avoid that," said Rem. "We want him safe and sound, without a lot of attention." He looked around the shop. "Someone, a man, called his mother yesterday, saying Jerry was safe." He looked back at Bertrand. "Jerry doesn't know many older men that he might trust enough to go to."

"Other than you, Mr. Bertrand," said Daniels. "And maybe a few staff members at the hotel where he worked."

Bertrand chuckled. "You think Jerry came here?"

"It crossed our minds," said Rem.

"Jerry would never come here," said Bertrand.

"Why not?" asked Daniels.

Bertrand shrugged. "His mom hates me, number one, and he didn't leave here on good terms. The little shit stole from me, and I kicked him out. I haven't seen him since."

Rem glanced at Daniels. Patricia hadn't said anything about Jerry getting caught stealing. "Does his mother know about that?" asked Rem.

"Hell if I know. I caught the kid with a pocketknife. I took it back, read him the riot act, and fired him. What he did after that is a mystery to me." Bertrand stepped back and crossed his arms.

Rem studied Bertrand, wondering if he was telling the truth.

"Mr. Bertrand," said Daniels. "Jerry Lee's in a lot of trouble. He did nothing wrong, but we need to find him. His life may depend on it."

"Then I hope you locate him," said Bertrand. "Although he has issues, I still like the kid. I wouldn't want anything bad to happen to him."

"Do you have any idea where else he may have gone?" asked Rem.

Bertrand shook his head. "No idea."

Frustrated at their lack of progress, Rem pulled out his card. "If you hear from him or come across him unexpectedly, please tell him to call us. The sooner, the better."

"And you're welcome to call us too," said Daniels. "Should you have any sudden revelations about where he might be."

Bertrand took the card and tucked it into his shirt pocket. "Good to know. Thanks."

"And just to be clear," added Rem, "anyone harboring Jerry Lee is in just as much danger."

Bertrand smirked. "Good thing I don't have to worry about that."

Daniels rested his hand on the counter. "In your line of work, I assume you're well versed in protection."

"Damn straight," said Bertrand. "No one touches my stuff. Especially employees."

"We're pretty good at protection, too," said Daniels.

Bertrand's smug look briefly dropped before it returned. "Cops nowadays? I trust 'em as much as I trust my customers. If Jerry Lee's smart, he'll stay hidden."

Rem hardened his tone. "He can trust us."

Bertrand stared back with as much intensity as Rem. "Isn't that what they all say?"

"You seem like a man with a chip on his shoulder," said Daniels.

"More like a boulder." Bertrand looked between them. "Anything else?"

Rem decided that they'd have to do a lot more digging into Arnold Bertrand. "Hold on to that card. And use it if you need it. Any time of day or night."

Bertrand patted his pocket. "I doubt I'll need it, but I'll keep it. We don't get much police protection around here." He smirked again. "Good luck in your search. I hope you find Jerry."

Daniels tapped on the counter. "There's one more thing. We're not the only ones looking for Jerry. If a woman comes by asking about him, call us. We need to know."

"I don't suppose you could offer any more detail than that?" asked Bertrand.

Rem hesitated, but determined it was best to tell Bertrand what to expect. "She's a killer, and Jerry witnessed her latest act. She's smart, dangerous, and an accomplished liar."

"And a master of disguise," added Daniels.

"And if we connected you to Jerry Lee, she'll do the same." Rem glanced at the front door. "So watch your backside."

Bertrand raised the side of his lip. "I'm used to dealing with dangerous people. I can handle myself."

Rem imagined he had a weapon behind the counter. "Mr. Bertrand. Don't assume you can outsmart this woman."

"If she's threatened, or believes you're hiding Jerry," said Daniels, "she won't hesitate to use her considerable skills against you. If she comes in here, just redirect her. Or, if possible, stall her and call us."

Bertrand slid his hands into his pockets. "If she comes in, I'll tell her the truth. I have no idea where Jerry is."

"As long as that's true, you should be okay," said Rem, "but if you're lying..."

Bertrand jangled the keys in his pocket. "I'm not lying."

Rem held his gaze, but Bertrand didn't waver.

"We appreciate your time." Daniels turned and headed for the door.

Rem offered Bertrand one last look before turning and following Daniels out of the door. He walked to his car, but instead of getting in it, he walked to the back and leaned against the trunk.

Daniels joined him. "Well, what do you think? Is Bertrand lying to us?"

Rem crossed one ankle over another. "Hard to say. He's a cool customer."

"Maybe a little too cool?" asked Daniels. "We just told him a killer may come into his shop looking for Jerry. He didn't act too concerned."

"Do you buy the whole stealing thing?"

"Everything we've heard about Jerry is that he's a stand-up kid."

"And Bertrand emphasized no one stole from him." Rem crossed his arms. "I think we need to do a little background check on Arnold Bertrand. See what pops up."

"I was thinking the same."

Pensive, Rem stared off.

Daniels glanced over. "You've got that glazed look. What's going on in that head of yours?"

Rem scratched his jaw. "Maybe while we're at it, we should check out Elsa Crow, too."

Daniels frowned. "How do you propose to do that without her finding out?"

Rem looked over. "Like you said, it doesn't have to be us doing the checking."

"You mean Lexie? You heard Crow. She told us to keep Lexie out of it."

"She told us to keep Lexie out of our investigations. This is different."

"Not really, but I see your point. You think Crow's trying to impede our black bird research?"

Rem scoffed. "After that meeting? I don't trust that woman as far as I can throw Lozano. She basically told us we were idiots."

"She did come on pretty strong. But she's a woman in a male-dominated position. She's trying to prove herself."

"Well, alienating yourself from the detectives who work for you isn't a great way to start." Rem pointed. "I'm telling you. The black birds are involved with Lozano's suspension, and with Crow's sudden promotion. We just need to prove it."

Daniels expelled a breath. "Any ideas where to start, other than asking Lexie to check out our new boss?"

Rem thought about it. "Actually, yes." He pushed off the car's trunk. "I know we planned to talk to Lozano tomorrow after our meet up at the storage unit..."

Daniels straightened. "...but maybe we should move that timetable up?"

Rem eyed his watch. "Feel like stopping by Lozano's on the way back to the station?"

"I think we can spare a few minutes." Daniels turned toward the car door. "What about our homework? Are we going to include this little visit in our report to Crow?"

Rem headed to the driver's door and opened it. "What visit?"

"We'll tell her we stopped for ice cream."

Rem half-smiled. "I'll even tell her what flavor and how many scoops we got."

Daniels walked to the other side of the car. "Plus, how much we paid, where we parked, and how many customers were in the store."

"She's gonna love it." Rem slid behind the wheel.

"I'm sure we'll get a lecture about our poor use of time, but I can live with that." Daniels got into the passenger seat and shut the door.

"Course, you know what that means." Rem shut his door.

Daniels eyed Rem with a knowing look. "You want to stop for ice cream on the way to Lozano's, don't you?"

"I wouldn't want to lie to Crow." He smiled, started the car, and backed out of the parking space.

Daniels rolled his eyes. "Perish the thought."

· · · · · • · · · · ·

Arnold Bertrand watched the detectives from the side of his dirty front window. They stood near their car for a few minutes, talking, before finally getting in their car and leaving. Satisfied they were gone, he locked the front door and flipped the *Open* sign to *Closed*. He left the store through the door marked *Private* and headed down the stairs. Jerry was sitting at the table, staring into space. The TV was on, and Bertrand could see the grainy black-and-white image of the interior of his pawn shop on the screen.

Bertrand stopped beside Jerry. "Did you watch?" he asked, gesturing toward the TV.

Jerry nodded. "Yes."

Bertrand pulled the detective's card from his pocket. He pulled his burner phone from his pocket, took a picture of the card, and handed the card to Jerry. "Here. Take this."

Jerry eyed the card and took it. "You want me to call them?"

"No, I don't. It's still too hot. But if things go south, and you've got no other option, use it."

Jerry widened his eyes. "Things go south?"

Arnold pulled out a chair and sat. "You heard them. There's a killer looking for you. I pride myself on certain abilities, but if I always knew what I was doing, I wouldn't own a pawn shop in this crappy neighborhood. I'll do my best for you, kid, but it may not be enough."

Jerry's face paled. "You think she might kill you to get to me?"

"Based on what those two said, and they made it pretty clear, yes. This woman would kill me to get to you."

Jerry wrapped his fingers around the card. "I don't want you to get hurt."

"Believe me. Neither do I. And I'll do whatever I can to prevent it, but it would be silly not to have a backup plan."

"A backup plan?"

Arnold scratched his jaw. As much as he considered himself a man who could take care of himself, the detectives had convinced him he wasn't invincible. "Yes. If something happens to me, you need to get the hell out of here."

Jerry nibbled his lip. "But...but...where will I go?"

Bertrand interlaced his fingers. "That's exactly what we need to figure out."

Jerry ran his trembling fingers through his hair. "I miss my mom."

"I know you do, kid, but believe me, if this woman can get to me, she can get to your mom too. You need to play it safe for now."

Jerry dropped his head into his palm. "Okay." He looked up. "But I have no other place to go."

Arnold chuckled. "Sure you do, kid. In my experience, there are always options, no matter how impossible it seems." His heart fell when Jerry dropped his head again. "And sometimes, that's when miracles happen."

Jerry raised his head again. "You believe in miracles, Mr. Bertrand?"

Realizing Jerry needed a little hope, Arnold smiled. "Sure I do, kid. You just got to have faith." He tipped his head. "Okay?"

Still somber, Jerry sat back. "Okay."

"Good," said Arnold. "Now let's get thinking."

· · · • • · • • · ·

Rhonda watched Daniels and Remalla leave the shop, stop and talk, and then drive off. The moment they were gone, she spotted a man inside the shop flip the *Open* sign on the door to *Closed*. Guessing that was Bertrand, she wondered why he felt the need to close his store after speaking to the detectives. Was Jerry Lee inside? Was Bertrand speaking to him now? Her heart thumping, she debated going to find out, but Monk's words echoed in her ears. *Wait,* he'd said. *There may be another option.*

Imagining all the ways they might use this situation to her and Monk's advantage, she smiled, started the car, and drove away.

Chapter Fourteen

CAPTAIN FRANK LOZANO SAT outside at his porch table, staring out at his small swimming pool. A book was beside him, but unable to concentrate, he'd closed it over an hour ago. His wife Sheila was at work, and he had the house to himself. Not much of a TV watcher, he'd made a list of projects to do around the house. If he was going to have all this free time, he might as well use it wisely.

But with his meeting with the FBI agents and his suspension fresh on his mind, plus worrying about his detectives and wondering who'd replaced him, he'd put the work on the back burner for now. Once he'd had a day or two to assimilate what was happening, he hoped he could focus on other things.

Glancing at his empty coffee mug, he debated making a fresh pot when his doorbell rang. Figuring it was a delivery, or the landscape people he'd called and barked at for neglecting his lawn, he stood and went to the door. Looking through the peephole, he cursed when he saw it was Daniels and Remalla. He opened the door. "What are you two doing here?"

"Good to see you, too, Cap," said Rem, holding an ice cream cone and a cup with two scoops of ice cream and a spoon. He offered the cup to Lozano. "I wasn't sure if you wanted chocolate or vanilla, so I got you a scoop of each."

Daniels held a cup with one scoop. "I told him just one scoop, Cap. I know you're watching your waistline."

Rem smirked. "The man just got suspended. That warrants two scoops."

Daniels eyed the three scoops of ice cream on the cone in Rem's hand. "What's your excuse, then?"

Rem slurped a drip running down the side of his cone. "It's been rough for me, too." He gestured at Daniels' scoop of vanilla with what appeared to be butterscotch sauce or caramel on top. "Don't get testy just because you denied yourself."

"I didn't deny myself. This is all I wanted." Daniels scooped out a bite and ate it. "At least my stomach won't hate me later, and I'll still want dinner."

Rem patted his belly. "My stomach is pretty happy right now, and since when has a snack ever stopped me from eating dinner?"

Daniels pointed his spoon at Rem's cone. "When that snack could feed an elephant."

Lozano took the cup of ice cream from Rem. "Thank you for reminding me that there are some things I don't miss."

Rem pursed his lips. "Cap. Don't hurt Daniels' feelings."

"I think he was referring to you, too, sport." Daniels stepped inside. "How are you, Cap? Hanging in there?"

Rem walked in too. "You miss us, you know you do."

Lozano stepped back as they entered his house and shut the door. "You two are not supposed to be here. Didn't the chief tell the squad not to contact me?"

Rem eyed Daniels. "Did he? I don't recall." He licked some ice cream.

"He sure did," said Daniels. He ate another bite of ice cream. "We're ignoring him."

Lozano grunted. "I'm surprised you didn't stop by yesterday." He waved his hand. "Come on in and tell me what trouble you're stirring up."

Daniels and Rem headed into the living area. "Head outside," said Lozano. "We can sit out there." He caught Rem licking ice cream off his finger. "So you won't drip all over my couch."

Daniels licked his spoon and sighed at Rem. "I can't take you anywhere."

Rem walked outside. "Call me the problem all you want, but Cap's the one getting into trouble around here."

Glad Sheila wasn't around to gripe about him eating sugar, Lozano sat at the porch table and scooped up some vanilla. "There's a first time for everything." He ate the bite and moaned. "That's good."

Daniels sat beside Rem. "Tell us what's going on, Cap," said Daniels. "What happened between you and those FBI agents?"

"Did you know they were investigating Durning?" asked Rem.

Lozano scooped up a bite of chocolate. "I had no idea. I doubt Durning's wife did either. She never mentioned it to me."

"How'd you get roped into it?" asked Daniels.

Lozano had been wondering the same. "I don't know, Daniels. Those two showing up surprised me as much as my suspension. It came out of left field."

"What did they ask you about?" Rem licked a scoop of ice cream.

Lozano lowered his cup. "Before we go any further here, you two know you could get suspended yourselves for being here."

"Being where, Cap?" Rem dragged his tongue over the edge of his cone. "Daniels and I are just enjoying a treat. God knows we deserve it."

Daniels scraped his spoon over the bottom of his cup. "Rem and I are aware of the risks."

Lozano grunted. "Just be careful."

"Always are, Cap," said Rem.

"Since when?" asked Lozano.

Rem shrugged. "We'll start today."

Lozano grunted and sat back.

"Tell us what happened, Cap," said Daniels.

Lozano stared out over his pool. "The agents asked me a lot of questions about Reggie. They wanted to know about his time as a prosecutor when I was a detective. I told them what I knew and could remember. Then they started asking about Emilio Hippolito."

Half of his ice cream gone, Rem lowered his cone. "Who is Emilio Hippolito?"

Lozano dug his spoon into another scoop. "Basically, a gangland boss. When I was a detective, he controlled a large section of the city and was involved in trafficking, extortion and multiple homicides. Everyone called him Hippo, and for good reason. The man easily topped the scales at three hundred pounds."

Rem whistled. "Sounds like a fun guy."

Lozano thought back. "My partner, Phelps, and I had been after Hippo for years, and were working with Reggie to bring Hippo down. Finally, we orchestrated a sting, and Hippo took a fall for ordering the murder of a rival gang leader. We arrested him and brought an airtight case to Reggie. Reggie was as eager as we were to get Hippo off the streets. Everything moved smoothly until two weeks before trial, when our key witness, who was a former associate of Hippo's, was murdered. After that, the case fell apart. Reggie dropped the charges and Hippo walked." Recalling the disappointment, Lozano slumped. "We never had the chance to get him again."

Daniels set his cup down. "You think Hippo got to the witness?"

Lozano pointed with his spoon. "Somebody talked. We had the witness under more security than a casino vault, but in the end, it didn't matter."

Down to his last scoop, Rem licked it and sat up. "Did the FBI ask about anything else?"

Lozano nodded. "They asked about the witness, and if I thought someone within the department had been involved in his murder."

Daniels lowered his cup. "Now it's getting interesting. They think someone on the inside gave up the witness?"

"That was the gist I was getting." Lozano ate a bite of chocolate. "If I'd known at the time they were looking at Durning, and possibly me, as suspects, I'd have asked for an attorney."

"They think you and Durning gave up the witness?" asked Rem.

"I wonder how long Durning's been in their sights?" asked Daniels. "And why you weren't questioned until now, Cap?"

"What's your opinion on Durning?" asked Rem. "You think he was on the take?"

Lozano shook his head. "No way Reggie would let Hippo walk."

"You sure about that?" asked Daniels. He ate the last remains of his ice cream and set the cup down.

"A sizeable chunk of money could make a man think twice." Rem bit into his cone and chewed. "Were you ever offered any money?"

Lozano nodded. "Course I was."

Daniels and Remalla stilled.

Lozano took another bite of his ice cream. "Haven't you guys been offered goodies from bad guys to look the other way?"

Rem pursed his lips. "Whitey Micklemore, who ran a tanning bed business, once offered me a year's free membership to let him skate on a breaking and entering charge. I declined."

"Maybe you should have taken him up on it," said Daniels. "You're looking a little pale."

Rem's face fell. "He offered you the same."

"No," said Daniels. "He offered me the free year, plus ten grand."

Rem's eyes widened. "What? How come he didn't offer me any money?"

"I guess he thought you were an easy mark."

Rem slumped.

"And you did need a little color in your cheeks," added Daniels. "Plus, I suppose he thought I'd split the money with you."

"Would you have?" asked Rem.

Daniels shrugged. "I never took the money, so I guess we'll never know."

Rem mumbled something unpleasant under his breath about partners and Daniels half-smiled.

"Hippo offered me fifty thousand to give up the witness," said Lozano. "Like you, Remalla, I declined."

Rem sat back in his chair. "That's way better than a tanning bed membership."

"And way more than ten grand," said Daniels. "Durning may have been more tempted than you realize."

"If the FBI has a money trail on Durning that could lead to Hippo, then that investigation could have ended Durning's career," said Rem. "And sent him to prison. No wonder he was stressed."

"The question is why did they suddenly zero in on you, Cap?" asked Daniels.

"I have no idea." Lozano poked at his ice cream again.

"I do," said Rem. "The black birds."

Surprised, Lozano straightened. "Why would they target me?"

"Because of your association with us," said Daniels. "We're investigating Durning's murder, and we're on Rhonda's trail. If we can link her or the murder to someone in their society, that's a risk they have to mitigate."

"And by getting rid of you," said Rem, "and putting in Elsa Crow, who's much less supportive of our black bird theory, they've put a big kink in our investigation."

"Elsa Crow?" Lozano had never heard the name. "She's my replacement?"

"She's from the Special Crimes unit," said Daniels. "And she doesn't like us very much."

Rem leaned up. "And her name's Crow." He took another bite of the remains of his cone.

Lozano didn't understand. "So?"

"Crow, Cap?" asked Rem. "As in black bird?"

Daniels rolled his eyes. "Rem, I think that's a coincidence."

"It's a big damn coincidence," replied Rem. "I think someone's telling us something."

"Either way," said Daniels. "Crow's not buying the black bird theory, or that Rhonda is our killer. She told us to work on finding Jerry Lee and to stop chasing secret societies and focus on the CIW staff and Durning's clients to solve his murder."

"I hate to tell you this," said Lozano, "but to a new captain, it would sound a little farfetched. If I didn't know you two so well, I might have scoffed at the theory, too."

"But you know us, and what we've been up against," said Rem. "And the fact that you've been suspended only proves the point that this society exists as far as I'm concerned. Now we just have to figure out how to clear your name and determine whether Elsa Crow is involved."

"How do you propose to do that?" asked Lozano. "If Crow is a member, everything you two do will go straight back to the society."

"Which is why we're going to have to be selective in what we tell her," said Daniels.

"That's tricky," said Lozano. "Crow finds out and it could be your jobs."

"My worry is they have bigger plans for us than just ruining our careers," said Daniels. "Whoever is behind this has been very careful with how they deal with us. First, they wanted us dead and then changed their minds. They recruited your cousin, Rem, and directed him to involve Erin, who has some connection to me. That suggests a methodical, drawn-out plan, and where it leads is anyone's guess, but I doubt it stops with Erin, Cain, and now Lozano."

Rem dropped the last bite of his cone into his mouth and chewed. "We nee to ca Reinar..."

"What?" asked Lozano.

"We need to call Reinart," said Daniels. "Remember Phoebe? From the Rowan Laroche case?"

"Course I do," said Lozano. "I marveled at her ability to deal with you two."

Rem licked his fingers. "She works for the FBI now, in Art Crimes. We're going to call her and hopefully discover what they have on you and Durning."

Lozano perked up. "You think she'd tell you?"

Rem wiped his fingers on his jeans. "Course she will. She can't deny my charm and good looks."

Daniels made a snort. "I think the Taco del Fuegos might impress her more."

Rem offered a look of disgust. "It's better than offering her one of your vile organic sprouted drinks."

Listening to his detectives, Lozano realized how much he missed being around the squad. "Whatever you do, keep it quiet. And tell Reinart to do the same. You don't want this to blowback on her either."

Daniels' phone rang. He pulled it out and eyed the display with a sigh. "I need to take this. Give me two minutes." He stood, answered the phone, and walked toward the pool.

Rem rested his elbows on the table. "You doing okay, Cap? This can't be easy on you."

His appetite waning, Lozano couldn't finish his ice cream. "It's been rough. After talking to the chief and realizing what I was dealing with, I have to admit, I've wondered if I'll be reinstated. Things like this leave a stain, Remalla."

Rem wiped up a drop of ice cream on the table with a napkin. "I get what you're saying, but hang in there. Give Daniels and me time to figure it out."

"Be prepared that you may fail. If these people want me out, they'll find a way."

Rem set the napkin aside. "You've told me more than once, when I was going through a lot, to hang in there." He interlaced his fingers. "And I did. Your words, and your loyalty, made all the difference to me. So now I'm telling you the same. Don't give up, no matter what they say they have, or what they threaten you with, you can't give in."

Lozano's heart thumped. It had always been him giving his detectives a pep talk, and now that it was the other way around, it felt wrong. "I've always believed that the truth will prevail, and in my experience, it usually does, but with something like this, I'm not so sure anymore."

"That's why you have to fight, Cap. These people revel in fear and misery. They want you to feel hopeless. They're used to winning, but somebody's got to resist and maybe cause them to lose a few rounds."

"I'm suspended. My ability to fight back is limited, and you two," he waved his finger between Rem and Daniels, "have gotten on their bad side. If they really want to mess with you, they will. You might win a few rounds, but that won't matter if you lose the war."

"Nobody's invincible, Cap."

Lozano pushed his cup with his half-melted ice cream away. "Emilio Hippolito was."

Quiet, Rem leaned back in his seat.

Daniels returned and sat. His jaw set, he slid his phone into his jacket pocket. "Sorry for the interruption."

"Everything okay?" asked Rem.

"That was the damn insurance company. I've been going back and forth with them about a bill from the hospital after my head injury. They were supposed to pay it, but now say it's my responsibility." He cursed and crossed his arms.

Lozano glared. "You were injured in the line of duty. They're supposed to pay for everything."

Daniels tossed out his hand. "Yeah, well, tell them that."

Rem sat up. "How much?"

Daniels expelled a long groan. "Let's just say Hippolito's bribe, plus a little extra, would come in handy right now."

Rem knitted his brow. "You're serious?"

Daniels eyed the awning over Lozano's porch. "I don't know. Between Marjorie's pregnancy, this bill, and now the black birds, I'm beginning to wonder if Bolivia is the better choice."

"I'll call the chief," said Lozano. "See if he can straighten any of this out."

"I doubt it will help." Daniels ran his hand over his head. "I've been to HR. I've submitted reports. I even talked to the head guy at the insurance company." He gripped the edge of the table. "Hell. If I'd known all of this would happen, I would have suggested Marjorie and I wait a little longer before trying again."

"Hang in there, partner," said Rem. "It will work out somehow."

Frustrated, Lozano waved his hand. "You put your life on the line for the job, and this is the thanks you get."

"You could say the same, Cap," said Daniels. "You've spent years working your ass off and building your reputation, and in one swoop, they can yank it all away from you." He cursed again. "It's infuriating."

"Hey," said Rem. "Listen to you two. We've all got too much at stake to let this crap take us down. Step back if you need a breather but come back swinging. We've got a lot riding on our ability to return from the brink. I've done it more than once, and so can you."

"Look at you, Mr. Positivity," said Daniels. "I've taught you well."

"Both of you have been there for me, and if I need to hold the line to get you over the hump, then I will." Rem put his hand in the middle of the table. "All for one and one for all."

Lozano raised his brow. "What is this? A pep rally?"

"It's *The Three Musketeers*, Cap." Rem shot a look at Daniels. "Surely you've heard of them?"

"Yes," Daniels grumbled. "I've heard of them. Are you suggesting we use their saying as some sort of rallying cry?"

"Sure. Why the hell not?" asked Rem. "It worked for them."

"They're characters in a book, Rem," said Daniels.

"And it was set in the sixteen hundreds in France," added Lozano.

"Does it look like I care?" asked Rem. "Now get your hands in here."

Lozano hesitated, but when Daniels caved and put his hand on top of Rem's, Lozano leaned up and put his hand over Daniels'.

Rem smiled. "Altogether now, and don't be a wimp about it. Ready?"

Daniels made a face. "Do we really—"

"Shh," said Rem. "On three. One...two...three..."

Lozano raised his voice, along with Daniels and Rem, and they all spoke at once. "All for one and one for all."

Rem grinned, and along with Lozano and Daniels, removed his hand, and sat back. "Now, doesn't that make you feel better? I betcha those blackbirds don't do that."

Lozano made a snort, and Daniels rolled his eyes.

Chapter Fifteen

Marjorie Daniels opened the fridge and pulled out the hamburger patties. Checking the time, she realized Erin was due to arrive soon and Gordon was running late. He'd called, telling her he was on his way. Eager to do something, she'd set the table, made some brownies, and put them in the oven. Seeing and smelling the patties, her stomach flipped, and she took a slow breath until it settled. Three months into her second pregnancy, she missed the ease of the first one. This time around, her nausea came and went at a whim, and her fatigue could knock her flat, no matter how much rest she got. Her doctor had told her to take it easy, and Gordon was watching her like a hawk. He didn't like her driving since the doctor had told her to limit her activities until this phase ended. She still drove to work, but Gordon preferred to take her to her appointments, and Marjorie's sister helped with J.P. whenever she could. Since tonight was a big deal, her sister had picked J.P. up at daycare and had taken him home with her. Gordon would pick him up after dinner.

Grabbing a bag of chips from the pantry, she heard the back door open and Gordon's voice. "I'm home."

She turned as he walked into the kitchen. "Hey, honey," she said.

"Hey, babe. Sorry I'm late." He frowned at the patties. "What are you doing?" He took the chips from her. "You're supposed to be resting."

"Honey, I can remove the patties from the refrigerator and the chips from the pantry."

He sniffed the air. "Did you make brownies?"

She put her hand on her hip. "It's a box mix. I added the ingredients and stirred."

"I could have done that." He tossed his keys on the counter, unclipped his badge, and sat it next to the keys. "And with your stomach, you may not even be able to eat them."

"We have guests coming, and Rem will certainly enjoy them."

He took his jacket off and removed his gun and holster. "Rem will survive without dessert."

"Maybe so, but as a host, I like to have a dessert. Plus, it may come in handy. Dessert can be a nice ice breaker. It may help Erin open up."

"If we were talking about Rem instead of Erin, I'd agree with you. But if Erin doesn't start talking before then, I'd say our chances are slim of getting her to reveal her secrets." He kissed her forehead, went to the front closet, and put his gun in the safe.. "I'll start the burgers."

"She agreed to this meal, so that's a good sign."

Daniels walked to the sink and flipped on the faucet to wash his hands. "I hope you're right. I made Rem promise to be on good behavior. He's dubious about her."

She walked up beside him. "I suspect that has more to do with protecting you. He can see what I see."

Daniels turned off the sink and dried his hands on a towel. "What's that?"

"That you like her. Whatever this connection is, you feel it too."

He turned toward her. "Babe, I just want to be sure Erin's safe. I realize we know very little about her, but she's willing to risk her safety to help us."

Marjorie rubbed his arm. "The only reason she's risking her safety is you."

Daniels sighed. "What are you saying? You think she likes me?"

"Not that way, but I sense she wants to know you better. I'm hoping after we actually meet face-to-face and talk, I can see if Rem has a reason to worry." She glanced toward the door. "Where is he, by the way? Did he stop to pick up Mikey?"

"He stayed to finish the report we have to email Crow at the end of each day. Then he's going to stop and grab some beer. Mikey didn't want to be late, so she'll come on her own. She should be here soon." He reached around her. "I should get the patties on the grill. Erin will be here soon, too."

Marjorie leaned to let him reach around her. "How was your day? Does Rem have anything interesting to report?"

Holding the tray, Daniels grabbed a spatula from a drawer and walked out to the back porch. Marjorie stood at the back door. "I wish. We've been spinning our wheels. There's still no sign of Jerry Lee, and we've spent most of our time on Durning's client list and the staff list at CIW. We called Phoebe Reinart, though, to ask if she could dig into the FBI investigation into Lozano. We left her a message. Hopefully, she'll call back soon."

"I always liked Phoebe. We should ask her back to dinner. Find out what she's up to."

"Sounds good to me."

"Did you go to the storage unit with Lexie?"

Daniels sat the tray with the patties and the spatula next to the grill and turned the grill on. "We did."

"I'm guessing since I didn't hear anything that it was a bust?"

"We found a lot of old furniture and clothes, boxes of albums, and costume jewelry, but no secret drive. Rem and I could only stay so long and had to leave Lexie behind. She was still going through stuff when we left. Rem talked to her later, but she'd found no secret USB."

"That sucks."

"I don't know if it does or not. At this point, I don't know if it's better to let sleeping dogs lie."

"You mean you don't want to find it?"

"I mean, I don't know what happens if we do. If there are names listed that we're not prepared for..." He shook his head and rubbed his neck, as he often did when he was stressed. "...I don't know."

"Hey," she jostled his arm. "What's bugging you?"

He glanced at her. "Now is not a good time to be upsetting the apple cart. We have a two-year-old and a baby on the way, an enormous bill to pay, and Lozano's not around to watch out for us." He shrugged and spoke softly. "I just feel like we're biting off way more than we can chew."

Understanding, Marjorie nodded. "I get it. There's a lot to think about. But what happens if you do nothing?"

He stared off.

"You still have the same things to worry about, plus we're not any safer. None of us are. Until you and Rem figure out what's going on, you'll never relax. You'll always be waiting for the next bomb to drop."

His gaze met hers. "As Rem always says, I hate it when you're logical." He wrapped his arms around her. "I just don't want anything to happen to you or J.P. We've all been through enough."

She hugged him back. "The fastest way to be sure of that is to stop this weird society, or at least figure out why they've made you and Rem targets." She rested her head on his shoulder. "And I don't like worrying about you either, but it comes with the territory."

He tightened his hold on her. "I love you. You know that?"

Marjorie looked up at him. "I love you, too." She gripped his hips. "We'll get through this, like we always do."

He kissed her forehead again. "If we can survive this dinner, that will help."

Smiling, she kissed his cheek. "Something tells me Erin is the least of your problems."

"Guess we're about to find out." His phone rang, and he pulled it from his pocket. "It's Rem."

"I'll go inside and wait for Mikey." She patted his butt and entered the house.

·········

Daniels answered. "You better not be backing out."

Rem responded. "I'm not. I just finished the report and emailed it."

"Did you include our lunch break?"

"I even mentioned your kale salad."

"And your chili dog with extra onions?"

"Of course. But that's not why I'm calling. Guess who just contacted me?"

Daniels pulled the cover off the patties. "Reinart?"

"Actually, yes. She called back and said she'd see what she could find out, but that's not who I'm referring to."

"Then who?"

"Patricia Caruso. She wanted to know if the reporter had made any progress in locating Jerry Lee."

Not understanding, Daniels frowned. "Reporter? What's she talking about?" He heard a car door slam over the phone and figured Rem was in his car and on his way out.

"Get this. Patricia said Lexie stopped by her house yesterday, asking all sorts of questions about Jerry Lee. She said Lexie told her we sent her to help find him. When I asked her to describe this woman, she described Lexie."

"We never asked Lexie to do that."

"I know."

"Did you call Lexie?"

"I sure as hell did. She didn't go to the Caruso house. Knows nothing about it."

Daniels opened the grill. "Then who—" He froze, still holding the grill handle. "No..."

"That's what I'm thinking. It's Rhonda."

"Son-of-a-" Daniels couldn't believe it. "She just walked in there? Where the hell was the patrol?"

"Out front, probably watching TikTok. I got in touch with him, and he had the balls to tell me he was looking for Jerry Lee, not some chick. Needless to say, he's no longer on patrol duty."

Daniels grabbed the spatula. "I don't believe this. What did Patricia tell her?"

"What we already know. She asked about Jerry's friends and male acquaintances. Patricia told her about the phone call she received."

"Rhonda's on the hunt."

"She sure is. The question, though, is what do we do about it? If she went to Patricia, her next stop is anyone Jerry might go to for help."

"We've already made those rounds."

"Which means she'll make them, too."

"You think we need to warn them?"

"I called Jerry's friends and told them if a female reporter comes around, asking questions, to call us. The only positive is Rhonda won't hurt them. She just wants information."

"Unless she thinks they've got Jerry."

"His friends are safe. They don't have Jerry. I doubt the staff at the hotel are in danger either. It's Bertrand that worries me. He's cocky enough to set her off. And we can't rule him out as far as harboring Jerry. He has the means to do it."

"You think we need a patrol to watch Bertrand's pawn shop?"

"Already requested an unmarked car. It's better Bertrand doesn't know and hopefully, if Rhonda shows, she won't notice."

"Don't count on it. Rhonda has better radar than Area Fifty-One."

"It's all we can do for now until we get another lead on where Jerry might be."

"Lexie must be thrilled Rhonda impersonated her."

Rem snorted. "She's mad as hell."

"I bet. What did you tell Patricia?"

Rem went quiet.

Daniels added a patty to the grill. "You told her, didn't you?"

"Not exactly."

Daniels tensed. "You didn't say anything?"

"What was I supposed to do? Tell her that the reporter was actually the assassin, and that Patricia may have endangered her son by helping this woman? She's upset enough as it is."

Daniels sighed. "I see your point."

"I just told her she shouldn't talk to anyone else about Jerry but us, and if Lexie returns, to call us first." He paused. "I don't think that's a concern, though. Rhonda got what she wanted. She wouldn't be stupid enough to return when she knows we'll be watching for her. I told the new patrol guy to look for Jerry and any woman who approaches the house. I don't care if she's a Jehovah's witness or Cher."

"You tell Crow?"

"I added a little P.S. at the end of the report."

"She's gonna love that."

"She'll probably just accuse Lexie of lying. And if Crow's going to hate us, what's one more thing to add to the pile of complaints?"

"I guess we'll just do what we always do."

"What's that?"

"Deal with it tomorrow. Where are you?"

"On the road. I'm about to get the beer. Mikey should be there any minute. Has Erin arrived?"

"Not yet. I'm starting the burgers."

"Don't eat without me."

"Then move your ass."

"It's shaking as we speak. See you."

"See you." Daniels hung up, and still trying to comprehend the repercussions of Rhonda's visit to Jerry Lee's mom, he added another patty to the grill.

· · • •· • •· · ·

Holding two wine bottles, Mikey rang the doorbell to the Daniels' home. Wondering again what to expect from this dinner, she smiled when Marjorie opened the door.

"Hey," said Marjorie. "Come on in." She pulled the door open.

"Thanks." Mikey entered and held out the bottles. "One fully loaded for me, and one with none of the good stuff." She raised the sparkling grape juice. "For you."

"I'll take it." Marjorie took the bottle. "Thank you." She entered the kitchen. "Let's open that other one, though. At least I can vicariously enjoy it through you."

"It's too bad you can't have any," said Mikey. "Tonight is the night you need it."

Marjorie held her stomach. "Honestly, the way my stomach's been, I doubt I could drink it."

Mikey looked her over. "You look great, though. How are you feeling?"

"Thank you. The nausea and fatigue come and go. Today's a good day, though. Let's hope it lasts." She opened a drawer and pulled out a wine opener.

Mikey looked around. "Am I the only one here?"

"Gordon's out back, starting the hamburgers. He said Rem's on his way."

Mikey nodded. "He just texted. He's getting the beer." Marjorie started to open the wine, but Mikey took it from her. "Here. Let me. Go sit. You're supposed to be resting."

Marjorie put her hand on the counter. "You, too, huh?"

Mikey set the bottle on the table. "Am I wrong?"

Marjorie opened her mouth but paused. "Actually, I am a little spent. This whole Erin thing has got my heart racing." She went to sit at the dining table.

"Me, too," said Mikey, opening the wine bottle. "I don't know what to think about any of this." She popped the cork. "I'm still surprised Erin agreed to come over." Mikey opened a cabinet and pulled out two wineglasses.

"Me, too." Marjorie leaned up. "You're the intuitive one. Are you getting any hits about her?"

Mikey grabbed the grape juice and twisted the cap off. "I've never met Erin, so no. I'll let you know after dinner, though, if any alarm bells go off."

"I'd appreciate that. I'm hoping to get some sign myself about this woman's connection to Gordon."

Mikey poured grape juice into one glass. "I'm not the only one who's intuitive. It wouldn't surprise me at all if you got some hits about who she might be."

Marjorie rubbed her forehead. "The only time I've seen her is when I caught her watching me and J.P. at the playground, and then outside the house, and I didn't get anything bad then. I just sensed she was curious."

Mikey set the juice bottle down and picked up the wine. "Then I'd trust that. First impressions are usually pretty accurate." She poured wine into the second glass.

"I hope so, for Gordon's sake. If she turns out to be dangerous, he'll be furious. At her and at himself."

Mikey handed the glass of sparkling juice to Marjorie and took the glass of wine for herself. "I think if he trusts her enough to invite her into his home, he's had a few intuitive hits himself." She sat next to Marjorie at the table. "Cheers." She raised her glass.

Marjorie clinked her glass against Mikey's. "Cheers." She sipped the drink. "Not bad, for juice."

Mikey sipped her wine. "It doesn't achieve the desired effect, but it will do in a pinch."

Marjorie set her glass down. "I'm hearing Rem's not too sure about Erin."

"Rem's BS meter is rarely turned off. He thinks the worst until proven otherwise." She swirled the liquid in her glass, recalling her talk with Rem about giving Erin a chance and not to grill her the moment she walked through the door. He'd told her he'd already promised Daniels that he would behave. She hoped Erin wouldn't give him a reason to break that promise.

"To be honest," said Marjorie, "I'm kind of glad he's on alert. It makes me feel better."

"Daniels is on alert, too. It's just not as obvious."

Marjorie sat back in her seat. "Maybe we should have a secret signal."

Curious, Mikey set her glass on the table. "What do you mean?"

"You know, just in case one of us gets a hit on something. If you see something I don't, or vice versa, or we need to handle a problem, then we need a signal that says we're on the same page, and we can help each other out."

Mikey thought about it. "You mean if I suspect Erin's up to something, or Rem's getting snarky, I brush my nose with my finger, and what, we make an excuse to go to the bathroom together?"

Marjorie rubbed her stomach. "I'll say my stomach's upset and excuse myself. Gordon will want to come with me, but I'll tell him to stay with our guest, and you can offer to join me."

"You think?"

"We may not need it and I'm probably overreacting, but just in case something smacks one of us between the eyes, we can discuss it sooner rather than later."

"What if it's something minor, like she's got bad breath or horrible social skills?"

Marjorie chuckled. "That stuff doesn't worry me. I just need to know if you think she might want to kill us or has a deep dark secret that may change our lives forever. Or if she's a shapeshifter."

Mikey smiled. "Any of the above are possible."

"That's what concerns me."

Mikey brushed her finger over her nose. "You got it."

Marjorie brushed her finger over her nose. "Thanks." She knitted her brow. "Didn't they make the same gesture in the movie *The Sting*?"

"Sure did," said Mikey. "It's one of my favorite movies."

"You can't go wrong with Paul Newman and Robert Redford."

Mikey sighed softly. "No, you can't." She raised her glass to drink more wine when the doorbell rang.

Marjorie stilled and Mikey gripped her glass. "Could that be Rem?" asked Marjorie.

"We'd have heard him before he ever rang the bell," said Mikey.

"Silly question." Marjorie took a deep breath and stood. "You ready?"

Mikey stood, too. "Are you?"

Marjorie smoothed her shirt and nodded. "I am." She headed toward the door. "Time to meet Erin."

Chapter Sixteen

HER HEART POUNDING, MARJORIE opened the door and came face to face with the woman they'd all been wondering about for months. Erin stood on the porch, clutching a small box with one hand and her small purse with the other. Marjorie could sense her nervousness, and half expected her to turn and run. Her blonde hair was longer than Marjorie remembered, and she had manicured nails with a pretty blue polish on them. She wore jeans, a collared white shirt and a leather jacket.

Marjorie told herself to relax and softened her stance. "Hi, Erin."

Erin let go of her purse and tugged on her jacket. "Hi," she said. "Marjorie, right?"

"Yes." Marjorie stepped back. "Come on in."

Erin hesitated but stepped inside.

"It's nice to meet you." Marjorie gestured toward Mikey. "This is Mikey Redstone." She shut the door.

Mikey stepped closer. "Hi. Nice to meet you, Erin." She held out her hand and Erin shook it.

"Nice to meet you, too." Erin looked around the house.

"If you're looking for Gordon, he's out back, making the hamburgers." Watching her, Marjorie had the oddest sensation that she'd met this woman before but couldn't place from where.

Erin tugged on her jacket again. "Okay."

Looking into Erin's eyes, Marjorie was convinced she somehow knew this woman. "Have we met before?"

Erin shook her head. "No." She fiddled with the box and handed it to Marjorie. "I wanted to bring something but didn't know what. I saw these in a store and thought you might like them."

Marjorie took the box. "You didn't need to bring anything but thank you."

"You can set your purse here if you want," said Mikey, gesturing at the entry table. "Why don't you come into the kitchen? Would you like some wine?"

Erin set her purse down, and her gaze darted around the house again. "Sure."

Marjorie wondered who else she was looking for and suspected it was Rem. "My husband's partner, Aaron Remalla, he'll be here soon." She waved toward the dining table. "Have a seat. Let's relax a little. I know this dinner is making us all a little anxious."

"A little." Erin walked toward the kitchen, and Mikey grabbed another glass and poured some wine for Erin.

"Here you go," said Mikey, handing Erin the glass.

"Thank you," said Erin.

Feeling a little calmer, Marjorie opened the box. Inside was a set of socks for infants, all in different colors. "Erin, this is so sweet." She took out the socks and admired them.

Erin held her wineglass. "Gordon told me you were expecting. I figured every baby needs socks."

Marjorie felt how soft they were. "You're right. We can use them. Thank you."

Mikey smiled. "You picked well, especially since nobody knows the gender yet."

Erin half-smiled. "I thought of that, plus I hate it when my feet are cold."

"Me, too," said Mikey.

That same odd sensation fluttered through Marjorie. Where had she met this woman? She glanced at Mikey and caught her studying Erin, too.

"Gordon's going to love these. He always wanted to keep J.P.'s feet covered. He didn't like thinking they were cold, either." She set the socks back in the box. "Thank you again."

"You're welcome." Erin took a small sip of her wine. "Can I help with anything?"

Marjorie set the box on the counter to show Gordon when he came in. "No. There's not much to do. I've got brownies in the oven, and Rem's bringing the beer. The table is set, and the chips are out. All we need is the condiments, but we can get those when the burgers are ready."

Erin leaned a hip on the counter. "Okay." She took another sip of wine and raised the glass. "This is good."

Mikey picked up her wine from the table. "It's one of my favorites." She sipped from her glass. "I'm glad you're having some because Marjorie's on the wagon."

"I am." Marjorie walked over and picked up her juice. Her stomach turned, and she clutched it. "But I'm not missing it right now."

"You okay?" asked Mikey. "You look a little pale."

Marjorie nodded as her stomach settled. "It comes and goes."

"Morning sickness?" asked Erin.

"Yes," said Marjorie. "Only it's more like all day and night sickness."

"Maybe you should sit," said Erin. "And rest."

Something about the way she said it made Marjorie's heart thump. Mikey glanced at her with a look of surprise. Her mind whirling, Marjorie tried to grasp what had her on edge when Gordon came in from outside.

He held the empty tray and stopped when he saw Erin. "You're here."

Erin turned toward him. "I'm here."

He set the tray in the sink, picked up the kitchen cloth, and wiped his hands. He eyed Marjorie and Mikey. "I see you met my wife and Mikey."

Erin nodded. "I did."

"Good." He walked over. "The burgers will be done soon." He glanced at Marjorie. "You okay? You look pale."

Marjorie fanned herself with her hand. "I'm, okay, hon. Just had a brief spell."

"You should sit." He pulled out a chair for her.

"I'm fine," she said. "I'm just glad Erin is here. It's nice to meet her."

"It's nice to meet you too, but he's right," said Erin. "You should take it easy."

"She brought the new baby some socks." Marjorie pointed toward the box. "They're perfect."

Daniels turned and picked up the box. "You didn't have to do that, Erin." He opened the box.

Erin's nervous expression returned, and she rubbed her neck. "It's nothing, but I wanted to bring something, you know, for the baby."

Marjorie almost gasped at the familiar gesture. The reason she thought she knew Erin became clear. Glancing between her husband and their guest, she compared their eyes and posture.

Daniels smiled when he picked up the tiny set of socks. "These are great. I hated it when J.P.'s feet were cold. These will come in handy. Thank you."

Marjorie's heart pounded again when she compared her husband's smile to Erin's and realized how similar they were. She caught Mikey staring and realized Mikey was making the same comparisons.

"You're welcome." Erin shifted on her feet and sipped some more wine.

"You sure you're okay, babe?" asked Gordon. He put the socks back and set the box on the counter. "Is it the smell of the burgers?"

Marjorie caught Mikey sliding her finger over the side of her nose. "I...uh...no." Marjorie debated what to say, but her shock made it hard to think. "I mean...yes." She held her stomach. "It might be..." She shot a look at Mikey. "I may just run to the restroom."

Daniels' worried look returned. "You need some help?"

"No," said Marjorie, abruptly, and immediately softened her tone. "I mean, don't be silly, Gordon. I'm fine. You stay with Erin."

Mikey set her glass down. "I'll go with her. Make sure she's okay."

Gordon frowned. "You're sure?" he asked Mikey.

"It's fine, Gordon." Marjorie walked toward the hall. "Stop worrying." She shot another look at Mikey, who walked over to her. "Why don't you take Erin outside? Have her help you with the burgers?"

Gordon's stare told her he was wondering what was up. "You sure you're all right?"

"She's great," said Mikey. "We're great." She waved her hand. "You two go grill. We'll join you in a second."

"But isn't it the smell that's bothering you?" asked Erin.

"I...um...well, it comes and goes. I just need to step out for a second." Marjorie tried not to ramble. "I'll use the bathroom, and Mikey can stand outside just to be sure I don't faint or something."

"Do you feel faint?" asked Gordon.

Marjorie cursed at herself. She was not handling this situation well. "No. It was just an expression." She spoke to Erin. "Erin, why don't you grab the cheese slices from the fridge, and the buns from the counter? Take them out to the grill. You and Gordon can catch up."

"Catch up?" asked Gordon.

"You know," said Mikey. "Chat." She took Marjorie's arm. "I'll make sure Marjorie's okay. C'mon, Marjorie." She tugged Marjorie's elbow.

Marjorie ignored Gordon's narrowed eyes. "Show Erin the backyard, honey."

"She's seen the backyard," he said.

Marjorie headed toward the restroom behind the stairs. "It's nice out. Enjoy the weather. Be right back."

Hearing Gordon grunt, she headed down the short hall with Mikey. She heard Gordon tell Erin where to find the cheese in the fridge and heard the back door open and close. Mikey stood beside her, listening too.

As soon as it went quiet, she went into the bathroom with Mikey and shut the door.

Mikey faced her with wide eyes. "Tell me you saw what I saw," said Mikey.

Marjorie shook her head in shock. "I can't believe it." She again compared her husband to Erin. "Her eyes...her smile..."

"Her mannerisms...and body language," said Mikey.

"They're so similar." Marjorie rubbed her head. "This big secret of hers..."

"I think it's obvious," said Mikey.

Marjorie took a deep breath. "She's his sister, isn't she?"

"Well, she can't possibly be his daughter, and I don't think cousin warrants this level of secrecy, so yes. I think the obvious choice is sister."

"Oh my God." Marjorie gripped her head. "How is this possible?"

"I think the bigger question is, how did Daniels not notice?" Mikey paced in the small bathroom. "I mean, it took us just a few minutes."

Marjorie tried to gather her thoughts. "It's not the same for him. He doesn't see himself the way we see him, and the absolute last thought he would ever have is that his father would do something like this."

"You think it's possible his parents had another child he knows nothing about?"

Marjorie shook her head. "No. And remember, the first time he saw Erin is when he caught Raymond talking to her at that hotel in LA."

"Hell." Mikey huffed and put her hands on her hips. "Raymond had a secret family? That's hard to imagine."

Still in disbelief, Marjorie put her hand on the wall to steady herself. "Is there any way we're wrong about this? Could their similarities be some crazy coincidence?"

Mikey paused. "Considering everything we know? Her talk with Raymond? Her weird behavior around Daniels? The way she watched you and J.P.? How much she and Daniels are alike?" Mikey leaned back against the wall. "I can't think of any other explanation. And my gut tells me we're not wrong."

Marjorie hung her head. "My gut too." Worried about how her husband was going to handle this when he found out, she looked up. "What do we do?"

Mikey eyed the ceiling. "Obviously, she's terrified to tell him. It's taken her months to work up the courage to even walk into this house. I'm afraid if we push this, she'll bolt."

"So let her take the lead and tell him when she's ready?"

"Ideally, yes."

"Mikey, I can't keep this to myself. If she doesn't tell him today, I have to say something. He's my husband. He deserves to know."

Mikey pushed off the wall. "If she can't reveal her secret, you can tell him later. But at least let's give her the chance to spill it. Maybe that's why she's here today."

Marjorie groaned. "How are we supposed to sit through dinner and not say something?"

"She didn't have to come over. It's clear she wants to get to know Daniels. I think she wants to tell him, or she could have steered clear and never involved herself. I sense she's eager to say something, so let's give her a chance. Maybe this dinner will trigger Daniels, too. I don't think it's going to take much for him to realize that she's related. The more time he spends with her, the more likely he'll figure it out."

Marjorie tried to put herself in Erin's shoes and could imagine how nervous she would be. The fear of rejection would be immense. "That makes sense. Let's give her the evening to settle in and get comfortable. Maybe that will put her at ease enough for her to open up."

"And once she sees we're pretty normal, she won't be so scared."

Talking it through, Marjorie felt better. "Okay. I'm willing to let her take the lead. Let's see what happens and go from there." She eyed her reflection in the mirror, smoothed her hair, and straightened. "You ready to go back out there?"

Mikey nodded. "I—"

A booming male voice traveled from outside the door. "Hey. Where is everybody?"

Realizing Rem had arrived, Marjorie sucked in a breath. "Oh, hell."

Mikey's eyes widened. "If he sees Erin..."

"He'll know before we did. We've got to tell him." She flung the door open. "Rem?" Marjorie caught Rem holding a six-pack and heading into the kitchen. "Rem. Wait."

He swiveled toward them. "There you are. I knocked, but nobody answered. I used my key." He smiled at Mikey. "Hi, honey." He gave her a quick kiss. "What are you two doing in the bathroom?"

"Rem. Honey," said Mikey. "We need to talk to you."

He turned back and went into the kitchen. "I got the beer, and it's cold if you want one. Where's Daniels?"

Marjorie ran into the kitchen. "He's out back. With Erin."

"She's here?" he asked. He grabbed a beer and opened it. "Good. I'm glad she showed."

"We need to talk to you," said Marjorie. "It's important."

He glanced at her and Mikey. "What's wrong? You two look like you saw a ghost."

"Honey," said Mikey. "It's about—"

The back door opened, and Daniels and Erin walked in.

· · · • • · • • · ·

Erin saw him and stopped. Daniels entered behind her and, seeing Rem, he glanced at Erin, who stood with uncertainty in the kitchen. "You made it," he said to Rem. "Just in time for the hamburgers."

"I'm never late for food." Studying Erin, Rem unscrewed his beer top and tossed the cap onto the counter.

Daniels gestured at Rem. "Erin, this is my partner, Aaron Remalla."

"It's nice to meet you," said Rem, "instead of chase you."

She shifted on her feet. "Nice to meet you, too."

"Rem, honey," said Mikey, pulling his arm. "Can you come outside?"

Erin moved farther into the kitchen, and studying her wine, leaned against a counter.

Not taking his eyes off Erin, Rem answered. "Come outside? What for?"

"I...um...I think one of my tires is low." Mikey pulled harder on his arm. "I need you to look at it."

Marjorie stood in front of him, breaking his gaze. "Go check on the tire. Better to do it now, before it gets dark."

Rem looked around Marjorie and watched as Erin continued to study her wine glass.

"Marjorie made brownies, buddy," said Daniels. He grabbed a beer from the six-pack on the counter. "Thanks for the beer."

Something about Erin tugged at Rem. "That's great."

Daniels frowned at him. "You in there?" He waved his hand.

Mikey pulled on him again. "Let's go check that tire. Marjorie's right. You wait and you'll forget."

The oven timer dinged.

"That's the brownies," said Marjorie, loudly. She yanked open a drawer, pulled out some potholders and waved them at Rem. "Would you like to do the honors?"

Erin glanced over at him and, seeing his scrutiny, she tensed, looked away, and ran her hand over her shoulder.

"Everything okay, partner?" asked Daniels. He glanced at Erin, who wouldn't make eye contact.

Marjorie waved the potholders in front of his face. "The brownies, Rem?"

"Yes," said Mikey. "Get the brownies and then we'll go to the car. But hurry. Those hamburgers will be ready soon."

Daniels shot a look at Marjorie and Mikey. "And what's up with you two? Why are you acting so strange?"

Marjorie lowered the potholders. "Nothing. I just thought Rem would like to get the brownies."

"And the last thing I need is a flat tire," added Mikey.

Rem took a sip of his beer. "I'll tell you why they're acting strange."

"Why?" asked Daniels.

Rem raised his beer at Erin. "It's her."

Erin looked over at him and knitted her brow. "Me?"

Seeing the grip on her wineglass and getting a good look at her, Rem debated what to say, but went with his gut, as he usually did. "Have you told him yet?"

Erin's face fell, Mikey clutched his arm, and Marjorie closed her eyes.

"Told me what?" asked Daniels.

Staying cool, he spoke to his partner. "Your detective skills need work, partner. You can't see that Erin's your sister?"

Erin paled.

Marjorie groaned and dropped her head.

"Rem, you're supposed to behave," whispered Mikey.

"What?" asked Rem. "I said it nicely."

Daniels stared in shock. "What the hell are you talking about? Erin is not my—" He looked over and Erin studied the floor. "—sister. Right, Erin?" He scoffed. "I mean that's crazy." He glared at Rem. "What is the matter with you? Why would you say that?"

"Because it's obvious, and nothing else makes sense." Rem waved his hand toward Erin. "How can you not see what I, and obviously Mikey and Marjorie, see? Why do you think they're trying to distract me? They see it too."

Daniels looked between his wife and Mikey.

"Honey," said Marjorie, walking over to him. "Don't freak out. Maybe we should all calm down a bit. This is a lot to take in."

"Everything about her screams Daniels," said Rem. "If I'd had another minute at that restaurant in LA, or at the coffee shop, or when we found her at her work, I would have caught it then." He spoke to Erin, who looked like she wanted to curl up into a ball. "I'm not wrong, am I, Erin?"

Her face paling more, she finally looked at Daniels but didn't say anything.

His eyes wide, Daniels walked over to her. He set his beer on the counter. "Erin," he said. "Is it true?"

Erin didn't say a word, but she set her glass down and hugged herself. Nobody else said a word, either.

"Erin...," said Daniels, waiting.

Erin clutched her elbows and met Daniels' gaze. She took a deep breath and answered. "Your father and my mother had an affair."

Daniels dropped his jaw.

Chapter Seventeen

DANIELS DIDN'T KNOW WHAT to say. Utter shock prevented his brain from working.

"They were together for two years," said Erin. "And when she got pregnant with me, Raymond dumped her. Told her I wasn't his and left the relationship." She glanced at the others, who were just as mute as Daniels. "Mom raised me on her own, sometimes working two to three jobs to keep food on the table, until I got sick when I was five. When I ended up in the hospital, she lost two jobs because she had to take care of me and almost lost the third. That's when she finally confronted Raymond. Told him to start contributing to my care or her next call would be to his wife. Mom told him she'd happily consent to whatever paternity testing would be required. He started paying after that." She paused and her face regaining some color, she straightened her shoulders. "That allowed mom to stick with one job, be home with me more often and pay off some debt. When I hit eighteen, though, he stopped paying. But that was fine because we'd both saved enough for me to go to community college. I got my degree in computer programming, and Mom and I lived our lives. I graduated, got a job, and we stayed in LA, but I couldn't help but be curious. I wanted to know where I came from. So I took a weekend and went to your hometown."

Daniels blinked. "You what? You visited Dad?"

Erin shook her head. "I didn't intend to. I asked around and found him in one of his hardware stores but was too scared to confront him. I went to your family's house and watched. I knew from my mom that he had two daughters and a son, and I'd heard that one of your sisters had died. I never saw you. I think you'd left home by then, but I saw your sister."

"Shelly?" asked Daniels. "Did you talk to her?"

Erin set her jaw. "I didn't plan on it, but before I left town, I gathered my courage and went back to the hardware store. Raymond saw me. He wasn't thrilled and told me to come to his office, where he said I shouldn't be there and that he wouldn't be blackmailed for any more money by me or my mother."

Marjorie sucked in a breath. "He didn't."

Erin's eyes glistened with unshed tears. "I was furious. And when I left, I bumped into Shelly in the parking lot. I was so angry I told her who I was, and she laughed at me, and called me a liar. Told me to get out of town or she'd call the cops."

"That sounds about right for Shelly," said Rem.

Daniels' brain was in overdrive. He couldn't comprehend that his father had lied to everyone about an affair and a secret child, and that Shelly had known and said nothing.

"I left and never intended to see Raymond again. Then Mom got sick." Erin's voice tightened, and she cleared it. "Cancer." She paused and cleared her throat again. "She didn't survive." Erin swiped at her eye but held it together. "After she died, I got out of town and came here. Found an apartment, got a job, but my anger was building. Before Mom died, she told me I'd have to deal with Raymond eventually and made me promise to come to terms with him in whatever way worked for me. So I did. I called him and told him I wanted to see him."

"Is that why you two were in the hotel in LA?" asked Rem.

She nodded. "Yes. He wanted to meet in the hotel where he and Mom would get together. Can you believe that?" She scoffed. "I wanted to know why he'd treated me and Mom the way he had. Why he'd denied my existence and why he'd been so cruel to us." Her face tightened, and she sneered. "And all he could do was continue to deny I was his child, when look at me," she waved at herself, "I look like his son." She cursed. "Then he went on about how I wasn't going to get one red cent out of him, and if I told anyone, he'd deny everything." She narrowed her eyes. "He was a complete and total asshole."

"I recall you saying so on the way out," said Rem.

A tear escaped, and she angrily wiped it away. "I left and went home, and not long after that, I met Cain. He asked a lot of questions about my family, and I opened up to him about my father and lost siblings. And then you showed up where I worked and freaked me out. That's why I ran."

Daniels couldn't find the words. "Erin...why didn't you tell me sooner?"

Her jaw clenched. "So you could deny me, too?"

Still in denial, Daniels took a step back and tried to think, but his mind struggled to work. The only thing that came to mind was the hamburgers. He ran a hand through his hair and expelled a breath. "I need a second." He turned and walked outside. His stomach twisting and his hands shaking, he opened the grill. Seeing the burgers were almost ready, he lowered the heat, grabbed the cheese slices and added them, then opened the buns and set them on the top rack of the grill. Waiting for the cheese to melt, he spied a brick on a stair that led to the grass. He'd brought it out from the garage to put under a potted plant but hadn't used it.

Seeing it, an unexpected rage rippled through him, and he picked up the brick, and bellowing, he stomped down the porch steps and heaved the brick into the air. It hit the back fence and took a chunk of wood out of it. Furious, he made another bellow and added a variety of curse words to it while stomping through his yard.

"Feel better?"

Breathing fast, Daniels swiveled to see Rem standing on his porch. He hadn't heard him come out. "Where's Erin? She still here?"

Rem nodded. "Marjorie and Mikey are talking to her." His hands in his pockets, he stepped down into the yard and joined Daniels in the grass. "You okay?"

"Am I okay?" he yelled. "No, I'm not okay." He shot out a hand and resumed his pacing. "How am I supposed to deal with this? My father had a child with another woman? That he denies to this day? That my mom and I never knew about?"

"You assume your mother doesn't know."

Daniels whirled on him. "You think she does?"

Rem shrugged. "I'm just saying. Women aren't stupid. These sorts of things are hard to keep hidden."

Daniels cursed again. "I don't believe this. My dad is the most strait-laced, upstanding, by-the-book, puritanical man I know."

"Those are the ones most likely to cheat. Look at Reginald Durning."

Daniels glared. "How could I not have known?"

"Because he didn't tell you. And how could you have?"

"He lied and cheated on my mother for two years," he yelled.

"Is that any worse than six months, or a one-night-stand?" He paused. "It could have been worse. He could have continued to see her."

Daniels gripped his neck and stared up. "I don't understand any of this."

Rem took a step closer. "What's so hard to understand? Your father strayed outside of the marriage. It happens. And he got another woman pregnant, probably not long after you were born. And instead of being a stand-up guy about it, he panicked, probably because he was terrified of losing his family, his friends finding out, and losing his reputation, so he denied the whole thing. He didn't know what else to do."

"Of course, he panicked, but he's had years, Rem. I'm all grown up now. So is Erin. Why not take responsibility? He could have told me at any time during our trip to Elmwood. Why didn't he?"

"Because you're his son, and he doesn't want to lose your respect, and he knows you'd tell your mom." He sighed. "He's still just as scared as when he first heard about Erin." He grunted. "Can you imagine carrying this for as long as he has? And the stress of it all? It's a shock he hasn't had a heart attack."

Daniels pointed. "Don't take his side."

Rem raised his hands. "I'm not taking his side. I'm on your side. And I can imagine this is hard. But it's also not the end of the world."

Daniels couldn't believe what he was hearing. "It's pretty damn close." He paced again. "All this time..." he mumbled to himself.

Rem let him pace. "I know you're still absorbing all of this, but keep in mind you've got a sister in there who wants to get to know you."

Daniels stopped pacing. "You sure about that? This family has given her nothing but trouble."

"She moved to San Diego after her mother died. Why would she do that when she had a million other places she could go? She knew you were here, Daniels."

"Then why didn't she tell me sooner?"

"After the way your father and Shelly treated her? I'm sure she expected a repeat performance from you."

Daniels studied the ground, but didn't respond.

"You lost one sister you were close to, and you barely speak to your other one." He gestured toward the house. "Now you've got a new one that walks in off the street who obviously is desperate for some connection to a family. Now I'm not saying I trust her yet. We don't know much about her, but she's worth getting to know. And we still need her help to get close to Cain."

Daniels' anger bubbled up again. "You still want her involved in all of this mess?"

"She is already involved in all of this mess. And she offered. Remember?"

"She offered because she wanted to get close to me." Daniels pointed at himself. "I didn't know why at the time, but I do now, and there's no way she's going to keep doing this."

Rem hesitated. "I understand your need to protect her, now that you know you're her brother, but that doesn't change the fact that—"

"It changes everything, Rem. What if she was *your* sister?"

Rem hesitated and crossed his arms. "I'd feel the same as you, but I'd give her the choice. Not tell her what to do."

"Bullshit."

"And if the situation were reversed, you'd tell me the same thing I'm telling you."

Frustrated, Daniels turned away.

"Erin's a big girl, Daniels. You heard what she said. Cain targeted her after that meeting with your dad in LA. What does that tell you?"

Daniels thought back. They'd assumed Cain had approached Erin because he'd known about her connection to Daniels, but now how much he'd known was obvious. He turned back toward Rem. "How could he have known she was my sister?"

"Because the black birds told him."

"But how did they know?"

"Rhonda might have mentioned Erin if we talked to Raymond about her during our Elmwood trip, but I suspect the real reason is we were being watched. Someone saw the interaction between Erin and your dad and then you and Erin, and reported back to Mr. Big Bird himself. If her name was on the reservation for that restaurant, it wouldn't be hard to do a little digging. It's the only thing that makes sense." Rem paused. "It could be what stopped them from killing us, when they decided they could have a little fun with us instead."

Daniels shook his head in disbelief. "Who would want to do this?"

"I don't know, but whether you like it or not, they involved her and Cain, and walking away is no longer an option."

Daniels cursed again.

"Just be careful, partner. She may be your sister, but for all we know, Cain recruited her. And she could easily use her connection to you to twist us into pretzels. So until we can be sure, be cautious of what you tell her."

Daniels dropped his hands. "Are you suggesting she could be a double agent?"

"I'm saying don't let your emotions mess with your head."

Daniels walked toward Rem. "I just found out I have a long-lost sister, and your first thought is she could be using me?"

"You said it yourself. This family has given her nothing but trouble. What better way for her to get payback than to screw with her brother?"

"That's not what she's doing."

"You sure about that?"

Daniels shut his mouth, not trusting his next words. "I understand your concern, but you're wrong."

"I'm just saying to be careful. Your heart's in a delicate place right now. Just watch who you trust it with. Okay?"

Daniels set his jaw, but not wanting to argue with Rem, he returned to the porch. "I'm going to get the hamburgers."

· · • · • · • · ·

After Daniels brought the hamburgers inside, Rem stayed in the backyard, thinking. Daniels wasn't the only one reeling from Erin's revelation. Now that they knew her secret, it changed things. Rem would have to be on alert. His partner, despite his well-honed cop instincts, would instinctively want to protect Erin, and Rem understood why. Even with Cain's misguided decisions and anger at Rem, Cain was still family, and Rem felt protective of him. As Daniels' sister, Erin now fell into that category, but until she proved she could be trusted, Rem would have to monitor her involvement as best he could, with or without Daniels' help.

Telling himself to take it slow and give Erin, and Daniels, time to adjust, Rem went back inside. Daniels was at the sink, washing his hands, and Marjorie and Mikey were prepping their burgers. He didn't see Erin.

"Don't tell me she left." Rem went to the sink to wash his hands after Daniels.

Marjorie added lettuce, tomato, and ketchup to her burger. "She's in the bathroom. Mikey and I had to convince her to stay. She was sure Gordon was going to throw her out."

Daniels stepped aside for Rem to use the sink. "That's silly. I would never throw her out."

Marjorie added chips to her plate. "Based on her experiences, I understand her concerns. It's no wonder she's a wreck."

Mikey added mustard and pickles to her burger. "She'll be okay. She just needs time to collect herself. And a nice normal dinner will help."

Rem rinsed the soap from his hands and shut off the faucet. "I think nice and normal have left the building."

"It won't be gone long," said Mikey, "especially if you're the charming and kind man I know and love so well." She smiled at him and ate a chip.

Daniels grabbed a plate and put a burger on it. "I'm glad someone thinks he's kind and charming."

Rem dried his hands on a towel. "Jealous, partner?"

Daniels pulled Marjorie close. "Nope, because I've got someone who thinks I'm kind and charming, too." He kissed her.

Marjorie smiled at him and whispered. "Remember that when Erin comes back to the table."

He nodded. "I'm okay. The shock is dwindling. Besides, I've got questions."

"So do I," said Rem, reaching for a plate.

Marjorie frowned at both of them. "Don't drill her. Let her at least get a hamburger first."

Rem heard the bathroom door open, and they all went quiet. Daniels prepped his burger, and Marjorie and Mikey sat at the table when Erin came around the corner. She stopped when she saw Daniels and Rem, and didn't move.

Daniels grabbed a plate and handed it to her. "Food's getting cold. Dig in."

She hesitated and eyed the plate.

"Daniels makes a mean burger," said Rem. "Plus, we've got all the fixins. You can leave if you want, but nobody here wants you to."

Erin studied the plate, and after a pause, took it. "Thanks."

She walked to the counter as Daniels added chips to his plate and went to sit next to Marjorie. Rem doctored his burger with almost everything on the counter, grabbed some chips and his beer, and went to sit next to Mikey.

After adding some mustard to her bun and a few chips to her plate, Erin found her wine glass and joined them at the table. They sat quietly and ate before Daniels finally broke the silence. "Listen, Erin. I know this is difficult for all of us, and we all have some adjusting to do, but I want you to understand that, as my sister, you're now part of the family, and that includes everyone at this table." He ate a chip. "You okay with that?"

Erin stopped in mid chew and looked around. "Are all of you?"

"Of course," said Marjorie.

"I am," added Mikey.

They all looked at Rem, and he caught Mikey's look that said to behave himself. He lowered the chip in his hand. "I'm fine with it, as long as you know that just because we're family doesn't mean we put up with bullshit. If something's off, we say it. We rely on each other a hundred percent, we're fiercely loyal, and trust each other implicitly. We'll expect the same from you, but you can also expect it from us. How's that sound to you?"

Erin studied the burger in her hand. "I've never had a big family before. It was just me and Mom."

"Well, you've got one now," said Daniels. "As long as you agree to the terms which Rem eloquently stated, which is unusual for him."

Rem munched on a chip. "It also comes with a lot of badgering from your brother, so get ready. And I hope you like green juice."

Erin eyed Daniels. "Never been a fan."

"That's fine," said Marjorie, patting Daniels' hand. "Neither am I, and I still manage to live with him."

"I haven't given up on you yet," said Daniels, squeezing Marjorie's fingers. "Rem, though, is a lost cause."

"Which I'm fine with." Rem bit into his burger.

Mikey picked up a chip. "So, Erin. Are you in?"

Seeing the hopeful gleam in Daniels' eyes, Rem chewed and waited to hear Erin's answer.

She studied each of them and, after a pause, nodded. "I'm in."

"Good." Daniels sat back and wiped his fingers. "I'm glad."

Rem shot a look at his partner and prayed they hadn't just made a deal with the devil.

Chapter Eighteen

FEELING BETTER AFTER EATING his burger, Daniels finished his beer. Sitting at the table, he watched the group in front of him, glad they were all together for Erin's revelation. Even though the news had slowly sunk in, he still had his questions and while they ate, he'd asked Erin about her upbringing and her mother, and she'd asked about his childhood, his mother and Raymond.

Despite their differences, they found they had several similarities. Neither one of them enjoyed a great relationship with Raymond, although Daniels believed he and his father had grown closer after their trip through Elmwood. Daniels suspected, though, after he confronted Dad about Erin, that their truce might be short-lived.

Realizing he and Erin had dominated the conversation, Daniels spoke to Mikey. "Any news with you? How're Mason and Trick?"

"They're fine," said Mikey. She told them about Mason's latest case and explained Mason's work as a paranormal medium and PI to Erin.

"I've heard of that stuff, but never really believed in it," said Erin.

"Hang around us long enough," said Rem, "and you soon will."

"We've got some stories," added Daniels.

"We'll save those for later. We don't want to scare Erin away." Marjorie munched on a chip and spoke to Mikey. "How's it going with the upstairs closet? Have you two gone through it?"

Rem eyed Mikey, and she nodded. "We're getting there."

Marjorie widened her eyes. "Oh, dear. Should I not have asked? I'm sorry."

Rem shook his head. "It's fine, Marj. Nothing you can't bring up. It's slow going, and it brings up a lot of crap, but we're getting through it."

Daniels saw Erin's look of confusion. "You mind if I tell Erin?" asked Daniels.

Rem shrugged. "Sure. She's family now."

Daniels told Erin about Jennie.

"I'm surprised Cain didn't mention her," said Erin.

"Cain never met her," said Rem. "My relationship with him has been frosty for a while."

"I'm sorry you lost her," Erin said softly to Rem. "Losing my mom has been the hardest thing I've ever dealt with. I don't think I'll ever adjust to life without her."

Daniels thought of his sister, Melinda, and how he still missed her. "It's never easy. But time helps."

"So does dealing with stuff you'd rather avoid," added Rem. "I found some items, though, that I didn't expect." He wiped his fingers on his napkin. "I found a box with my dad's gun. A 38 Special. Mom gave it to me after he died. I forgot I even had it."

"Did he ever use it?" asked Daniels.

"He did. He'd take it to the shooting range and even took me a few times."

"You going to keep it?" asked Marjorie.

"He wants me to have it," said Mikey. She made a face. "But I'm not so sure I want it. I've never been a fan of guns."

"Honey," said Rem. "It wouldn't hurt for you to practice. You don't have to travel with it, but at least it will be in the house should you need it. With everything going on right now, it would make me feel better."

"It's not a bad idea," said Daniels. "Marjorie is well trained, and we have an extra gun in the house."

Mikey sipped her wine. "I know she is. I saw her in action when we were up in the mountains in those damn woods."

Rem blanched. "Don't remind me."

Erin frowned. "Those damn woods?"

"One of those stories we're not going to tell," said Daniels.

"I'll fill you in later," said Marjorie to Erin. "But you're going to need something stronger than wine."

"I'll think about going to the shooting range," said Mikey. "But something tells me I don't have a choice." She eyed Rem.

"Not really. I want you to be safe." Rem grabbed his empty plate and the others' empty plates and brought them to the sink.

"He's right, Mikey," said Marjorie. "It can't hurt to learn to use it. The more knowledge you have, the better."

"Thanks Marj. Maybe you can convince her." Rem poured more wine for Mikey and Erin, got Marjorie a water, and grabbed another beer for himself and Daniels. He sat, opened his beer, and eyed Erin. "Speaking of safe, not that I want to disrupt this joyous family reunion, but we need to ask you about Cain. You still okay with helping us, or do you want to back out?"

Erin paused and opened her mouth to answer, but Daniels interrupted. "She shouldn't be doing any of this." He faced Erin. "It's too dangerous."

"Isn't that up to her?" asked Rem.

Daniels scowled. "She's my sister."

"Who, last I heard, has a mind of her own." Rem gripped his beer. "And I just asked her if she wanted out, so why don't we let her answer?"

Annoyed, Daniels sat back and told himself to relax. There was no reason to get mad at Rem, but now that he had a new sister in his life, he felt more protective than ever. "Fine." He took a breath. "Sorry." He looked over at Erin. "What do you think?"

Erin rested her elbows on the table. "I'm still in. I want to help you."

"That's great." Rem sipped his beer.

Daniels leaned up. "No, it isn't. You don't realize how dangerous these people are, Erin."

"We talked about this, and I understand the risk," said Erin. "Cain is using me to get to you. It's the whole reason he met me. He can't get away with that."

"It's not your job to catch him," said Daniels. "It's my job."

"And how are you going to do it without my help?" she asked. "I'm there. And you're not."

Daniels struggled to get her to understand. "And if he finds out what you're doing—"

"He won't find out," said Erin. "He's not that smart." She looked at Rem. "No offense."

Rem sipped his beer. "None taken. I'm well aware."

"I don't like it," said Daniels.

"You don't have to like it. Just accept it," said Erin.

Daniels sighed with frustration.

Marjorie sat her napkin on the table. "She's got the Daniels' stubbornness, honey. That's obvious."

"Now you can see how irritating it is," replied Rem.

Daniels gave in. "I deal with you every day, partner, so I'm familiar. I just didn't expect to have to deal with more of it."

"Just be careful, Erin," said Mikey. "It's never as easy as you expect. Watch your back with Cain. Those Remallas can be sneaky."

Holding his beer, Rem shot a knowing look at Mikey. "We can be a lot of other things, too."

Mikey held his gaze, and her cheeks turned pink.

Marjorie chuckled. "I think we need to get back to Cain." She spoke to Erin. "Does he know you're here tonight?"

Daniels perked up at that question and saw Rem do the same.

"He does," said Erin.

"How did he react to that?" asked Daniels.

"He thought it was a good idea but told me to be careful. Said his cousin would try to warn me about him, and that you," she gestured toward Daniels, "couldn't be trusted, even if you are my brother. Cain said your loyalty is to your partner, not me."

"Cain certainly thinks highly of us, doesn't he?" Daniels asked Rem.

Rem sat up. "Did he suggest you try to get information from us?"

Erin swirled her wine. "He told me to see what I could find out about your current investigation. When I told him I wasn't comfortable with that, he told me I was missing out on a big opportunity. I could be rewarded if I got information."

"He means he would be rewarded," added Daniels.

"I doubt you would get much credit," said Rem. He sighed and looked at Daniels. "What do you think?"

Daniels hated involving Erin in this mess, but since she refused to change her mind, they had to determine what to do next. "Tell him we're backing off the black birds and focusing on our case."

"And we're trying to help Lozano," added Rem. "He's our captain who's currently on suspension pending the outcome of an FBI investigation."

Erin narrowed her eyes. "Captain Lozano?"

Daniels noted her curious expression. "Have you heard that name before?"

"Yes," she said. "Cain mentioned him the other night when we were talking about me coming here for dinner. He warned me not to get too close and when I asked what that meant, he chuckled and said your Captain Lozano was about to get a visit from the FBI, and that would be just the beginning."

Daniels gripped his beer. "He knew about Lozano?"

Rem cursed. "That confirms it. The black birds are targeting us and using Lozano to do it. And what's worse is they're involving Cain, which suggests he's moving up the ranks."

"I wonder what else he knows?" asked Daniels.

"I tried calling him twice," said Rem. "He doesn't answer."

"He left town on a sales trip two days ago," said Erin. "He comes back tonight. And he's taking the day off tomorrow, so he'll be home."

Rem took a drink of his beer. "Then maybe it's time I stop by."

"You want company?" asked Daniels.

Rem took a second to think. "Let me deal with him on my own. If we both go, it looks like we're ganging up on him."

"Just be careful." Daniels eyed Erin. "When do you see him again?"

Erin tapped on the tabletop. "He'll probably call me tonight, but I don't have plans to see him yet."

"Can Cain access your phone?" asked Daniels. "We have to be sure you and I can communicate without him knowing."

Erin scoffed. "Hell, no. We're close, but I keep up my boundaries. And I've told him that won't change."

"Are you sure you're comfortable with this, Erin?" asked Mikey. "I hate to ask this, but do you have feelings for him?"

Daniels wished he'd thought to ask the same.

Erin studied her wine but shook her head. "No. I don't. He has a charming quality about him, and of course, he's attractive, but once I found out why he showed interest in me, I cut off all ties with him."

Daniels hadn't heard that before.

"Then how are you with him now?" asked Rem.

"When I realized you two were investigating this group Cain's caught up in, it seemed obvious I could help. I went back to him and told him I wanted to be friends. That I admired him and his ambition, which boosted his ego. He wants more than friendship and I told him I need time. Cain can't imagine a woman actually not liking him, much less using him to get information, and so far, he's going along with it." She stared off. "Strangely, I think he enjoys having a female friend. I don't think he's ever had one before. Although I doubt that's what he's telling his society buddies."

"I'm sure he's lording over his conquest of you," said Mikey.

"Let him play the conquering hero," said Erin. "I don't care. I just want to find out what he and his cronies are up to."

"That's a pretty smart set up," said Rem. He chuckled at Daniels. "You're almost as smart as she is."

Daniels aimed a steely gaze at Erin. "We'll see how smart you are as this plays out. I want you to promise me that if you get a whiff of things turning in the wrong direction, you get out. You don't owe me anything."

"And your life isn't worth revealing this society's secrets," said Marjorie. "Or Cain's."

Erin sighed. "I'll get out if I sense trouble."

"Thank you." Feeling some measure of relief, Daniels drank some more beer. His phone buzzed, and he picked it up and read his text message. "It's Josh Durning." He spoke to Marjorie. "Looks like there's a good chance I'll be testifying on the day of your doctor's appointment. You mind if Rem takes you?"

Marjorie patted his knee. "Honey, that's unnecessary. I can take myself to the doctor."

"I don't want you going by yourself."

"I don't mind, Marj," said Rem. "I know Daniels worries about you. I can sit in the waiting room and make phone calls to CIW staff members who've never worked for Durning." He rolled his eyes.

"Please, honey," said Daniels. "You told me you almost had to pull over the other day because you were about to puke. Did you talk to Jackie about carpooling to work?"

Marjorie hesitated and slumped. "She's picking me up tomorrow. But that doesn't mean—"

"Hon, when you're past this phase, you can drive yourself to San Francisco if you want, but for now, humor me. Okay?" He offered her his most sincere look.

"He's aiming those baby blues at you, Marj," said Rem. "You're toast."

Marjorie took Daniels' hand. "I was toast the first time I saw them." She squeezed his fingers. "Fine. You win."

"I'd take you, Marjorie," said Mikey, "but Mason's got me going to some paranormal medium conference with him downtown."

"That's fine, Mikey," said Marjorie. "Rem and I can hang and maybe stop for donuts on the way back. My treat."

Rem smiled. "If that's the case, I may take you to all your appointments." He stood. "And speaking of sweets, those brownies are calling my name."

Marjorie stood too. "I can start the coffee and clean the dirty dishes."

Daniels took her elbow. "No, you won't. You'll sit right there."

Marjorie sighed. "I'm not porcelain, honey."

"You are to me." Daniels' phone beeped again. Groaning, he reached for it. "What does Josh want now?" He read the text message, and, not understanding, read it again. "It's Lexie." Wondering what was going on, Daniels stood and pushed his chair in. "She's outside."

Rem's eyes widened. "Outside? Here?"

"Lexie Logan?" asked Marjorie. "That's good. I'm eager to meet her."

"Me too," said Mikey.

Daniels' mind raced. Why was Lexie at his house? "I think it's better you three stay inside. Rem and I will talk to her."

Rem headed to the front door when Daniels' phone buzzed again with another text message from Lexie. Reading it, he scratched his head.

"Now what?" asked Rem. "Is she bitching because we're taking too long?"

Daniels shot out his thumb. "She's in the backyard."

"How'd she get in the backyard?" asked Rem. "Your gate's locked."

Daniels had no idea. "You three stay put."

"Guess I'll be making the coffee after all," said Marjorie. She huffed when Daniels protested. "Don't argue with me. Let me feel useful while you and Rem meet your rogue reporter." She dropped her napkin on the table.

"And if you're bold enough, invite her in for a brownie. We'll pull the shades."

"We're not inviting her in for brownies," said Daniels. "Tonight's had enough excitement as it is."

Rem left his beer on the table and headed toward the back door. "C'mon. Let's find out what Lexie Logan has on her mind."

Chapter Nineteen

LEXIE SAT AT THE porch table, her big purse beside her, holding her head.

"Lexie," said Daniels. "What are you doing out here?"

She looked up, and Rem saw a scrape on her cheek and dirt on her forehead and hands. Recalling when two men had assaulted her and taken Ackerman's box, he sat beside her. "Are you okay?"

Her elbow on the table, she rested her chin in her palm. "I'm great."

Daniels sat on the other side of her. "How did you get back here?"

"I scaled the fence." Her words ran together, and she smiled.

"That's an eight-foot fence," said Daniels. "How'd you get over it?"

She glanced back at the yard and whispered as if someone was listening. "Your neighbor left his trashcan out. I got on top and pulled myself over." She giggled.

Rem took a good look at her. "Are you drunk?"

She moaned, sat back and closed her eyes. "Maybe a little. I didn't want to come to the front door." She stopped as if that explained everything.

"Please tell me you didn't drive," said Daniels.

"Nope," she shook her head. "I called a rideshare." She opened her eyes. "The driver dropped me off in the alley." She groaned, dropped her head on the back of the chair, and sighed. "I'm so going to pay for this tomorrow."

"No doubt." Rem wondered what was up. Lexie, as far as he'd seen, had never been the type to get drunk enough to jump a friend's fence. "Did you come here to say hi to Daniels, or do you have some other reason?"

She gaped at Rem. "I could ask you the same. Don't you two ever separate?" She snorted and rested her head back. "And I'm the crazy one," she murmured and shut her eyes again.

"Oh, boy," said Daniels. "I think we need some coffee." He stood.

"Make it two," said Rem.

"I'll make it three." He leaned over Lexie. "Hey." He poked her arm.

She winced and raised her arm. "Ouch."

Rem could see an angry red and raw scrape running down the inside of her forearm. "What the hell did you do to yourself?"

Lexie sucked in a breath when Daniels inspected it. "I must have done it climbing over the fence."

"I'll get something to clean it. Stay put." Daniels pointed at Rem. "Better yet. Tell him what you're doing here, and don't pass out or puke on my porch."

She made a face at him. "I'm not that bad."

"You're pretty close." Daniels went inside.

Rem turned his chair to face her. "What's going on, Lex?"

She inspected her injured arm. "I met with Miguel, from CIW."

That got Rem's interest. "This evening? Where?"

"I called him. Told him I was a producer for a podcast called *Don't Kill Me Because I'm Beautiful*. It's about femme fatales." She smiled. "Pretty good, huh?"

Rem frowned at her. "Is that a real podcast?"

"No. I made it up."

"What's beauty have to do with it? It's about women killing men."

She rolled her eyes. "You don't have the agile mind for creativity that I do." She put her hand on her chest. "Miguel loved it."

"That explains a lot. For both of you." Moving on from the title of the podcast, he focused on Miguel. "I'm guessing it worked."

"Like a charm." She rested her ankle on her knee. "We met in a bar."

"Obviously. Do you normally drink like this during an assignment?"

He expected an argument from her, but she stilled and studied her fingers. "I don't normally drink at all." She paused. "I tend to overindulge."

Rem recalled the background check on Lexie he and Daniels had done when they'd first met her. It had been clean other than an arrest for a DUI a few years back. "What was different about tonight? Surely Miguel wasn't that persuasive."

She rubbed her forehead. "I got a stupid text from my ex as I was walking out the door. It...threw me off." She let out a deep breath. "I thought I'd have just one drink, but that never works. At the time, though, it felt great."

Rem suspected there was a lot he and Daniels didn't know about Lexie Logan. "When did you leave the bar?"

"I don't know. About an hour ago. Maybe two."

"Did you go somewhere else and drink?"

"No. I just went somewhere else."

"And you're still drunk?"

She sighed, opened her bag, and pulled out a flask. "This didn't help. I grabbed it on the way out of my apartment. I'm not even sure what's in it, but I think it's tequila."

Rem took the flask from her. "You're officially tapped out." He stood, opened the flask, and poured the remains into the shrubs.

Lexie gripped her temples. "You're as bad as my mom."

Rem recapped the empty flask and dropped it in Lexie's purse. "It's only because I care." He sat. "Now tell me about Miguel."

Daniels returned to the porch, carrying a small bag. "Coffee's almost ready." He sat and pulled out some cotton and a bottle of peroxide. "Let me see your arm."

"Is that going to sting?" asked Lexie.

"It'll help sober you up," said Rem. "Now tell us about Miguel."

Lexie reluctantly held her arm out. "I told him I thought he'd be an excellent candidate to create a podcast of his own, especially since he has knowledge of Reginald Durning's murder." She gasped as Daniels cleaned her wound.

"Sorry," said Daniels. "Keep talking."

Lexie cursed as Daniels moved up her arm. "I asked him about Durning, and he said he was a nice guy and well-liked, until the last year."

"Nothing new there," said Rem. "Did you ask about clients and staff?"

Daniels dabbed on a deeper part of the scrape. "God. I hope so."

Lexie bit her bottom lip. "He couldn't tell me much about the clients, but he had some insights about the staff. There were three women he thought could be suspects." She sucked in another breath. "Damn. I wish I had that flask."

"What flask?" asked Daniels.

"It's not important," said Rem. "Who are the three women?"

Lexie nodded toward her purse. "Grab that purple notebook."

"The infamous purse." Rem opened the purse and found the purple notebook in between a red and green one. He pulled it out.

"Go to the last page."

Rem flipped to the last page and studied it. "Am I supposed to be able to read this?" He flipped the notebook around to show Lexie.

"I write fast, plus...I was tipsy." She leaned to look. "The first name is Nicole Bartleshein...Bartemshine...something like that."

"Barstein," said Daniels. "I recall her name from the staff list."

"Close enough," said Lexie. "She used to be an intern that worked for Durning." She winced as Daniels focused on a tender spot. "Word was the two worked a lot of hours together and the rumors flew they were involved. Then, one day, another attorney told Miguel that Durning and Nicole had fought. The next day, she was transferred downstairs to a different division. She didn't go quietly, though, and made it obvious she was unhappy. CIW ended up firing her two months ago."

"Interesting," said Daniels. "Who else?"

Lexie read her scribbles. "Electra Kentworth."

"Electra?" asked Rem. "I don't recall that name on the list."

Lexie narrowed her eyes at the paper. "Sorry. It's Elana. Miguel and I had a brief conversation about female superheroes."

Rem raised his brow. "I'm starting to worry about the reliability of your notes."

"They're just fine," said Lexie, with another wince.

Daniels studied Lexie's arm. "Tell us about Electra." He focused on a few more scrapes, then set the cotton down and grabbed some ointment.

Lexie frowned at him. "Electra...I mean Elana, she was part of a big case that Durning was working on with another attorney. Miguel said they eventually won the case and went out to celebrate. From what he heard, there was a lot of drinking and Durning and Elana disappeared for a while, and when they returned, Durning left and she left right after. Everyone assumed they'd hooked up."

Rem rested his elbow on the table. "It's definitely looking like Durning thought little of his wedding vows."

Daniels delicately rubbed the ointment along Lexie's arm. "That gave Rhonda an easy way in." He wiped his fingers on a small towel.

"Rhonda," said Lexie with a sneer. "If I ever meet up with her, I'm going to—"

"Steer clear," said Rem. "She'd eat you alive."

Lexie set her jaw. "She impersonated me."

"She's doing it on purpose," said Rem. "To get under your skin."

"Forget about Rhonda," said Daniels, putting the ointment away and pulling out some gauze. "Continue with Electra. What happened after the party?"

"Do I need gauze?" asked Lexie.

"It'll keep it clean," said Daniels. "Continue."

Lexie watched Daniels work. "She and Durning no longer worked together, and the rumors died, until six months ago when Alice Sutton, the firm's most strait-laced and religious member, walked in on Durning and

Electra in the maintenance room, apparently having sex. Alice about had a stroke, and Miguel had to call paramedics."

"I can empathize with Alice. Nobody likes surprises," said Daniels, rolling gauze around Lexie's arm.

Rem guessed Daniels was thinking about Erin. "I'm sure Alice has moved on despite her trauma," added Rem. "What happened to Electra?"

"Miguel didn't see her again after that, but heard she was given a nice sum of money to move on."

"CIW paid her to leave?" asked Rem. "I wonder why?"

"The rumors were that she threatened a lawsuit against Durning and the partners." Lexie flexed her fingers as Daniels wrapped tape around the gauze to secure it.

Daniels set the tape down. "Then why would she kill Durning?"

Lexie pulled her arm back. "Miguel thinks Durning may have brought up a few dubious activities from Electra's background. She got paid, but not as much as she wanted." She checked her bandage. "That feels better. Thanks."

"You're welcome. Just keep it clean. You should be able to take the gauze off tomorrow." Daniels returned the items to his bag. "I'm going to check on the status of the coffee." He stood, grabbed the bag, and went inside.

"Who's the third lady?" asked Rem.

Lexie's phone buzzed. She studied her purse, but didn't look for her phone.

Rem imagined why. "You think it's the ex?"

"Probably."

"He been bothering you?"

She rested her injured arm in her lap. "I hadn't heard from him in a while until this evening. I ignored him until I had a few drinks, and then...I may have gone off on him." She eyed her purse. "I'm sure that's his response."

"It's probably better to ignore it until you sober up and can think with a clear head."

Lexie brushed her hair back. "Probably."

Rem noted the dirt under her nails. "Did you get that dirt from falling over the fence?" He pointed at her fingers.

She looked at them. "Nope. I'll get to that in a second."

Rem wondered why she was being so cryptic. "So, who's the third?"

The back door opened, and Daniels brought out a mug and set it in front of Lexie. "Black with two sugars. Will that work?"

Lexie reached for it. "That's great. Thanks."

"How's it going in there?" asked Rem.

"Fine. They're talking about our trip to the mountains."

Rem's heart thumped. "A memory I'd just as soon forget."

"I'd offer you my flask if I still had anything in it," said Lexie.

Daniels went back inside and returned with two more cups.

Rem took his mug from Daniels and sipped some coffee. "Now I just need that brownie."

"Later," said Daniels, eyeing Lexie. "Who's number three?"

Lexie eyed her notebook, took another sip of her coffee, and set her mug down. "Delaina Desmond."

The name surprised Rem. "Crenshaw's personal assistant? Did Durning sleep with her too?"

"According to Miguel, Delaina went after Durning." Lexie sat back and rubbed her temples.

"Feeling better?" asked Daniels.

"Ask me tomorrow." Lexie blew on her coffee and took a sip. "Miguel says Delaina is Crenshaw's mole. Whatever information she gets goes straight to Crenshaw. Miguel thinks Delaina was asked by Crenshaw to do some digging. She used her significant appeal to woo Durning, but it backfired. He saw right through her and tossed her out of his office. Word is she doesn't take rejection well."

"How does Miguel know all this?" asked Rem. "And not Martha Cravitz?"

"Martha told us she doesn't listen to gossip," said Daniels.

Lexie nodded. "Miguel told me that Martha was intensely loyal to Durning. She rarely ate with the other staff and refused to discuss anything negative about anyone, much less Durning. As a result, she doesn't know much about this and certainly wouldn't make any assumptions."

"Smart lady," said Daniels. "Too bad there aren't more like her."

"It's not too helpful with police investigations," added Rem. "But it does beg the question, how much of this is accurate? Is Miguel blowing smoke up your ass because he thinks you're going to give him a podcast?"

"Podcast?" asked Daniels.

"About femme fatales," said Lexie, scowling at Rem. "I think it's a winner."

"Not with that title, it isn't." Rem ignored Daniels' confused look. "So, where does this leave us? We've got three scorned women, plus Rhonda." He scratched his head. "We still think Rhonda killed Durning, right?"

Daniels drank some coffee. "We'll follow-up but it's good fodder for our reports to Crow. It will make her happy while we search for Rhonda. Plus," he held up his finger, "when we talk to Ingram and Willoughby, we can talk to Delaina too."

"She's not going to say a word to us," said Rem. "She'll be just as tightlipped as Crenshaw."

"You never know with assistants," said Daniels. "It can't hurt to try."

Lexie closed her notebook. "Miguel said Barb Ingram returned to the office yesterday."

Rem wondered what the other two partners might offer. "Looks like we're visiting CIW again tomorrow, partner. That should be fun."

"Can't wait." Daniels glanced at Lexie's nails. "You go digging in the flowerbed when you came over the fence?" He sipped some coffee.

Lexie studied her fingers again. "About that. When I was talking to Miguel, he said something to me that made me wonder about Ackerman."

Daniels set his mug down. "What was that?"

"During our talk, and after several drinks, I told him about my stupid ex, who I was furiously rage texting..." She stared off. "And he told me he used to have an ex like that, that he couldn't seem to get rid of." She poked at the edge of the table. "His shrink recommended he perform a ceremony to exorcise her."

"That's outside the box," said Rem. "Did he do it?"

"He did," said Lexie. "He wrote down all his frustrations and disappointments on a piece of paper and added that he forgave her and was ready to move on. Then he put the paper in a small box and buried it in his backyard. He even added a tiny tombstone and wrote on it. It said 'Here lies the failed relationship with so-and-so. May she rest in peace.'"

Daniels pursed his lips. "Did it work?"

"He said it did." Lexie rubbed her bandage. "When he would get upset or caught up in the past, he'd look at the little tombstone, and it clarified everything and comforted him."

"What does that have to do with Ackerman?" asked Rem.

"Ackerman talks a lot about his late wife in his files. Plus, he kept all that stuff of hers in that storage unit. My guess is he went there to feel closer to her."

Rem thought of Jennie's closet. "Makes sense."

Lexie picked at some dirt under her nail. "And after what Miguel told me, I wondered if Ackerman found comfort at his wife's grave." She paused. "So after I left Miguel, I went to the cemetery where Ackerman's wife is buried."

Rem almost choked on his coffee. "You did what?"

Daniels looked just as surprised. "You went to her grave?"

"I did," she said, "and I started digging."

Rem sputtered. "What for?"

The back door opened, and Marjorie poked her head out. "Honey? Rem? There's a car out front. We think it's watching the house."

Daniels was up on his feet, and alarmed, Rem joined him. He grabbed Lexie's purse. "Come inside, Lexie."

Lexie stood. Rem took her elbow and followed Daniels into the kitchen. He set her purse on the counter. "Were you followed?"

Looking pale, Lexie shook her head. "No."

"How can you be sure?" asked Rem. "You were drinking." He went to the front window and looked outside. The sun was almost down, but across the street, one house away, Rem saw a dark SUV with tinted windows. From his viewpoint, he could see a driver in the front seat. "You see that car in the neighborhood before?" Rem asked Daniels.

Daniels pulled the cord and closed the shades. "No. Have you, honey?" He asked Marjorie, pulling down a single slat in the shade to keep looking.

"No," said Marjorie, "but that doesn't mean they aren't visiting someone."

Lexie came up behind them and peered out. "That car was there when my driver drove by. I saw it when I told him to go around to the alley."

"Were there people in it?" asked Rem.

"I'm not sure," said Lexie.

"I'm Marjorie, Lexie," said Marjorie. "And this is Mikey and Erin."

"Nice to meet you guys," said Lexie. "Sorry I barged into your party."

Rem continued to watch the car. "What do you think, partner? Should we go out and say hello?"

Daniels closed the blind and turned. "Who noticed the car?"

"I did," said Erin. "I've seen a similar one like that once or twice outside Cain's. It made me suspicious."

"That's all I need to hear." Rem pulled his weapon from his holster. "All of you, get into the laundry room and close the door."

Daniels went to the front closet and accessed his gun.

"Are you serious?" asked Lexie. She put a hand on her head. "Man, I wish you hadn't emptied my flask."

Daniels checked his weapon. "Do what Rem says. Everyone in the laundry room and don't come out until we tell you." He spoke to Mikey. "Keep an eye on Marjorie, Mikey."

"I will." She went with Marjorie, Erin, and Lexie to the laundry room and looked at Rem. "Be careful."

"I will, sweetheart." Rem headed to the front door.

"Honey," said Marjorie. She held Daniels' gaze. "I love you."

"I love you too, and I'll be fine. Now go." He waited for them to get into the room and closed the door behind them. He looked at Rem. "Ready?"

"As I am for that brownie. Let's go." He went to the front door and opened it. They peered out. The SUV remained where it was.

"Let's take a stroll." Walking casually, Daniels walked out of his house, keeping his gun at his side.

Rem stayed beside him as they walked to the sidewalk and then down it, toward the vehicle.

Within seconds, the vehicle started up, and the engine roared as the driver gunned it, and the SUV raced down the street. They ran toward it, and Rem got the license plate, but the SUV squealed around the corner and disappeared from sight.

Breathing fast, Rem re-holstered his weapon. "What do you think of that?"

Daniels stared off toward the empty street and then glanced behind him. "Let's get back to the house. We'll call in the plate."

They headed back to Daniels' home and closed the door behind them. Daniels went to the laundry room, and Rem called in the license plate.

Still in shock, Marjorie, Mikey, Erin and Lexie returned to the kitchen. Lexie wiped dirt off her pants. "That's one way to get to know everyone."

"Everybody okay?" asked Daniels, sliding his gun into his waistband. Marjorie came over, and he put his arm around her.

Everyone nodded, and Mikey came over and wrapped her arm around Rem. Talking on the phone, he pulled her close. He spoke to someone in Research who told him the plates were registered to an eighty-year-old woman who'd reported her car stolen two weeks earlier. Rem hung up. "No luck with the plates. They're stolen."

"What happened?" asked Marjorie.

"He took off when he saw us," said Daniels.

"Who do you think it was?" asked Erin.

"If it's a similar vehicle to the one you saw at Cain's," said Rem, "it's got to be the black birds."

"But why come here?" asked Marjorie. "Why watch us tonight? Did something happen that made them nervous?"

"Maybe Erin's dinner with us made them curious," said Mikey.

Rem looked at Lexie. "You're sure that car was there when you arrived?"

She nodded. "It was."

Rem thought about what she'd said outside. "You said you went to Ackerman's grave and dug into the dirt." He paused. "Did you find something?"

She swallowed and looked at the faces studying her.

"Lexie?" asked Daniels.

Lexie reached into her pants pocket and pulled out a small, worn and dirty plastic bag. Rem could see what looked like a thumb drive inside. She held it up. "Ackerman's secret file."

Chapter Twenty

REM TOOK THE STAIRS up to Cain's apartment. After waking early from a restless night's sleep, he'd gone for a five-mile run to clear his head. Still uncertain about how to handle this conversation, he reached Cain's floor and headed to his door, but stopped outside of it. Thinking, he stepped back and leaned against the wall.

Thoughts of his previous evening raced through his mind. Lexie's revelation had eclipsed Erin's, and after holding up that plastic bag, they'd all stared at her, none of them knowing what to say or do. Daniels had acted first. He took the bag from Lexie and strode upstairs to the extra bedroom, where he had a desk and a computer. Lexie and Rem followed, telling Marjorie and Mikey to stay with Erin and keep an eye out in case the SUV returned.

Rem recalled Daniels inserting the drive and opening it. They'd all studied the screen, barely breathing, when the information popped up. Leaning in, Rem had cursed when none of it was readable. The file had been encrypted.

Disheartened, they'd debated what to do. Lexie insisted on making copies and Daniels had found some fresh thumb drives and created two copies—one for him and one for Rem. He gave Lexie the original.

Deciding the obvious next step would be to find someone to decrypt it, they'd left the bedroom and returned downstairs. They'd had no choice but to tell Erin about the file and its contents. Daniels had put his copy in his safe and Lexie had tucked hers into her purse, saying she'd start a search for a reliable decrypter who could be trusted. Rem didn't like Erin knowing about the drive, but there was nothing he could do about it, and she'd promised to keep it a secret. Because she was Daniels' sister, he wanted to trust her, but until she proved herself, his doubt would remain. It was just his nature.

After a crazy evening of surprises, they'd all agreed to call it a night. Erin had left and Marjorie gave Rem and Mikey brownies to take home, and they'd dropped Lexie off at her apartment on the way.

The shock and risk of it all still weighed on Rem. After getting home, he'd been half tempted to ask Mikey to stay with Mason for a while, but knew that if the black birds wanted to get to her, Mason couldn't stop them. He'd put his copy of the drive in his safe and after a long talk with Mikey about her safety while they shared a big brownie, they'd gone to bed.

His attempt at sleep and his jog had done little to allay his fears, though. That USB drive supposedly held the names of the society's members, and once revealed, could take down a potentially vast network of conspirators. It didn't escape Rem that those threatened would kill to keep it hidden, and Rem sensed he and Daniels had crossed a threshold there was no return from, and it unnerved him.

Knowing his cousin would be a critical source of information if they couldn't decrypt the drive didn't help his anxiety. Rem needed Cain to tell him who he'd been talking to, but barging in and insisting his cousin reveal his source was the fastest way to failure. He had to break down Cain's walls and wasn't certain how to do it. Normally skilled at interrogating suspects, Rem had prided himself on getting information, but Cain was different. This was his cousin. Someone with whom he'd once had a close relationship and wanted to help before Cain got in too deep. Convincing Cain of that might be the only way to get through to him.

Taking a deep breath, Rem pushed off the wall, prepared to knock, when the neighbor's door opened. A man, dressed in a robe, stepped out, holding a bag of trash. Seeing Rem, he stopped. "Morning."

"Morning," said Rem.

The man headed toward the stairwell. "You here to see Cain?"

"I am."

"Tell him to keep it down. I banged on the wall last night for a reason." He opened a chute in the wall and tossed down his bag of trash. "Next time, I'm calling the cops." He returned to his apartment.

"I'll tell him."

The man went inside and, curious about what the neighbor had heard, Rem knocked on Cain's door. When there was no answer, he knocked again. "Cain? It's Aaron. Open up." He listened but didn't hear anything, and suspected Cain had been up late and was sleeping in. He knocked louder. "I'm not leaving, so you might as well let me in. We need to talk."

After several more seconds, Rem was about to knock again when the door abruptly opened. Cain stood there in his robe, his hair disheveled and his eyes shooting darts at Rem. "What the hell are you doing here?"

Rem didn't wait to be invited and entered the apartment. "I need to talk to you."

Cain looked down the hall. "Where's your beloved partner?"

"Not here."

Cain closed the door. "That's a first." He tightened the belt on his robe. "What do you want?"

Rem told himself to stay calm because getting upset would only cause Cain to retreat. "We had dinner with Erin last night."

"I heard."

Erin had said she expected Cain to call her after he got back into town. "Did she tell you about how it went?" asked Rem.

"She did. I heard she told your partner she's his sister."

Rem arched his brow. "Did you already know that?"

"I did."

"Who told you first? Her or your black bird buddies?"

Cain stilled and didn't respond.

"I guess that's my answer. Guess my next question. How'd they know?"

"If you came here to interrogate me, you've wasted a trip."

Rem told himself to slow down. Making Cain angry would get him nowhere. "Did you two argue about her revelation, or anything else?"

Cain frowned. "No. Why would we?"

"I saw your neighbor. He told me to tell you to keep it down."

Cain scoffed. "Guy's an idiot."

"If you weren't arguing with Erin, who were you arguing with? Did someone stop by last night?"

Cain glared. "None of your business." He went into the kitchen and grabbed a mug from a cabinet.

Rem leaned against the door frame between the kitchen and living room. He wanted to ask about Captain Lozano, but didn't want to reveal Erin's disclosure. "How's it going with your new friends?"

Cain grabbed a coffee pod from a drawer, added it to a coffee machine, and placed his mug on the holder. "I don't know what you're talking about." He closed the top portion of the machine over the pod and hit a button. The machine whirred to life and began to pour coffee into his mug.

Rem stepped forward and tapped the tattoo of the black bird on Cain's wrist. "I'm talking about them." He stepped back.

Cain sneered. "Like I said. None of your business."

"Is that who you argued with? Did they want an update after you got home?"

Cain's face clouded. "What did Erin tell you last night?"

Rem wondered what that meant. "Just that she was worried about you. She considers you a good friend and doesn't want you to get hurt."

"Why would I get hurt?"

"I think she's worried for the same reasons I am. She cares for you, and these people you're involved with don't."

He scoffed again. "Are you trying to say you care for me?"

"Of course I do. You're my cousin. And no matter what we've been through, you're still family. That won't change."

"Bullshit. You're just out to take down this society. You don't care about me. Would you even be here if it wasn't for your investigation?"

"Not at this moment, no. But I've made efforts, Cain, which you've consistently rebuffed."

Cain raised his voice. "Because you lied to me."

Rem raised his voice, too. "When did I ever lie to you?"

"I told you things that you used against me and my friends, and now you want to do it again, and you expect me to trust you?" He shot out his hand. "You're not here for me. You're here for you. You're a cop first, and family second."

"Cain—"

"Am I wrong?" shouted Cain. "You want information. You want me to turn on the people who've been there for me when you weren't?"

"It's hard to be there when you won't let me in."

"I idolized you and you betrayed me," yelled Cain.

"I didn't betray you," Rem yelled back. "Those kids weren't your friends. They would have used you just like this society is doing. Can't you see that by now?"

"The only thing I see is a pathetic cop looking to make a score so he and his partner can polish their records and reputation, which have suffered lately."

Rem didn't understand. "What are you talking about?"

"It's not so easy now, is it? When your buddy-buddy captain isn't there to hide your mistakes and protect you from yourselves."

Rem tensed at Cain's mention of Lozano. "How do you know about my captain?"

Cain tensed too, and Rem guessed he didn't mean to say that much. "Never mind," said Cain.

"Too late. Did you know Lozano would be suspended?"

Cain studied his coffee mug.

"You did, didn't you?"

Cain still didn't answer.

"The society set him up, didn't they?"

The coffee machine slowed to a drip, and Cain grabbed his mug.

"Why?" asked Rem. "Because of me and Daniels?"

Cain opened his fridge and took out some cream.

"What are they planning, Cain? What's coming next that requires Lozano to be out of the way? Or is Lozano just an unfortunate casualty because he's an ally of ours?"

Cain added cream to his mug and stirred it with a spoon he took from a drainer beside his sink. "I don't know anything."

Rem's patience was dwindling, and he fought not to yell but failed. "Don't lie to me, Cain. What did these people tell you?"

A bang on the wall made them both turn. Cain muttered a curse, and Rem reminded himself to follow his own advice. Yelling at Cain wouldn't work.

Cain rinsed the spoon and returned it to the drainer. He lowered his voice, but his animosity remained. "If you came here expecting me to tell you anything, you should have stayed home. And if you think your little dinner with Erin convinced her you and Daniels are two white knights ready to defend her from the evil bad guys, it won't work. She sees through you two, just like I do." Looking satisfied, he sipped his coffee.

Rem gritted his teeth and forced himself not to react. If it had been anyone else, he'd have grabbed that mug and thrown it against the wall. Taking a calming breath, he crossed his arms and set his jaw. "Listen to me, Cain."

"I'm done listening."

Holding his mug, he started to walk out of the kitchen, but Rem stood in his way. "Not yet, you're not. Like it or not, we're family. You can hate me all you want, but I'm not going anywhere."

Cain glared at him.

Rem glared back. "If you choose to stick with these guys, I can't stop you. You're all grown up and can decide for yourself. But if that's what you want, make sure you do it for the right reasons. Not to get back at me for some perceived slight. Not to impress Erin, and not to inflate your bruised ego."

Cain's glare deepened.

"Do it because you legitimately want to hurt and bully people. Do it because you like power and lording it over others for your own gain. Do it because you like to lie and cheat and steal. If that makes you feel good and makes you proud, then go for it. You've teamed up with the right people. But don't think for one second they're your friends. They don't value loyalty. Once they're done with you, they'll bulldoze right over you, because they'll no longer need you, and you'll be a liability."

Cain stared him down. "You don't know what you're talking about. You think you know everything." He scoffed. "Don't you ever tire of being so smart?"

Rem didn't move. "I've been a cop for too long and I've seen too many bad people. I know what I'm talking about, and I know you know that. Behind all that bravado, I think you're desperate to prove yourself." He paused. "You're not dumb, Cain. Never were. You knew those kids in school were using you, just like you know this society is using you, and what I don't get is why you let them."

Cain's expression darkened further. "I'm not letting them do anything."

"Yes, you are. You're letting them control you. You're letting them manipulate you."

"No. I'm not."

"If you could see that you've always had what you wanted. You've always had my respect, and your family's. And it doesn't require money, or status or power. You have it because you're you, Cain. You don't have to prove anything to us."

Cain's grip on his mug tightened.

"I always thought, and I still do, that you're a good guy. You've got a good job, a nice place to live, a mother and sister and plenty of family who love you, and a lady who might even like you enough to have a relationship with you. You've got it all, Cain, and you don't even know it."

Cain lowered his mug. "What is this? Your lousy attempt to tell me you love me? That you're my buddy? My pal?"

"I do love you, Cain. Why wouldn't I? You haven't done anything bad enough to stop that, and you never will."

Cain looked away.

"Just do one thing for me, okay?" asked Rem. "Think about what I said. Please. Consider the long-term implications of what you're doing. Where do you want to be in a year? Five years? Ten years?"

Cain knitted his brow.

"Because if you attach yourself to these people's coattails, there may not be another five or ten years. There may not even be a year."

"You're just trying to scare me."

"I'm being honest with you. There is no future with these people."

Cain paused. "Are you done?"

Rem studied him but then stepped to the side. "I'm done."

Cain walked past him. "Good. You know where the door is." He walked into the living room and sat on the couch.

Rem sighed and followed Cain to the sofa. "Can I make one request before I leave?"

"Like I have a choice." Cain groaned and sat back. "Make it quick."

Rem took a second to think. "If you want nothing to do with me, I can live with that. That's your choice."

"How kind of you."

"But if you find yourself in trouble, or if it occurs to you that you've fallen down a hole you can't climb out of, you can call me."

"I'll be just fine."

"And it doesn't have to be as a cop. It can be as a cousin. Or as a friend. Or just someone to talk to."

"Like you wouldn't turn me in if you could."

"All I can do is promise to help you in the best way I can."

Cain set his mug on the coffee table. "You just made my point."

Rem stepped closer, leaned over, and got in Cain's face. "At some point, you're going to need someone you can trust, Cain. And when that time comes, just know you can rely on me."

Cain hesitated and held Rem's look, but didn't respond.

Rem pulled back. "I'll see myself out." Having said and done all he could, he walked to the door and left.

Chapter Twenty-One

SITTING AT HIS DESK, Manetti reviewed his notes. Monk sat across from him, studying his monitor. Manetti glanced at the clock. "What time is our witness coming in?"

Monk scratched his jaw. "Anytime now."

Manetti nodded. They'd been investigating a recent assault and robbery of a man in an alley. Similar to another assault three blocks from the scene, Manetti and Monk questioned whether the crimes were related. A witness to the attack, a cook who'd been smoking in the alley, was coming in that morning to talk about what he'd seen. Considering what he wanted to ask, Manetti scribbled some questions in his notebook.

The squad doors opened and Remalla walked in, looking serious and not saying anything. He headed to his desk and sat. Rocking back in his seat, he stared off as if deep in thought.

"Everything okay, Rem?" asked Manetti. "You look like you paid for three Taco del Fuegos and only got one."

Rem glanced over at him. "Yeah. I'm okay. Just a lot on my mind." He eyed Daniels' empty desk. "Daniels isn't here?"

"Haven't seen him." Manetti flipped a page in his notes. "Anything you want to talk about?"

Rem paused, looked between him and Monk, and shook his head. "No. I'm good. Thanks, Manetti." He grabbed a mug from his desk, stood, and went to the coffee machine. He eyed Crow's empty office. "Where's our illustrious captain?" He poured himself some coffee.

Monk made a soft chuckle.

"Haven't seen her either," said Manetti. "Any movement in the Durning case?"

Rem returned the pot to the machine. "Is Elsa Crow warm and lovable?"

Manetti smiled. "Sorry to hear it."

Monk looked away from his monitor. "It's always darkest before the dawn."

Rem shot a look at him but didn't respond. He added cream and sugar to his mug.

Monk resumed his study of his monitor. "At least that's what I've been told."

Rem stirred his coffee.

The doors opened again, and Daniels entered, looking just as intent as Rem felt.

"There you are," said Rem. He sipped some coffee and sat at his desk.

Daniels took off his jacket and draped it over the back of his chair. "How was your morning?"

Rem rocked back in his seat again with a grunt. "About as delightful as you can imagine."

"That good, huh?" asked Daniels, sitting in his chair.

"I'll fill you in later." Rem sat up. "Where've you been?"

Daniels glanced in Manetti and Monk's direction. "I'll fill you in later."

Monk turned from his computer and smiled. "You two want Manetti and I to leave? Give you some privacy?"

Daniels glowered.

"You can leave whenever you want, Monk." Rem scowled. "The sooner, the better."

Monk stared back. "Somebody got up on the wrong side of the bed."

"C'mon, you guys. Just take it easy." Manetti tried to change the mood. "This job's hard enough as it is without us picking on each other."

"That's good advice," said Daniels. "Maybe you should tell your partner to follow it."

"I could tell you the same," replied Monk.

Feeling the tension in the room amp up, Manetti set his pen down. "How's Marjorie doing, Daniels?" He hoped the change in subject would help. "She feeling better?"

Daniels turned his attention to Manetti after a glare at Monk, who went back to studying his screen. "She's hanging in there. How's Annabelle?"

"She's doing the same. The last trimester is tough, though, so I'm trying to distract her."

"How's that going?" asked Rem.

Manetti nodded. "Not bad. I took her shooting after work yesterday."

"Really?" said Daniels. He looked at Rem. "We were just talking about that last night."

Rem set his coffee down. "I'm trying to convince Mikey to do the same. I found my dad's old gun in a closet recently. I want her to have it, but she's hesitant. Doesn't like guns."

"I get that," said Manetti. "Annabelle wasn't sure either, and then I took her, and she loved it." He recalled her delight when she'd hit the target dead center. He eyed Daniels. "Does Marjorie shoot?"

Daniels nodded. "All the time before J.P. was born. She's good. I wouldn't want to meet her in a dark alley."

"Neither would I," said Rem.

Manetti smiled. "You think it's bad for the baby, though? I wondered if it was too loud."

Daniels shrugged. "Not that I'm aware of."

"You can always research it," said Rem. "But I'm sure going to the range every once in a while is fine."

Manetti felt the same, but he was glad to hear it from Daniels and Rem.

Monk's phone rang, and he answered. "Monk."

"Well, partner," said Daniels. "You ready to tackle CIW again?"

Rem sighed. "Can I bring my coffee?"

Daniels stood. "Only if you say please." He grabbed his jacket. "I called Miguel and told him we were coming. Ingram and Willoughby will be there, anxiously awaiting our arrival." He pushed his chair in.

"Just as it should be." Rem stood, pulled a thermos from his drawer, and poured his coffee into it. "Let's go." He glanced at Manetti. "Duty calls, Manetti." He capped his thermos.

"See ya, Manetti," said Daniels, as they headed out.

"See ya." Manetti closed his notebook as Monk hung up.

"Our witness is on his way up. You ready?" asked Monk.

"I am." Manetti grabbed his notebook and pen and stood.

Monk joined him as they left the squad room and met their witness at the top of the stairs. They showed him into an interview room, and he sat at the table. Manetti offered the man a drink, and he requested a coffee.

"Sure." Manetti turned to leave when Monk patted his jacket pocket.

"While you're out there, grab my phone, will you? It's in the top drawer of my desk."

"Will do," said Manetti. He left, returned to the squad room, filled a Styrofoam cup with coffee, and put a lid on it. He went to Monk's desk, set the coffee down, and opened the top drawer. Seeing the phone, he reached for it and hesitated. He thought back on Vera Canmore's file, which Monk had found despite it not being in the search results. Still mulling over it, Manetti had held off asking Monk about it. It was as if his partner had known the name all along, but Manetti figured there had to be another explanation.

If Lozano had been around, Manetti would have likely asked him what to do. Now, though, standing at Monk's desk, with no one else around, he eyed the drawer. Telling himself it was just a drawer, he went casually through it but found nothing other than basic supplies. He grabbed Monk's phone and closed the drawer, but after another hesitation, he opened a side drawer. Inside were file folders, notebooks, a package of pens, and some bags of crackers and dried fruit, which Monk liked to snack on. Manetti closed it, too. After another glance around the squad room, he opened the other side drawer.

There were more files, a bottle of water, a package of coffee grounds, and a book. He picked it up and saw it was *Moby Dick*. Manetti returned the book, telling himself he was an idiot for searching Monk's desk, and almost closed the drawer when he saw a rumpled looseleaf paper sticking out of one file. He almost ignored it, except it looked like a drawing.

Curious, he pulled it out, and his heart thumped. Blue swirls drawn in crayon decorated the paper and a barely legible name was written in the corner. Sucking in a breath, Manetti recognized it as the drawing Margaret Redstone had given Monk when they'd visited her at the psychiatric facility three months ago. Wondering why Monk would want to keep it, Manetti quickly returned it and saw another rumpled paper in the file. He pulled it out and dropped his jaw. Red circles surrounded by dense black strokes of crayon covered most of the paper. It was the drawing Margaret Redstone had given Manetti before they'd left. She'd called it Bloody Tears in Hell. When they'd returned to the station, Manetti couldn't get rid of it fast enough. He'd balled it up and tossed it in his trash basket. Why had Monk fished it out and kept it?

"You lose your partner, Manetti?"

Manetti jumped. He lowered the paper and saw Elsa Crow standing in the squad room. His heart thumping harder, he returned the drawing to the file. "No. He's in the interview room. I'm about to join him." He closed the drawer.

Her brow furrowed, she studied him. "You looking for something?"

Manetti kept a flat expression on his face. "Yeah." He grabbed Monk's phone and held it up. "Monk's phone." He picked up the coffee cup. "I should get back."

She stepped closer. "Were those drawings?"

Manetti thought fast. "Yeah...um...Monk's taking some classes."

"He is? I didn't know."

"He's...uh...keeping it to himself. I saw them, and I took a quick look. He never shows me anything." He lowered his voice. "Don't tell him, though. He'd kill me if he knew."

Elsa half-smiled. "Don't worry. Your secret's safe with me." She walked toward her office and turned back. "Just between you and me, though, he needs more practice."

Manetti tried to breathe normally and chuckled. "No kidding."

Crow went into her office, and Manetti walked into the hall, trying to calm down. He'd almost told Crow the truth about the drawings, but didn't want to risk her asking Monk about them later. He jumped again when Monk's phone buzzed with a text notification. Glancing at it, Manetti caught the brief drop-down box that displayed a number and a truncated version of the text. All he saw was *The plan is in place for Dan.* The text cut off, and the display disappeared.

Manetti frowned, wondering what the plan was and who was Dan?

Telling himself the text was none of his business and wondering why Monk would want to keep drawings from a psychopath, Manetti took a few deep breaths, stretched his neck, and returned to the interview room.

•••••••••

Finishing his coffee after telling Daniels about his visit with Cain, Rem rubbed his temples and sighed. "I don't know what else to do."

Daniels pulled into the parking lot of the office building where CIW was located. "You've done your best. That's all you *can* do. He's made his choices."

Rem set his empty thermos on the floor of the car. "He knew about Lozano. God knows what else they told him. I was hoping he might tell me something."

"Give him time. Maybe something you said will sink in." Searching for a space, Daniels drove through the lot. "Did he mention Erin?"

"He said they talked, and she told him about our dinner and her revelation. He didn't deny that the society initially informed him about her being your sister."

"I doubt he'll ever admit it." Daniels shot him a look. "Cain doesn't know Erin told us about Lozano, does he?"

Rem shook his head. "No. I told him Erin cares about him and is worried. I'm hoping that might encourage him to talk to her."

Daniels gripped the wheel. "I just don't want him thinking she's helping us."

Rem's doubts bubbled up. "Just so long as she is."

"She is, Rem."

"How can you be so sure?"

Daniels narrowed his eyes. "She could have told him about the USB, and obviously she didn't."

Rem had to admit that was true. "I'll give her that much. Assuming they're not holding off on killing us until later."

"Why don't you trust her?"

"Why do you? Despite all that talk about family, you barely know her."

"She's my sister."

"And your other sister would betray you in a heartbeat."

"That's different."

"Is it?"

Daniels pulled into a parking space. He turned off the ignition and faced Rem. "Erin's not going to betray me. Give me a little latitude here. I have to trust my gut, which is something you're familiar with."

"I'm all for trusting your gut, but your hope that she's the sister you can have a relationship with could cloud your judgement. That's all I'm saying." He paused. "She's not Melinda, Daniels."

Daniels stilled. "I never said she was."

"But you're hoping."

Daniels faced the wheel again. "What are you saying? That I should back off? Not try to be a brother to her?"

"No. I'm not saying that. Just be careful. Let's go slow with her. Give her some time to show us she can be trusted. That's all I'm asking."

Staring out the windshield, Daniels paused and sighed. "You need to know something."

Rem shifted in his seat. "Don't tell me. You ate one of those bran muffins and there's going to be several bathroom breaks today." He reached for the door handle. "I'm sure there's a restroom in the lobby."

Daniels spoke quickly. "I gave Erin a copy of the USB."

Unsure he heard right, Rem swiveled back. "You did what?"

"That was my errand this morning. After everyone left last night, Erin called me. She offered to decrypt the drive."

Rem couldn't believe what he was hearing. "And you agreed?"

"She's good with computers, Rem. She works with security systems. Says she knows a friend who might help."

Shock rippled through Rem. He didn't know what to say.

"I stopped by her place this morning. Brought her some donuts so it wouldn't look suspicious."

Facing his partner, Rem pressed his palm against the dash. "Well, thank God you brought her donuts. Nobody would suspect that."

"Rem, listen. I know what you're thinking..."

"What happened to the guy who didn't want his sister involved? The person who was trying to convince *me* not to push her."

Daniels shifted back toward Rem. "I don't like it either, but she's our best shot at getting this information. And we need it now, not later. For Lozano's sake, as well as our own."

"What caused this sudden turn of events? How'd you go from keeping Erin out of this, to dumping her square into the middle of it?"

"I thought about it all night, and talked to Marjorie about it—"

Rem's anger grew. "Funny. I didn't get a phone call."

"Because I knew what you would say."

"I'd have said no," yelled Rem. "You just handed the woman all the secrets of the black bird society. If she's caught with that thing, or God forbid, tells them about it—"

"She won't tell anyone, Rem. I swore her to secrecy, and she knows the risks. She'll be careful."

Rem scoffed. "Well, now I feel so much better." He fought the urge to call Daniels a name best left unsaid. "And did you forget about the car outside your house last night?"

"No. I didn't forget."

"Did you stop to think they could have been following her? She said she'd seen a similar car outside Cain's."

"Because they were watching Cain, not Erin. And Cain knew about our dinner and likely told his bird buddies, so they watched Erin."

"The same night that Lexie found the USB drive."

"That's coincidental."

Rem couldn't believe Daniels' justifications. "You're making a lot of assumptions about them, and Erin. All of which could be wrong."

"I told Erin to keep an eye out for anyone suspicious, and if she sees anything, to call me."

"Is that before or after she hands the USB drive over to Cain or whoever the hell else she could be working with?"

Daniels shot out his hand. "How is this any different from us trusting Lexie?"

Rem widened his eyes. "Lexie got her ass kicked trying to protect Ackerman's stupid box and has been searching for that drive for months. And she's been with us since day one. What the hell has Erin done? Stalk you and hook up with Cain?"

Daniels took a long, slow breath and, after a second, spoke softly. "I did what I thought was best. For both of us."

Rem studied him. "Thanks, buddy. I appreciate it. But next time you decide to risk my life by giving a near *total stranger* something she could use against me, you, Lexie, and our loved ones, I'd appreciate a heads up."

Daniels scowled. "That's not going to happen, Rem."

"For your sake, and mine, I pray you're right." Giving up before he said something worse, Rem opened the door. "Let's go talk to CIW." He got out and slammed the car door shut.

·········

The ride up in the elevator was a quiet one. Rem wasn't talking and Daniels gave up trying to explain. As much as he wanted to keep justifying his actions, he couldn't because if the situation were reversed, he'd likely feel the same as Rem. Daniels had gone from wanting Erin out of danger to, as Rem said, dropping her square in the center of it. For the millionth time, he questioned if he'd done the right thing. He understood the repercussions if the existence of the drive became known to the black birds. And he knew the black birds were aware of Erin and her relationship to him, and to Cain.

But as Erin had told them, Cain wasn't smart enough to think she'd play both sides and he no doubt would convey that to the black birds. Erin could fly under the radar and hide in plain sight. At least he prayed she could. If this didn't work, or Rem was right, and Erin betrayed them, Daniels would have to live with the repercussions for the rest of his life.

That's why he hadn't made the decision lightly. After talking to Erin on the phone and seeing her that morning, he'd sensed her need to help, but she'd told him it was more. Her desire to be a part of his life, and the two of them working together, was a goal she'd set for herself since she'd traveled to his hometown. Their father and shared sibling had been an enormous disappointment, but Daniels didn't have to be. And Daniels couldn't deny that Rem was right. Daniels wanted the same and after losing Melinda, he'd never expected to have it again.

So, after a long conversation with Erin and drilling into her the risks, what to do if she suspected trouble, and giving her the short version of where the drive came from, he'd given her a copy. He realized Rem would be unhappy, but Daniels was determined to do his best to explain his reasoning to his partner.

So far, though, that reasoning was failing miserably.

The elevator stopped and opened on the main floor of CIW's offices. Rem strode out. Wondering how they were going to get through this questioning, Daniels followed.

They approached the front desk where Miguel sat and looked up. His eyes were bloodshot and puffy, and Daniels guessed Lexie wasn't the only one who'd drank a lot at the bar.

"Hello, Detectives." He picked up his phone. "I'll let them know you're here."

"Thanks, Miguel," said Daniels.

Miguel called, spoke to Delaina, and hung up with a long sigh.

"You feeling okay?" asked Daniels.

Miguel lowered his voice. "I drank too much last night. I should know better." He looked around the front lobby. "But on the plus side, I may have my own podcast soon."

Daniels nodded. "Good for you."

"What are you going to call it?" asked Rem.

He leaned closer. "You two ever listened to *Don't hate me because I'm beautiful*?"

"Never heard of it," said Daniels.

Rem rolled his eyes. "Don't bother. It's terrible."

Miguel widened his eyes. "Seriously?"

"If you work with whoever created that podcast, get a better title. One that makes sense." Rem eyed the door into the offices.

"Good tip." Miguel picked up a pen and wrote something on a piece of paper.

Seeing Delaina approach the glass doors, Daniels stepped up next to Rem. "Don't get cranky with him just because you're mad at me."

"Who's cranky? I'm telling him the truth."

Daniels put his hand on Rem's arm. "Rem, before we go—"

"Too late," said Rem. "She's here."

Delaina opened the glass door and stepped back. "This way, Detectives."

"Thank you." Rem headed down the carpeted walkway. Daniels shook his head and followed.

Approaching Crenshaw's office, Delaina waved at a nearby door. "You're in the main conference room today."

"How nice...and we don't have to wait," said Rem.

"That's the benefit of calling ahead," said Delaina with a smile. She opened the door and ushered them in.

Ben Crenshaw sat at the end of a long oak table, talking to another man of similar age with silver white hair, wearing a pristine suit and a gold and diamond watch. Across from him was a woman with reddish brown hair pulled up into a loose bun, perfectly manicured nails, heavy makeup, and also wearing an expensive suit. She was younger than the other two, though. Daniels put her around her mid-fifties.

Crenshaw looked up at their entrance. "Detectives." He stood. "Nice to see you again." He gestured toward the man. "This is Charles Willoughby."

Daniels and Rem held out their badges and introduced themselves.

Charles stood. "Nice to meet you, Detectives." He shook their hands.

Crenshaw gestured at the woman. "And this is Barbara Ingram."

Barbara didn't stand and didn't offer to shake their hands. Her gaze traveled over each of them and settled on Rem. She narrowed her eyes. "Hello," she said with little emotion.

Crenshaw and Willoughby sat. "Have a seat, gentlemen," said Crenshaw.

Daniels sat at the table, and Rem took the seat beside him. "We appreciate your time," said Daniels.

"And we appreciate you trying to find Reginald's killer," said Charles. "This is so horrible."

"Have you made any progress?" asked Crenshaw.

"We're working our way through the client and staff lists you provided," said Rem.

"I hope they've been helpful," said Crenshaw, offering a look of sincerity Daniels didn't buy.

"They have been," said Daniels. "I feel we've made some progress, don't you, Rem?"

Rem glanced at him. "Definitely." He looked back at the partners. "But before we get into all of that, I'd like to ask Mr. Willoughby and Mrs. Ingram here a few questions."

"Good idea," added Daniels.

"Call me Charles," said Willoughby.

"And it's *Miss* Ingram," said Barbara coldly. Daniels wondered about her attitude. It was clear she didn't like him or Rem.

"All right, Charles," said Rem. "And *Miss* Ingram."

She crossed her arms.

"Since we're all together," said Daniels, "we'd like to know about your relationship with Durning. How well did you know him?"

"Not that well personally," said Charles. "But he was an excellent attorney. He worked hard, won his cases and his clients liked him. He was on track for a partnership."

Barbara remained quiet. "Do you think the same, Miss Ingram?" asked Daniels.

She pushed back in her seat and crossed one leg over another. "I did until this past year. Then it seemed to be too much for him. He couldn't handle the stress. And I disagree about the partnership. He wasn't cut out for it."

Crenshaw interlaced his fingers. "As you can see, we have different opinions."

"That's pretty obvious," said Rem. He regarded Barbara. "Why do you think he wasn't capable of becoming a partner?"

She shrugged. "Because of what I just said. He couldn't cope with the stress. He had a lot on his plate, and he handled it with a bottle of booze and a slew of mistresses." She leaned forward and tipped her head at Daniels. "If your partner handled stress like that, would you want to work with him?" She sat back with a smug look.

"That would depend on what he'd been assigned," added Rem. "Even the best cop can make poor choices."

Rem's comment stung, but Daniels stared straight ahead, as did Rem.

Rem continued. "But as a partner, I'd support him. Not kick him to the curb. If Durning was the excellent attorney you say he was, maybe he was worth saving."

Crenshaw chuckled. "I think you're getting the wrong impression. We didn't kick Durning to the curb." He eyed Barbara. "Did we Barb?"

Barbara didn't answer him.

"I actually talked to Reginald about his behavior," said Charles, "but he said he didn't need my help. He said he was handling it and would be fine."

"What exactly was he handling that was so difficult?" asked Daniels. "From everything we've heard, he managed big cases like a pro and won them. Why did that change?"

Crenshaw chuckled again. "I'm not sure why you're taking this line of questioning? Durning was murdered by a woman he'd taken to a hotel. Not by anyone here at CIW."

"That woman at the hotel was paid to kill him," said Rem. "And we want to know why."

Charles dropped his jaw. "What?"

"You heard him, Charles," said Daniels. "This isn't about a spurned ex. Reginald Durning was the victim of an assassin who's already murdered two other men and will probably murder more."

"Then perhaps a spurned ex hired this assassin," said Barbara. "I assume you've considered that."

"We have," said Daniels. "Which is why we want to ask about three women. Nicole Barstein. Electra Kentworth—"

"Elana," said Rem.

"Sorry. Elana..."

Barbara interrupted. "Neither of those women works at this firm anymore."

"And neither of them would hire an assassin," said Crenshaw. "That's absurd. Nicole Barstein now works for another firm and, from what I hear, is thriving, and Elana Kentworth was paid handsomely to leave."

"We heard not handsomely enough," said Rem. "And Barstein was forced out after Durning dumped her. Thriving job or not, women have been known to carry a grudge."

Crenshaw's face fell.

Barbara's face tightened. "Men are just as good at carrying a grudge, Detective." Her gaze bore into Rem's.

Daniels looked between Rem and Barbara and got the distinct impression Barbara didn't like his partner. "Do you know something, Miss Ingram?" asked Daniels.

Barbara relaxed. "Just that I can see why you two are detectives, and not attorneys."

"Thank God for small miracles," muttered Rem.

"Who's the third woman?" asked Charles.

Daniels rested his elbow on the table. "Delaina Desmond."

Crenshaw's eyes widened. "My assistant? Are you serious?"

"Is Miss Ingram difficult to talk to?" asked Rem.

Barbara squinted.

"According to the people we've spoken with," said Daniels, "you sent Delaina after Durning to use her significant appeal to get information from him."

Crenshaw glared. "I would do nothing of the sort."

"If we needed to talk to Reginald, we did it ourselves," said Charles.

"You knew about his mistresses," said Rem. "Something was troubling Durning those last few months of his life. We heard you and Durning argued, Ben, not long before he died."

"That's not unusual," said Barbara. "As partners, we sometimes have to push some buttons if an associate is not pulling their weight."

"Did you ever talk to him, Miss Ingram?" asked Rem. "Put some pressure on him, too?"

Barbara's lips tightened, but she didn't respond.

"This whole thing is ridiculous," said Charles. "Delaina had nothing to do with Reginald's death. Whether Ben asked her to get close to him or not."

"I didn't," said Ben. "Who said that to you?"

"Sorry," said Rem. "That's classified."

"If someone's spreading lies about us, we have every right to know," said Barbara.

"You know that's not the way it works," replied Rem. "I guess that's why we're detectives, and you're not."

Barbara's glare returned.

"Since you're shocked and appalled by this accusation against you and Delaina, then you won't mind us talking to her?" asked Daniels.

Crenshaw set his jaw. "That's fine. You can set up a—"

"Today," said Rem. "Before we leave."

"This is a murder investigation," added Daniels. "Not one of your criminal cases."

Charles regarded Barbara's and Ben's glowers. "Well, of course you can talk to her today," said Charles. "Why on earth not? Let's get this misunderstanding cleared up."

Crenshaw sat back and straightened the cuff on his shirt. "By all means. Let's get this cleared up."

"Thank you, Ben," said Rem with a smile Daniels could see right through. "We so appreciate it."

"Is there anything else?" asked Crenshaw, standing. "Before I call in Delaina? As you can imagine, we're all very busy."

Daniels raised his finger. "Actually, there is."

"We're not quite done," said Rem.

Daniels sat forward. Despite their argument, he and Rem had slipped right back into their routine with ease. After years together, it was as natural as the sun rising.

Frowning, Crenshaw sat. "What is it, Detectives?"

"Don't tell me," said Barbara. "Do you want to accuse Rico, the facility manager? Maybe Durning was a slob, and Rico hired a killer to take him out."

"No doubt, he's on the staff list," said Daniels, flatly.

"Right along with the window washers," added Rem.

"Barbara, please," said Charles. "They're just doing their jobs."

Barbara's look told Daniels if the window was open, she'd throw Charles out of it.

Charles spoke to Rem. "What's your question?"

Looking satisfied in taking his time, Rem swiveled his seat back and forth. "We've also been going through the client list…"

"I hope they've all been cooperative," said Crenshaw.

"Oh, very," said Daniels. "But it appears a name is missing."

Looking bored, Crenshaw sighed. "What name is that?"

"We're not sure," said Daniels. "All we know is that Durning had a client named Dirk. With no last name. Does that ring a bell?"

The energy in the room shifted. Crenshaw's grip on his armrest tightened and Barbara visibly tensed. Staring at his partners, Willoughby went quiet.

Rem glanced back at Daniels. "Seems we hit a nerve."

"Seems so." He waited for one of the partners to answer. "Who is Dirk?"

Crenshaw slowly smiled. "I think the rumor mill has gotten the best of you two."

"Why is that?" asked Rem.

"Because there is no client named Dirk." He stole a glance at Barb and Charles, who remained silent.

"That's not what we heard," said Daniels.

Barbara finally spoke. "Did you talk to this Dirk?"

"No. We don't know his full name," said Rem.

"Do you even know if it is a man?" asked Ben. "How do you know it's not a woman? Did your source tell you?"

Daniels recalled Martha telling them she'd never met Dirk. "We assumed it was a man."

"Of course you did," said Barb with a scoff. "How do you know Dirk is not another one of Durning's mistresses? By your own account, he had several of them."

"Apparently," said Rem, "Dirk was a big deal. Durning would take the morning to meet with him outside the office."

Barbara laughed. "I think you're proving my point."

"And you, Ben," said Rem, pointing at Crenshaw, "would join them." He waved his hand at Barbara. "If Miss Ingram is right, Durning's not the only one having fun on the side."

Crenshaw's face turned red. "That is outrageous. You have no basis for an accusation like that. And if that ever gets out, I will sue both of you and your entire force for slander."

Rem raised his eyebrows. "Wow. That's a lot of indignation." He swiveled toward Daniels. "Don't you think?"

"My hair almost curled," said Daniels.

"I almost peed my pants," added Rem.

"Are you two jokers finished?" asked Barbara. "This entire line of questioning is abysmal. I have a mind to report you to your captain."

"She'd love that," said Daniels.

"Give her one more thing to bitch about." Rem swiveled back toward the partners. "But if you're so adamant you weren't sleeping with Dirk, Ben, then why were you meeting with him and Durning?"

Daniels waited for the answer with interest.

"That's simple, Detective," said Ben. "because there is no Dirk." He straightened his shirt and composed himself. "At least not one that I'm aware of. Just because Durning and I were both out of the office doesn't mean we were together."

"That seems obvious," said Barbara with a smirk. "At least to smart people."

"You're pretty quiet, Charles," said Rem. "Do you know who this Dirk is or why Durning met with him...or her?"

Charles studied his hands and shook his head. "No. I can't say that I do."

Daniels leaned forward. "You can't say or don't want to say?"

Charles, his face paler than before, clasped his hands together. "I can't help you, Detective."

Knowing something was up, Daniels sat back. "Then maybe Delaina can help us, since all of you seem to be having a memory lapse."

"I object to that insinuation," said Crenshaw, tensing up again.

"Object all you want, Ben," said Rem. "But this isn't a court of law."

Daniels studied each of them. "I hate to tell you all this, but for attorneys, you're all the worst set of liars I've ever seen."

"And we've seen a lot," said Rem.

"Accuse us of whatever you want," said Barbara. "But as of now, this questioning is over, at least for me." She stood. "And if I have anything to say about it, your careers as detectives will be short-lived."

"Promise?" asked Rem.

"We'd appreciate it," added Daniels.

"I'd suggest you call security, Ben, and have these two escorted out." Her eyes shooting lasers, she stomped to the door and left.

"What's with all the escorting?" asked Rem. "We know how to walk in and out of an office."

"Then why don't you two escort yourselves out right now?" asked Ben.

"Love to," said Daniels. "Right after we talk to Delaina."

"At this point, I'm not sure that's wise," said Ben.

"Why?" asked Rem. "She got something to hide?"

"For God's sake, Ben," said Charles. "Let her talk to them. Let's get this cleared up now. Not later."

Crenshaw hesitated, and after a long pause, he walked to his desk and picked up his phone. He hit a number, listened, and spoke. "Delaina, would you come in here, please?" He hung up and returned to his seat just as the door opened, and Delaina poked her head in.

"Yes, sir?"

Ben waved her inside. "Please join us, Delaina. These detectives have a few questions for you."

"Me?" She stepped into the office and closed the door behind her.

"Have a seat, Delaina," said Charles, gesturing at the chair vacated by Barbara.

"We just have a few questions," said Daniels. "I don't suppose we could talk to you alone?"

"Absolutely not," said Ben. "As her attorneys, Charles and I will be present."

"Does she need an attorney?" asked Rem.

"No, I do not," said Delaina. "I have nothing to hide, but it's fine if they stay. It won't change my answers." She smiled and settled back in her seat. "Fire away."

Ben and Charles didn't move, and Daniels spoke first. "How well did you know Reginald Durning?"

She tucked a strand of her blonde hair behind her ear. "Not that well. We were friendly when we saw each other, but that's it."

Rem tapped on the table. "Did Ben Crenshaw ever instruct you to get close to Durning to get information from him?"

Her forehead furrowed. "Excuse me? Why would he do that?"

"That's what we're trying to find out," said Daniels. "But if I were to guess, Durning had been tasked with a major case and an important client."

"Someone who the partners needed to keep happy," added Rem.

"And who perhaps Durning didn't like or didn't want to work with," added Daniels.

"And when he balked," said Rem, "or didn't behave as expected," he tipped his head at Ben, "Ben here, panicked, and sent you in to do damage control."

"Why would he ask me to do that?" asked Delaina.

"It's no secret that Durning was swayed by the opposite sex," said Daniels.

Rem leaned up. "And as Ben's loyal assistant, who I assume he trusts and pays well, you'd be the perfect choice."

She straightened. "Are you insinuating that Ben asked me to sleep with Durning for information?"

Rem nodded. "Yes."

Daniels held up his hands. "And there's no need for shock and indignation. We've had plenty of that. Just a simple yes or no will do."

She sputtered and glanced at Ben, who surprisingly stayed quiet. "Absolutely not," she said. "Ben would never make such a request of me."

"So, he's never asked you to get information?" asked Daniels, raising his brow.

Her body language shifted, and her outrage diminished. "Of course, sometimes I've spoken to staff and followed up on questions from Mr. Crenshaw, but only in a limited capacity. And certainly not in the way you're suggesting."

Rem studied her. "Do you know anything about what Durning was working on the last month he was alive?"

She shook her head. "No." She sat back and pulled on the hem of her jacket. "I don't."

"What about the name Dirk?" asked Daniels. "Are you familiar with it?"

Delaina immediately glanced at Ben and Charles, who remained quiet, but Ben shifted slightly in his seat.

"They can't help you, Delaina," said Rem. "And remember. You're talking to the police. We'd appreciate the truth."

Delaina looked back at them. "No. I don't know any Dirk."

"And if we were to get a warrant for Ben's calendar for the past year?" asked Daniels. "Would we see the name Dirk on it?"

She crossed her arms the way Barb had. "No. You would not."

Ben smiled. "You see, Detectives? We've got nothing to hide." He stood. "Is there anything else?"

Rem glanced at Daniels, who raised his brow at him. "Not at the moment," said Rem, standing, "but I don't believe for a second that this firm, and you, have nothing to hide."

Daniels stood too. "We'll be in touch." He eyed Delaina. "And there's no need to see us out."

"We know the way." Rem stepped toward the door with Daniels, and they left the conference room.

Chapter Twenty-Two

RIDING DOWN THE ELEVATOR, Rem's mind raced with what had occurred during the meeting and before it.

Daniels stood beside him. "I know you're mad, and I get it, but we're going to have to get past this if we're going to move forward. We have a lot to do."

Still angry with Daniels, Rem realized he couldn't keep up the silent treatment and successfully work with his partner to complete the investigation. They'd have to find a workable solution to handle both. Tempted to mention that what came next wouldn't matter if Erin spilled the beans about the secret file, Rem faced his partner. "I understand we've got things to do, but I'm still pissed and may be for a while."

Daniels studied the individual floor lights that illuminated as the elevator descended. "I get it and you're right. I should have told you first."

"No. You should have asked me first. We're partners, Daniels. Decisions like these should be made together."

"I realize that, but it all happened so fast."

"It didn't happen fast enough that you couldn't take five minutes to call me. I know why you didn't. You'd made up your mind, and you didn't want to argue about it. Figured you'd rather ask for forgiveness instead of permission."

"That's not—"

"Yes. It is. Because that's exactly what I would have done."

"And have done."

"Not with something as important as this. And you know it." His anger percolating again, he took a breath and faced the doors again.

The elevator reached the lobby and stopped. Daniels spoke softly. "She's not going to betray us, Rem."

The doors opened, and Rem turned. "Whether or not she does doesn't change the fact that you went behind my back. Maybe that's okay with you, but it's not okay with me. Now I'm big enough to handle that disappointment and focus on this case, but if you think that means I'm over it, I'm not." He turned and strode out of the elevator.

Daniels walked beside him. "We need to work through this. Staying mad is not good right now. We've got a case to solve, and based on what happened in that conference room, CIW's got a client named Dirk nobody wants to discuss."

"You should have thought of that before you gave that USB to Erin." Rem reached the lobby doors.

"C'mon, Rem." Daniels pushed on a door and walked outside along with Rem. "Give me some leeway. She's my sister."

Rem stopped next to a large fountain in the center of the outside courtyard. "But she's not mine. And family or not, Erin's still got a lot to prove, at least to me. You, too, because you don't know her any better than I do. And you need to tell Lexie what you did. She should know."

"Of course I will."

"Fine." Rem turned toward the parking lot. "Then let's talk about the case because I'm done talking about Erin. What's done is done."

"But you're going to stay angry?"

"Pretty much. Now, let's get back to the case."

Daniels ran his hand through his hair. "Fine." He blew out a long breath. "What'd you think about that whole Dirk conversation?"

"They're lying through their teeth. But what I don't get is why? What client could generate that level of fear?"

"If this Dirk is the one who hired Rhonda, then that suggests he's a black bird member. Maybe that explains the fear."

They approached Daniels' car and Rem walked to the passenger side. "Did you see Charles' face? He certainly didn't enjoy discussing Dirk."

"Neither did Delaina." Daniels stopped near the front of his car. "And Barbara Ingram's got a chip the size of this building on her shoulder, and she didn't like you at all."

"Some women are repelled by my natural charisma and charm." He reached for the door handle.

"Don't you mean most?"

Rem smirked and was about to open the car door when a woman walking through the lot approached him. She wore black slacks, a collared shirt and a jacket and her dark hair brushed her shoulders. "Excuse me. Are you Detective Aaron Remalla?"

Thinking the worst, Rem went for his gun. Daniels pulled his too when a broad-shouldered man, dressed similarly to the woman, approached from the other direction.

"Stay right where you are," said Rem, aiming his weapon at the woman. "Who are you?"

Daniels aimed his gun at the man. "And who are you?"

The man, who was easily three to four inches taller than Daniels, held up his hands. "Name's Tito. You Gordon Daniels?"

"Never mind who we are," yelled Daniels. "What do you want?"

"Stay cool," said the woman, who was also holding her hands up. "I'm Tina. Somebody wants to talk to you two."

Rem tightened his grip on his gun. "Ever hear of a phone?"

Tito smiled. "You guys are jumpy."

Daniels spoke with ire. "We don't like it when strangers appear out of nowhere and approach us in a parking lot."

"Who wants to talk to us?" Rem envisioned Erin handing the mysterious Dirk the USB file and Dirk sending his people to kill them.

The woman lowered her hands. "Take it easy. We didn't mean to spook you."

Her arm brushed her jacket and when it moved, Rem caught sight of a holstered gun at her waist. He assumed Tito had a weapon, too. "You're armed."

"We are," said Tina. "But we have permits. We're not here to harm you, fellas. Just to communicate."

"Our boss wants to talk to you," said Tito. He pointed. "He's over there. In the limo."

Rem glanced toward the far side of the lot, where he saw only a few cars parked. A long black stretch limousine was idling on the curb, near the street. Rem imagined Dirk sitting in the car and assumed what that meant. "If you think my partner and I are stupid enough to get in that limo to speak to some mysterious black bird member who wants to kill us, you're stupider than you look."

Tina's forehead furrowed. "What's a black bird member?"

Daniels kept his gun aimed at Tito. "Don't play stupid. We've dealt with you people before and almost got killed. You expect us to do it again?"

Tito lowered his hands. "I don't know what you two do in your free time, but I suggest a nice, long vacation." He glanced toward the limo. "Our boss is in the car and for good reasons, he can't get out of it. He came a long way to talk to you and he doesn't know a thing about any black birds, sparrows, hummingbirds, or whatever the hell you're talking about."

"How are we supposed to believe you?" asked Rem, his heart racing.

Tina threw out her hands. "Guys. Look where we are. In a parking lot in front of an office building where there are plenty of cameras." She pointed at one in the lot. "If we wanted to kill you, it sure wouldn't be here."

Tito gestured at another camera in another area of the lot. "And those same cameras will see you get in the limo, so it's a stupid plan to kill you there, too."

"Our boss only wants to talk," said Tina. "We saw you stop here and figured this was a good place to approach."

Rem lowered his weapon when a man and woman walked through the lot and stared at the four of them. He pulled his badge and flashed it at the couple, who hurried into the building.

"Now you've got two witnesses who saw you guys with us," said Tina.

His heart rate slowing, Rem held on to his gun. "Who is this boss of yours?"

"It's better if you see for yourself," said Tito. "But you're going to want to talk to him."

"What's this about?" asked Daniels, lowering his weapon.

"Your current case," said Tito.

Rem glanced at Daniels, who stared back at Tito. "We're keeping our guns," said Daniels.

Tito frowned. "Keep them holstered."

"We'll holster them when we get to the limo and see who we're talking to." Rem waved his free hand at Tina. "After you."

Tina turned toward the limo. Holding their weapons at their side, Rem and Daniels followed. Tito took up the rear, but along with Daniels, Rem kept his eye on him.

They approached the limo, and Tina knocked on the rear door. The tinted window rolled down, and Rem gaped at the man in the back seat. It was Sammy Caruso.

· · · • • • • • · · ·

Looking over Rem's shoulder, Daniels couldn't believe his eyes. The powerful senator who'd almost become president was sitting in the back of the limousine.

Caruso smiled. "Detectives. Please join me."

Tina opened the car door and stepped back.

Rem straightened and met Daniels' gaze. Daniels hesitated, but then nodded. They might as well hear what the man had to say.

Rem turned, holstered his gun, entered the limo, and got in the back. Daniels did the same. With Caruso in view, they sat in the back seat, separated from the driver by a closed partition. Caruso's salt and pepper hair, round face with creases at his eyes, rings on his fingers and impeccable suit, gave him the look of a made man, which Daniels supposed was fitting, since that's what he was.

Tina closed the door, and Caruso studied them. He held a crystal glass half-filled with an amber colored liquid. He gestured at a bar along the side of the limo. "You two want a drink?"

"We're on duty," said Rem.

"I won't tell," said Caruso with a chuckle. He swirled the liquid in his glass. "I apologize for the abrupt introductions, but under my current circumstances, I have to be careful."

Daniels recalled reading that Caruso's trial was due to start soon in Illinois. "Are you supposed to be in this state?"

Caruso narrowed his eyes at Daniels. "Which state would that be, Detective Daniels?"

Daniels got the implication.

"I'm guessing Illinois?" asked Rem.

"Exactly," said Caruso. "I never left. Right?"

"Right," said Daniels. "And we never saw you."

"Good." He rested his glass on his knee. "Now that you're here, let's get to the point." He lowered his voice. "Where is my grandson?"

"We've been asking ourselves the same question," said Rem.

"You two are investigating Reginald Durning's murder?" asked Caruso. "The murder Jerry Lee witnessed?"

"We are," said Daniels.

"And how the hell is it possible that you can't find Jerry Lee?" asked Caruso, showing signs of agitation.

"Mr. Caruso," said Rem, "there's an APB out on Jerry. Every cop out there is looking for him."

"We've checked with his family, friends, and acquaintances," said Daniels, "but he hasn't turned up."

Caruso scowled. "I just left my distraught daughter. Jerry Lee is twenty years old. How is he outsmarting two seasoned detectives?"

Rem adjusted his position on the seat. "We believe he's found someone to hole up with until the heat dies down, or until the killer is found."

Caruso's gaze turned steely. "You think this killer is looking for him?"

"We're sure of it," added Daniels.

Caruso's voice turned icy. "And how can you be sure this killer hasn't already found him, and my grandson's body isn't floating down some river?"

"Because if that were true, we'd have discovered him by now," said Rem.

"Why is that?" asked Caruso.

"Because we're familiar with this killer," said Daniels. "She's an assassin, and she's not shy. If Jerry Lee were dead, she'd want everyone to know it, especially her boss."

Caruso's eyes glittered with anger. "An assassin? Jerry Lee saw an assassin murder her target? Shit." He took a drink of his beverage. "You know who this assassin is?"

Rem glanced at Daniels. "We have some history with her. We call her Rhonda, but that's not her actual name."

"Who does she work for?" asked Caruso.

"If we knew that, we'd arrest him," said Rem.

Caruso snorted. "Would you?"

Daniels bristled at the question. "We're not on the take, Mr. Caruso. We want to find and protect Jerry Lee and arrest Rhonda and whoever she's working with, but it's not that simple."

"If Jerry were to come out in the open now," said Rem, "we'd give him protection, but that's no guarantee. We have reason to suspect that the people Rhonda works for have friends in high places." He paused. "And to be honest, until Rhonda is found, it might be better that Jerry isn't."

"You're saying he's safer in hiding?" asked Caruso. "Who are these people?"

"We don't know, but we're working on it," said Rem. "We know Rhonda's looking for Jerry, but if we can find her first—"

"You won't find her," said Caruso. He gripped his glass. "Not alive, at least."

Daniels didn't like the sound of that. "What do you mean?"

Caruso met his gaze. "I will do whatever it takes to protect my grandson."

"You don't know who or where she is, either," said Rem.

Caruso took another drink, reached for a bottle on the bar, and added more liquor to his glass. "The person who hired her will kill her for her dumb mistake. The only way she can save herself is to kill Jerry first. And if you arrest her, and Jerry comes forward, Jerry's life is still at risk while your assassin lives." He set the bottle of liquor down. "Which is why Rhonda has to die." He recapped the bottle.

"You kill her, and you could make a new enemy," said Daniels. "This boss of hers may not like your involvement."

Caruso's tone turned menacing. "I have plenty of enemies, Detectives."

"Not like this one, you don't," said Rem. "We've learned firsthand that this enemy will use the ones you love to get what he wants."

Daniels shifted forward. "If he's willing to let Rhonda kill Jerry to protect his organization, then he's willing to do anything. But even with Rhonda's mistake, she's still a valuable asset, and he'll likely want to keep her around. If you get involved, there's no telling what he'd do."

"If he keeps her around," said Caruso, "he's a fool." He sneered. "And if Rhonda hurts Jerry, her fate is sealed. I don't care who she is or who she works for."

"What about your daughter?" asked Daniels. "Unless she agrees to go back with you to Illinois, you're putting her at risk."

Caruso arched an eyebrow. "He wouldn't be stupid enough."

Rem sighed. "Mr. Caruso. We understand your worry and need to protect your grandson. But before you send your goons to look for him, or go after Rhonda, give us some time." He paused. "We may be on the verge of some revelations that might give us some insight into who this boss and Rhonda are, and that could lead to a slew of other conspirators who might be just as dangerous as Rhonda."

"Right now," said Daniels, "Jerry Lee is safe. We don't know where he is, but neither does Rhonda, and that may be the best possible solution, for the moment."

Rem nodded. "We know his mother is scared, but someone called her and told her Jerry was alive."

Caruso lowered his voice. "For all you know, that man is dead now, and so is Jerry Lee."

"If that's true, we'd know it," said Daniels. "Jerry Lee is out there, and he's scared and wants to come home, but he hasn't."

"He's with somebody who obviously knows the stakes, and so far, they've protected him," added Rem. "We'll still do everything we can to find him and bring him in safely, but as a second option, it's not a bad one."

Caruso leaned forward. "My grandson is being hunted by a killer that you two can't find. And he's being protected by some stranger you two can't find, either." He aimed a finger encircled by a large diamond ring. "And you expect me to believe that you guys can figure this shit out before Jerry winds up dead?"

Daniels understood how it looked. "We know it's not ideal."

"Ideal?" yelled Caruso with a glare.

Caruso's ire almost made Daniels go for his gun.

Caruso pointed with two fingers. "Let me tell you bozos something. If Jerry Lee dies, and you two clowns are still walking around, the three of us are gonna have a little chat, and believe me, only one of us is walking away from it."

Rem straightened. "You're threatening two police officers."

Caruso cackled. "You must be the bright one."

His heart thumping, Daniels spoke calmly. "Threatening us won't make us work any harder. We're already dealing with one dangerous boss. Two doesn't make much more of a difference."

Caruso downed his whole drink, and with a grimace, he set the glass down beside the bottle. "I don't care who or what you're dealing with. And if I have to go to war to protect my family, I will. I'll burn the whole house down if I have to." He narrowed his eyes to slits. "Nothing is more important than my family."

"We understand that," said Rem.

"Good. I'm glad." Caruso sat back. "You do what you have to do, and I'll do the same."

"Mr. Caruso, we'd highly encourage you to let us do our jobs," said Daniels. "Let us try to figure this out with as little bloodshed as possible."

Caruso studied them with fiery eyes. Twirling his pinky ring, he cursed and set his jaw. "I'll give you guys two days. You don't figure this out by then, then it's my turn, and believe me," he sat back and ran the back of his fingers over his jaw, "I don't play by the rules."

Rem sighed. "Mr. Caruso—"

Caruso rapped on the window. "We're done here."

The door opened, and Tito looked into the car. "Right this way, gentle-men." He waved his hand at the parking lot.

Caruso looked out the opposite window as if he'd dismissed them and moved on to the next problem. Deciding that arguing with a mobster was a poor choice, Daniels climbed out of the car and Rem joined him. Tito got into the limo and closed the door. Tina got into the front passenger seat, closed the door and the limo drove off, leaving Rem and Daniels standing in the parking lot.

Daniels stared in disbelief as the limo turned onto the street. "I can't believe that just happened."

Rem cursed. "We just got threatened by a mobster."

"Even worse, we've got forty-eight hours to find Rhonda, save Jerry, and take down the black birds." He put his hands on his hips and eyed the ground.

"I guess it's better than twenty-four."

Daniels looked up. "What do you want to do?"

Rem paced. "As much as I'm pissed at you for giving that USB to Erin, you better pray she comes through for us." He put his hands on his hips. "On the plus side, Caruso didn't say he'd kill us. He just said he'd start his own search if we didn't find Jerry."

Daniels watched the limo turn a corner and disappear. "If Caruso's goons start making waves, there's no telling what they'll stir up."

"Never mind that. If Jerry Lee winds up dead, we're officially toast."

Daniels remembered his schedule. "And I've got to be in court tomorrow." He shook his head at the insanity of it all. "Even though you're pissed at me, I hope you'll still pick up Marjorie."

"I'm mad at you, not her. Of course I'll get her." Rem started walking toward Daniels' car. "Maybe while I'm waiting for her, I can figure out our route to Bolivia."

Daniels sighed. "I'll pack a bag."

Chapter Twenty-Three

MIKEY OPENED HER EYES, uncrossed her legs, and shook out her hands. Grounding herself as Lena had taught her, she stretched her arms and neck, stood, and stretched some more. She'd been meditating since Rem had left for work. He'd been up early and so had she, since she wanted to get in a meditation session before Mason picked her up for the paranormal medium conference.

Feeling more centered, she sat on the couch and reviewed what she could recall. Since her last session with Lena, Mikey had been focusing less on the cigarette smoking man and more on Vera. Not much had happened in her last two meditations, but in this one, Mikey had sensed a difference. Now that she and Rem were cleaning out the upstairs closet, her sessions had felt less cumbersome, and she'd entered them with less friction. This morning, she'd slipped right into it.

She recalled watching the people around the fire at the grove, seeing her sister, Margaret, and the masked man smoking his cigarette, and Victor. Observing Vera and Nathan kneeling in front of the fire, Mikey would usually feel her panic and fear rise, but this time, she'd been calm and detached, as Lena had advised her. She'd simply watched the scene unfold, only this time, the masked man didn't fire the gun. Margaret moved in front of him, blocking Mikey's view, and Mikey had focused on Vera and Nathan. For a second, Vera had turned her head, seen Mikey, and smiled.

Entranced, Mikey had stared back, until Victor had stepped toward the fire, breaking the connection between her and Vera. Startled, Mikey had come out of her meditation, but without the ache of regret and loss.

Relieved to have made progress, she stood and walked into the kitchen. Checking the time, she saw she had fifteen minutes before Mason picked her up. She was tempted to call Rem and tell him about her success, but she decided to wait until later.

Grabbing some apple juice from the fridge, she pulled a glass from the cabinet and poured herself some. She returned the bottle to the fridge and reached for her glass when a strange tingle ran up her spine. The unexpected sensation made her shiver. Wondering what was happening, she closed her eyes and tuned in. The tingles grew and ran down her arms, and suddenly nervous, she opened her eyes, half expecting to see someone standing in the room with her.

Not seeing anyone, she rubbed her arms as the tingles lessened, but the sense of presence did not. Certain she wasn't alone, she walked back into the living room, and then into the bedroom, but no one was there. Unnerved, she double checked the locks on the front and back doors, but they were secure.

She returned to the kitchen, and with shaky fingers, drank her juice, wondering what she'd felt. Had she connected with someone from the other side? Had Vera made a tentative attempt at communication? Mason felt tingles when a spirit was nearby. Was that what she was picking up on?

Making a mental note to ask her brother several questions on their way to the conference, Mikey went into the bedroom to grab her jacket and purse.

· · • • • • • • · ·

Rem sat at his desk, reviewing his notes to determine what to do next. After Sammy Caruso's visit, he and Daniels made another stop at Patricia Caruso's to discuss her father. All she told them was that she'd asked him to go home and stay out of it, but he'd insisted she return to Chicago, where he could keep her safe. She'd refused, though. Until Jerry Lee was found, she wasn't going anywhere. He'd left frustrated and angry.

After leaving Patricia's, they'd made another run by Bertrand's pawn shop, but it was closed. They talked to the undercover officer watching the store, who'd told them Bertrand had arrived as scheduled that morning, but had left an hour later, and hadn't returned.

They'd spent the rest of the day digging into Elana Kentworth, Nicole Barstein, and Delaina Desmond, following up with clients on the client list, and finding out what they could about Arnold Bertrand, Ben Crenshaw, Charles Willoughby, and Barbara Ingram. Arnold's background check had revealed a stint in the military and a few years when he'd fallen off the map, but nothing else of much consequence. He'd lived in the area for ten years and his shop had been open for nine of them. As far as the rest, they'd learned nothing new and found no red flags.

Rubbing his eyes, Rem sat back in his seat and laid his head back. It had been another night of not great sleep, and he wondered how much longer he could go with just coffee and sugar to keep him awake. After Daniels had left to go to court, Rem had snuck one of his partner's protein bars out of a drawer and ate it. It helped a little, but not much.

Cracking an eye open, he checked the time. He'd have to leave in fifteen minutes to pick up Marjorie for her appointment. Looking around the squad room, he saw it was quiet. Monk and Manetti weren't at their desks and Crow was in Lozano's office, talking on the phone. A couple of other detectives were at their desks, working.

Thinking of Sammy Caruso again, he wondered about Erin. Daniels had contacted her about moving fast, and she'd said she was doing her best. Rem still didn't like it, but all he could do was hope she wasn't lying to Daniels. After Daniels had told Lexie what he'd done, she'd been just as shocked as Rem. She'd questioned Daniels about the wisdom of his decision, but Daniels continued to assert Erin's trustworthiness. In the end, Lexie could only do the same as Rem—hope and pray for the best.

Standing to refill his coffee mug, Rem stopped when his phone rang. He set his mug down, and seeing Cain's name on the display, his heart thumped, and he answered. "Cain?"

"Aaron?"

Hearing his cousin's strained voice, Rem sat in his seat. "You okay?"

"I need to talk to you." His voice shook.

"What's wrong?" asked Rem, alarmed. "Where are you?"

"I...I'm at my apartment. Can...can you stop by?"

Rem checked his watch. "I've got to be somewhere."

"Please. It's important."

"What is it? Are you in trouble?"

"I...I just...I need to talk. I promise. It won't take long. But it needs to be now. Please."

Rem debated what to do. Knowing it was critical to talk to Cain, he made a quick decision. "Wait there. I'm on my way."

"Thank you." Cain whispered and hung up.

Cursing, Rem quickly dialed Marjorie's number. She picked up on the second ring. "Don't tell me," she said. "You're grabbing coffee on the way, and you'll be late."

"Hey, Marj. No coffee, but I will be late. Any chance this doctor can take you a little later?"

"How much later?"

Rem held his head. "How about thirty minutes later?"

She chuckled over the phone. "Are you kidding? He's always running behind. I'll call and tell them we're on our way, but are slightly delayed. No big deal."

Relief flooded through Rem. "Marjorie, you're a peach. Just stay put and I'll be there as soon as I can."

"Okay. See you soon." She hung up.

Rem hung up too, grabbed his jacket and ran out of the squad room.

· · · • • • • • • · ·

Waiting for Rem, Marjorie sat on the couch, grabbed a magazine, and flipped through it. She'd taken the morning off work and after her mother had picked up J.P. to take him to daycare, she'd showered, had breakfast and done what she'd been doing for the last three months–rested. Hopeful that after this appointment, the doctor would clear her for more activities so Gordon could relax, she flipped through the magazine, reading about the proper soil in which to grow herbs and glancing at various recipes.

Bored, she closed it and stood to use the restroom when her phone rang. She picked up, and not recognizing the number, she answered. "Hello?"

"Is this Marjorie Daniels?" asked an unfamiliar male voice.

"Yes. This is she."

"Mrs. Daniels. I'm a nurse at Mercy Hospital. Your husband's just been brought into the emergency room in critical condition."

Marjorie's heart stopped. "What are you talking about? He's supposed to be in court today." Fear rippled through her, and she clutched her chest.

"There was a shooting. Your husband was hit. I was told to call you because he's...he's...well it's very serious."

Marjorie dropped her jaw. "How serious?"

"Mrs. Daniels. It's imperative you get here as soon as possible. He...may not have long."

Terrified, Marjorie tried to breathe. "I...I'm on my way." She hung up, and barely able to think, she grabbed her phone and purse and ran out the door.

···•••••···

Frustrated, Rem pounded on Cain's door. "Cain? Answer the door." He'd arrived a few minutes earlier and had been knocking since, but Cain hadn't answered. Halfway tempted to break the door down, he smacked his palm against the door again. "Cain? Are you in there?"

He grabbed his phone to call his cousin when the neighbor's door opened. He stepped out and glowered at Rem. "Hell. I can't get a moment's peace even when he's gone."

Rem lowered his phone. "I'm here to see Cain."

"That's obvious, but he's not home."

"How do you know that?"

"Because I heard him leave. In case you haven't realized, the walls are thin around here."

"You sure it was Cain?"

"Who else would it be?"

Rem cursed his cousin. "Thank you."

The neighbor returned to his apartment. Rem called Cain, but it rang and went to voicemail. Cain never picked up.

Rem ran to the stairs and raced down them. He dialed Cain's number again, but still didn't get an answer. He left a stern message for Cain to call him as soon as possible and explain what was going on. Hoping to get to Marjorie's before she was too late for her appointment, he jumped in his car, backed out of the space and headed toward Daniels' house.

Twenty minutes later, Rem pulled up into the driveway of Daniels' home and saw Marjorie's car wasn't there. Concerned, he parked, got out, and jogged up to the door. "Marjorie?" He knocked, but no one answered. "Marjorie?" He tried the door again.

When she didn't show, Rem used his key to open it. He pushed the door open, but the house was quiet. "Marj? Where are you?" He stepped inside. "Hello?"

Seeing no one, he tried calling her phone, but it went to voicemail. "Hey, Marj. It's Rem. I'm here, but you're not. If you went to the doctor on your own, don't tell Daniels, because he's going to kill me for being late. Please call me when you get this." He hung up and, uncomfortable, he shut the door and looked around, hoping she'd drive up after running a quick errand. When she didn't, something nudged at him, but he didn't know what. Angry at Cain for ditching him and making him late, he tried his cousin again but still got no answer.

After waiting a while, he guessed she'd gone to the doctor on her own, and uncertain of what else to do, he left the house, locked up, and headed back to the station. On the way, he continued to call Cain and Marjorie, but neither answered. That same anxious feeling crept through him as he returned to the squad room. Manetti and Monk were still gone and Crow remained in Lozano's office.

Seeing him through the glass, she waved him in. Groaning to himself, he walked to the office door and opened it. "You want to see me?"

"Come in. Have a seat."

Telling himself to stay cool, he entered and sat across from her.

"How's it going with the Durning investigation?"

Rem shrugged. "You know what we know. You get our report every evening." That was only a partial lie. Since she'd be required to report it, they'd left out Sammy Caruso's visit.

"About those daily reports, I know you two think you're funny, but you can leave out the lunch and bathroom breaks."

"You said you wanted to know what we were doing." He sat back. "Now you know."

"Listen, Remalla. I know you and Daniels don't like me, but I'm here because the chief assigned me, and it's not my fault Lozano's in trouble."

"We never said it was."

"Your attitude says otherwise."

"That may have something to do with our first meeting."

She tossed her pen on the desk. "What? Did I hurt your feelings?"

Rem set his jaw and took a breath. "If you want this relationship to improve, you're going to have to make more of an effort."

"That goes both ways."

"Daniels and I are all for it, but when you tell us how to do our jobs, we have a problem with that."

She scoffed. "Men. So damn sensitive." She sat back.

"I'm sure HR would love to hear that."

She frowned at him. "You hear from Daniels today?"

Rem shook his head. "No. And I don't expect to. He could be in court for a while." He asked the obvious. "Any word on the internal investigation of Lozano?"

"You know I'm not privy to that."

Rem wondered if that was true. "Can't hurt to ask."

"I'm sure we'll hear something soon enough." She moved a file on her desk. "What are you working on while Daniels is out?"

He gave her a quick update on his plans when he got back to his desk.

"About that stakeout of Bertrand's shop. I'm removing it after tomorrow."

"What for?"

"Patterson has drilled into me to watch our expenses. I can't justify an undercover car watching a pawn shop that's shown no activity other than customers pawning their goods."

"In other words, you want to impress the chief."

"Wouldn't you?" She sat up. "You give me good reason to keep up the surveillance, I'll do it. But until then, it's over."

Rem didn't like it but couldn't offer anything credible to change her mind.

"And I think it's time to go public with Jerry Lee Caruso."

Rem shook his head. "I don't think that's a good idea."

"I'm aware, but if someone's seen him, we need to know. You can't argue with that, but you're probably going to, anyway."

Rem understood her logic. Using the media was a good way to find Jerry Lee, but it could also get him killed. "All I want to do is keep him safe."

"I want the same. We played it your way for a while. Now it's time to change tactics." She dropped her pen into a jar of them. "Let the mother know so she doesn't freak out when she sees it on the news."

Rem debated arguing, but based on Crow's tone, it was pointless. "I'll tell her."

"Good." She asked several more questions and, antsy, he squirmed in his seat. It bothered him that neither Marjorie nor Cain had called him back. Ready to get out of there, he leaned up. "Anything else you'd like to tell me how to do?"

Her eyes narrowed at him. "I admire Lozano more and more each day."

"The man knew what he was doing."

She stared at him. "That's it. You can go."

"Thank you." Rem stood when his phone rang. He left Lozano's office and hopeful it was Marjorie or Cain, he frowned when he didn't recognize the number on the display. He answered. "This is Remalla."

"Rem? It's Parsons."

Rem recognized the name of the patrol officer. "What's up, Parsons?"

"I'm at the scene of a traffic accident. We arrived not long after it happened."

That anxious feeling bloomed, and Rem instantly relived the night another officer called with news of Jennie's accident. "What's wrong?" His heart raced, and he felt slightly dizzy.

"A car drove into the intersection and was broadsided. The ambulance just took the injured driver away."

Rem held his breath. "Why are you calling me?"

"I tried Daniels, but he's not answering. It's his wife, Rem. The vic is Marjorie Daniels."

Everything spun, and Rem took a second to collect himself. Feeling sick and keeping Parsons on the line to get more information, Rem sprinted out of the squad room.

Chapter Twenty-Four

Anxious, Rem sat in the emergency room waiting area, his head in his hands. Immediately after arriving, he'd checked in up front and they'd told him Marjorie had arrived, but because he wasn't family, he couldn't go back. He'd told the nurse about Marjorie's pregnancy and the nurse told him she'd let the doctor know and to have a seat.

That had felt like hours ago, but he knew it was maybe an hour at most. He'd called everyone he could think of to get a hold of Daniels, and his partner had finally called him back, saying little more than he was on his way to the hospital. Rem had heard the worry and fear in his voice but also his questions. Rem could imagine what he was thinking. Why was Marjorie driving? Where had Rem been?

He heard the outer doors open, but instead of Daniels, he saw Mikey run in. Seeing Rem, she ran over.

"Rem. Honey," she said breathlessly. She sat beside Rem. "I came as fast as I could. How is she?"

Rem sat up. "I don't know. They won't tell me anything. Parsons, the officer who called me, said he was sure she had a concussion. She wasn't lucid at the scene and couldn't tell him anything about what happened."

"What about the baby?"

Dejected, Rem shook his head. "I don't know."

"Where's Daniels?"

"On his way." He set his elbows on his knees and held his head again. "This is all my fault."

"Honey, no it isn't." She put her hand on his back.

"I was supposed to be there." He looked up. "I was supposed to pick her up."

"You told her that. She said she would wait. You couldn't have known."

Rem glanced at the doors leading into the treatment area. "It doesn't matter. I never should have gone to see Cain." Worried, he bounced his foot.

"He told you he wanted to talk." Mikey slid her hand into his. "This isn't on you."

Glad she was there, Rem squeezed her fingers. "I just want to know that she and the baby are okay." He eyed the ceiling. "God, please let them be okay."

"They will be. Marjorie's a tough lady." She leaned close. "Just take a breath. It will be fine."

Rem went back to studying the floor. "How'd you get here?"

"I called a rideshare. Mason would have come, but he's got a presentation. I told him I'd call him as soon as I heard anything."

Distracted, Rem kept staring at the closed doors, willing a nurse or doctor to come out and give them an update, but they didn't. The outer doors did open, though, and Daniels ran in, his hair disheveled and his eyes wide.

Rem stood.

"Where is she?" asked Daniels, running over.

"Still in emergency," said Rem. "I haven't heard anything."

Daniels eyed the front desk where a nurse sat and raced over. "I'm Detective Gordon Daniels. You brought my wife in. Marjorie Daniels. I need to see her."

The nurse checked a monitor. "Be with you in a second, Mr. Daniels. Have a seat."

"I don't want to have a seat. I want to see my wife. You know she's three months pregnant?"

The nurse was unfazed. "We do, and you'll see her soon." She left the desk and went behind a partition.

"Damn it." He gripped his head.

Rem, his stomach churning, put his hand on Daniels' elbow. "She'll be okay."

Daniels whirled on him. "What did Parsons say?"

Rem reiterated Parson's account of what happened—that Marjorie must have run the light and was broad-sided by a delivery van. Parsons suspected she had a concussion because she was in and out of consciousness and not lucid.

Daniels cursed, started to pace, then stopped and stared at Rem. "Where were you?"

Rem's heart fell. "I got a call from Cain. He said he wanted to talk, and that it was important. I called Marjorie and told her I'd be late. She said that was fine."

Daniels' eyes widened, and he yelled. "You went to see Cain?"

Rem slumped. "Yes."

Daniels set his jaw. "And what did he tell you?"

"Nothing. He wasn't there."

Daniels' look of shock became a glare. "And now my wife is in a hospital because you put Cain first?"

"Daniels, I—"

"Don't you dare say you're sorry. Don't you dare. You yelled at me when I trusted Erin...and now you go off and trust Cain? When he's done nothing but lie and accuse you?"

"Daniels, I understand why—"

Daniels raised his finger. "Don't go there. Don't tell me you understand." He aimed his finger at the nurse's desk. "My wife is in the hospital. She's pregnant. I trusted you to take her to the doctor because I didn't want something like this to happen. But you didn't show, and she drove herself, and now...now..." He gripped his neck. "God. If...if..." He turned away.

Rem made one last attempt. "I know you don't want to hear it, but I am sorry. She said she would wait. I don't know why she left...I...I..." He dropped his head. "I don't know what else to say." Mikey came up beside him and put her arm around him.

Daniels turned back, his eyes flashing. "I think you've said enough."

Rem understood his friend's anger and accepted it, because it wasn't any worse than the anger he felt for himself. He knew how it looked.

The doors to the treatment area slid open, and a nurse stepped out. "Mr. Daniels. You can come back. The doctor's with her now."

Without saying a word, Daniels followed the nurse behind the doors.

Crestfallen, Rem leaned over, put his hands on his knees, and tried to breathe. Mikey stroked his back. "He's upset. Don't take anything he said seriously."

"He's right. I let him down. I should have been there."

Mikey tugged his arm and pulled him toward a chair where he sat. "He'll understand once he realizes Marjorie's okay. You two have been through worse than this."

Rem groaned. "I don't know. This is pretty bad. And we don't know yet if she and the baby are okay. If they're not..." Weary, he looked up at Mikey.

"Let's not think the worst, all right? Let's deal with this one step at a time." She squeezed his arm.

Rem put his hand over hers. "I'm glad you're here."

She took his hand again and rested her head against his shoulder. "Me too."

Rem's phone rang, and he pulled it out of his pocket. "It's Parsons." Wondering why the officer was calling him again, Rem answered. "This is Rem."

"Rem? How's Mrs. Daniels?"

Rem could hear traffic in the background. "Don't know. She's still in Emergency. Where are you?"

"Still at the scene. We've cleared out the vehicles, but Reagan and I are investigating what happened."

His head throbbing, Rem pinched the bridge of his nose. "What'd you learn?"

"We were certain she must have run the light, but now we're not so sure."

Rem sat straight. "What do you mean?"

"Well, we've got a witness here who says it was intentional."

Rem sucked in a sharp breath.

"I know you're at the hospital, but is there any way you can come to the scene? I think you're going to want to talk to this guy."

Rem stood. "Text me the address. I'll be there as soon as possible." He hung up.

"What is it?" asked Mikey.

"It's about Marjorie's accident." He eyed the doors Daniels had disappeared behind. "Can you stay? In case Daniels comes out and needs company?" He tucked his phone back into his pocket.

"Of course." She stood. "What's going on?"

Rem gave her a quick kiss and ran toward the exit. "I'll call you." He dashed out of the hospital and into the parking lot.

·········

Approaching the intersection of the accident, Rem pulled into a gas station at the corner where a police cruiser was parked. One lane was still closed as firefighters cleared debris from the streets, but otherwise traffic moved smoothly. Trying not to think about Marjorie, he parked near the cruiser and got out. He spotted Parsons and his partner, Jim Reagan, talking to a man outside the gas station, and he jogged over. "Parsons."

Parsons looked over. "Hey, Rem. Thanks for coming. Any word on Mrs. Daniels?"

Rem shook his head. "No. Nothing." He said hello to Reagan, who gestured at the short man standing with them. "This Eric Lamar." Middle-aged with brown hair and a mustache, Eric shook Rem's hand.

"Mr. Lamar, this is Detective Aaron Remalla," said Parsons. "Can you tell him what you told us?"

Lamar nodded. "Sure. Yeah. I was at the intersection when the accident happened. I was in the left lane, behind another car and I could see the lady who got hit."

"What happened?" asked Rem.

"She was in the middle lane, at the front, and another car came up behind her. It hit her."

Rem stilled. "What do you mean? By accident?"

"No," said Lamar. "It was intentional. It happened so fast, it was hard for me to comprehend. This car pulled up behind the lady's and hit her. The lady's car jolted forward, then the second vehicle hit the gas. I could hear tires squeal. And the lady's car got pushed right into oncoming traffic. I saw the whole thing."

"What happened next?" asked Reagan.

Lamar waved at the intersection. "The accident happened. That poor woman got hit. All the traffic stopped, and the other car sped around the damage and took off."

"Did you get a license plate?" asked Rem, praying the answer was yes.

The man sighed. "No. I didn't. But I told these guys the type of car it was and who I saw behind the wheel."

"We've got an APB out on the car," said Reagan.

Rem's hope bloomed again. "Who was behind the wheel?"

"Blonde lady," said Lamar. "Pretty. I only saw a profile, but for a second, she touched her face, and I saw her nails. She was wearing blue nail polish. I don't know why I noticed that, but I did. I hope it helps."

Rem almost had to sit down. His stomach twisted, and it was hard to catch his breath.

"You okay, Remalla?" asked Parsons.

Rem shook his head to clear it. "You sure about this, Mr. Lamar?"

Lamar put his hands on his hips. "Sure, I'm sure. It's why I stuck around after the accident. To tell the cops what happened."

Parsons shot a thumb at the gas station. "We checked the video from the station. There's a camera that caught part of the intersection. Mr. Lamar is right. Another car pushed Marjorie Daniels' vehicle straight into traffic. We can't see the plates or the driver, but it confirms Mr. Lamar's account."

Cold fury raced through Rem, and he had to take a second to calm himself. Based on Lamar's description and recalling Erin's blue nail polish from the other evening, Erin had been the woman behind the wheel. "Thank you, Mr. Lamar. You've been very helpful."

"What do you want us to do?" asked Parsons.

"File your report," said Rem, "and I'll take it from here. Thanks."

"You got it," said Parsons. "Tell Daniels we're all praying for Marjorie."

"I will." Rem turned and ran back to his car.

Chapter Twenty-Five

REM WAITED AS THE elevator ascended to the eighth floor of the office building where Smith Electronics was located. After leaving the scene of the accident, he'd debated what to do. He'd called Mikey, but she didn't have any updates. Then he'd called Erin. Daniels had given Rem her number, but he'd never used it until now. When the voicemail picked up without it ringing, his stomach dropped again. Her phone was either dead or turned off. Hanging up without leaving a message, he made up his mind and headed to her place of business. If she was there and had been all day, then she'd have her alibi, but if she wasn't...

The elevator dinged, stopped, and Rem raced off when the doors opened. He approached the receptionist sitting beneath the big block letters that said *Smith Electronics* and flashed his badge. "I'm Detective Aaron Remalla. I need to see Erin Gerard immediately."

The receptionist's brow furrowed, and she picked up the phone. "Let me see if I can reach her."

Rem waited as she dialed a number and spoke to someone. She lowered the phone. "I'm sorry. Erin didn't come in today."

That same fury rushed through him. "Is that her supervisor you're speaking with?"

"It's a coworker. Her name's Nancy."

"Can I talk to Nancy, please?"

The receptionist told Nancy that she was handing the phone over to Rem. Rem took it and kept his voice steady when he spoke. "This is Detective Remalla, Nancy. Do you know why Erin didn't come in today?"

Nancy paused. "Um, well, she called and said her aunt up in LA had some sort of medical episode and she needed to drive up and see her."

"What Aunt is that? Do you remember?"

Nancy's voice dropped in volume when she spoke to someone else and then came back on the line. "I think she said it was her Aunt Valora? Something like that. Why? Is everything okay?"

"Everything's great. Thanks, Nancy." He handed the phone to the receptionist. "Appreciate your help." He jogged back to the elevator, recalling the conversation from dinner the other night. After Erin's revelation, she and Daniels had discussed their pasts. Erin had confided that her mother had worked as an accountant at a well-known beverage company for years. Their only close relative had been her mother's best friend, Valora Mitchell, who Erin had affectionately called Aunt Valora. Valora and Erin's mother had worked together for over two decades at the same company.

Glad he'd been paying attention, he took the elevator back down to the lobby and returned to his car. Sitting behind the wheel, he grabbed his phone and searched the internet for the contact information of the beverage company in LA. He found it and called and after several redirections and waiting on hold, he finally got hold of someone who'd worked with Erin's Mother and Valora. He introduced himself and said he was trying to reach Valora.

The woman told him to hold on. He waited again, and after a few seconds, another woman answered.

"Yes?" she said. "This is Valora."

Rem sat up and told Valora who he was. "This is the Valora who knows Erin Gerard?"

"It is. What's this about? Is Erin okay?"

"She's fine. I know this may sound odd, but can you tell me if you've been at work all day?"

She paused. "That's a strange question. But yes. I have."

Rem closed his eyes in defeat. "Have you seen Erin lately?"

"No. Not in several weeks. Detective, you're scaring me. What's going on?"

Rem gripped the wheel. "I'm sorry, Valora. I didn't mean to worry you. Erin's fine. When I see her, I'll tell her to give you a call."

"But—"

Rem hung up the phone. Anger, sadness, and dejection bubbled up. Erin had not only betrayed them, but she'd gone after Marjorie. If Daniels didn't kill her first, Rem certainly planned to. "She can call you from prison, Valora," he muttered to himself. He threw the car in reverse, backed out of the space, and screeched out of the lot.

His next stop was Erin's apartment. Not caring who saw him or what attention he attracted, he banged on her door, yelling her name, but she didn't answer. He continued to call her phone, but the voicemail always picked up without the phone ringing. He didn't leave any messages because he didn't trust what he would say to her. Imagining she was halfway to Bolivia by now, he gave up on her apartment and returned to his car, prepared to put out an APB on her when his phone rang.

Seeing it was Mikey, he quickly answered. "Mikey? Any news?"

"I saw Daniels, honey." Her voice was quiet. "Marjorie's got a severe concussion, a broken rib and wrist. They're keeping her overnight. Marjorie's sister and Lozano just arrived too."

Rem gave thanks that Marjorie's injuries weren't worse, and that Lozano and Marjorie's sister were at the hospital. "How's Daniels?"

"He's a mess. They're trying to find a room for Marjorie. He just needed a breather because...because..." She paused and her breath caught.

"Because what?" Rem held his breath when he heard her voice shake.

Mikey cleared her throat and spoke softly. "Oh, honey...she lost the baby." Her words faded as she spoke, and she took a shuddered breath.

Rem's world shifted, and his vision briefly spun. "No." He shut his eyes. "Don't tell me that. Please don't."

Mikey composed herself. "The good news is that she's okay. She'll make a full recovery."

Rem dropped his head. "No. She won't." Emotion rippled up inside him and he found it hard to breathe.

"Daniels, he's in a daze. He came out for a second and went back in to see her. Marjorie's still in and out. I'm not even sure how much she knows yet."

Rem leaned his head against the wheel, trying to pull his jumbled thoughts together. He thought of Daniels and could only imagine how his partner must be feeling. No matter how mad Daniels might be, Rem knew he had to be there. "I'm on my way." He said his goodbyes to Mikey, hung up, and, unable to move, stared blankly out the windshield.

Chapter Twenty-Six

Sitting in the small lounge area on the hospital floor where Marjorie's room was located, Rem did much of what he'd been doing since hearing the awful news—sitting and staring at nothing.

After returning to the hospital, he'd been told that Marjorie had been moved upstairs. He'd gone to the floor and, seeing Mikey and Lozano talking at a small table in the sitting room, he joined them. Marjorie's sister had been with Marjorie and Daniels. Mikey had told him that Daniels had not made an appearance since telling them the heartbreaking news.

Once Marjorie's sister re-emerged, she'd told Mikey that Daniels wanted to see her. Mikey had gone to the room and returned soon after. Since Marjorie's sister had to return to her own home and family, Daniels had asked Mikey to go to the house to get some things for him and Marjorie, since he planned to stay the night with her. Mikey had agreed, but Rem was reluctant to let her go. Since Marjorie had been targeted, he couldn't be sure Mikey wouldn't also be in danger. He planned to join her, but Lozano had offered to take her and bring her back so Rem could stay at the hospital.

After they'd left, Rem remained on the small sofa next to the table. The sitting area also contained a refrigerator, sink, and counter with a coffee-maker on it. Rem couldn't even bring himself to make coffee. He didn't think his stomach could handle it. Wondering how Marjorie and Daniels were doing and what he would say if Daniels made an appearance, Rem rested his head back, stared at the ceiling, and wondered what to do about Erin. He hadn't put out the APB yet because he needed to tell Daniels what was going on. He felt his partner should know first that his own sister had tried to kill his wife. Maybe it was wrong to wait, but Rem had to go with his gut.

His phone rang, and he sat up. He pulled it out of his pocket and saw it was Lexie. Realizing she had no idea what was going on, he answered. "Hey, Lexie."

"Hey, Remalla. You got a second?"

Rem eyed the room he was in and almost laughed at the absurdity of the question. "You could say that." He poked at a hole in the vinyl-covered sofa.

She paused. "Everything okay? I don't hear any annoying Remalla sarcasm."

Rem told her where he was and about the events of the day. The only thing he left out was the likelihood that Erin was the driver of the vehicle that struck Marjorie.

Lexie went quiet, as if trying to comprehend what Rem had told her. "She lost the baby? Oh, Rem. I'm so sorry."

Rem rested his forehead on his palm. "So am I."

"Is there anything I can do?"

"No. There isn't. But I suggest you be careful. Whoever came after Marjorie could come after you. Until we figure out what's going on here, no one is safe, and Daniels and I are out of commission at the moment, so watch your back."

"I will. You do the same. And that includes not blaming yourself."

"That's going to be hard."

"That's never stopped you before."

Rem sighed heavily. "It's going to take some time." Deciding he needed to change the subject, he cleared his throat and sat up. "Were you calling about something?"

"Yeah. I was. I got some info for you on Elsa Crow, your new captain."

Rem had almost forgotten that he and Daniels had asked Lexie to see what she could find out about Crow. "What'd you learn?"

"I've got a friend. He used to be a detective but left the force and became a PI, but he's still got connections. He made a few phone calls and learned that Elsa Crow is legit. She was on her way to being promoted in Special Crimes when Lozano's spot became available. From everything my friend learned, she's a good cop with a good arrest record. No red flags. Not with her, at least."

"What does that mean?"

"This is where it gets interesting. Her father is Chogan Crow. You familiar with that name?"

"No. Should I be?"

"He's the city council president. A prominent position with lots of connections." She paused. "Who's also very good friends with the chief of police."

That got Rem's interest. "You think Chogan Crow had something to do with Elsa getting Lozano's job?"

"Chogan Crow isn't as clean as his daughter. He's had his hand in a few pies that many have found questionable. That whole Pinnacle Properties thing? Where they're putting in that new development?"

"Don't remind me."

"Crow's a big proponent of it."

"That's not an indictment of him."

"No, but he's helped pave the way for Pinnacle to get properties at the expense of the property owners. He's not too popular with the people who've been pushed out."

"You think he's benefiting in a less than legit way?"

"You mean, is he in someone's pocket? I think that's pretty likely."

"Does he have the kind of clout that could sway the chief to make Elsa our captain?"

"It wouldn't surprise me."

Rem rubbed his eyes. "Could he be a black bird member?"

Lexie grunted over the phone. "Only a certain item can tell us that."

Rem thought of the USB drive. "Any luck in that area?"

"Not yet, but I'm working on it." She paused. "What's even worse is the possibility your police chief could be a member, too."

"God. Don't even say that." Wondering how to translate this new information, Rem pushed his hair out of his face. "This is good info, Lexie. Thanks."

"Do with it what you will, but don't assume anything about Elsa. Could be she takes after her father. That may be the reason she wants you to back off of the black bird angle in your investigation."

"Yeah. I know. You be careful, okay? And keep me posted," he said, referring to the USB drive.

"I will. And tell Daniels..." She sighed. "Hell. I don't know what to tell him."

That same heaviness filled Rem's chest again. "I'll tell him you called and that you're thinking of him and Marj."

"Doesn't seem like much, does it?"

"Maybe not, but every bit helps."

"You take care too, Rem. This is killing you as much as it's killing Daniels."

Rem doubted that. "I will. Thanks, Lex."

They said their goodbyes and Rem hung up. He slipped his phone back into his jacket pocket and went to stand to stretch his legs when Daniels walked in.

Seeing Rem, he froze.

In mid-stance, Rem froze, too.

After a second, Daniels went to the fridge and opened it. "What are you doing here? Mikey said you went to the accident scene." He pulled out two small cartons of orange juice.

"I did. I came back."

Daniels closed the fridge and stared at Rem. His eyes were red and puffy, and he looked like he hadn't slept in days. "You heard?"

Rem's stomach fell and that awful tightness intensified. "Mikey told me."

Daniels nodded and stepped to the counter.

Rem stepped around the small table. "Daniels, I—"

"Don't," said Daniels, his voice tight. "Just don't." He grabbed two straws.

Rem stopped. "I'm so sorry."

Daniels turned abruptly. "I said don't. I don't want to hear how you're sorry that you didn't...you weren't..." His voice caught, and he set his jaw. He looked away. "You should have been there."

Rem's heart broke at the pain in his partner's voice. "You're right. I should have been. I made a mistake." He took another step.

Daniels held up his hand. "Don't."

"Don't what?"

Daniels' gaze hardened. "Don't give me that *I'm here for you* look. Don't act like you're my friend right now."

"But I am, Daniels. I want to help."

"To allay your guilt?" yelled Daniels. "To make yourself feel better?"

Rem stiffened at the amount of anger coming from his partner.

"My wife is devastated. She barely remembers her own name and she can't stop crying, and there's nothing I can do about it. You want to handle that one, *partner*?"

Rem stepped back.

"You want to do something?" asked Daniels. "How about you leave? That's the best thing you can do for me and Marjorie right now."

Rem took the hit and wanted to buckle to the floor, but he couldn't. No matter how much pain and anger his partner was in, Daniels had to know the truth. "Okay. If that's what you want, I'll leave, but you need to know what I learned at the crash site." He took a deep breath and pushed past his misery. "This was deliberate, Daniels. Marjorie didn't run the light. She was pushed into the light. By a driver behind her."

"What?" Daniels' eyes glittered. "Who would do that?"

Rem hesitated, unsure of how to say it. "I don't know why Marjorie left without me, but someone was waiting. I talked to a witness at the scene. He saw the whole thing. He said the car behind Marjorie hit the gas and pushed her car into the intersection. He said the driver was...was a female, and blonde, and...she was wearing blue nail polish." He paused, waiting for Daniels' reaction.

Daniels didn't move, but his eyes said everything. "What are you saying?"

Rem swallowed, bracing himself. "You know what I'm saying. His description matches Erin's."

Daniels set his jaw. "You think Erin, my sister, tried to kill my wife?"

Tense, Rem curled his hands into his fists. "I went to where Erin works..."

"You what?"

"She wasn't there. Her coworker said Erin called this morning and told them she was going to LA to see her Aunt Valora, who was sick, but I tracked down Valora..."

The juice cartons bulged with Daniels' grip on them.

"...Valora said she wasn't sick, had been at work all day, and hadn't spoken to Erin in a while..."

Daniels spoke with menace. "None of that means—"

"Erin doesn't answer her phone. It goes straight to voicemail. I went to her apartment, and she's not there."

Daniels took a long, shaky breath and spoke with quiet intensity. "Did you put an APB out on my sister?"

Rem, his hands shaking, shook them out. "No, but I—"

Daniels erupted. "My sister did not try to kill anyone, much less my wife."

Rem composed himself. "Then who did?"

Daniels raised his voice. "C'mon, Rem. Blonde hair and blue nail polish? That's all you've got? How do you know this isn't Rhonda?"

"How would Rhonda know about the nail polish? And how do you explain Erin's lie about work? Why doesn't she answer her phone?"

"I don't know, Rem, but before you label my sister as a killer, maybe you should find her first."

"What do you think I've been trying to do?" yelled Rem. He cursed and softened his voice. "Daniels, I know this is a lot—"

Daniels' eyes flashed again, and Rem prepared himself. "A lot?" yelled Daniels. "Did you just say a lot?" His gaze bore into Rem's. "I just lost my child, and I damn near lost my wife, and now you're trying to take my sister away from me?"

Rem shook his head. "That's not—"

"Is this some messed up attempt to ease your guilt? By going after Erin? So you can prove you were right about her, and I was wrong?"

Rem couldn't hold back his shock. "No. I would never do that. I would never—"

"How can you be so cold and cruel? Don't you understand what we're going through right now?"

Rem hung his head and thought of Jennie.

"Get out of here, Rem." Daniels stepped away, but stopped. "You do what you have to do, but..." His voice trembled. "...I...I can't deal with this right now." He paused and looked back. "You're wrong about Erin."

Rem summoned the will to respond. "I hope I am."

His eyes swirling with unshed tears, Daniels turned and walked out of the lounge.

Devastated, Rem took long breaths, but it was hard to take in air. He pulled out a chair and sat at the table, trying to pull it together. He hadn't expected that level of animosity from his partner, but thinking of his own experiences with Jennie, he understood Daniels' tenuous emotional state and immediately forgave him. Rem couldn't imagine what he would do if the situation were reversed.

After several minutes of sheer misery, he decided he would honor Daniels' wishes and leave. The last thing he wanted was to make Daniels feel worse. His partner's words echoing in his ears, Rem determined that he'd give Erin one last chance. He'd go to her apartment one more time to find her. If she wasn't there and still didn't answer her phone, Rem would have a hard decision to make.

He stood on shaky legs, and pulled out his phone to text Mikey, when it rang. Cain's name appeared on the display. Fury rippling through him, he answered. "Cain?" he said with a hard edge. "Where the hell have you been?"

Cain's voice shook. "Rem?" His breathing came in rapid gusts. "I...I'm sorry." He paused. "I didn't know. I didn't mean to...to..."

Hearing the fear in Cain's voice, Rem gripped the phone. "Cain? What's wrong?"

"I...I...screwed up. I didn't know."

"You didn't know what?"

Cain spoke fast. "What would happen. They just said to call you and then call her." He whimpered on the phone. "I didn't know what...what...that meant."

Rem recognized that this wasn't some false flag from his cousin. "What did you do, Cain?"

Cain cried into the phone. "I need help, Rem." He could barely speak through his sobs. "Can you come over? Please. I'll tell you everything."

Rem ran out into the hall and toward the elevator. "I'm coming right now. Do not go anywhere. Do you hear me? Promise."

Cain sucked in air. "I won't. I promise. Just hurry."

Rem punched the *Down* button on the elevator. "Stay on the line with me, Cain."

"I have to go. Just hur...hurry."

"Cain, if this is some sort of trap…"

"I need your help, Rem. I'm in too deep, and I don't know what else to do."

The elevator doors opened, and Rem jumped inside. "Stay put and stay calm. I'm on my way. Don't hang up. Keep talking to me."

"I…can't." Cain sucked in another breath and groaned into the phone.

"Cain…" Rem willed the elevator to move faster.

Cain responded in a whisper. "I'm…sorry."

Rem cursed when the line went dead.

Chapter Twenty-Seven

REM RACED UP TWO stairs at a time to Cain's floor. After reaching it, he ran down to Cain's apartment, prepared to bang on the door, but stopped short when he saw it was slightly ajar. Instinct took over, and he pulled his weapon and stood to the side of the frame. "Cain?" he yelled. "You in there? It's Aaron."

Not hearing anything, Rem used his foot to push the door open wider, and he peered around the frame and into the apartment. Not seeing Cain, he swiveled around and took a step inside. "Cain? You home?"

He heard a moan, took a step around the couch, and stood in shock. Cain was lying on his back on the floor with an ugly wound in his chest. Blood pooled beneath his body in a wide circle. "Oh, my God." Rem holstered his gun, and ran to Cain's side, where he dropped to his knees in the blood. "Cain?" Based on the look of the wound, Cain had been shot. "Cain?" he yelled. "Can you hear me?" He leaned over his cousin. "Talk to me."

Cain's eyes were closed, but his lids fluttered. Rem spotted a T-shirt on the couch. He grabbed it, balled it up, and pressed it against Cain's injury.

He heard an audible gasp and looked up to see Cain's neighbor standing in the doorway, holding what looked like a grocery bag. Watching the scene, his eyes went wide, and his face was quickly losing color.

"Call nine-one-one. Now." Rem pressed harder with the T-shirt and Cain moaned. "Stay with me, Cain," he yelled.

The neighbor dropped the bag and grabbed his phone. "Nine-one-one. Okay. I'm dialing." He put the phone to his ear and stepped into the hall.

Cain's eyes opened to slits. "R...Rem?" he whispered.

"I'm here," said Rem, frantic. "I'm right here. Just hang on."

"I...I'm sorry." Cain muttered softly. "I...I...didn't..."

"Try and relax, Cain. Reserve your strength. Help is coming."

Cain feebly raised his bloody hand. "Don't...don't leave me," he said, placing his fingers over Rem's.

"I won't. I'm right here." Rem prayed to any god that would listen to save his cousin. "Just keep looking at me, okay?"

Cain blinked, and tears escaped from the sides of his eyes. "I'm scared."

Rem felt his own tears welling up. "Don't be scared. I'll stay with you."

Cain coughed, and blood speckled his lips. "You were right, cou...cousin." His grip tightened on Rem's hand. "You were...right."

"That doesn't matter, Cain. I don't care about any of that. I just want you to stay alive."

Cain's eyes closed and opened again. "I'm try...trying."

Rem stayed with him while Cain took shallow, shaky breaths and gripped Rem's hand. "You're doing great," said Rem. "Just keep breathing." He could hear the distant wail of a siren. "Hear that? They're coming. Just hang on."

Cain released a deep moan and coughed again. Blood escaped his mouth and ran down the side of his cheek. "Re...Rem..."

"I'm right here."

Cain slowly blinked and stared at the ceiling. "I...I...can't feel...anything."

Rem gritted his teeth. "Don't worry about that. Just take it easy."

"They...they lied to...to...me."

"Who lied to you?"

"A...a man. I bel...believed him." He clenched his eyes shut and moaned. "Stu...stupid."

"Take it easy." Rem squeezed Cain's fingers.

Cain opened his eyes. "Can't...can't tr...trust him."

"Who, Cain? Who did this?"

"He said...he...said...to tell you..."

Rem struggled to hear and leaned closer. "I'm listening."

"T...Tex."

Raising his head, Rem's blood turned cold. Tex was the nickname of one of the men who'd almost killed Daniels and Rem in Elmwood.

"Co...come closer." Cain's voice was losing strength.

Rem steeled himself. "Cain, please. Don't give up."

"Rem." It was so quiet, Rem could barely hear it.

His chest tightening into a vise and his emotions bubbling over. Rem stayed close to his cousin. "I'm right here," he whispered.

The sirens wailed from below. The neighbor appeared at the door. "They're here. I'll bring them up." He ran off.

"Rem," whispered Cain.

Rem let go of the T-shirt and gripped Cain's hand in return. "I'm with you. I'm not leaving."

Cain gasped and forced out three words. "Please...for...forgive...me."

Rem met his cousin's gaze and set his jaw as his own tears fell. "I do, Cain. I do." He could barely speak. "Don't worry about Mabel and your mother. I'll look out for them."

"Th...thank y..." Cain's grip on Rem's hand weakened, his eyes went glassy, and a long, soft breath escaped his mouth and brushed against Rem's cheek, but there was no inhale.

"No," yelled Rem, desperate to save him. "No, Cain." He raised up again and pressed the now bloody shirt against his cousin's chest. "You can't die." He frantically pumped his palms up and down on his cousin's chest as paramedics ran into the room. They pushed Rem out of the way and began to work on Cain, pulling out equipment, taking his vitals and beginning life-saving measures.

Distraught, Rem stepped back from the fray and watched the flurry of activity, but in his heart, he knew it was too late. His cousin was dead.

··········

Sun filtered through the closed blinds, and Daniels blinked and shifted in his chair. Stiff from trying to sleep in it, he groaned at the ache in his back. Sitting forward, he studied Marjorie in her hospital bed. The bruise on her swollen cheek had grown darker. Her eyes were closed, but Daniels knew she'd slept little. A nurse had been in every hour throughout the night to check that Marjorie's head injury didn't show signs of worsening. Thankfully, Marjorie had passed all the tests she'd been through and, as long as there were no additional complications, she'd be able to go home later today.

After Mikey had brought the items Daniels had requested from home, he'd done his best to make Marjorie comfortable. The concussion made it hard for her to focus, and although she understood what had happened to her, she couldn't understand why. She had no memory of the accident or the hours leading up to it.

Wanting to comfort her, Daniels had wet a cloth and gently wiped the grime of the accident off her skin. He'd requested Mikey bring Marjorie's body lotion, and he'd delicately rubbed it over his wife's face, arms, and legs. She'd been quiet during his ministrations as silent tears ran down her face. Afterward, he'd helped her into a soft pair of pajamas and settled her back into bed, where he'd laid beside her as she continued to cry. There seemed to be no end to her tears. Finally spent, she'd fallen asleep on his shoulder, and he'd almost punched the nurse when she'd come in to wake Marjorie to evaluate her.

Thankfully, though, Marjorie did not resume her tears, and when the nurse left, she'd fallen back asleep on Daniels' shoulder. That continued until, needing to use the bathroom, he'd slipped out of bed. Marjorie had shifted at his movement, but her eyes remained closed.

After leaving the bathroom, he watched her rest, until the nurse came again to check her. Restless and needing a distraction, he'd flipped on the TV, and muted it, then went to sit in the chair for the rest of the night.

As the sun brightened the room, Daniels tried again to come to terms with all that had happened. He'd spent the last twenty-four hours worrying about his wife, grieving the loss of their baby, thinking about what Rem had told him, and refusing to believe Erin had any part of this. But as time passed, his doubts intruded, which only made him madder at Rem for suggesting Erin's involvement.

He sighed, stood, and stretched. Recalling his argument with his partner, Daniels wondered where Rem was. When Mikey had brought their things from home, she'd told him Rem had left the hospital, and Daniels had a brief regret over what he'd said, but when Marjorie had moaned again, the anger had returned, and he'd pushed any regrets to the side and gone to his wife. But now that it was quiet, his thoughts returned to what Rem had told him about Erin. Whether or not she was involved, Marjorie's accident had been deliberate. Someone had come after her, and when he found out who, nothing would stop him from putting that person behind bars for the foreseeable future.

Once again, the nurse returned. She jostled Marjorie's shoulder and Marjorie opened her eyes. She answered the nurses' questions; the nurse checked her vitals, made notes in her tablet and left. Marjorie shifted in the bed and winced. Daniels went to her side and took the hand of her good arm. The other one was in a cast from the elbow down.

She opened her eyes.

"Hey," he said. "Good morning."

She blinked at him. "Hey." She squeezed his fingers and looked around the room. Her face fell. "It wasn't a dream, was it?" Fresh tears swam in her eyes.

Feeling his own sadness return, Daniels stroked her cheek. "No, it wasn't a dream." He grabbed a tissue from a nearby tray table and used it to brush away a tear that had fallen down her cheek.

She pulled on the sheet. "I can't seem to stop crying."

"Nobody said you should." He noted her brighter eyes and was happy she seemed more clear-headed. "Cry as much as you need to."

She sniffed. "What time is it?"

He eyed the clock. "Almost seven."

"You should go home," she said. "You look exhausted."

"I will. Later."

She ran her hand over his palm. "It's okay to go." She sniffed again. "I won't fall apart."

His own emotions swirled. "You don't have to be strong."

"Neither do you."

Pulling himself together, he gripped her hand, leaned closer to her, and kissed her forehead. "I love you."

"I love you too," she whispered. She wrinkled her nose. "But you need a shower."

He chuckled, glad to see some of his wife's personality return. "Your mom said she'd bring J.P. by when he wakes up. Is that okay?"

"More than okay. I want to see him."

"Just don't push it, okay?"

"I won't." Her eyes flicked to the TV screen. She studied it and frowned. "Isn't that your witness' mother?"

Daniels turned and saw Patricia Caruso on the screen. Curious, he stood, grabbed the remote, and turned up the volume. It was the early morning news, and the TV broadcaster was speaking about a reward that Patricia Caruso was offering to anyone who could locate her son, Jerry Lee, who'd been missing since the murder of Reginald Durning at the hotel where Jerry Lee worked. Daniels guessed Elsa Crow had made good on her word to use the media to find Jerry Lee, but he hadn't expected this. Patricia told the reporter that a benefactor had come forward to put up the money for the reward of $62,148.

The reporter asked her about the odd amount, but Patricia had said that her benefactor had chosen it. She didn't know why and didn't care. She just wanted the safe return of her son.

"I thought you wanted to keep Jerry Lee out of the news," said Marjorie.

"Obviously, that's changed."

The news report ended, the broadcasters went on to other news and Daniels lowered the volume. The obvious assumption was that Patricia's benefactor was Sammy Caruso, but why he'd picked such an odd total for a reward eluded Daniels.

"That's a strange amount," said Marjorie. "But I understand her desperation."

Daniels set the remote down. "I hope she knows what she's doing. Somebody finds Jerry, and that could make him an easy target."

"I'm sure she's hoping whoever's hiding him will turn him in. That's what I'd want." She gripped the tissue Daniels had left on the bed.

Forgetting about Jerry, Daniels returned to her bedside and sat beside her. Seeing her fiddle with the tissue, he took her hand again. "What's on your mind, besides the obvious?"

She looked up from her lowered lids. "I know I had some visitors yesterday."

"You did." He gestured at the flowers. "They were all very worried about you."

"I don't recall seeing Rem."

He tightened the hold on her hand.

"Honey," she said, softly. "This isn't his fault."

He studied their hands. "He was supposed to be there. He was supposed to take you. If he had…" His throat closed and he stopped talking.

She let go of his hand and cupped his jaw. He looked up and stared at her shimmering eyes. "He's your best friend. We can't lose him too."

Thinking of his conversation with Rem, his chest tightened. "I know. I just need some time." He blinked back his tears. "I just wish I could understand."

"Understand what?"

He cleared his throat and told her the truth. "Babe, what happened to you yesterday wasn't an accident."

Her eyes rounded. "What do you mean?"

"Rem went to the scene. He said he spoke to a witness who said he saw your car struck from behind at the light." He paused. "Honey, you were pushed into that intersection deliberately."

Her face froze. "Who…who would do that? And why?"

He shook his head. "I don't know." He refused to tell her that Rem suspected Erin. "But I damn sure plan to find out." He sighed. "They must have been waiting for an opportunity. I don't know how else…" He saw Marjorie look away, her face draining of color. His heart thumped with concern. "Honey? What's wrong? Is it your head?"

"Yesterday…" She looked back at him and squeezed his wrist. "Somebody called me."

He didn't understand. "Who called you?"

Running her hand over his arm and shoulder as if to ensure he was there, she stammered. "I remember. Rem…he called me. I…said I would wait." She clutched his elbow. "Then there was another call. From a man."

Worried, Daniels sat closer. "What man?"

"He said he was a nurse, calling from a hospital." She put her palm on her forehead. "He said you were hurt. Said there'd been a shooting, and it was urgent. He…he said I…I had to get to the hospital…I panicked, grabbed my purse...and left." She stifled a sob. "That's why I was driving. To get to you."

Daniels' body flared with heat, and he wanted to throw something.

She pulled him forward, and he leaned in and held her. "I thought you were dying," she whispered through fresh tears.

Daniels did his best to keep his fury under control. He stroked the back of her head. "I'm okay, sweetheart." His heart raced faster, and he set his jaw in anger. "Did you recognize this man's voice?"

She shook her head against his shoulder. "No."

Daniels pulled away from her and brushed her hair away from her face, but it was impossible to hide his rage from her.

"Honey," she said, wiping away a tear. "I understand your anger, but none of this is Rem's fault."

Daniels cursed at the implications of what Marjorie had told him. The whole thing had been a setup. Someone had known Daniels would be in court and that Rem was picking up Marjorie. They'd delayed Rem, called Marjorie, scared her enough to drive and had caused her accident. Daniels blaming Rem had no doubt been an extra benefit. The only thing he didn't know was who and why. Had Rem been right? Had Erin duped Daniels and gone after Marjorie at the behest of Cain and his black bird friends?

Furious, he stood and paced. Holding his head, he tried to think, but there was only one thing he knew to do—call Rem.

He reached for his phone and pulled out the charger Mikey had brought him the previous day. Before he could dial, though, his phone rang, and Mikey's name appeared on the display. He answered. "Mikey?"

Mikey's pleading voice replied. "Daniels. I'm so sorry to bother you, but I don't know who else to call." She paused. "It's Rem."

An icy shiver ran up Daniels' spine and he recalled his angry words directed at his partner. "What's wrong?"

"I...I can't find him." Her voice caught. "It...It's Cain. He's dead."

Daniels felt the blood leave his face. "What?"

"Oh, God, Daniels. Cain called Rem yesterday, and he went over, but when he got there, Cain had been shot. Rem tried to help him, and the paramedics came, but it was too late."

His body going numb, Daniels sat in the chair.

Mikey rambled. "Rem called me from the hospital. Cain's mother and sister were there and when the doctor told them Cain was gone, Rem couldn't handle it. He left. I told him I'd come get him and to wait for me, but he said he needed to drive around for a while. He...he sounded...so lost. He's been gone all night. He was texting me until a few hours ago, but hasn't since. I don't know where he is and I'm terrified. The only person I could think to call is you." Her voice cracked, and he heard a muffled sob.

Imagining his partner's mental state, Daniels' brain flipped to all the places Rem would go, and he landed on one spot. "Mikey, listen to me. Can you come to the hospital and sit with Marjorie? I don't want her to be alone."

"I'm fine, honey," said Marjorie.

Mikey took a deep, trembling breath and sounded more composed. "Yes. I'm on my way." She hung up without saying goodbye.

Daniels hung up and told Marjorie what was happening.

Marjorie held her chest. "What is going on? First me and now Cain?"

Daniels realized that this had been an attack against both him and Rem. "That's why I don't want you to be alone."

"My mother will be here soon."

"Mikey will be here sooner. You two stay here until you hear from me."

"Where exactly am I going to go?"

Daniels had another idea. "I'm calling Lozano. He can come here and keep an eye on things until I find Rem and get back."

"Are you sure?"

Daniels grabbed his phone again. "Until we find out what's going on, no one is safe." Worrying about Rem, he dialed Lozano's number.

Chapter Twenty-Eight

HEARING MABEL'S WAIL ECHO in his mind, Rem jolted awake and opened his eyes. Uncomfortable and stiff, he groaned and sat up, blinked at the sunlight, and rubbed his weary eyes. Eyeing his surroundings, he saw the tombstones, and the bench he'd fallen asleep on and the tree he sat beneath. He couldn't understand how everything was still moving and why the world hadn't stopped. He'd felt the same after Jennie's death. Everyone going about their lives as if nothing had happened felt so wrong.

That familiar ache returned, and visions of Cain dying, the paramedics fighting to revive him, driving to the hospital, contacting Cain's mom and sister, and waiting for what he knew was the inevitable news swirled in his mind. He could still hear the doctor telling them they'd done all they could, but Cain had not survived. Cain's mother had dropped to her knees and Mabel had wailed in a way that Rem would never forget.

The police arrived and Rem told them what had happened and when other family members joined them at the hospital, Rem, in complete overwhelm, had left. He needed to get as far away as possible to deal with Cain's loss, although no place was far enough. He'd stayed in touch with Mikey and told her not to worry, but realized that was impossible. His grief and despair were obvious, but he couldn't bring them home to her. Not yet. He needed to be alone to think, but all he could contemplate was his mistakes. There were so many things he could have done differently that might have saved Cain, but Rem had charged in like a bulldozer, trying to pressure his cousin, but it had only backfired, and Cain had paid the price with his life.

He'd ended up at the cemetery where Jennie was buried. He'd come here frequently after her death. The first year, he'd sit and talk to her at her tombstone, and the second year, he'd sit on the bench he was sitting on now and appreciate the quiet and peace of the setting. Her tombstone was visible from the bench, and it brought him comfort. It had been months, though, since he'd been here, and although he didn't talk to her like he used to, he still knew she was near.

Checking the time, he realized he couldn't sit there forever. He had to get home. Realizing he'd fallen asleep on the bench and hadn't texted Mikey, he reached for his phone. But when he picked it up, he saw a smear of blood on the screen and his stomach lurched. Had that smear been there the whole time? His previous evening was such a blur, he couldn't recall. Staring at his fingers though, he saw the blood on them, too. The memory of him leaning over Cain, clutching his hand, and Cain asking for Rem's forgiveness before he died, almost buckled him.

He thought of Daniels, wishing he could talk to his partner, but Daniels had his own grief to deal with and needed to be with his wife. Plus, Rem could still see the anger on Daniels' face when he'd told him about Erin. Dropping his head into his hands, he wished he could be anywhere but here. His gut churning, memories swirling and tears returning, Rem made an audible moan. Misery was too kind a word for how he was feeling.

Hearing soft footsteps approach, Rem straightened, sniffed, and wiped his eyes, thinking another mourner was there to visit a loved one. He turned and froze when he saw Daniels walk up from behind. Rem didn't say a word as Daniels came around to the side of the bench and sat beside him.

· · · · • · • · · ·

Seeing his partner, Daniels had to force himself not to gape in shock. Rem was covered in blood. His jeans from the knees down were stained a dark red, his hands and nails were crusted with it, and he'd obviously wiped his fingers on his shirt because streaks of red covered the front of it. Seeing his partner's grief, his own grief returned, and it was hard not to cry himself. Both of them were in terrible shape.

"Hey," he said softly.

Rem wiped his wet face with his shirtsleeve and sat back. "Hey." He composed himself and cleared his throat. "How'd you find me?"

Daniels eyed Jennie's grave. "This is where you come when you need some quiet or have something on your mind."

Rem stared straight ahead. "I haven't been here in a while."

"I figured old habits die hard."

"I guess they do." He glanced over at Daniels. "How's Marjorie?"

"Better today. More alert."

Rem looked away. "Good." He studied his hands. "Mikey call you?"

"She did. You need to text her. She's worried sick about you."

Rem cursed and grabbed his phone. "I fell asleep on the bench." He quickly typed out a message and sent it.

"You've been here all night?"

Rem nodded. "I didn't know where else to go."

"What about home?"

Rem went still and the muscle in his jaw flexed. "You know...about Cain?"

"Mikey told me."

Rem's phone beeped, and he sent another text. "Mikey says thanks for finding me."

"I told her to stay with Marjorie. I didn't want either of them to be alone right now."

Staring at nothing, Rem nodded. "Yeah."

Hoping to pull Rem out of his despair, Daniels faced his partner. "Mikey said you were the one who found Cain?"

Rem eyed his phone. "Um...yeah. He called me after our...well...after you and I talked yesterday."

Daniels shut his eyes. "Rem, what I said..."

"Is completely understandable. You're right. I shouldn't have gone to see—" His brow furrowed, and he looked away.

"You didn't do anything wrong, partner, by going to see Cain."

Rem looked over at him with a tortured look. "I should have been there for Marjorie."

Hating the look on Rem's face, Daniels put his hand on his friend's elbow. "Listen to me. What I said to you was stupid and cruel. I should never have said it. And I never should have implied that you didn't understand how I felt, because I know how well you understand loss. I apologize for that."

"You don't need to apologize. You've lost your child. I feel terrible." More tears swirled in his eyes.

Daniels' own emotions swirled. "And you've lost Cain. I'm sorry you had to lose him like that."

Rem shut his eyes, and tears slipped down his cheeks. "He asked me to forgive him. Can you believe that?" His breath caught. "When it's my fault he died." He brushed the fallen tears away with his fingers.

Daniels' anger returned. "The hell it is." He blinked back his own tears. "That's what I need to tell you. This whole thing was a setup."

Rem sniffed and opened his eyes. "What do you mean?"

"Marjorie remembers getting a phone call after you talked to her. She said a man called. He said he was a nurse at the hospital and that I had been injured in a shooting. He told her it was urgent she get there and implied I wouldn't survive." His body shook just saying it. "That's why she left, partner."

Rem stared for a second, as if confused. "You mean this whole thing was planned?"

"I think Cain called you to delay you. Then someone called Marjorie and scared her enough to get in the car and drive, and whoever rammed her car was watching and followed her."

Rem's eyes widened. "But why yesterday? They could have done it at any time."

Daniels had been wondering the same on the drive to the cemetery. "This was an attack against us as much as it was against Marjorie and Cain. They knew I was in court. They knew you were picking Marjorie up. They knew how it would look. If Marjorie had died," his pulse quickened at the words, "you would have blamed yourself and I would have let you."

Rem stared blankly out at the cemetery. "It would have destroyed us," he said softly.

"I don't know if that was their ultimate plan, but they got close enough."

Rem sucked in a breath and grimaced. "Cain...he said something else, before he...he died."

"What?"

Rem looked over at him. "He told me he was sorry. That he didn't know. That all he was supposed to do was call me and then call her..."

Daniels tensed. "He must have been the one who called Marjorie."

"He said they lied to him. That he didn't expect what happened."

"I bet he didn't." Daniels tried to think. "I'm sure they told him it was no big deal and no one would get hurt."

"That's why he called the second time," said Rem. "He realized what he'd done and regretted it. He said he would tell me everything." He slumped and held his head. "But I didn't get there in time. Those bastards got to him first. Somehow, they knew he was going to talk."

Another realization hit Daniels. "Maybe not. Maybe they were there the whole time."

Rem sat up. "You mean they told him to call me? To get me to come over?"

It made sense to Daniels. "They threaten him, and he calls you, thinking it'll save him, but it doesn't. They shoot him and leave him there, so you'll find him like that."

Rem stared off again and gripped his stomach. "Son-of-a-bitch."

Daniels gritted his teeth at the damage that had been caused. "They sure as hell know how to twist the knife, don't they?"

After a long pause, Rem's eyes narrowed. "Cain told me who did it."

Daniels hadn't expected that. "He told you who shot him?"

Rem's fingers curled into fists. "He said it was Tex. Cain even said Tex wanted me to know it was him."

Shocked, Daniels recalled the man who'd almost killed them in Elmwood, and didn't even know how to respond. "We're in deep trouble here, Rem. Someone went to an awful lot of trouble to screw with us."

"But what was the point?"

"I'd say whoever it is really hates us." He thought of Marjorie and the baby, and his partner losing his cousin, "but when I find him, he's gonna find out how much I don't like him either."

"Something tells me there's more than one."

"I'm sure there is, but they're all serving one master, and that's the one we have to find."

Rem hesitated. "There is one person we can talk to, if we can find her."

Daniels knew who he meant.

Rem's face fell. "I didn't put out the APB." He paused. "If you want me to hold off, I will. I'll do whatever you want me to do."

Recalling his angry words directed at his partner, Daniels flinched. "I didn't handle that very well, either." He hated to think Erin could be a part of this. "But I can see why you'd suspect her."

"I don't want to."

"I know you don't." Daniels put his hand on Rem's shoulder. "But I appreciate you holding off until we can talk to her."

"Assuming we still can."

Daniels straightened at the implication. "Hell, if she was responsible for the accident, could they have killed her too? Once it was done?"

Rem shook his head. "That's not what I meant."

"But it could be possible. Maybe that's why she's not answering."

Rem softened his gaze. "If that were true, I think we'd know. They'd want to use that against us, too. You probably would have gotten a phone call from her, like I did from Cain."

Daniels couldn't imagine that, but suspected Rem was right. "Then where is she?"

Rem slumped again. "I wish I knew." His phone rang and Daniels could see Phoebe Reinart's name on the display.

Groaning, Rem picked up his cell and took a deep breath. "Maybe Reinart will have some good news."

"Don't count on it."

Rem answered and talked to Phoebe. Daniels was relieved to see Rem's mood improving after finding him despondent over Cain. He figured any distraction was good for both of them.

After talking a few minutes, Rem hung up. "Reinart came through. She got info on the FBI investigation on Durning and Lozano." He attempted to wipe a smear of blood off his screen, but failed, and slipped the phone into his pocket. "They think Durning took bribes as a prosecutor to ensure certain people went free. Hippolito is one of the men on their radar."

"There are more?"

"There are, but Reinart can't determine who." He brushed back his hair with a bloodstained hand. "A tip came in on their hotline that put Durning on the hot seat. They've been investigating for six months. Lozano wasn't part of it until two weeks ago, when his name suddenly turned up as a possible accomplice."

Daniels didn't buy that. "They've been investigating for six months, and they just now suspect Lozano? That makes no sense."

Rem rested his elbows on his knees. "Apparently, they've found a money trail."

Daniels leaned in. "What kind of money trail?"

Rem glanced over with bloodshot eyes. "An offshore account with ties to both Durning and Lozano, worth over a million."

Daniels gaped at him. "That's ridiculous."

Rem sat up. "I know that, and you know that, but the FBI doesn't."

Daniels' mind raced. "Whoever did this to us is doing the same to Lozano."

"Probably to screw with us." Rem fell back against the bench. "And Lexie called yesterday about Elsa Crow." Rem told Daniels about Elsa's background, her father Chogan Crow, and his ties to Chief Patterson. "We're in some deep shit here, partner," said Rem. "and I don't even know where to start digging to get out."

Daniels stared out over the tombstones. Trying to grasp the situation, his head pounded, and it occurred to him that neither he nor Rem had gotten any sleep. Blinking his tired eyes, he shot a look at his exhausted partner. "We're not going to solve it sitting here."

Rem eyed his bloody hands. "What do you propose?"

"Let's go back to my place. Get cleaned up. I need to take something before this headache gets worse." He gestured at Rem's shirt. "And you need a shower."

Rem looked down at himself. "I know."

Daniels pulled on his own sleeve. "So do I. Then we'll go back to the hospital and figure out our next steps."

"Hopefully, sleep will be one of them."

Daniels stood and held out a hand to Rem, who took it and pulled himself up with a groan. He swayed for a second but found his balance.

"And hey," said Daniels softly.

Rem met his look.

"I'm sorry about Cain." He took a second. "I know you loved him."

Rem's lost look returned. "I did and thank you." His voice tightened, and he cleared his throat. "And I'm so sorry about the baby. But thank God Marjorie's okay."

His eyes filling at the grief they both felt, Daniels nodded. "I appreciate that."

Trying to keep it together, Rem sniffed. "No matter what happens, Daniels, we can't let them tear us apart. If they do that..."

Daniels met Rem's watery gaze. "...then they win."

Rem nodded.

Realizing how much more they could have lost, Daniels stepped closer. "Come here, partner." He wrapped Rem in a bear hug and Rem hugged him back tightly. They held the hug for several seconds, both needing the connection, before stepping back. "Somehow, we're gonna get through this," said Daniels, his voice taut with emotion.

Rem wiped his eyes on his sleeve again. "I know we are. Let's just pray no one else gets hurt."

Daniels brushed away a tear that slipped down his cheek. "The rate we're going, that's no guarantee."

Rem nodded. "Once we get over this hill, we'll figure out what to do."

"I hope you're right." Weary and depleted, Daniels thought of Marjorie and all he and his wife had been through. "I don't know about you, but I feel helpless."

Rem put his hand on Daniels' shoulder. "I get it. But we have to stick together and do what we do best, partner. Lean on each other. It's all we've got."

Understanding, Daniels met Rem's gaze. "I know." He squeezed his throbbing temples. "One step at a time, right?"

"Even if they're baby steps. Just so long as we're moving forward."

Daniels lowered his hand. "I'm tired of moving backward."

"Me too." Rem turned to head back to the parking lot. "C'mon. Let's get you a pill before you end up with a doozy."

A doozy, the term Rem used to refer to Daniels' severe headaches, was the last thing Daniels needed. More composed, Daniels walked quietly with Rem back to their cars. They walked past the tombstones and Rem eyed his bloody shirt. "Do I have a change of clothes at your place?"

Feeling better after their talk, Daniels stretched his tight neck. "You've still got clothes there from that time you used our washer and dryer after your machine broke. They've been sitting there for weeks. I've almost donated them twice."

Rem perked up. "Is that where my purple anteater socks are? I've been looking all over for them."

Happy to hear their much-needed banter slip back into place, Daniels couldn't help but smile.

Chapter Twenty-Nine

AFTER ENSURING MARJORIE WAS sleeping, Daniels came down the stairs to see Mikey and Lozano in the kitchen and Rem talking on the phone in the living room.

Mikey swiveled in her chair. "How is she?"

Daniels entered the kitchen. "Finally got her settled. Hopefully, she can get some sleep. Can you check on her in an hour?"

"Sure."

Daniels nodded. "Thanks." After leaving the cemetery, he and Rem had returned to Daniels' house. He'd taken something for his headache and called Marjorie, who'd been visiting with her mom and J.P., Mikey, and Lozano. She told him and Rem to take a few hours and get some sleep. The doctor had not been in yet and she doubted she'd be released until later that afternoon.

After quick showers, and confident that Marjorie and Mikey were safe, Rem had taken the couch, and Daniels had lain down upstairs. After an hour, though, Daniels had given up and gone downstairs to see Rem sitting on the couch with his feet on the coffee table, watching TV. Neither of them had the capacity for rest when so much was going on.

They'd headed to the hospital and stayed with Marjorie until the doctor cleared her to go home. Rem had spent much of that time on the phone with family, dealing with Cain's loss and funeral arrangements. Daniels was glad Rem could do it with him and Mikey around, because it clearly took its toll on his partner.

Once they returned home, Marjorie's mother had grabbed some items for J.P. and had taken him back to her house. Daniels got Marjorie comfortable upstairs, Rem was back on the phone, and Mikey and Lozano sat in the kitchen.

Lozano checked his watch. "I can stay another couple of hours. Then I have to meet with my attorney."

Daniels and Rem had informed him of what Phoebe had learned. As expected, he had no knowledge of any offshore account in his or Durning's name. "You have a lot to discuss with him," said Daniels.

"I do," said Lozano. "Mostly about what I can do to take the offensive. I'm clearly a target of whoever is after you two."

Daniels poured himself a glass of water. "Just be careful, Cap. They obviously want you out of the picture, and until Rem and I figure out who's behind this, it may get worse before it gets better."

"I'll watch my backside," said Lozano, drinking some coffee from a mug he held. "You two do the same. If what you say about Elsa Crow's father is true, you can't trust Elsa either. You have no idea what she's telling him."

"We'll take precautions, but the only way to find these people is to get out there and look."

"I can stay with Marjorie the rest of the day," said Mikey. "Don't worry about her."

"Thank you." Daniels set his water glass on the counter. "Hopefully, Rem and I will be back before Lozano has to leave." Neither Mikey, Marjorie, nor Lozano knew about Erin's potential involvement in Marjorie's accident. And until he was certain Erin was at fault, Daniels planned to keep it to himself.

Rem walked into the kitchen, looking weary.

"How's it going?" asked Mikey.

Rem slid his phone into his back pocket and rubbed his face. "Uncle Horace is taking charge of the funeral, which is good for Mabel and her mom, and me, too." He grabbed a half-filled mug from the table and dumped the contents into the sink. He grabbed the almost empty coffeepot and added more coffee to his mug. "I think I've talked to every family member I have. Everyone's in shock and wants to know why this happened, but I can't answer them." He added cream and sugar to his mug and stirred it. "It's hell."

Daniels could only imagine. "Give them a couple of days. It will settle down."

Rem leaned against the counter. "On the plus side, I talked to Elsa Crow. She gave us the day off." He sipped some coffee.

"That's good, since we haven't been there," said Daniels. "What about tomorrow?"

"She said to let her know." Rem took another drink of his coffee. "Guess what else she told me?"

Daniels set his water glass in the sink. "I'm afraid to ask."

Rem lowered his mug. "She assigned Cain's case to Monk and Manetti." He snorted. "Can you believe that?"

Daniels widened his eyes. "She did what?"

"That ought to be interesting," said Lozano.

"Detective Monk almost arrested me for murder," said Mikey. "And now he's investigating Cain's murder?"

"To say he was overzealous is an understatement," said Lozano. "I wrote him up for his behavior, but he couldn't have cared less."

Daniels eyed Rem, and they exchanged that look that said they knew something the others didn't. Was Monk part of the black birds, an unfortunate victim of them, or just took his job too seriously?

"They want to talk to me tomorrow," said Rem, setting his mug down. "That should be fun."

"I'll bring the party hats," said Daniels.

"Please do," said Rem. "I'm wondering if I should call Lurch."

Daniels recalled another one of Rem's cousins, who was the attorney who'd represented Mikey when she'd been a suspect in Vera Canmore's murder. "You think that's necessary?"

Rem shrugged. "I was the one found with Cain. I had his blood all over me. And the neighbor heard me arguing with him. And we all know Monk doesn't like me much."

"None of that means you killed him," said Mikey.

"Maybe not to you and me," said Rem, "but to Monk, who knows?"

"Did you see a weapon at the scene?" asked Daniels.

Rem shook his head. "No, but I wasn't looking either."

"Let's not jump to conclusions," said Lozano. "Don't forget Manetti's part of this too. He handles Monk pretty well."

"Let's hope so, Cap." Rem spoke to Daniels. "You ready?" He took a long gulp of his coffee and set the mug in the sink.

"I am." Daniels grabbed his jacket. "You two help yourself to whatever is in the kitchen. Make yourself at home. We'll be back soon." He put a hand on Mikey's shoulder. "And call me if Marjorie needs anything."

"I will," said Mikey.

Rem walked over and gave her a kiss. "You stay inside with Lozano. Don't open the door to anybody."

"We'll be okay," said Lozano. "Go do what you have to do."

"Thanks, Cap," said Rem. "We'll stay in touch."

Daniels opened the door, and they both stepped onto the porch, and waited to hear the lock turn. Once it did, they headed toward Daniels' car. Looking up and down the street, he searched for a dark SUV but didn't see one.

"Hey," said Rem. "One sec."

Daniels turned. "What?"

"I didn't mention this inside, but Crow assigned Marjorie's case to Mel and Garcia."

Daniels stopped.

Rem stopped beside him. "I didn't say a thing about Erin, but we'll have to talk to Mel and Garcia."

Daniels started walking again. "Then it's good thing we're going to clear this up with Erin today."

"About that," said Rem. "I called Erin again. This time, her phone rang, and then went to voicemail, instead of going straight to voicemail. Her phone is back on."

Daniels hesitated. "Then why the hell doesn't she call us back?"

"I don't know. Maybe once we get to her apartment, we can find her and ask her."

Worried, Daniels opened his car door and slid behind the wheel. Rem got into the passenger seat. Before starting the car, Daniels' phone rang. He pulled it from his pocket and stilled when he saw it was Erin calling.

Rem saw it too and stared at Daniels, who listened to it ring. "Whatever she says, partner," said Rem. "We'll handle it."

Daniels took a second and answered.

· · · • · • · · · ·

Rem listened as Daniels spoke to his sister. He asked her where she'd been the last twenty-four hours and why she hadn't answered her phone. He listened, glanced at Rem, and told Erin they were headed to her apartment. He paused again, frowned, and told her to text him the address. "We're on our way." He hung up and started the car.

"What did she say?"

Daniels backed out of his driveway. "Said she's been in LA."

Rem groaned. "We know that's not true."

"She said she would explain everything but didn't want to over the phone. She told us to meet her, but not at her apartment."

"Then where?"

Daniels' phone buzzed. He accessed his texts and handed his phone to Rem. "There. Plug it into your navigation. Tell me where we're going." He pulled onto the street and glanced in his rearview mirror. "And make sure we're not being followed."

Rem put the address into his phone and studied the screen. "Straight ahead." He glanced behind him and then looked more closely at the map. "This is where that new development is going in." He looked up. "Why are we going there?"

"Because that's where she said to go." Daniels drove down the street. "Said it would be quiet."

Rem couldn't help but think the worst. "You sure about this, partner?"

Daniels shot a look at him. "You think this is some sort of ambush?"

"The thought didn't occur to you?"

"No. It didn't."

Rem told him to turn at the light. Deciding to go with his partner's gut, he sat back against the seat. "I hope you know what you're doing."

"Erin didn't do this, Rem."

Rem sighed, and keeping his concerns to himself and watching to ensure they weren't being followed, he guided Daniels toward the address.

Several minutes later, they arrived at an office building with no people in sight. "Where the hell are we?" asked Rem.

"Erin said this place is due to be bulldozed to make room for new construction. She said to meet her in the underground parking."

Rem watched as Daniels took a ramp down into a dark lot. "Are you serious? You don't see the obvious problems with this? How do we know this isn't another setup?"

"My sister is not trapping us. She's being careful." He slowly drove toward the back. "She said to park near the elevators."

Rem looked around, but the lot was empty. His heart thumped. "This is a little too cloak and dagger for me." He paused. "Can we at least back in? So we can make an easier escape?"

Daniels arched his brow, but after looking around, he did as Rem asked and backed into the space. "Just relax. I'm sure it's fine. I told her to be careful when I gave her that USB, remember?"

"And if she hadn't disappeared yesterday and lied about her whereabouts, I'd have less reason to worry. For all we know, she gave that USB to the people who killed Cain and almost killed Marjorie. We could be next."

Daniels gripped the wheel and studied the lot. He glanced at Rem as if considering his theory, but before he could respond, another car entered the lot and drove toward them. "There she is."

Not taking any chances, Rem pulled his weapon from his holster. The car approached and pulled up next to them. He saw Erin behind the wheel, but no one else was in the car. Daniels got out, and so did Rem.

Erin left her vehicle. A purse hung from her shoulder, and she approached Daniels. Rem gripped his gun, prepared in case Erin put her hand near her purse. He moved closer to her car and peered inside it, but it was empty. "Were you followed?" he asked and eyed the entrance to the lot.

"No," she said. "I was watching, but didn't see anyone."

"Where have you been?" asked Daniels.

"I went to LA." Erin clutched her purse closer.

Rem walked up next to Daniels. "To see Aunt Valora?" Rem couldn't keep the sarcasm from his voice.

Erin eyed the gun in his hand, and then her gaze met Rem's. "How did you know about Aunt Valora?"

"We've been looking for you, Erin," said Daniels. "A lot has happened in the last twenty-four hours."

"I called your work," said Rem. "They said you'd gone to see Valora. I tracked down Valora..."

Erin's eyes rounded. "You did what?"

Rem ignored her shock. "Valora told me she'd been at work and hadn't talked to you in a while."

"Why did you do that?" she asked.

"Because you wouldn't answer your damn phone," yelled Rem. His voice echoed through the empty lot.

Erin tightened her hold on her purse.

"Rem," said Daniels, putting his hand on Rem's arm. "Let me handle this."

Rem huffed and leaned back against the car. "She's all yours." He kept his gun in his hand.

Daniels faced Erin. "Erin, there was an orchestrated attack against us yesterday. Marjorie was in a car accident. Someone hit her car from behind and she...she..." He set his jaw. "...she went to the hospital."

Erin dropped her jaw. "Is she okay?"

Daniels took a heavy breath.

"Marjorie's okay, but she lost the baby," said Rem.

Erin's face tightened. "No." She studied Daniels. "Gordon, I'm so sorry."

Rem studied her for any deception but couldn't be sure if he saw any. "I talked to a witness at the scene. The vehicle that hit Marjorie and drove her into the intersection was driven by a female who was blonde and wore...blue nail polish." He eyed her nails.

Erin stared for a moment and then her face fell, and she glanced at her blue fingernails and then at Daniels. "Wait a second. You think it was *me* that hit Marjorie?"

"He doesn't," said Rem. "But *I* have my doubts. That description matches you, Erin. That's why I tried to find you, and when I learned you lied about where you were, and you wouldn't answer your phone, I had to wonder."

Erin shook her head. "It wasn't me."

"Then where were you?" yelled Rem again. Daniels looked back at him and Rem forced himself to calm down. "Listen, Erin." Rem softened his voice. "I want to believe you. Not for your sake, but for Daniels. He has been steadfast in his belief that you are not involved, and I pray to God he's right, because if you've betrayed him, I will personally escort you downtown and happily lock you behind bars."

Erin looked at Daniels. "It wasn't me. But I was in LA."

"Why?" asked Daniels.

"I told you I had a friend who could help me decode that drive. That's where I went, but I couldn't tell anyone that. That's why I made up the story about Valora." She shot a look at Rem. "And I didn't answer my phone because I turned it off. I watch too many crime shows and I got paranoid that someone could track me." She spoke to Daniels. "You grilled me about being careful and after Cain stopped by my place yesterday morning, I—"

"Cain did what?" asked Rem.

"When did he stop by?" asked Daniels.

Erin looked between them. "He came by early, which surprised me. He was acting weird and asked me to hang out and play hooky from work, which was odd since he's a workaholic. I told him I had to go see Valora in LA and he backed off and left. Said he'd see me later and to call when I got back."

Daniels stared off. "He would have seen your nail polish."

Holstering his gun, Rem thought it through. "He told someone, and they used that detail to make the driver look like Erin." He cursed. "It must have been Rhonda. The polish was a nice touch." He glanced at Erin. "...and once Cain learned you'd be out of town..."

"He assumed you wouldn't have a good alibi," said Daniels. "At least not at first..."

"I wonder if that was the plan," said Rem. "Cain was supposed to get Erin away..."

"Where she'd be hard to reach?" asked Daniels. He nodded. "Maybe. But unless he planned to kill her, he could be her alibi."

Rem hated to think about what his cousin had been up against. "Not if he lied."

Erin furrowed his brow. "What are you two talking about? Are you saying Cain was setting me up to make it look like I hurt Marjorie?"

Rem's grief bubbled up. "Cain was only taking direction from others. They were using him."

"You mean the black birds?" asked Erin. "Did you ask him about this? I hope to God you confronted him."

That familiar constriction returned, and Rem looked away.

"Cain is dead, Erin," said Daniels, softly. "They killed him."

Erin's eyes widened, and her jaw dropped. "What? When?"

"Cain called Rem yesterday," said Daniels. "He wanted to talk. Said he'd gotten in too deep, but by the time Rem got there, it was too late. He'd been shot."

Holding her chest, Erin turned away. "I don't believe it."

After a pause, Rem pushed back his grief and refocused. "Someone did this on purpose, Erin. You knew I was taking Marjorie to her appointment, and I had to wonder if you were involved. When I couldn't reach you, I feared the worst." He shook his head. "I don't know who to trust anymore."

Tears swam in her eyes, and she took a second to adjust to the news. "I'm sorry about Cain." She blinked back her tears. "Despite all his bravado, I think he loved you a great deal." Her voice caught. "He just didn't know how to show it."

Rem forced his emotions back. Now was not the time to lose it. He swallowed and took a second to compose himself. "Thank you." He shook out his hands and cleared his throat. "But now that we know where you were, how come we're just now hearing from you?"

Daniels patted Rem on the shoulder for support and regarded Erin. "What happened with the USB drive? Did you make any progress?"

Erin wiped a tear from her cheek. "We worked most of the night, trying to decode it. It's pretty sophisticated. I didn't get home until early this morning. All I could do was jump in the shower and get some sleep. I didn't even turn my phone back on until I was getting ready to call you. I wondered about all the missed calls, but figured I'd find out what was up soon enough."

"Yeah, well. Now you know," said Rem. "Just tell me you guys made some progress with that drive."

Erin dug through her purse. "I'll do you one better. This Mr. Ackerman was smart, but not smart enough." She pulled out a folded white piece of paper and waved it. "We decrypted it."

•••••••••

Daniels stood in disbelief. Erin handed him the paper, and he took it from her. "We printed what we found," said Erin. "I hope that's okay."

"It's fine." Daniels unfolded it and saw a list of names. "I don't believe it." His hands shook.

"Bring it over here," said Rem. "Put it on the hood." He pulled out his phone and flicked on the flashlight.

Daniels turned and put the paper on the hood of his car. Rem came up on his right with the light, and Erin on his left.

The first set of names had question marks next to them. Daniels read *Dirk*, *Winnie*, and *Denise Simmons*. Daniels pointed at Denise's name. "That's Rhonda's real name."

"Which she unfortunately no longer uses," said Rem. "I guess Ackerman couldn't identify these members, either." He tapped on Winnie's name. "Winnie is Margaret Redstone's accomplice. He's got to be the smoker who shot Vera and who Mikey's trying to remember."

"Who's Dirk?" asked Erin.

"No idea," said Daniels. "But he's a big player."

"Maybe the biggest," said Rem. "He's at the top."

Below the first three names were four more, with asterisks next to them. They were *Donald Morgans, Rex Beelson, Reginald Durning, Rita Vittorio*.

"That's our three vics," said Rem, "plus a new name. Who's Rita?"

"Maybe another victim we haven't found?" asked Daniels. "I don't know."

"Maybe that's the list of targets who owed a big debt, and three of them couldn't pay up," added Rem.

"If Rita's alive, that could be interesting," said Daniels.

"Very," said Rem.

Below the asterisked names was a long list of more names, most of them Daniels didn't recognize.

"Look," said Erin. "Cain's on there." She pointed at the paper.

Rem cursed. "This must be a list of members."

"You think some of these people owed debts too?" asked Daniels. "And may still be under the group's control?" He eyed Rem. "Like Cain?"

"It's possible." Rem eyed the list. "How much you want to bet Tex's actual name is listed here? His buddy Tommy's too?"

"I'd say it's highly likely," said Daniels.

"Who's Tex?" asked Erin.

Rem glanced at her. "He's in deep. He may be the one who killed Cain. And tried to kill us, too." He looked back at the paper and spoke with an edge. "I look forward to finding him."

"Rhonda told us his debt was paid, though, so why is he back?" asked Daniels.

"Guess he's an overachiever," replied Rem.

Daniels pointed at another name. "Rem. Look."

Rem cursed again. "Judge Thomas Gunderson. Bingo. Now we know why he signed that warrant to let Monk search my house. I knew that was suspicious."

"I don't see Monk's name on here. That's a good sign." Daniels kept reading and stopped again. Rem saw the name at the same time. "Holy...Barbara Ingram," said Rem. He eyed Daniels. "Maybe that's why she's got an attitude. That means she's got to know this Dirk."

"And it explains how Durning may have gotten caught up in all of this." Daniels couldn't believe what he was reading. The list of names was lengthy. "Rem, if all these people are involved..."

Rem tapped on the paper. "Then finding this is just the start. Who knows who all these people are or how they're implicated?"

Realizing the depth of what they'd uncovered, Daniels kept reading and pointed again. "What do you know? Chogan Crow, Elsa's dad."

"Unbelievable," said Rem. "At least I don't see Elsa listed." His gaze traveled over the names. "Please tell me Chief Patterson isn't on here."

Hoping the same, Daniels scanned the list. "I don't see him."

"Thank God," said Rem, dropping his head. "That's all we need."

"Your Captain Lozano isn't listed either," said Erin.

Daniels and Rem both gaped at her.

"What?" asked Erin. "That's good, isn't it?"

Shaking his head, Daniels went back to reading. He stopped on a name toward the end and sucked in a breath. "Rem."

His partner looked back at the paper. "What?"

Daniels pointed. "At the bottom."

Erin leaned closer. "Who is it?"

Rem spotted the name. His eyes widened and his face turned pale. "You got to be kidding me."

Shocked, Daniels eyed the name again and almost hated to say it out loud. "Victor D'Mato."

Chapter Thirty

THE BUZZ OF HER phone startled Mikey out of her meditation. She picked it up and saw a text from Marjorie asking for water and some peanut butter crackers from the pantry. Mikey texted she'd be right up and stood from the couch. Lozano had left ten minutes earlier and Rem had texted soon after that he and Daniels were on their way back.

Since it was quiet, she'd taken advantage of the silence and sat on the couch to meditate to calm her nerves. After all that had happened, she needed a respite. Planning only to clear her mind, she'd quickly found herself back at the grove, watching the activity around the fire. Despite the expected outcome, Mikey had remained detached, and before the worst could happen, Vera had again turned her face toward Mikey and smiled. She watched Mikey until the text interrupted the meditation.

Thinking about Vera, Mikey walked into the kitchen, found the crackers, and filled a glass of water for Marjorie. Turning, she stopped when tingles ran up her back and that strange feeling of being watched returned and made her shiver. Mason had told her that usually meant a spirit was present and recommended that Mikey go still and listen.

Looking around the kitchen, Mikey waited, but not seeing anything, she shook off the tingles and went up the stairs. She softly knocked on the bedroom door. "Marjorie?"

"Come in."

Mikey opened the door and saw Marjorie awake in the bed. Her arm with the cast lay outside the covers. The bruise on her face had traveled and the skin beneath her eye was purple. "Hey," said Mikey, noticing Marjorie's puffy eyes. "I got your water and crackers."

"Thank you." Marjorie sniffed and wiped her cheek with the fingers of her uninjured arm.

Concerned, Mikey set the water down and grabbed a tissue from the nightstand. "How are you?" She handed the tissue to Marjorie.

"Thanks." Marjorie took the tissue. "It comes and goes. I woke up and just started crying." She wiped her nose.

Mikey opened the crackers and recalled her grief after losing her mother. "That's normal. You're processing a lot right now." She held out a cracker.

"Thanks." Marjorie took it. "I'm not hungry, but should probably eat something. At least, that's what Gordon would tell me."

"He's right. It'll keep up your strength. He and Rem are on their way back. They should be here soon." She picked up the glass. "You want some water?"

"Please." She finished the cracker and drank some with a grimace.

Mikey took the water and set the crackers aside. "Are you comfortable?"

Marjorie tried to shift, but gasped. "My rib is killing me. Can you help me move the pillows?"

"Sure." Mikey helped raise Marjorie enough to fluff and arrange the pillows behind her. "How's that?"

Marjorie rested back. "Much better. Thank you."

Mikey pulled out another cracker and handed it to Marjorie. "Here. Have another."

"Thanks." Her tears slowing, Marjorie took a bite and studied Mikey. "How are you doing?"

"Me?" asked Mikey.

"I feel like everyone's been worrying about me, Gordon and Rem. But you're in the middle of this too."

Mikey poked at the edge of the blanket. "I didn't lose a baby or a cousin."

Marjorie chewed and swallowed. "Out of all of us, you're the most empathic. I know you feel others' pain, especially Rem's. Don't tell me this hasn't been difficult."

Mikey met Marjorie's gaze. "No. It hasn't been easy. I've learned to put up boundaries, but I still feel things." She paused. "I just..."

"You just what?"

Mikey considered how much to say. "You're right. I feel the intensity of Rem's guilt and grief. I want to be there for him, but I'm not sure he wants that."

Marjorie lowered her cracker. "He does. He's just not ready to let you in yet."

"Did Daniels tell you he went to Jennie's grave after Cain died?" Mikey hated to admit that had bothered her.

Marjorie's face softened, and she took Mikey's wrist. "He went there all the time after he lost her. But don't think he doesn't want to be with you. It's just his process. After Jennie died, it was pulling teeth to get him to talk about it. I've known him a long time, but Gordon knows him best, and even he couldn't get Rem to open up, until one day, all it took was one trigger for it to all come crumbling down."

"I'm trying to avoid that," said Mikey. A memory flashed of her bringing Rem dishes to smash when it looked like Daniels might die after his head injury.

"And he's trying to protect you. He wants to be strong but knows you can feel his pain. But when he's ready, you'll be the first one he goes to." Marjorie squeezed Mikey's hand. "He loves you, Mikey. I think more than you realize. Just be patient with him."

Unexpected tears surfaced, and she smiled softly at Marjorie. "I love him too, you know. So much."

"I know you do. Which is why he's in good hands. He'll be okay, and he knows you'll be there to catch him if he falls. He'd do the same for you in a heartbeat."

Mikey recalled Rem holding her in a running shower when, after re-membering Vera's murder, she'd fallen apart. She squeezed Marjorie's hand in return. "Thanks, Marjorie. I needed to hear that."

Marjorie popped the rest of the cracker in her mouth. "You're wel-come." She finished the cracker, and Mikey handed her the glass of water.

Marjorie took a sip. "And can I make another suggestion?"

"Sure."

Marjorie handed the glass back to Mikey. "Take Rem's advice and learn to shoot that gun."

Mikey hesitated. "You think it's that important?"

"I do." She shifted and winced again.

"You okay?"

"Yeah. It just hurts when I breathe."

"Sorry about that. You want another cracker?"

Marjorie shook her head. "No, thanks." She pulled up the blanket. "Rem and Gordon are out there now, trying to find who caused all of this. And as much as they want to protect us, they can't be everywhere at once, which means it's important to take our safety seriously. We have to assume that whoever did this will try again, and it may be up to us to protect ourselves."

Mikey recalled her conversation with Rem, where they'd discussed the dangers of him pursuing the black bird group and of her trying to retrieve her memories. "I know you're right, but it didn't really hit home until now."

"This time around, it was me, but next time, it could be you. We have to be prepared, Mikey."

"I took a self-defense class a while back. Maybe it's time to refresh my skills."

"When I'm better, I'll join you. We'll work on it together."

"I'd like that."

Marjorie eyed the ceiling. "These people, whoever they are, underestimate us, and I'm tired of being used as a pawn to hurt my husband."

Mikey didn't like the thought of being Rem's weak spot, either. "I think that attempt to pin Vera's murder on me was a way to get to Rem."

"Exactly. It pisses me off."

Mikey asked the hard question. "Do you ever regret marrying a cop?"

Marjorie met her gaze. "The better question is, do I regret marrying Gordon? And the answer is no. We've had bumps along the road, and we work at it, but there's no one else I'd rather be with." She paused. "Do you regret meeting Rem? If you could go back, would you do it differently?"

Mikey didn't hesitate. "No. Never. I can't imagine being with anyone else."

"Then, since we're crazy enough to attach ourselves to two men who seem to attract a lot of trouble, we have a responsibility to take care of ourselves." She pointed. "Which means you're going to learn to shoot that gun. Okay?"

Mikey nodded. "And when you're strong enough, you're going to take that self-defense class with me."

"You're on."

Mikey smiled. "Rem and Daniels may not be so thrilled."

"They'll get over it." Marjorie blinked heavy lids.

"I'll let you rest, so you can be ready sooner rather than later. You need anything, let me know."

Marjorie relaxed against the pillows. "Thanks, Mikey." She closed her eyes, and Mikey stood, but paused when Marjorie opened her eyes. "I'm glad we talked," said Marjorie. "You and I need to stick together. Nobody else can understand."

Mikey put her hand over Marjorie's. "I'm glad we talked, too. We should do it more often."

Marjorie closed her eyes again. "We will."

Grateful for their much-needed conversation, Mikey left the water glass and remaining crackers on the nightstand and crept out of the room. Closing the bedroom door, she turned and froze when the tingles abruptly returned, this time much stronger. They ran up her back and down her arms. Going still, she tuned in and gasped when, down the hall, the air swirled and coalesced. Too scared to move, Mikey stood in shock as the swirls condensed, took shape, and Vera appeared.

Her heart racing, all Mikey could do was stare. Vera, wearing what Mikey recalled from the grove, stared back. She made no attempt to communicate but simply watched Mikey. The light from the window at the end of the hall fluttered through her.

Wondering what Mason would do, Mikey heard a door open and close from below and Rem's voice. "We're back."

Mikey glanced toward the stairs.

"Hello?" said Daniels.

"Up here," said Mikey. Looking back, she saw no one in the hall. Vera had vanished.

Chapter Thirty-One

RHONDA SAT IN HER car at the end of the street and watched the entry to the pawn shop. It had been quiet, with little activity. Two customers had come and gone, so she knew Bertrand was present.

She patiently waited while running through her plan in her mind. It had been an active few days, but now that they'd gotten to this point, she could relax. The harder stuff was done and had gone exactly as she and Monk had hoped. Now, all she had to do was deal with Bertrand and kill Jerry Lee, and then she could take a few days off. Maybe she'd go to the beach and soak up some sun. She was long overdue.

Her phone rang, and picking it up, she smiled and answered. "Calling instead of texting? You must be alone and feeling frisky."

Monk chuckled. "I'm always frisky when I talk to you. And yes. Manetti's not here at the moment, and Remalla and Daniels are out of the office, just as I'd hoped."

"Perfect."

"It is. Feel free to move forward as planned."

She eyed the pawn shop again. "I will."

"You're sure Caruso is there?"

"I am. I followed Bertrand the other day to the grocery store. I doubt his eating habits are great, but there's no way he eats that much junk food by himself."

He chuckled over the phone. "Text me when it's done. And don't forget the cameras."

"This isn't my first rodeo."

His voice deepened. "Once it's done, we'll celebrate."

She rested her head back. "I was thinking the beach."

He chuckled again. "I'll see what I can do."

"Good. You know how I like to be spoiled."

"And I enjoy doing the spoiling, especially when you're naked."

She sighed into the phone. "Don't distract me. I have work to do."

His tone shifted. "Manetti's back. Go do your thing."

"See you, baby."

"See you. And good luck." He hung up.

Rhonda ended the call, silenced her phone, and slid it into her purse. She opened her door and whispered. "It's never been about luck, baby." Before exiting the car, she grabbed her cane and studied herself in the rearview mirror. Satisfied, she got out, and using the cane, limped toward the pawn shop.

· · · • · • · · ·

Listening to his son giggle and splash in the water while his grandmother gave him a bath, Daniels walked down the stairs, carrying the dirty plate and glass he'd brought up with Marjorie's lunch.

After meeting with Erin the previous day and reviewing Ackerman's list, he and Rem had to make some quick decisions. They'd told Erin to get in touch with her Aunt Valora and make sure no one else had called to verify where Erin had been the day before. Then they encouraged her to convince Valora that if anyone called, to lie and say Erin had been with her. They'd also told her to stay with a friend for a few days since it was best not to be alone. Daniels wanted her to stay with him and Marjorie, but after discussing it, they decided it was better to act as if there was some distance between Daniels, Rem, and Erin after Cain's murder and Marjorie's accident.

After leaving Erin, they called Lexie, told her they needed to discuss what happened to Cain and Marjorie, and asked to meet her at a coffee shop. Thirty minutes later, after stopping at a print store to make additional copies of the list of names, they sat at a small table with Lexie and went over the events of the previous day. They told her they needed to back off the black bird investigation since it was too dangerous and encouraged her to go stay with her mother for a little while. While she argued for all the reasons they should move forward, and why she didn't need to go to her mom's, Rem asked her to open one of her notebooks. Curious, she'd complied, and he'd taken one of her pens, written *We have the list of names*, and slid her folded copy between the sheets of the notebook. Then he'd written *For once in your life, listen to us and go stay with your mom. We'll get in touch soon.*

She'd read the note, stared at them, slammed the notebook shut, and stood, telling them they were making a mistake, but she understood their concerns, hoped they could stay in touch and stomped out as if angry.

Daniels and Rem hadn't known whether that performance had been necessary, but now that they had decoded the drive, nothing could be assumed, and safety was a priority.

After returning home and talking to Marjorie and Mikey about Erin and the decoded list, he and Rem took the following day off so Daniels could stay with Marjorie and J.P., Rem could be with his relatives, and they could decide their next steps.

Weary after a restless night of sleep, Daniels went into the kitchen, rinsed the plate and glass and put them in the dishwasher. Grateful his mother-in-law had come over to help with Marjorie and J.P., Daniels poured himself some apple juice and sat at the table.

A knock on his door startled him out of his thoughts. Cautious, he walked over and peered out the peephole and saw Rem. He opened his door. "Hey. I thought you'd be with family all day."

Looking as weary as Daniels felt, Rem sauntered in. "I've been with them all morning. If I stay any longer, you're going to have put me in the same institution Margaret's in."

Daniels closed and locked the door. "That's not a bad idea, since she knows who Winnie is."

Rem scowled at him. "That's not even funny." He sat at the table.

"You suggested it. Not me." Daniels joined him at the table. "Where's Mikey?"

"At SCOPE. I drove her in and told her to call me when she's done, and I'd pick her up." Rem scratched his head. "How's Marjorie?"

"Better. She's upstairs with her mom, helping give J.P. a bath. I asked her not to overdo it, but J.P. makes her feel better, so she's getting some leeway."

"J.P.'s good for the soul." He eyed Daniels' juice. "You got any more of that?"

"What? No coffee?"

"I've been drinking it all morning. I could run around the block about ten times."

Daniels stood. "I'll get you some."

"Thanks."

Daniels grabbed another glass, poured some apple juice into it and brought it over to Rem. "Drink up." He sat at the table.

Rem took a long drink and set the glass down. "So, what happens tomorrow? We go about our business as usual?"

Daniels scratched his head. "I've been thinking about that. We need to find Durning's killer and locate Jerry Lee."

"We know who killed Durning. Rhonda. Going through CIW's client and staff list, while enlightening, is a waste of time."

"It's not a total waste of time. Barbara Ingram is on that staff list, as well as Ackerman's."

"What do you propose? Questioning Barbara about Ackerman or the black birds? That would tip our hand, plus she won't tell us anything."

"It's a given she knows this Dirk."

"And we know how well that went over when we asked her, Crenshaw, and Willoughby about him."

"Maybe if we got her alone, she might be more willing to talk."

Rem snorted. "Did you see the way she looked at us? She'd probably accuse us of assault."

"She's a player in this game, Rem. We need to get her to talk."

"Last I checked, my torture skills were rusty, but I suppose I could find some bamboo shoots to jam behind her fingernails."

Daniels leaned back with a sigh. "There is another option." He swirled his juice. "But you're not gonna like it."

"What is it?"

"Talk to Margaret Redstone."

Rem almost choked on his drink.

"I said you weren't gonna like it. But she was close to Winnie and D'Mato. She likely knows about the black birds, and maybe even knows Dirk."

Rem groaned. "These options suck. Is there a third?"

"The next obvious thing is to research every name on that list, especially Rita Vittorio, and find out who we're dealing with, but we have to be careful. If somebody starts asking questions, we need to be able to answer them."

"You know Lexie is already on that."

"Well, she can't be the only one researching. We need to do something. There's no point in having the list if we don't use it."

Rem rested his elbows on the table. "How about this? Our best bet is to find Rhonda. We do that, and we can better protect Jerry Lee and find Cain's killer."

"How do you propose we do that?"

Rem straightened. "We start with the men on the list."

"Why the men?"

"Because one of those men is Tex. And Tex knows Rhonda. And since Tex is back on the payroll, he may know Winnie and maybe even Dirk. We find him and it could open up this whole thing." He pointed. "Including finding out who's framing Lozano."

Daniels considered that. "Us looking for him would make sense, since he tried to kill us in Elmwood, and he's connected to Rhonda." He eyed Rem. "Crow might go for that."

"Unless she's a pipeline of information to her father, so we have to watch what we tell her. If the black birds learn we're looking for Tex, that makes him a liability."

Daniels nodded. "They'd kill him like they did Cain."

"I could live with that if he wasn't a potential source of information. I'd like to kill him myself."

"Careful, partner. You still need to talk to Monk and Manetti about Cain. Best keep that thought to yourself."

Rem rubbed his temples. "At least they agreed to push back my questioning until tomorrow, so they can't be that eager to arrest me."

"Guess you'll find out tomorrow."

"Assuming they don't put me in cuffs, hunting for Tex is our best bet. We can use the staff and client lists as an explanation for researching the names. Crow won't know the difference."

Daniels couldn't think of a better idea. "Then that's where we'll start."

"It's damn sure better than talking to Margaret."

"I doubt she'd tell us anything," said Daniels. "But it's an option if we need to use it. But let's not forget Rita. If she's alive, she could be useful, too."

"If she's alive, we'll have to be cautious. We can't reveal how we found her name."

"The same goes for Tex."

Rem finished his juice. "Let's see what we find first and go from there. Hopefully, somewhere along the way, we'll find Jerry Lee, too."

"With that reward money, somebody may find him for us." Daniels had told Rem about the news report he'd seen regarding Patricia Caruso and the odd amount of reward offered to anyone who could locate her son. "Which is another thing to consider. The two days Sammy Caruso gave us are up. Which means he's going to get involved."

"You think he put up that reward money?"

Daniels thought about it. "It doesn't sound like his style. Plus, he offered it before our two days were over. Why not wait to see if we could find Jerry first?"

Rem's cell rang, and he took it out of his pocket. "It's Crow." He answered. "Remalla speaking."

Daniels watched as Rem listened, and his eyes widened. "What?" he asked. "When?" He eyed Daniels.

Daniels waited to hear what was going on.

Rem nodded. "Yeah. No. I'm glad you called. Daniels and I are on our way." He hung up.

"What's wrong?"

Rem stood. "Arnold Betrand is dead. He was found shot to death in his pawn shop."

Shocked, Daniels stood too. "Any sign of Jerry Lee?"

"None, but there are signs he was there." He eyed the stairs. "I can go on my own if you want."

Daniels grabbed his jacket. "Let me tell Marjorie."

Chapter Thirty-Two

REM SQUATTED NEXT TO the covered body. He lifted the covering and studied the corpse of Arnold Bertrand.

"He took two shots to the chest," said Brann, the same officer who'd been in charge of Durning's crime scene. "And a third one grazed his head and went into the wall behind him."

Daniels leaned over Rem. "He's got a gun. Did he fire it?"

"Looks like he got off one shot," said Brann. "Bullet's in the wall over there." He pointed toward the far side of the shop. "We'll dig it out and get ballistics on it."

"Thanks," said Rem, lowering the covering. "Find any casings, or blood other than his?"

"No on the blood and just one casing. It's likely from the vic's gun, though. It was found near him."

Rem nodded and stood. "Any indication that anyone else was in the shop other than our killer?"

Daniels audibly groaned. "Please tell me there isn't another witness."

"None that we know of," added Brann.

Shaking his head, Daniels looked around the shop. "Anything stolen?"

"Doesn't look like it," said Brann. "Money's still in the register. Shop looks undisturbed. And Bertrand's wallet is untouched."

"Anything in it of interest?" asked Rem.

"Just cash, couple of credit cards, and receipts," said Brann. "That's it." He gestured toward the open door marked *Private*. "The basement's interesting, though. It looks like he'd been staying here a while."

Rem moved away from the body, followed Daniels through the door to the basement, and walked down the steps. "Look at this," said Rem, seeing the kitchenette, cot, table, and TV. A ladder was against the wall beneath a small window.

"All the comforts of home," added Daniels.

Brann came up behind them. "Looks like the cot's been slept in. There's food and drinks in the cabinets and fridge. Judging by what's in the trash, two people were down here."

"Jerry Lee," said Rem with a sigh. "Damn it. He was here all this time." He wanted to kick something.

Daniels walked to the ladder and studied the window. "Since Jerry's not around, I'm guessing he made his escape." He gestured toward the window.

"Smart move," said Rem. "Bertrand must have prepared him, in case something like this happened." He cursed again. "If Crow hadn't pulled the surveillance...this might have turned out differently." He had to wonder if she'd removed it deliberately.

Brann pointed at the TV. "You can see the interior of the store here."

Rem walked over. "Please tell me there's footage of what happened."

Brann shook his head. "No such luck. Footage was wiped clean. We'll dust the equipment for prints, though. Maybe we'll get lucky."

"Don't count on it," said Daniels.

"Have you found a murder weapon?" asked Rem.

"Nope. Killer took it with him," said Brann.

"You mean her," said Rem.

Brann shrugged. "No way to know."

"Trust me," said Daniels, stepping around a photographer taking photos. "We know."

"You start a canvas?" asked Rem.

"I've got a few guys on it," added Brann. "Hopefully, someone saw or heard something."

Rem doubted it. Neighborhoods like this rarely liked to share. "Keep us posted and make sure they're asking about Jerry Lee, too."

"Will do." Another officer appeared at the top of the stairs, asking for Brann, and the officer returned to the first floor.

Rem walked over to the ladder and stared up at the window. Daniels joined him. "We're going to have to call Patricia Caruso," said Daniels.

"That'll be fun." Rem hated the thought of telling Jerry Lee's mom that Jerry Lee had escaped another attempt on his life and vanished again. Trying not to think about it, he eyed the room and the ladder and made some deductions. "So Rhonda shows as a customer, probably in disguise. Bertrand helps her, but she pulls a weapon and so does he. He gets a shot off, but not before she kills him." Rem glanced at the TV. "Jerry sees the whole thing and escapes out the window. Rhonda gets down here, doesn't find Jerry, but finds the footage and erases it." He crossed his arms. "Stupid. Why didn't Bertrand trust us?"

"He didn't seem like the trusting type," said Daniels. He gestured at the TV. "And if Jerry Lee could see us from down here, why didn't *he* trust us?"

"I'm sure Bertrand gave Jerry a million reasons why he couldn't."

"And now Bertrand's dead."

"And Jerry Lee's back on the run."

"With Rhonda on his heels." Daniels rubbed his neck. "Sooner or later, she's going to catch up to him."

"How the hell did she know Jerry was here?"

Daniels surveyed the room. "She played a hunch, which paid off. Maybe we should have done the same."

Rem heard the dejected tone in Daniels' voice. "This isn't our fault. We came here. We told Bertrand the deal. Both he and Jerry had the option of accepting our help, but they didn't. We don't have the option to bust in and search the place, unless you want to do it like Rhonda did, and pull our weapons. But attorneys frown on that."

Daniels slid his hands into his jacket pockets. "Jerry's just a kid, Rem, and probably scared to death. We should have pushed harder."

"And where would that have gotten us?"

"Jerry Lee could be in our custody right now."

Rem lowered his voice. "And you saw Ackerman's list. For all we know, there are cops on it. Jerry Lee may not be any safer with us."

Daniels met Rem's gaze. "If that's true, then what are we doing? If we can't keep Jerry safe, or the people we love, who can?"

Understanding his partner's frustration, Rem stepped closer to him. "Like we said in the cemetery, we do what we always do. Trust each other. Plus, there's Lozano, and Lexie, Marjorie and Mikey, and now Erin. Manetti, too. We do the best we can with what we have. It's worked before, and it will work again." He paused. "At some point, you just got to have faith."

Daniels stared up at the window, and his look of melancholy remained. "I hope someone told Jerry Lee that." After a pause, he turned from the window and walked away.

•••••••••••

The next morning, Daniels sat at his desk. Rem was in an interview room, with Manetti and Monk, talking to them about Cain. After a discussion with Lurch, Rem had decided not to bring him into the meeting. He wanted to see how it would go first and then determine whether he needed an attorney. Rem didn't want to poke the bear if he didn't have to. But if Monk became acrimonious, Rem would end the questioning and call Lurch. Lurch had also advised Rem to keep the black birds out of the discussion if possible until they had more proof of Cain's role within the group. Until then, bringing them up would involve Monk and Manetti and could spur more retaliation. And it could make Rem look suspicious if Monk and Manetti believed he was lying to protect himself.

Working on the list in front of him, which contained the last few names from the client list, Daniels picked up his phone to make a call when a tall man with thinning salt and pepper hair, an angular narrow face, and wearing an expensive suit, entered the squad room. He stopped and looked around, and Daniels swiveled toward him. "Can I help you?"

"I'm looking for—" He smiled. "There she is."

Elsa Crow emerged from her office. "Hey, Dad." She walked over and gave the man a hug. "You're early."

Daniels, realizing the man was Chogan Crow, focused on his list.

"I got out of my meeting sooner than expected. Figured I'd head over. You ready?" asked Chogan.

"Sure. Let me grab my purse. Oh, by the way, this is Detective Gordon Daniels."

Daniels straightened and swiveled back toward Chogan.

"Daniels," said Elsa. "This is my father, Chogan Crow."

Daniels stood. "Nice to meet you." He held out his hand.

Crow paused, and his eyes narrowed. He looked at Daniels' hand and shook it. "Nice to meet you, too." He glanced at Rem's desk and Daniels wondered if he expected to meet Rem.

"Dad and I are headed to lunch." Elsa went into the captain's office.

"Elsa tells me she's settling in, despite a few bumps in the road," said Crow.

Daniels imagined what Elsa had told her father about him and Rem. "I suppose that's expected, considering how she got here." His words sounded harsher than he intended, but he wasn't lying.

The sides of Crow's lips raised. "It's unfortunate what happened to your captain."

"We expect he'll be exonerated soon."

"Assuming he's innocent."

Daniels sensed Chogan Crow was used to intimidating people, but Daniels didn't plan to be one of them. "He is. That will be proven soon enough."

Daniels and Chogan stared at each other until Elsa returned. "I'm ready."

Chogan broke the look and glanced at his daughter. "Good. Let's go." He spoke to Daniels. "Nice to have met you."

"You, too." Elsa and her father left the squad room, and Daniels absorbed that he'd just met another black bird member. He sat heavily in his chair and groaned. Had Chogan played a role in what had happened to Marjorie and Cain? Had he been part of it since the beginning, when Daniels and Rem had traveled through Elmwood?

Daniels pulled out his notebook, flipped to a blank page, and wrote Chogan's name on it. That was one name on the list he could say he'd spoken to.

The squad doors opened, and Daniels turned to see Rem return to the squad room. "How'd it go?"

Rem plopped into his seat. "Better than I expected. They just asked the basics, and Monk was even nice to me."

Daniels sat up. "Really? Someone must have put sugar in his cornflakes this morning."

"He was almost in a good mood." Rem shivered. "It kind of weirded me out."

"Speaking of being weirded out, guess who I just met?"

"The Mothman? Godzilla?"

"Try Chogan Crow?"

Rem's face fell. "I wish it had been the Mothman."

"He…Crow, not Mothman…picked up Elsa for lunch. She introduced him to me, and warm and fuzzy is not a description I would use."

"That's too bad. Were you warm and fuzzy?"

"Not exactly."

"Good."

"I got the impression Elsa did not sing our praises to him."

Rem lowered his voice. "If Crow's in the you-know-what group, then he already hates us."

"Good point." Daniels closed his notebook. "Did you get any information out of Manetti or Monk about who might have killed Cain?"

"I tried, but they were tightlipped about it. I told them about what Cain said, though, about Tex being the one who killed him."

"How'd they take it?"

"They asked about Tex. I told them he was one of the men who came after us in Elmwood. I mentioned his tattoo but kept the rest of the bird stuff out of it."

Daniels returned his notebook to his drawer. "Well, who knows? Maybe that will help find him."

"And maybe I'll turn vegan."

Daniels chuckled and swiveled as Monk and Manetti returned. They sat at their desks, and Manetti opened his notebook.

"Hey, Manetti," said Rem. "I know I'm not on Cain's case, but he is my cousin. Keep me posted on whatever you can."

Manetti looked up and nodded. "Of course."

"Hey, Manetti," said Monk. "We can tell him about the weapon. That won't hurt anything."

Rem perked up. "Did you find a weapon at the scene?"

Manetti shook his head. "No such luck. But ballistics came back from the bullet that kill…well, struck Cain." He shifted in his seat toward Rem. "Forensics is pretty confident it came from a .38 Special."

Recalling Rem's father's gun was the same, Daniels went still, and Rem didn't move, either.

Monk rocked back in his seat. "I don't suppose you know anyone who owns one, do you, Remalla?" He twirled his pencil around his fingers.

· · · ● · ● · ● · · ·

With a monumental effort, Rem kept his shock off his face and stared at Daniels, who was doing the same.

"Don't push it, Monk," said Manetti.

"It's a good question, Manetti," replied Monk, staring at Rem.

Rem forced a disinterested gaze on his face. "Nobody I know."

Manetti dropped his pen onto his desk. "You think of someone, tell us." He stood. "You ready, Monk? We're supposed to meet with Cain's neighbor."

Monk stood. "Ready when you are." He glanced at Rem and Daniels. "See you guys."

"See ya," said Daniels.

Monk grabbed his jacket, and he and Manetti left the squad room.

Rem shot out of his seat. "Did you hear that?"

Still in his chair, Daniels pushed away from his desk. "It could be just a coincidence."

Rem, his heart thumping, knew it wasn't. "And...again...I could go vegan." He paused. "There's one way to be sure. We need to go to my house."

Daniels stood. "If your dad's gun isn't there..."

"I'm way past screwed."

Daniels reached for his phone when it rang. He picked it up. "Hold on. It's Marjorie." He answered. "Hey, honey. Everything all right?"

Rem tried not to think about what would happen if his father's gun was no longer in his upstairs closet. He paced, waiting for Daniels, when Daniels' brow furrowed.

"What do you mean?" asked Daniels. "It's what? But how...?" He paused. "No. I didn't do anything." His eyes widened, and he looked at Rem. "Say that again. It's how much?" Daniels closed his eyes and sat again. "Yeah. I know. It's the same." He gripped his neck. "I have no idea."

Wondering what was happening, Rem stepped closer.

Daniels leaned over and rested his head in his palm. "Let me see what I can find out. You get some rest, okay? Let your mom help with J.P. Don't overdo it." He paused. "Yeah. I will. I love you, too." He hung up.

Rem pulled his chair closer and sat. "What's wrong? Is Marjorie okay?"

"She's fine." Daniels set his phone on his desk. "She was catching up on email. You know that medical bill I owe from my head injury?"

"Yeah."

"It's been paid in full."

Rem narrowed his eyes. "What? By who?"

"No idea."

"When?"

"Two days ago."

Rem didn't understand. "Why would...?"

"Guess what the amount was?"

"Daniels, I don't—"

"$62,148."

Rem dropped his jaw. It was the exact reward amount offered by Patricia Caruso for Jerry Lee's return. "What in the hell is going on here?"

"Think about it. Cain's shot with a .38 Special, I get my debt paid off..." He stilled.

"What is it?"

Daniels cursed and reached for the landline phone on his desk. "Give me a second." He picked up the landline and dialed an extension. After a pause, he spoke. "Hey Wilhelm? It's Daniels. You get the ballistics back on the bullets pulled from Arnold Bertrand?" He eyed Rem, whose heart dropped. "Yeah. I'll wait."

Rem closed his eyes, praying Daniels wouldn't get the answer Rem feared.

"Yeah. I'm here," said Daniels. He listened, sighed, and gripped the phone. "You're sure?" He paused. "Okay. Thanks, Wilhelm." He hung up and stared at Rem. "Wilhelm believes Bertrand was shot with a .38 Special, and worse, the bullets came from the same gun that killed Cain. He's writing the report now."

Dejected, Rem fell back in his seat.

·········

Daniels waited downstairs as Rem raced up to the second floor of his home to check the closet for his dad's gun. Chester, Rem and Mikey's cat, which at one point belonged to Mikey's sister, Margaret, appeared and rubbed against Daniels' ankle until Rem ran back down the stairs, holding a small box. Chester ran off and Rem opened the box. Daniels peered in and cursed when he saw it was empty.

Rem threw the box across the room, put his hands on his hips and paced. "Now what do we do?"

Daniels eyed the ceiling, wondering how to answer, when he recalled the amount of the reward. "Patricia Caruso."

"What about her?" asked Rem, still pacing.

"Whoever put up the reward knew the exact amount I owed." He raised a brow at Rem.

Rem gazed back with a knowing expression. "Let's go talk to Patricia." He headed for the door.

· · · · ● · ● · · ·

After driving as fast as possible without causing an accident, Rem pulled up to Patricia Caruso's house. He and Daniels got out and, after a wave at the patrol car out front, they ran up to the door and knocked.

A few seconds passed, and Patricia opened the door. "Have you heard anything about Jerry Lee?"

Rem pulled the screen door open. "No, but we need to talk to you."

She stepped back. "Okay." Rem walked in along with Daniels, and they headed into the living room.

Patricia closed the door. "What's this about?"

"We need to ask about the reward you offered for Jerry's safe return," said Daniels. "Who put up the money?"

"Was it your father?" asked Rem.

Patricia walked over to the couch. "No."

"Then who was it?" asked Daniels.

Patricia wrung her hands.

"It's important," said Daniels.

Patricia sat on the couch. "A man came to the house."

Rem sat in the love seat across from her and Daniels sat beside him. "What man?" asked Rem.

"He was around your age. Handsome. He was wearing sunglasses and a baseball cap, but I could see he had brown wavy hair and a muscular build. He wore gloves too, which I thought was odd. He told me he wanted to help find Jerry. I was suspicious, but he said his boss was watching the news and wanted to get involved."

"Who's his boss?" asked Daniels.

"He wouldn't tell me."

"What did he say?" asked Rem.

"He said his boss wanted to offer the reward. He'd lost someone too, and knew how difficult it could be, and he wanted Jerry Lee safely home. When I asked about the odd amount, the man said that was his boss' decision, and he was only the messenger." She clutched her hands together. "I didn't care about the amount. I just want Jerry back, so I agreed to offering the reward, but the man said there was one stipulation."

"What was that?" asked Daniels.

"He said not to tell you two about him until you showed up asking. And when you did…" She stood, went to a drawer, and pulled out a manilla envelope. "I was supposed to give you this."

Rem stared at the envelope, wondering what they would find inside. Daniels took it from Patricia and opened it. He pulled out a piece of paper and Rem leaned to read it. It said, "Let's talk." Beneath the words was a phone number. Daniels looked inside the envelope and pulled out a small phone. He shot a look at Rem before dropping the paper and phone back into the envelope.

Rem's heart hammered. "Patricia," he said, meeting her gaze. "Did the man you spoke to have a name?"

Patricia, who stood rigid in the room, nodded. "He said to call him Tex."

• • • • • • • • •

Sitting in the passenger seat of Rem's car, Daniels held the envelope. "Well? What do you think?"

Rem gripped the steering wheel. "He wants to talk? Then let's talk."

"We could try to get prints off the note and phone."

"What for?" asked Rem. "So Forensics can find ours and Patricia's? He wore gloves, remember?"

Daniels paused. "Okay. Here goes." Taking a breath, he removed the paper and phone. He used the phone to dial the number and listened to it ring. It rang several times without an answer and no voicemail picked up. "That's helpful," said Daniels, lowering the phone. "A cryptic message and a number no one answers."

"Maybe we caught him in the bathroom."

The phone buzzed, and Daniels raised it. "It's a text message."

"What does it say?"

"It's an address." He held the phone up for Rem to see.

Rem studied the screen. "Let's not keeping him waiting." He started the car and drove off.

· · • • • • • • · ·

Rem pulled up in front of a quiet gas station with a garage in the back. A *Closed* sign was in the window. "Is this it?"

Daniels studied his phone. "This is it."

Rem killed the engine, and they both got out. Rem walked up to the entrance and peered inside. "Nobody's here."

Daniels looked around. "This neighborhood is part of that new development. They probably sold this place." He eyed the garage. "Let's go back there."

They walked past the station toward several bays that were all closed and locked.

"Rem," said Daniels, seeing a black SUV parked in the back. He pulled out his gun, crept up to it, and peered in. "It's empty."

"Daniels." Rem tipped his head and hurried over to a door just past the SUV. Holding his weapon, he moved to one side of it. Daniels went to the other. He tried the knob, and it turned. Rem nodded and Daniels pushed the door open. Rem swung around, his gun out, facing the interior. He stepped inside and Daniels, aiming his own weapon, came in behind him. Inside the murky space was a table with chairs, a dirty window with a view of the alley, and a large mirror that hung from the wall parallel to the table. One light bulb above them illuminated the space, and the room was empty.

Rem lowered his gun. "Nothing."

Squinting in the minimal light, Daniels saw another door in a small, recessed alcove behind the mirror. "Hey," he said to Rem. He came up beside the door and Rem joined him. Daniels tried the knob, but it didn't turn. "It's locked."

"Figures."

Daniels stepped back and looked around. "What the hell is this place?"

"Must have been the owner's old office," said Rem.

"But why bring us here?" asked Daniels. He looked at himself in the mirror.

Rem swiped his fingers over the table. "They must have expected us." He held up his fingers. "No dust."

"And the light's on," said Daniels.

"Hello, Detectives," said a male voice.

Daniels swiveled toward the sound, and Rem raised his gun. "There," said Rem. "In the corner."

Daniels squinted and saw a small speaker at the back of the room. He glanced back at the mirror and guessed someone was behind it. "Who are you?"

The male voice responded. "I will answer your questions as soon as you place your weapons on the table."

Daniels hesitated, and Rem responded. "We're not going to do that."

The voice returned. "If we wanted you dead, you'd be dead. This is about protecting me. Don't worry. You can have them back after we talk. I don't want them."

Rem eyed Daniels, who reluctantly lowered his gun. As much as Daniels preferred not to put down his weapon, he needed to know who was talking and what they had to say. He stepped to the table, and he, along with Rem, set his gun on it.

"Okay," said Rem. "They're on the table."

"Phones, too. And turn them off."

Cursing, Rem pulled out his phone, turned it off, and set it on the table. Daniels did the same.

There was no response from the speaker, but Daniels swiveled when the door in the alcove behind the mirror opened. A tall, bald man with massive shoulders and enormous arms stepped out. Daniels looked up at him, and Rem stiffened. "What do you eat for breakfast?" asked Rem. "Small children?"

The voice returned. "Kindly stand still while we check you for listening devices."

The big man pulled a wand-like device from his pocket. Daniels and Rem raised their arms, and the man waved the wand over them. When he was done, he returned the wand to his pocket and stepped toward the open door where Daniels and Rem had entered the room. He shut it and stood beside it with his arms crossed. A second passed, and a second man stepped out from the alcove door behind the mirror. Daniels' stomach clenched when he recognized Tex.

· · · ● · ● · · · ·

Seeing Tex, heat bloomed in Rem's gut, and thinking of Cain, he strode toward him just as the big man stepped in front of Tex, and Daniels grabbed Rem's arm.

Tex smiled at Rem. "I suggest you step back."

Daniels pulled on Rem's arm. "C'mon, partner. Not yet."

Rem reluctantly let Daniels pull him away.

The big man relaxed and went back to guarding the door.

Tex slid his hands into his pockets. "Nice to see you two again."

Rem fought another urge to rush at him. "Why are you here?"

"Rhonda said your debt was paid," added Daniels.

Tex shrugged. "It was. I went back to my life, but I've learned that sticking around can be very lucrative." He raised his hand and showed the tattoo of the black bird on his wrist. "Maybe you guys should consider joining."

Daniels glared. "Tell us why we're here." He eyed the mirror.

Rem eyed it too. It had to be two-way, and Tex had been watching them since they'd entered the room. He wondered who else was watching.

"First off," said Tex, "my condolences to you both. You've had a rough few days."

"You killed Cain, didn't you?" asked Rem.

"Who went after Marjorie?" asked Daniels, his voice taut. "Rhonda?"

Tex stepped closer to the table and put his palms on the back of a chair. "Your cousin was a necessary piece of the puzzle, Remalla. Too bad he didn't listen to you."

Rem stiffened, and Daniels put his hand back on Rem's arm.

"And Marjorie," said Tex, "well, you got lucky, Daniels. You know how Rhonda can be. She rarely leaves her victims alive."

Daniels took a step toward Tex, and Rem turned and put his hand on Daniels' chest. The big man at the door glared. "Like you said, not yet, partner," said Rem. He lowered his voice. "But there will come a time."

Daniels met Rem's stare, hesitated, and stepped back.

Tex chuckled. "If you two kill me now," he raised his hands, "then you'll never learn why you're here." He studied Rem. "Don't you want to know where your gun is?" He eyed Daniels. "Or who paid your debt?"

Shaking with rage, Rem faced Tex. "Cain and Bertrand. They were shot with my gun?"

Tex smiled. "They were."

Rem muttered a curse. "Where is it?"

"You can have it back. But first you need to do something." Tex spoke to Daniels. "And your debt payment? Never has to come to light."

"You set us up," said Daniels. "Why?"

Rem's heart pounded. "What do you want from us?"

"Both excellent questions," replied Tex. "I'll do my best to answer." He glanced at the mirror. "But some things are up to others to reveal."

Rem glanced at the mirror, too. "Who else is watching?"

"One question at a time," said Tex. "First off, let's talk about your debt to us."

"*Our* debt?" asked Rem, incredulous. "We owe you nothing."

Daniels gestured at the mirror. "Or whoever else is behind there."

"I guess that depends on who you're asking," said Tex. "Call it whatever you want, but if you two don't want to go to prison for bribery and murder, then you need to prove you're worth saving."

Rem braced for whatever he was about to hear.

Tex hardened his tone. "This witness you're looking for? He can never go home."

Rem held his breath, and Daniels didn't move. "You want us to kill Jerry Lee Caruso?" asked Daniels.

"You can do it however you want," said Tex. "But he can't survive."

Rem tried to absorb Tex's words. "Because he can identify Rhonda?"

"He's a liability," said Tex, "and my boss doesn't like liabilities."

"Rhonda's already tried twice and failed," said Rem.

"Which is why it's now up to you two," replied Tex.

"Jerry Lee is the grandson of Sammy Caruso," said Daniels.

Tex nodded. "We know, which is why it's preferable you kill him."

"So Caruso can come after us?" Rem scowled at the mirror. "Instead of your boss?" He scoffed. "How stupid do you think we are?"

"That's your problem. Not mine." Tex tipped his head. "But there are ways to make it look like you're innocent."

"What if Rhonda gets to Jerry Lee first?" asked Daniels.

"Rhonda has been pulled off this job. For now." Tex waved his hand at Daniels and Remalla. "The boss thinks you're the next best option."

"I bet he does," said Rem, trying to think. "And if we don't do it?"

Tex shrugged. "That .38 Special will be found in your car, or a place specifically tied to you, Remalla, and your paid debt," said Tex to Daniels, "will be reported by an anonymous tip."

Rem didn't say a word and Daniels clenched his jaw.

"And who knows?" said Tex. "Before the gun's found, it would be awful if it were used again."

Rem tensed.

"Especially against a nosy reporter...or a newly discovered sister." Tex smiled.

Daniels rushed at Tex. Rem got between him and Tex before the bodyguard could. Daniels sneered and pointed at Tex. "You touch a hair on Erin's head, or Lexie's, or anyone I know and love, and you're a dead man."

Tex stepped back and raised his hands. "There's no need for threats, Detective Daniels. All of this is easily solved." His voice became threatening. "As long as Jerry Lee Caruso doesn't live long enough to see the inside of a police station."

Rem gritted his teeth. He pushed Daniels back until Daniels broke his glare at Tex and stopped fighting Rem. "You okay?" asked Rem.

"Yeah," said Daniels, breathing hard. "Until I get him alone in a dark alley."

"Just so long as I'm with you." Rem patted his partner's shoulder. He eyed Tex and then Daniels. "You trust me, partner?"

Still glaring at Tex, Daniels nodded. "Of course."

"Good." Rem turned toward Tex. "We'll consider it."

"What?" said Daniels.

"On one condition," added Rem.

Tex snickered. "I don't think you're in a place to be making conditions."

"I think I am." Rem stepped toward Tex. "Your boss wants us to kill a twenty-year-old kid to save our hides. But he's forgetting one thing. We know about this black bird society."

Tex stopped snickering. "You don't know shit, Detective."

Rem took another step closer. "You're wearing a pretty bird tattoo. So did Cain. And Tommy? Your little buddy from Elmwood? So did he. Should we take a guess whether your boss has one?"

Tex made a snort. "Tattoos are all you have?"

"We saw Ackerman's box," said Rem. "And what was in it."

Tex's face fell. "Which was taken from you."

"Was it?" asked Rem. He held Tex's gaze and didn't move.

Tex paused, and his face tightened. "You're bluffing."

"Maybe I am, and maybe I'm not." He narrowed his gaze. "Mom always told me I was good at poker."

"If you had it," said Tex, looking slightly less confident, "you would have exposed it by now."

"Not necessarily," said Daniels from behind Rem. "Information is power, Tex." He came up from behind Rem. "I suspect your boss knows that very well."

Tex's gaze moved between Rem and Daniels. "What's your condition?"

Rem pointed at the glass. "I want to know who's behind that mirror."

Tex hesitated. "That's not up to me, fellas."

Rem didn't ease up on his glare. "Then who," he said, his voice dripping with acrimony, "is it up to?"

A moment of silence passed, and the door behind the mirror opened. Rem heard a footstep, and an older man stepped out, wearing a crisp suit and tie, and polished shoes. "It's up to me, Detectives."

He moved into the light and, noting the man's perfectly cut hair and weathered tan face, Rem dropped his jaw and muttered. "The most interesting man in the world."

Daniels, his eyes wide, stared with shock. "Damien Rook."

Chapter Thirty-Three

STUNNED TO SEE ROOK, Daniels didn't know what to say. Rem stared open-mouthed as well. Daniels' mind whirled, and he put two and two together. "You're Dirk."

"Damien Rook?" asked Rem. "Owner of Rook Enterprises? You're Dirk?"

Rook didn't deny it. "Now you know who I am. Pretty smart bluff, Detective," Rook said to Rem. "But whatever information you have amounts to nothing."

Rem shut his mouth. "Why kill Durning?"

Daniels wanted the answer to that, too. "You were his client?"

Rook stepped farther into the room. "Crenshaw assigned him. Said he could handle certain issues I needed to go away." He swiped something off the cuff of his sleeve. "Durning handled the mess for a while, until he balked, and started to grow a pair." He scoffed. "Apparently, whatever Crenshaw had on him wasn't quite enough. Just goes to prove that if you want something done, you do it yourself." He leaned back against the table. "Durning threatened to go to his buddy Lozano. I obviously couldn't have that, and I don't abide disloyalty."

"You had Durning killed, and you set up Lozano," said Daniels.

Rook crossed his arms. "Maybe it's time you two started respecting my society a little more." His voice held a hard edge.

"*Your* society?" asked Rem.

"Rook." Daniels tried to breathe normally, but his heart was racing. "It's another word for a crow. You lead the black birds."

"Among others," said Rook. "It's a shared ideology and responsibility."

"You have people killed," said Rem. "What kind of ideology is that?"

"A necessary one," replied Rook. "One I believe you'll come to respect."

"You've set us up to manipulate us into killing an innocent kid that witnessed your assassin murder Durning." Daniels smirked. "Why don't you clean up your own mess?"

Rook's gaze turned ominous. "Don't act so innocent, Detective. I know how you two work. You've both killed people and used innocent victims to get what you wanted. Don't act like you're any better than me."

"We're detectives," said Rem. "We have a job—"

"You're murderers!" yelled Rook, his voice shook.

Surprised by Rook's vitriol, Daniels went quiet along with Rem.

After a pause, Rook relaxed his face, smoothed his jacket, and collected himself. "And as such, you'll fit right in."

"Fit right in with what?" asked Rem.

"With the black birds," said Rook.

Daniels sputtered. "No offense, Rook, but we don't care to join."

"I'm not a fan of your silly tattoos," added Rem. "Are you?" he asked Daniels.

"I prefer butterflies," replied Daniels.

Tex, who'd stepped back and was leaning against the wall, scoffed.

Rook looked between Daniels and Rem. "The tattoos can come later. Right now, all I need is for you two to kill Jerry Lee Caruso. After that, we'll see."

Daniels stared in disbelief. "What are you telling us?"

Rook pushed off the table. "I'm saying you two belong to me now." He ran his fingers down his tie.

"We what?" asked Rem.

"I think you heard me just fine, Detective." Rook aimed his fiery gaze at Rem. "I don't like you."

Rem looked down at himself. "Why not? I'm a nice guy." he spoke to Daniels. "Aren't I?"

Daniels played along. "You could work on your eating habits, and maybe buy some new jeans, but yeah, you're very nice."

"See?" Rem asked Rook.

Rook's glare intensified. "Your stupid games may have duped others, but not me. I've worked hard for what I have, and two idiot detectives aren't going to tear it down." He softened his shoulders. "I value wisdom, talent, and planning. I almost let my personal agenda get in the way with you two, but I caught myself before that happened, and now, here we are, and I've got you both right where I want you."

Hearing the odd tone of Rook's voice, as if he was planning a board meeting agenda instead of threatening two detectives, Daniels asked the obvious. "And where is that?"

Rook adjusted the cuff of his sleeve. "Who needs Rhonda when I have you two?"

Rem widened his eyes at Daniels. "We aren't assassins," said Rem.

"You are now." Rook straightened his shoulders. "You're going to do exactly as I tell you, and that starts with Jerry Lee Caruso. You choose otherwise..." He offered a cruel smile. "And I'll destroy you."

Rem's face paled. "Why do you hate us so much? If you're so certain our information from Ackerman's box is worthless, why involve us?"

Rook's icy stare at Rem returned. "I know all about you and your partner. I've done my research. I know your skills, habits, loved ones, and all about your friendship. I know what books you read, and TV shows you watch. I know where you live and breathe. Your weaknesses and strengths are my playground. I can use them against you and pit you against each other." He shot a look at Daniels. "You made me an enemy, Detectives.

And because of that, I plan to make you the very thing you despise the most."

Daniels fought the urge to step back. "What's that?"

Rook spoke calmly. "Evil."

Astonished, Rem shook his head. "You sound like a nutcase. I don't suppose you know Margaret Redstone?" He spoke to the immense bodyguard. "What do you think, Tiny? He a nutcase?"

Tiny scowled and Rook sneered at Rem. "You will either kill Jerry Lee Caruso or you will go to prison for the murder of your cousin and Arnold Bertrand, along with your friend Lexie Logan," he tipped his head toward Daniels, "and his sister Erin Gerard. And while you're incarcerated, I promise, every prison inmate will know you're a cop."

"Wait a minute...," said Daniels.

Rook whirled toward Daniels. "And maybe he'll do time for your death, too, Detective. But if he doesn't, then you can sit behind bars for bribery and accessory to murder, and your destitute wife and son will be forced to survive without you."

Daniels stood in shocked silence.

"We know about you," said Rem, his voice quiet.

Rook whirled back at Rem. "What are you going to do? Accuse a prominent businessman of threatening you? Of being the leader of a secret society? Your partner made it very clear when we met how he disapproved of my company's plans to revitalize this area. I can provide plenty of reasons why you'd want to damage me and my reputation. I'm a millionaire with more clout and influence than your measly mind can imagine. You have no idea who's part of the black birds. Your career and reputation will take the hit, not mine, but that will be nothing compared to the ruin that will be your life. That sweet girlfriend of yours will run from you and your mess faster than the judge can slam his gavel and pronounce you guilty."

Rem paled.

Rook's glare shifted to a flat expression, and he buttoned his jacket. "I think I've said all that needs to be said." He headed toward the front door. "I expect to hear of Jerry Lee's death soon."

Tiny opened the door for Rook, and Rook looked back. "Tex, as you prefer to call him, will be your contact." He strode out the door.

Tex stepped away from the wall. "You heard the man. Use the phone from the envelope." He walked to the door. "I'll be in touch."

He exited the room, and without a second glance, Tiny followed and shut the door behind him.

· · · ● · ● · · · ·

Daniels stood frozen in utter disbelief. Trying to comprehend Rook's expectations, he couldn't utter a word.

Rem appeared just as stymied. He studied the closed door, clenched and unclenched his fingers and swiveled toward Daniels. "What just happened?"

Daniels walked to the table, grabbed his gun, and holstered it. "Apparently, we just became assassins." He picked up Rem's gun and held it out to him.

Rem walked over and took it. "We aren't assassins."

"I know that," said Daniels, more harshly than he meant to. He picked up his phone and turned it on. "Let's get out of here."

Rem holstered his gun and grabbed his phone. He followed Daniels out of the murky room and, not seeing the SUV, he passed the closed bays and returned to the car. Rem got behind the wheel and Daniels sat in the passenger seat. Neither moved.

Rem spoke first. "Let's get something to eat."

Daniels spoke in a rush. "You can eat after that?"

Rem started the car. "I'm not hungry, but I think better on a full stomach."

"That makes no sense."

Rem shot Daniels a look. "Nothing makes sense right now."

Frustrated, Daniels raised his voice. "And how is eating when you're not hungry going to help?"

Rem raised his voice in return. "Don't yell at me. Don't we have enough problems without us bitching at each other?"

Daniels deflated. He rested his elbow on the door and gripped his temples. "Sorry. I'm a little on edge."

"And I'm not?" Rem yelled. He sat back, expelled a long sigh, and held up his hand. "I'm sorry, too. I guess I'm a little flummoxed about becoming a hired killer."

"Me too." Daniels lowered his hand. "Let's eat then. I saw a diner on the corner. Let's go there and talk."

Rem pulled away from the gas station. Five minutes later, they were seated in a booth and the waitress handed them menus. "You have chocolate pie?" asked Rem.

The waitress smacked her gum. "Sure do. Homemade."

Rem held his menu out to her. "Give me the biggest piece you've got, and a cup of coffee."

"You got it." She took the menu from Rem and eyed Daniels.

"Ditto." Daniels handed her his menu. "And some water, please."

"Comin' right up." She took Daniels' menu and walked away.

Daniels set his elbows on the table and interlaced his fingers, and Rem stared out the window at the parking lot. "You know," said Rem, "after Jennie died, and Cain, too, I couldn't understand how the world kept turning." He sighed. "I feel the same way right now."

Daniels understood how he felt. "I'm not even sure where to begin."

Rem looked back at him. "How about how the founder of Rook Enterprises is Dirk? A man who apparently leads a secret society full of powerful people and hires assassins to get rid of the ones that don't do what he wants?"

Daniels rubbed his neck. "He could have easily killed us, but he didn't. Why?"

"Because he wants to punish us. Plus, we're way more useful to him alive."

"And under his thumb," added Daniels.

Rem reached for a sugar packet when the waitress brought two mugs, cream, and an insulated pitcher of coffee and set them down on the table. "And I still think he plans to kill us," said Rem, "whether we're his assassins or not."

The waitress stilled.

Rem glanced up at her. "It's a Dungeons and Dragons thing."

Daniels rolled his eyes.

"I'll get your waters." Her expression dubious, the waitress walked away.

Daniels did his best to collect his thoughts. Now that some of the shock had worn off, it was easier. "Okay. Let's think this through. He has your gun."

Rem added sugar and cream to his mug. "Which was used on Cain and Bertrand." He poured coffee into his mug.

Daniels pointed. "That's something. When Bertrand was shot, you were with your family. They can all vouch for your whereabouts."

Rem stirred his coffee. "Not exactly."

"What do you mean?"

Rem set his spoon beside his mug. "I stopped at the park on the way to your place. Mabel was upset that morning and got in my face about Cain. Said I should have prevented his murder. I know she was speaking from grief, but I couldn't tell her the truth, so I left. Went to the park and just sat for a bit."

"How long were you there?"

"Maybe an hour. Plenty of time for me to kill Bertrand, wipe the video footage and head to your place."

Daniels groaned. "That's not good."

"No, it isn't." Rem blew on his coffee.

"But what's your motive? Why would you kill him?"

"I'm sure they'll link it to Jerry Lee. And if Lexie and Erin are targeted, I'll be painted as some sort of psycho cop on a rampage." Rem sipped his coffee. "And we already know how the situation looks between me and Cain. That's no better." He paused. "You might get off easy. Apparently, you work for cheap. Sixty-two grand to help me bump off two, maybe four, people, assuming you're sharing? That's low for the going rate."

"Is it?" Daniels shrugged. "Hell. If they can plant fake offshore accounts on Lozano, they sure as hell can do it to me, too."

The waitress brought them two glasses of water. "Pie's comin' up."

"Thanks," said Daniels. The waitress walked away, and he picked up his water. "Monk and Manetti are going to learn that the same gun killed Cain and Bertrand, which means they're going to wonder why." He drank some water.

"We're going to have to work with them," added Rem. "That'll be fun."

"How do we do that without telling them what's going on?"

"I have no idea."

Daniels added cream to his mug and poured himself some coffee. "There's got to be a way out of this."

"What's your assessment of Damien Rook?" asked Rem.

Daniels stirred his coffee. "I think you're right. He's a nutcase."

Rem leaned in. "I think he's been listening to his own bullshit for too long. He's bought it hook, line and sinker. He thinks he's this all-powerful leader who's completely justified in his actions."

"But to what end?" asked Daniels. "Why create the black birds in the first place?"

"He likes power. That's obvious. And he likes control. Plus, he's way overconfident. Did you catch that?"

"You mean when you mentioned Ackerman's box? Yeah, I caught that. He didn't seem at all worried that we might still have access to the contents."

"Didn't even ruffle his hair." Rem drank more coffee and stared off. "That might be a good thing, though."

"Why is that?"

The waitress appeared with two pieces of pie, napkins, and forks. She set them in front of Rem and Daniels. "Enjoy."

"Thank you," said Rem. He picked up a fork. "Because if Rook's not worried about the box, then that means he's not aware of Ackerman's list of names. If he was—"

"His hair would definitely get ruffled." Daniels picked up a fork. "He gloated about us not knowing who the members are."

"And called us idiots." Rem dug his fork into his pie. "He looks down at everyone."

"I wonder how much the other members appreciate that."

"He implied it was a shared responsibility."

"Do you think he shares anything?" asked Daniels.

"I suspect he hogged all the Legos when he was a kid." Rem took a bite of pie and moaned. "That's good pie."

Daniels took a bite, too. Chewing it, he sighed. "What every newbie assassin needs before their first kill."

"That's not funny."

"I'm not laughing."

They ate and sipped their coffees in silence.

"You know, Rook never answered my question," said Rem, putting his fork down.

"Which one?"

"Why he hates us so much. Like you said, he could have handled us the way he handles everyone else who pisses him off."

"He could have sent Rhonda after us."

"He did, and Tex and Tommy, but then he called them off."

"He said his own personal agenda almost got in the way."

Rem added more coffee to his mug. "That's the key. This is a vendetta."

"Why?" Daniels set his fork on his plate. "We did something he didn't like?"

"Something that put us on his list, only killing us was too easy. He wants to turn us."

"Make us evil. That was a nice touch."

"So, whatever we did must have been pretty bad."

Daniels tried to think of what it could be. "Any ideas?"

"None."

"Great."

Rem snagged the last bite of his pie with his fork. "But we do have the list of names that Rook is oblivious to. And since he's so damn cocky that he's got us where he wants us, and can't even imagine us fighting back…"

Daniels picked up his mug. "…we can keep digging and maybe find someone who knows about this grudge against us."

"And maybe find somebody who isn't thrilled with Rook's leadership."

"Who might turn on him?" Daniels considered it. "You think that's possible?" He drank some coffee.

Rem chewed his last bite and swallowed. "Rook is as close as I am to you from becoming completely unhinged. I'd say we're not the only ones who've noticed."

"What do we do in the meantime?" Daniels pushed his plate back. "We're supposed to kill Jerry Lee, remember?"

"I haven't forgotten that little gem." He eyed Daniels' pie. "You gonna finish that?"

"It's all yours."

Rem pulled Daniels' plate closer. "I guess that means we have to kill him." He grabbed a bite of Daniels' pie with his fork.

Daniels clutched his napkin. "Excuse me?"

"If you can't beat 'em, join 'em."

Daniels narrowed his eyes. "You mean act the part?"

Rem shrugged. "Why not?"

"How do we do that?"

"It'll take some careful maneuvering, but I bet we can do it. They underestimate us, and that's their weakness." He paused and held his fork. "In fact..."

Daniels raised a brow. "I'm afraid to ask. I see that gleam in your eye."

"We should go all in. Instead of fighting Rook, let's join him."

Daniels paused. "I'm a little worried about you right now."

Rem ate the last bite of pie. "Think about it," he said through a mouthful. He sipped his coffee and swallowed. "How is this any different from going undercover?"

"Going undercover requires support and backup. People who can pull you out if needed."

"All of that is nice, but not necessary. Plus, we'll have each other, which is better than most of that other stuff." Rem pointed with his fork. "If we can get deep enough, we could bust this thing wide open. Find Rhonda, clear Lozano's name and ours, locate Winnie, and take down Tex, Rook, and his whole damn society."

"Now who's deranged?"

"You got a better idea?"

Daniels sat back and mulled it over. "It's not going to be easy. We're going to need help."

"We have people we trust. We'll figure it out. We always do."

"If we screw up, it could mean prison for both of us, or worse."

"And if we don't do it?"

Daniels blew out his cheeks and tossed his napkin on the table. "I see your point."

Rem set his fork on Daniels' plate and pushed it away. "So, you agree? We go undercover to expose Rook and his society."

"And try not to get killed or go to prison. Or get anyone else killed."

"That's the plan, partner."

"That's a tall order." Daniels took a second. "But I guess we don't have much choice, do we?"

"Not from where I'm sitting."

Daniels considered everything that could go wrong, and quickly deduced their odds of survival were low. His heart thumping, he touched his wrist. "I hope this doesn't require tattoos. Marjorie won't be happy."

"Maybe we can get away with fake ones. Rook wouldn't know the difference."

"Don't count on it."

Rem leaned closer. "Does that mean you're in?"

Daniels held his partner's gaze and thought back. "What was that saying? All for one and one for all?"

"I always wanted to be a musketeer."

Daniels refilled his mug with coffee. "Looks like you're about to get your wish." He set the pitcher down.

Rem smiled and held up his coffee cup. "Then a toast...to the newest members of the black bird society."

Praying they knew what they were doing, Daniels raised his mug and bumped it against Rem's. "God help us all."

What Happens Next?

Daniels and Rem take on their most dangerous assignment yet in *Black Bird*. They'll go undercover with the secret society to clear their names, protect their loved ones, and stop a deadly organization, but the risks involved could cost them everything worth fighting for. And when shocking revelations expose the truth of what they're up against, they'll have to reevaluate just how far they're willing to go to stop a madman.

Enjoy an excerpt below.

Want more from J. T. Bishop?

Subscribe at jtbishopauthor.com to get the Daniels and Remalla prequel novellas, *The Girl and the Gunshot*, and *The Magic of Murder*, plus future books, for free, in addition to extra content.

Did you know there's a Daniels and Remalla Prequel Novel, and an Omnibus?

Meet Phoebe Reinart in *Murder Unveiled,* the prequel novel to *Haunted River*. A prominent art dealer is found murdered after the unveiling of a famous, but cursed, painting. When Daniels and Rem are assigned to investigate, they'll learn that a curse may prove more deadly than a killer and they could be the next targets.

Or catch up fast on the series with *Secrets and Shadows*, the Detectives Daniels and Remalla omnibus, which includes *Haunted River*, *Of Breath and Blood*, and *Of Body and Bone*.

How did it all begin with Daniels and Rem?

Check out the *Family or Foe Saga* where we first meet the detectives. This four-book series focuses on a murderer with a mysterious background and unique abilities who's out for revenge against the family he believes wronged him. Can Daniels and Remalla stop him before he seeks his vengeance?

And meet the Redstones.

Mason and Mikey Redstone, introduced in *Of Breath and Blood*, book two of *Detectives Daniels and Remalla*, were so engaging and fun to write, they got their own series.

Mason, a former Texas Ranger turned medium and paranormal investigator, along with his sister Mikey and partner Trick, take the cases others won't and risk their lives in the process. If you like a little more paranormal thrown into your mystery thrillers, then this series is for you. Plus, there's the added bonus of appearances by Daniels and Remalla.

Note: Because the Daniels and Remalla books and The Redstone Chronicles are a spinoff and crossover series, they share an overarching story, and the characters from each are mentioned or appear in all the books, so reading both is ideal. The books published alternate between both series. A list of books in chronological order follows below.

Fan of Paranormal Romance, Urban Fantasy, and Light Sci-Fi?

Discover Bishop's first series, *The Red-Line Trilogy*.

Yanked from her predictable world, Sarah Randolph learns she's the key to unlocking a secret that will ensure the existence of a hidden community. One man, assigned to protect her from a dangerous adversary, will risk everything to keep her alive, but when he falls for her, will their destiny be enough to save them both?

In *The Fletcher Family Saga*, the four-book sister series to *The Red-Line Trilogy*, a distant but deadly threat risks the lives of three unique siblings, but life can't stop because of who they are. They'll endure love, loss and a dangerous enemy determined to destroy them all.

Either series can be read first. Take your pick. Boxed sets are available, too!

A Note From J.T.

IT WAS A THRILLING challenge to write *Vendetta*. After I finished *Illusions*, I had no idea what was going to happen next with Rem and Daniels. I knew the big stuff—who the bad guy was ultimately going to be, that Cain would have to die, and Marjorie would lose the baby. Those were significant plot points that had to be covered, but how they were going to unfold was a crapshoot. That's sort of how I'm feeling now when I think of the next book, *Black Bird*. I have some aces up my sleeve, but how they will be revealed is unknown. There's a lot going on with this secret organization and the players in it, and I want to give them all the justice they deserve. Will it all be resolved in *Black Bird*? The answer is, I don't know. We'll see how it plays out.

One element I loved about *Vendetta* was the big revelation of Erin as Daniels' sister. I know many of you already suspected who she was, but Daniels suspected nothing. The scene where Rem figures it out while Marjorie and Mikey try to distract him had been playing in my head for a while. It made sense that he'd know immediately and would blurt it out in front of everyone.

The other element I enjoyed was putting a little stress on Rem and Daniels' relationship. They've been through a lot together, but what happens when a loved one is hurt and one blames the other? Or when one of them does something questionable without talking to the other first? Marjorie, Cain, and Erin played integral roles to pull those scenarios off, and they did their jobs well.

Putting beloved characters through this tension makes a writer happy, but the most satisfying part was bringing the partners back together again. I love the emotion of the cemetery scene. It highlights the best features of Rem and Daniels' relationship–their ability to communicate, be honest and vulnerable, and hug each other, while still being badasses. It's the hallmark of their bond, and it's what keeps me (and I think you) coming back for more. I've got some big shoes to fill with *Black Bird*. And all I can say is that I'll do my best not to disappoint.

Reviews are a huge plus and big help for an author, and for potential readers. I would love it if you could please take a couple of minutes to leave a quick review for *Vendetta*. And if you'd like, please leave a few comments, too.

As always, thank you for your time and readership. It is deeply valued and appreciated.

Now, on to the next book!

Books in Chronological Order

Although recommended but not required, in case you prefer to read in order...

Lost Souls
Of Body and Bone
Lost Dreams
Of Mind and Madness
Lost Chances
Of Power and Pain
Lost Hope
Of Love and Loss
Lost Lives
Dominion
Lost Time
Illusions

Acknowledgements

Another book is complete, and again, I have many to thank. This doesn't happen alone, and I am indebted to family and friends for their help, support and encouragement. It is truly appreciated.

I also want to thank my Beta and ARC teams. You guys keep me on my toes, ensure I write a great story, and help with early reviews. Thank you for being honest and offering your guidance.

I love writing about the bonds between loving family, deep friendships and the ties that hold them together. Plus, my fascination with the unknown thrown into the mix makes for a satisfying story and hopefully, adds a little more thrill for my readers.

I especially want to thank my fans. Hearing from you and knowing that you're enjoying my books makes all the hard work worthwhile. None of this would matter without your tremendous support. If I can help you escape from this crazy world for a short period each day, then I've done my job.

Here's to more stories, more fun, and more time for yourself. If you can have a little of that each day, you're on the right track.

About the Author

AWARD-WINNING AUTHOR, J.T. BISHOP, is a writer of mystery thrillers with a paranormal edge. Growing up, she read Stephen King, Mary Higgins Clark, and Dean Koontz, devoured every episode of the X-files and watched plenty of TV shows with great partnerships that leave you wanting more. She loves tangled relationships, unexpected twists and turns, heart-stopping love stories and the complications that come with all the above. Throw in a little supernatural fun and she's hooked. Her evil plan is to hook you, too.

She's the author of *The Red-Line Trilogy* and its sister series, *The Fletcher Family Saga*, which features touches of urban fantasy, light sci-fi, and paranormal romance. She's also happily writing mystery thrillers featuring two charismatic detectives who may occasionally encounter a supernatural villain or two, and a crossover series which follows the exploits of a gifted, but troubled, paranormal P.I. and his spunky sister.

All the above keeps her busy, but in her spare time, she loves good movies, tasty food, an unfortunate sugar addiction, and traveling.

Enjoy an excerpt from Black Bird, Book Ten in Detectives Daniels and Remalla.

MARTIN BAILEY DROVE DOWN the dark alley. A soft rain fell, and his wipers squeaked as they slid over his windshield. Squinting through the wet windows, he drove beneath a dim light fixture that, along with his headlights, cast eerie shadows. His heart thumped, and looking for his destination, he slowed down. The rain picked up in intensity and he cursed, wishing he was back on his couch, drinking a beer and watching an old movie.

The moment he'd gotten the call, he'd dreaded every moment of this assignment. He'd done this twice before, but never in the rain, and never at this time of night. The first time he'd done it, he'd simply stopped in the alley beside a heavy metal door, and a man the size of a prizefighter had come out. Martin had popped the trunk, and the man had grabbed the box, shut the trunk, and Marty had driven off.

The second time, Marty had stopped at the door, but no one showed. After waiting several minutes, he'd received a text telling him to bring the box inside. He'd reluctantly left the car, collected the box, and had gone to the door. He'd knocked, but no one had answered. Uncertain, he'd opened the creaky door and stuck his head in. Not seeing anyone, he'd stepped inside.

Not sure what to do, he'd waited, and an awful smell made his hair raise. He'd held his nose and debated leaving the box when a man's deep voice pierced the quiet.

"Bring it here."

Trembling, Marty had cautiously walked down a hall and turned a corner. A room came into view that he could only describe as terrifying. Lighted candles were placed around the room at various heights, strange objects hung on the wall, and a circle had been drawn in chalk on the floor. The horrid smell had almost made him gag.

The voice spoke again. "Put the box in the circle."

Marty looked around but saw no one. He couldn't even identify the source of the voice. His heart hammering, he'd stepped into the room and approached the circle. Staring at it and the strange objects on the walls, he'd realized that whatever this place was used for, it wasn't good. He'd started to leave the box and, aware he was about to step inside the circle, he'd jumped back. An icy chill ran up his back and intuitively, he knew not to step past the chalk. He'd lowered the box, set it on the ground, and shoved it into the circle.

He'd heard a crackle, and chill bumps ran over his skin. "Leave," said the male voice.

Marty wasted no time. He'd turned, ran out of the building, jumped in his car, and squealed away.

Now, two months later, he was back, and the memory of that last visit made him tremble again. He prayed that this time around, the prizefighter would be back, and he wouldn't have to return to that room, and the awful smell.

Slowing more, he looked for the metal door. He passed another light fixture, and just beyond that, he spied where he'd stopped the previous two times. Saying a prayer, he pulled up and stopped. He waited, watching the door, hoping it would open, but it didn't. Groaning, he spoke to himself. "Take it easy, Marty. It's just a room. No big deal."

He thought of the box in his trunk and wondered what sort of delivery would warrant this level of secrecy. Whatever was in it had to be important, but to who and why was a mystery.

Several minutes passed, and Marty expected the text, but it never came. He debated whether to keep waiting or to bring the box inside when he saw headlights in his rearview mirror. The light fractured into irregular shapes on the wet glass as Marty watched through the mirror, and the car stopped behind him.

Expecting all he'd have to do was pop the trunk and let whoever was in the car take the box, Marty breathed a sigh of relief, thrilled he wouldn't have to return to the bizarre room. His phone buzzed with a text notification, and he picked it up and read it. "Bring the box to me."

Marty lowered his phone with a curse. "Figures I'm the one who has to get wet." He popped the trunk and opened his door. Stepping out into the rain, he pulled his hood over his head and grabbed the box from his trunk.

The car behind him idled, and the passenger door opened. A man wearing a dark raincoat with the hood pulled up got out. Holding the small box, Marty closed his trunk. He stepped to the side, expecting to hand the box over to the man, when the man stopped and slid his hands into his pockets.

Getting closer, Marty recognized him. "Croft? What'd you do wrong to have to come out in this crappy weather?"

Croft half-smiled. "I could ask you the same."

Marty grunted. "I'm just a messenger boy. You know that. I don't carry the clout you do." He paused. "Unless you're no longer Mr. Sidekick." He snickered. "Don't tell me. Did you finally tell the bossman the truth?"

Croft didn't move. "What truth is that?"

The rain fell harder, and Marty pulled his hood higher over his head. "You know what I mean. The rumors are circulating."

"What rumors?"

Marty wiped the rain from his face. "It's a mess out here. Can we get this over with? Pop the trunk or take the box. I'm getting wet and want to go home."

Croft's expression didn't change. "What rumors, Marty?"

Rain splattered against the box. "Seriously?"

"Seriously."

Marty scoffed. "I think you've gone as bonkers as him." He shook his head. "What's up with all this delivering strange boxes in the middle of the night crap?" He tapped the box. "What's in this thing?"

"Nothing that concerns you."

Marty squinted at Croft. "It concerns me when I have to deliver it to some crazy room with candles, circles, and weird stuff hanging on the walls. What the hell is going on, Croft? This is more than I signed up for. I'm all for the group support, and the nice paycheck, but this is getting strange."

"I'm sorry to hear that, Marty."

Marty pointed. "And I'm not the only one thinking it, either."

"Really? Who else is questioning their membership?"

Marty detected the clip in Croft's voice. "Hey, man. Don't take it personal. It's just that when you see and hear things, you have to wonder."

"Wonder what?"

"Just who exactly I'm working for." A clap of thunder and a flash of lightning made Marty grip the box tighter. The cardboard, softened by the rain, bent under his grasp. "You better take this box. It's getting soaked."

Croft remained still.

"C'mon, man. Don't just stand there." Marty shivered. "I'm freezing."

Croft's eyes narrowed. "I'm sorry, Marty."

"It's okay. Just take this already." He lifted the box.

Croft pulled his hand from his pocket. He was holding a gun. "As you say, it's not personal. But the boss does not abide disloyalty."

Marty widened his eyes in shock. "What the hell is this?"

"The group must remain cohesive, and those who stir the pot, well, they have to go."

Marty stared at the gun. "You want me out? Just because of a few rumors?"

"Rumors are just the beginning. If they aren't controlled, then it leads to more disloyalty."

Marty couldn't believe what he was hearing. "Are you listening to yourself? You're as bad as he is. He's crazy and you know it. Why aren't you questioning it, too?"

"I'm not the one who makes the rules. He is. And he pays the bills."

Scared, Marty raised his free hand. "You want me out? That's fine with me. I'm out. I'll drive off and you never have to talk to me again."

"You've seen too much." Croft glanced at the box. "You know too much." He glared. "And you talk too much."

Marty spoke fast. "I don't know shit. And who would believe me, anyway?"

Croft blinked, and Marty thought of his cat, whose eyes gleamed the same way when he was about to pounce. "And, if there's dissension in the ranks," said Croft, "someone needs to be an example."

Marty's mind whirled. How was he going to get out of this? "An example? Of what?"

"Of what happens when you question your superior and spread lies."

Marty gaped at Croft. "I won't say another word. I swear it."

"Put the box down, Marty."

It hit Marty that Croft was there to kill him. The box was secondary. Another crack of thunder jolted him into action. Panicking, he swiveled, dropped the box, and ran. The first thing he saw was the metal door. Thinking at warp speed, he imagined getting behind it and locking it. It could be the only thing that might save him. He raced toward it when a cold, sharp sting sliced into his back. Crying out, his legs gave way, and he crumpled into a puddle on the ground. His hood slid down, and rain pelted his head and face, but he crawled toward the door. He reached for it, grabbed the handle, and felt a measure of hope when it opened. But before he could get inside, another shot rang out. He fell forward, his face hit the wet pavement, and his last thought was of his cat, Butters.

· · · · ●·●·· · ·

Holding the gun, Croft walked past the taillights of Marty's car. He approached the door to the building, squatted in a puddle next to Marty's body, and checked his pulse. Feeling nothing, Croft stood and tucked his gun back into his pocket.

The driver's side door of his car opened, and the driver got out. He easily towered over Croft and had arms the size of basketballs. He wore a black knit cap, jeans, a sweatshirt, boots, and gloves, but no protection from the rain.

"Russell," said Croft. "Put the body in the trunk of his car." Thunder rumbled, and there was another flash of lightning.

Russell didn't say a word, but closed his door and approached Marty's body. Croft returned to the other side of their car to retrieve the box and stopped short when he saw the box had opened and its contents were strewn across the pavement. The tape must have loosened from the rain. Cursing, he raced to pick up what had spilled from the box, and hoped it wasn't damaged and could still be used. Rook would not be happy to know it had been exposed to the elements.

Squatting and picking up the contents, he heard Russell yell from behind him.

"Croft."

Hearing the big man's tone, he swiveled. Rain blew into his face, but it didn't prevent Croft from seeing swirling lights at the far end of the alley. He froze. "Shit," he said to himself. He had to assume it was a police car, and two cars parked in a dark alley on a night like this would likely draw their attention. "Get back in the car." He turned and raced to grab whatever he could from the ground and throw it into the box.

Russell hesitated. "But the body."

"Leave it." He thought fast. "Leave the bag, too. In the front seat." Croft stood with the box and raced toward his car. "Let's get out of here. Now." He slid into the passenger seat. After tossing the bag into the front of Marty's car, Russell raced back and jumped into the driver's seat next to Croft. He slammed it into reverse, and looking behind him, raced backward out of the alley.

www.ingramcontent.com/pod-product-compliance
Lightning Source LLC
Chambersburg PA
CBHW070618260626
47161CB00007B/2490